The Cowboy Who Heard Her

Sweet Workplace Christian Romance & Small Town Saga

Three Rivers Romance™
Book 7

Liz Isaacson

ISBN-13: 978-1-63876-433-5

Reader Note

Hello Fabulous Christian Cowboy Readers!

Oh, boy, it's Mitch's turn to find his happily-ever-after. As I'm sure you know, he's Deaf. He was born deaf and didn't have access to the language-rich environment necessary to learn how to speak or sign very well.

He's been in Virginia for over a decade, learning ASL, how to train hearing dogs, and teaching at a deaf college there...and now he's back in Three Rivers, ready to open an academy he hopes will bring the language development and education to those who need it.

I hope you love him and his story, and I hope to represent Deaf people well! My daughter is a Deaf Studies major, is fluent in ASL, and is learning to be an interpreter.

I had her consult with me on this book, and she read it as a sensitivity reader as well. Another interpreter did the same, as well as a Deaf college professor at my daughter's school.

I really hope I did Mitch and all deaf people justice, and that you *love* his love story with Lacy!

xoxo

~Liz

The Small Town of Three Rivers

W elcome to Three Rivers! There have been three complete series here already - Three Rivers Ranch, Seven Sons Ranch (Walker Brothers), and Shiloh Ridge Ranch (Glover Family).

That's 37 books. Loads of characters. I'm going to list them here, but you don't need to know them all comprehensively for this book. I just know some of you like seeing these amazing small towns and who lives here!

Shiloh Ridge Ranch:

   Lois & Stone (deceased) Glover, 7 children, in age-order: (Lois is now married to Donald Parker)

   1. Bear — Sammy, wife

- Lincoln (33), adopted son, married to Misty / Dallas (nickname: Diesel, son 6), Scout (son, 3), new baby coming)
- Stetson (Smiles, 26), son
- Russell (Rock, 24), son
- Heather (22), daughter
- Sunnie (18), daughter

2. Cactus — Allison, ex-wife / Bryce, son (deceased) // — Willa, wife

- Mitch (34), adopted son
- Cameron (29), adopted son
- Kyle (27), adopted son
- Charlie (Chaz, 25), son
- Lynn (22), adopted daughter
- Melissa (20), daughter

3. Judge — June, wife

- Lucy Mae (39), step-daughter
- Birch (20), son
- Willow (18), daughter
- Linden (15), son

4. Preacher — Charlie, wife

- Betty (23), daughter

- Hank (21), son
- Daisy (17), daughter

5. Arizona — Duke Rhinehart, husband, living at the Rhinehart Ranch, just south of Shiloh Ridge

- Shiloh (23), daughter
- April (20), daughter
- Dwayne (18), son
- Dallas (14), son

6. Mister — Libby, wife

- Bell (19), son
- Marley (17), daughter
- Hazel (14), daughter
- Brantley (11), son

7. Bishop — Montana, wife

- Aurora (39), step-daughter and married to Oliver Walker
- Robbie (27), son
- Georgia (21), daughter

Aurora and Oliver have 5 children, who are Bishop and Montana's grandchildren:

- Jewel (13), daughter
- Laramie (Lara, 10), daughter
- Mason (8), son
- Lennon (6), son
- Nicole (6 months), daughter

Dawna & Bull (deceased) Glover, 5 children, in age-order:

1. Ranger — Oakley, wife

   • Wilder (25), son
   • Fawn (23), daughter

2. Ward — Dot, wife

   • Glory Rose (25), daughter
   • Silver (22), son
   • Flint (20), son

3. Ace — Holly Ann, wife

   • Gunnison (24), son
   • Pearl Jo (22), daughter
   • Ashton (19), son

4. Etta — August Winters, husband

   • Hailey (32), adopted daughter
   • Joey (22), son
   • Nash and Nellie (twins - 18), son and daughter

5. Ida — Brady Burton, husband

   • Johnny and Judy (twins - 25), son and daughter
   • Riggs (20), son

- Sonora (17), daughter

Bull and Stone Glover were brothers, so their children are cousins. Ranger and Bear, for example, are cousins, and each the oldest sibling in their families.

Seven Sons Ranch:
Momma & Daddy: Penny and Gideon Walker
1. RHETT & EVELYN WALKER
Son: Conrad - 30
Triplets: Austin, Elaine, and Easton - 24

2. JEREMIAH & WHITNEY WALKER
Son: Jonah Jeremiah (JJ) - 27
Daughter: Clara Jean - 24
Son: Jason - 23
Daughter: Emily - 20
Daughter: Hattie - 19

3. LIAM & CALLIE WALKER
Daughter: Denise - 34
Daughter: Ginger - 30

. . .

4. Tripp & Ivory Walker
   Son: Oliver - 40 (and married to Aurora Glover)
   Son: Isaac - 30

5. Wyatt & Marcy Walker
   Son: Warren - 27
   Son: Cole - 25
   Son: Harrison - 24
   Daughter: Rachel - 20

6. Skyler & Mallery Walker
   Daughter: Camila - 27
   Son: Sawyer - 25
   Son: Gideon - 22

7. Micah & Simone Walker
   Son: Travis (Trap) - 26
   Daughter: Daisy - 24
   Son: Jensen - 20
   Daughter: Laurel - 18

Coyote Pass:

Alex Baxter, wife Nikki (twin boys - Shane and Hank, age 6)

. . .

Three Rivers Ranch:

Frank and Heidi Ackerman - patriarch and matriarch. Frank died 19 years ago; Heidi is remarried to Malcolm Rust.

Squire and Kelly Ackerman

Son: Finn - 38, wife Edith, Theo (son, 8), Bubba (son, 5), Dustin (1)

Daughter: Libby - 32, husband Rusty Jackson, Nora (daughter, 8 months)

Son: Michael - 29

Son: Samuel - 27

Pete and Chelsea Marshall (Chelsea is Squire's sister, and they own Courage Reins, which is housed at Three Rivers Ranch)

4 sons:

Paul - 34, married to Brielle

Henry - 32, wife Angel, son, Wrangler (18 months)

(Lone Star Ranch)

John - 29

Rich - 26

Reese and Carly Sanders: They're the admins for Courage Reins, Pete and Chelsea's equine therapy unit at Three Rivers Ranch. They have no children.

. . .

Garth and Juliette Ahlstrom (former foreman; vet technician)
> Son: Jake - 32
> Son: Carson - 29

Cal and Trina Hodgkins (he's the full-time vet at Three Rivers Ranch)
> Daughter: Sabrina - 41
> Daughter: Abby - 33
> Daughter: Olive - 29

Ethan and Brynn Greene (they own Bowman's Breeds, which is housed at Three Rivers Ranch)
> Daughter: Carolina - 30
> Son: Tyson - 29
> Son: Bryan - 26

Beau Peterson (foreman at Three Rivers Ranch) and Charlotte Wisenhouer
> Son: Walter - 15
> Daughter: Michelle - 11

. . .

Bennett and Ellie Peterson (he's a cowboy, she works on the finances on the ranch with Kelly)
>Daughter: Joy - 16
>Son: Jaxon - 13

Tad and Sandy Jorgensen (he's a cowboy, she owns the pancake house in town)
>Son: Nathaniel (Nate) - 29
>Daughter: Helen - 26

Kenny and Taryn Stockton (he's a cowboy, she works for a local online newspaper in town)
>Daughter: Joelle (Jo) - 28

Jon and Grace Carver (he's a cowboy, she helps Heidi run the bakery in town)

Andy and Lawrence Collins (he's a cowboy, she owns a clothing boutique in town)

Summer and Tanner Wolfe (he's a cowboy, she's a nurse at the hospital in town)

.   .   .

Gavin and Navy Redd - they own their own single-family ranch on the northeast side of Three Rivers

Boone and Nicole Carver (Squire's cousin) - they own and operate the full time veterinary clinic in town

Camila and Dylan Walker (he's a cowboy and an electrician, she owns a plumbing shop in town)

Rhinehart Ranch:

1. Dawson, wife, Caroline / Colt (son, 5), Joy (daughter, 18 months), due with a baby soon

2. Brandon (36)

Chapter One

Mitchell Glover glared at the text that had just come in on his phone. Yes, he'd gotten the invitation to Conrad Walker and Glory Rose Glover's wedding. It had been on his calendar for months. *Of course*, he was going to attend, and he felt like ripping off a text to his aunt to let her know that.

He'd told his mother he would be there, but he hadn't RSVP'd. He didn't see the point. Glovers far and wide knew about the wedding and would be there. His phone went dark, and he tapped to get it to come back on.

He supposed his aunt's question was valid. Would he be bringing a date?

He immediately thought of Lacy. His educational director and longtime crush had not received an invitation of her own. The one Mitch had gotten had only had his name on it, and he hadn't known—and still didn't know—how to bring it up with her.

Maybe you can just say you need an interpreter, he thought. That had worked a couple of times in the past, first for his uncle's birthday and then for the family Angel Tree celebration that happened every fall. Lacy had seemed to enjoy herself in his presence on both of those occasions, but Mitch hated using her as an interpreter.

He left his office and went into the kitchen, his phone still sitting on his desk. Everything had been going really well in his life in the past several years, and Mitch really couldn't complain. He had dated plenty of women over the years, some deaf and some hearing, and he hadn't liked any of them half as well as he liked Lacy.

He set the air fryer to preheat so he could make the chicken eggrolls he loved. She had found an amazing sweet and sour sauce at the grocery store, and Mitch got it out and poured a little bit into a glass bowl. He added salt, pepper, and garlic powder and mixed it all up, enjoying his "mad scientist moments" in the kitchen.

It was almost the weekend, with the Walker-Glover Wedding of the Year tomorrow morning. At first, Glory Rose had wanted to stage it in True Blue, but then she'd broken from family tradition when she decided to get married at the church.

Mitch's mother and Uncle Judge would perform the ceremony together, also something that had never been done. They would then move to True Blue for the luncheon to allow space for everyone to sit for the wedding, as well as have all of the tables and chairs set up for the luncheon without needing time for setup and takedown.

Mitch honestly had not given much thought to his own wedding, and as he closed in on thirty-five, he wondered if he'd ever get married at all. The work he'd been doing to become a Deaf advocate and fluent enough in Sign Language to teach it had dominated his life for the past decade, and the academy had been everything Mitch had breathed, eaten, or dreamed about in the past two years.

He put his chicken eggrolls in the air fryer, set the timer, and poured himself a cup of coffee. It was almost four o'clock, and he'd be awake all night if he drank too much. He stirred in some sugar and took his coffee cup to the front porch.

He took a sip as he gazed across the expansive front lawn, the roundabout he'd had put in with a fountain in the middle, and the lane that extended to the corner, where it narrowed to a single lane and led to the highway. All of the fields on the west side of the road had been left open, and Lacy had planted three pounds of wildflower seeds this past spring.

On the east side of the road, two beautiful dormitory buildings had been erected with a smaller, single-story building between them, which Mitch had designed and planned to house the administrative offices and classrooms for his Deaf academy. He and Lacy had been working tirelessly on it for the past seventeen months, and he had been dreaming about it long before that.

He planned to launch the website and open enrollment

the Tuesday following Memorial Day, which sat just another week and a half from now. Lacy had been working all of her contacts in the state, and Mitch had gotten all of his professors and friends from his time at Whispering Paws to spread the word.

He'd originally wanted to provide an academy for ages five and up, but he and Lacy had quickly learned that that would have to be something that they expanded into. He had amended his plans and made fourteen the minimum age.

They had curriculum built and ready to be taught for grades eight through twelve, and then advanced sign language in specialized topics after that. Anyone who enrolled at the academy could also live on site, and he and Lacy needed to get the registration open before he could hire anyone in any capacity.

The dormitories needed to be finished with furnishings, and they had moved into interviewing Resident Assistants, though he hadn't hired anyone yet. He couldn't until he knew how many people would be living at the academy.

You need a name too, he thought as he sank onto the bench on the front porch. Conrad Walker had built it for him, and his cousin, Clara Jean, had come over and equipped it with a plush cushion and back with pillows. Mitch had sat here many times and thought through things, because the decision fatigue he faced in putting together this academy had been monumental.

He couldn't have done any of it without Lacy.

He drained the last of his coffee as he tried to find a way

to ask her to be his date for the wedding. He didn't want to ask her to interpret. That was the coward's way out, and Mitch was done with it.

He wanted her to get dressed up and curl her hair and put on makeup for *him*. His heartbeat throbbed in his chest, and he looked over as the screen door opened and Lacy herself exited the house.

Your timer is going off, she said. *I pulled your chicken eggrolls for you.*

She gave him a pretty smile, which absolutely devastated Mitch. He scooted over on the bench built for two and patted the empty spot beside him. Lacy didn't hesitate as she moved over and sat down beside him.

Sitting side by side was not ideal for sign language. He had to be looking directly at a person to read their lips, and while he could probably read her hands just fine, she said nothing.

Mitch shifted slightly, and she looked at him. *My cousin is getting married tomorrow*, he said.

She nodded. *Yes, I know. It's been on your calendar for a long time.*

Yes, it had been, and he wondered if she'd thought at all about going with him. *There's going to be a lot of people there*, he said. *My momma is officiating the ceremony, and she said she would sign it all for me.*

Lacy smiled, and she looked like a golden angel straight from heaven. She'd cut her hair recently, but it still hung down past her shoulders, and she brushed it back now, as she nodded once again. *That's great,* she said. *Then you won't miss out on anything being said.*

He'd miss out on plenty, as he always did, and he frowned as he looked out over the academy. He caught her hands moving in his peripheral vision, but he didn't look at her.

His dog sat up and nosed his knee at the same time that Lacy put her hand on his leg. That was how he knew she'd said his name, as Champ had been trained to alert him when someone did so. Without thinking, he covered her hand with his and laced his fingers through hers. He felt her tense at his side, but she didn't pull away, and he didn't let go.

After several moments of pure bliss, his skin sizzling where it touched hers, he looked at her.

Her gaze hooked him in, and down, down, down. *Do you need an interpreter to go with you?*

He shook his head because no, he did not want an interpreter to attend a family function with him. His momma and daddy did a great job with sign language, as did Link. Misty got better all the time, and Chaz would be home, and he knew sign language really well.

He couldn't look away from Lacy's positively perfect blue-green eyes. He'd wished once upon a time that he'd been able to attend a deaf school that also taught him how to speak, but he hadn't.

He'd grown up with Signed Exact English until he was eight years old, and then he'd come to live at Shiloh Ridge Ranch. His momma had gotten better and better at sign language, but he'd never attended a specialized school, and he had been the only deaf person in Three Rivers for as long as he could remember.

He managed by typing things on his phone and gesturing, and when he really needed to be able to talk to someone, like at a doctor's appointment, he did get an interpreter. He hated that he had to do everything via video, but it was better than nothing.

He didn't want to remove his hand from Lacy's to be able to speak with her. As he'd explored the option of cochlear implants while living in Virginia, he'd been disappointed to learn that because he had never learned to speak, it would probably take him upwards of twenty years to do so, even after he got the implants.

Mitch had decided against getting them and had thrown himself into learning as much specialized sign language as possible, everything he could about Deaf culture in the United States and the world, and building this academy.

Lacy cocked her head, which was their universal sign for, *what's going on? Talk to me.*

Mitch did it without thought, and he hadn't realized it until Lacy had pointed it out to him. She'd laughed and said she always knew when he was trying to figure out what to ask next, or what to say, or what she had said, because he would cock his head.

Champ had laid back down, and Mitch finally lifted his hand from Lacy's so that he could talk to her.

I don't want you to come to the wedding as my interpreter, he said. *I want you to come as my date.*

Chapter Two

kay echoed through Lacy Hayes's mind.

She couldn't believe she'd said that word to Mitch, and now, fifteen hours later, she stood in her slip, trying to decide what she could wear to his cousin's wedding.

She saw the way his face had brightened, and he'd asked, *Really?*

She'd smiled, tucked her hair, and nodded. *Yeah, really.*

Then her phone had rung, and it was a call she needed to take from the groundskeeping company that they'd hired to beautify the land and erase all signs of construction around the dormitories.

Lacy had quickly excused herself and gone down the front steps, and by the time the conversation had ended, Mitch had vacated the bench. She'd heard him washing dishes in the kitchen, but instead of joining him, she'd tiptoed up to the third floor in the manor, where her apartment sat.

The wedding wasn't until eleven o'clock, with lunch afterward, and Lacy suspected that no one in Mitch's family would bat an eye at her being there. She'd attended a few family functions over the past year, and they knew her. "Yeah," she told herself, moving a pink dress out of the way. "As his interpreter."

He'd asked her out fifteen months ago and never brought it up again until yesterday. His discipline and his respect of her boundaries impressed her, and she'd been fighting her own feelings for the man for almost a year.

"He's not just a man," she whispered as she lifted a pretty emerald dress off the rack. "Mitch is a cowboy god."

And he was. He had taken mere ideas and shaped them into physical facilities. He'd attended a deaf college for a decade to make sure he had the skills and knowledge to open this academy. He could train dogs to be hearing helpers, and they adored him.

Lacy found herself wondering if he could take her broken and bruised heart and put it back together as well.

She put on the green dress and remembered why she didn't wear it very often. The straps sat a little bit too wide, and she couldn't wear a bra with the dress. That seemed highly inappropriate for a family wedding in a church, so Lacy quickly shed the garment and rehung it in her closet.

Mitch had texted her the details of the wedding last night, and he said he'd come pick her up on the third floor at ten-thirty. She'd brought in a mini-fridge and a microwave for when she didn't want to go down to the kitchen to make something to eat, and she padded out of the bedroom and into her faux kitchen to get a piece of string cheese and a pint of strawberries.

Since she lived alone on the third floor and always kept the door locked, she didn't need to worry about anyone seeing her in her slip.

Mitch had never once come to the third floor, and a quiet excitement began to grow inside her that today would be the first time. He'd held her hand for the first time yesterday, and Lacy had realized how starved for human touch she had become.

Her brother lived in town, and she'd been working with him as the physical facilities director here at the academy for almost a year. But Jacob was not the touchy-feely type of man, and Lacy couldn't remember the last person she'd hugged. Probably her mother, when she'd left San Antonio to make the move to Three Rivers almost eighteen months ago.

Tears filled her eyes, and she quickly blinked them back, as she had already done her makeup that morning. Lacy wasn't normally a weepy woman, and while she'd experienced some very difficult things in her life, the most crushing was the ever-present loneliness that went with her everywhere.

Her phone buzzed on the table, and she flipped it over. *Do you want breakfast?* Mitch asked. *I'm making omelets. I'm happy to bring you one.*

Lacy had eaten the piece of string cheese, but the strawberries still sat on the table in front of her. Her first instinct was to deny the omelet. She had food up here, and she had no idea what to say to Mitch.

You can't hide in your own house, she told herself, and she got to her feet and sent him a text as she hurried out of her rec room and into her bedroom.

Any chance of making it sausage and cheese? If so, I'm in.

Mitch sent back two laughing emojis and said, *Your wish is my command.*

She knew Mitch would deliver too, because he'd never let her down yet. She decided she didn't have time to choose a dress before breakfast, and she quickly shed her slip and stepped into a dark green pantsuit that her mother had made for her before she'd moved. The ribbed knit felt soft against her skin and simulated a warm hug for Lacy. She slipped on a pair of wide-foot sandals and headed downstairs.

For some reason, Mitch liked to play the radio when he cooked, though she'd asked him if he could hear, even a little bit, and he'd denied it.

It's what people do when they cook, he'd told her with a playful shrug. *My momma and daddy always listen to the radio while they work in the kitchen.*

Lacy's heart had warmed toward him then, seeing just a tiny bit into the things that had made Mitch into who he was today.

He had no idea how loud he set the radio, and this morning, it seemed to be blasting through the house, and she'd heard it from the third floor.

She entered the kitchen and stepped down the counter to turn down the radio. She could turn it off and he wouldn't know, so she did that. He turned toward her, more hope on his face than she'd seen in a long time.

Hey, he said. *Good morning.*

Good morning, she said back. She took in the mess on the island where he had been preparing ingredients for omelets. The man was a whirlwind in the kitchen, but everything she'd tasted that he'd made had been delicious. He told her he'd learned to cook in a few community classes here in Three Rivers before he'd moved to Virginia.

I'm doing your sausage right now, he said. *Do you want any veggies in your omelet?*

No, thank you, she said.

He nodded and went back over to the cutting board where he diced green peppers for himself. Besides the one that held her sizzling sausage, he had two empty pans sitting on the stove, but he hadn't turned on the flame under either of them yet.

Part of her wanted to simply ask him something and have him be able to continue to cook while he answered. But that wasn't a reality for a deaf person.

Mitch had to focus on what he was doing, and that included having a conversation. She could knock on the counter, and he'd feel the vibrations and look up.

It was a very common signal to get the attention of someone who couldn't hear. In fact, Mitch had filled his house with wood, as did a lot of Deaf people and Deaf-friendly places, as wood carried vibrations really well.

Lacy wanted to give Mitch the space he needed, so she waited while he finished with the onions and green peppers, turned back to the stove, and pulled her sausage off, draining it onto a plate covered with a paper towel.

He finally looked at her, and she raised her hand as if she needed him to call on her before she could speak. He did that adorable head tilt, and she asked, *Do you need any help?*

No, I've got it, he said. *You just relax.* He turned his back on her again, lit the flame under the pans, and moved like one of those chefs that cooked at a teppanyaki grill. Here, there. Spatula in his hand, this in the pot, that in the pan, and a few minutes later, he placed a perfectly folded sausage and cheese omelet in front of her. He carried his own plate around and sat beside her.

She looked at him. *Will there be dancing at the wedding?*

He cut off a bite of his omelet and nodded. She wished he would look at her again, but he didn't, and Lacy took the hint that he didn't want to talk. They ate in silence, though everything Lacy did with Mitch was in silence. She could only eat half of her omelet before she felt like she might pop, and she pushed her plate away a couple of inches.

Mitch looked at it and then her. *Are you done?*

Yes, she said. *You made an omelet for a giant.* Lacy grinned at him, glad when he returned her smile. He looked at his plate, where he only had two bites of omelet left. He forked them both up together and then signed with one hand, *I guess I'm a giant then,* and he put them in his mouth while she laughed.

She stood and took his plate, sliding hers on top of it. She looked right at him, feeling brave and bold. *I'll do the dishes.*

You don't need to do that, he said.

I want to. She moved away from him, cutting off eye contact and the conversation at the same time. Two could play his game.

He joined her at the kitchen sink, creating an intimate space between them as they stood hip to hip. She washed and he rinsed, setting their clean dishes in the drainer beside the sink. As she wiped out the sink and sprayed it with hot water to get it all cleaned up, he set his coffee mug in the dish drainer, and then turned toward her.

She flipped off the water and turned to look at him. He reached up and tucked her hair behind her ear, sending a shower of sparks down her neck and across her shoulder. His other hand slid along her waist and drew her into his chest. He stood a head taller than her, and Lacy fell motionless and weightless as he wrapped her up in his arms. Then she remembered how to be a human being, and she hugged him back.

She'd asked him if there would be dancing at the wedding, and as he started to sway back and forth with her, their bodies pressed chest to chest, Lacy whispered, "I want to dance with you today." She drew in a breath. "I want to go out with you."

Mitch pulled away, for she'd clearly alerted him to the fact that she had spoken out loud, something she didn't do often when it was just the two of them.

His eyebrows drew down, and he lifted one hand to the side and asked, *What did you say?*

Lacy wasn't sure she could repeat her thoughts now that he would understand them. She also didn't want to keep fighting her feelings, and she didn't want to go another eighteen months without hugging another human being.

You don't need another human being, she told herself. *You need Mitchell Glover.*

So she backed up a couple of steps and Mitch let her go. She held his gaze firmly as fear struck through her over and over as a rattlesnake did its prey. Then she raised her hands and drew a deep breath.

I said I'd like to dance with you at the wedding today.

He smiled. *Okay.*

And then I said I'd like to go out with you. She watched the smile drift off his face and his expression turn a bit guarded. He looked away, but Lacy held her determination not to be ashamed of what she'd said.

She simply needed to wait for him to answer.

Chapter Three

Mitch Glover couldn't force himself to look at Lacy's beautiful face. Indecision raged through him, and he wasn't even sure why. This was what he wanted, what he'd been waiting for. Something zinged through him, and he looked up. *I want that too*, he said, deciding to be honest.

But? Lacy asked, and it wasn't aggressive, but gentle and kind.

I'm worried, he said.

What are you worried about?

Mitch ground his teeth together and told himself to keep talking. *A lot of things, actually*, he said. *I think you should know that my history with girls—women—isn't great. I've never had a relationship that lasted longer than four or five months, and I can't lose you.*

He swallowed because that sounded extremely

personal, and he hoped that the ring of truth came through in his signing. He'd kept his signs quick and clipped, and he told himself to loosen up.

Lacy nodded, her own throat moving as she swallowed, but she didn't say anything.

You're my best friend, he continued, and his hands still whipped through the air. *I mean—outside of my family, and we work so well together. I don't want to lose either of those, and I just figure two out of three isn't bad, right?*

A frown appeared between Lacy's eyes and her mouth tipped down. *Two out of three isn't bad*, she said. *I guess not, but it's not great, either.*

It's a D, he said, and a D was so close to failing that Mitch's throat tightened. He took a step toward her, and then another, barely enough room for him to sign between them now. *I want to try*, he said. *And maybe if we're open and honest about things, even if you don't want to be my girl-friend anymore, we can still be friends and still work together.*

He knew he was hedging his bets, almost telling her she couldn't quit if they didn't work out. He hated himself for it, but the words had been said, and he couldn't call them back. He half-expected Lacy to call him on what he'd said, and at least four different emotions stormed through him as he watched her.

A blink of surprise crossed her expression and then...she nodded. Mitch moved into her and took her into his arms, the gathering of Lacy close to him so easy and so right. It felt so good, and the desire to hold her, kiss her, share intimate parts of his life with her, drove everything right now.

He tried to pull back to remind himself that if things didn't work out between them, he'd have *zero* of three things that he really wanted. He absolutely could not lose Lacy as his educational director, and he couldn't imagine working with someone that he didn't get along with—or that he'd hurt.

So you'll just have to figure out a way to be the one for her, he told himself in his grumpy, stern inner-cowboy voice. He could almost see his daddy saying it too in tight, terse hand movements, as he told Mitch plenty of things that he'd need to figure out.

Then, of course, his parents had dug in and helped him figure everything out, and Mitch wondered if he could take his romantic relationship to them the way he did all of the other complex things he needed help navigating.

He stepped back and met her eyes. *Well, I'm going to go shower. I can still pick you up at ten-thirty?*

Lacy pushed her hair out of her face and nodded. *Yep, I better go find something to wear.* She flashed him a smile and ducked around him, leaving the kitchen.

He turned to watch her go, praying for the first time in a long time that he wasn't making the biggest mistake of his life by trying to take her from friend to something more.

Mitch had fallen into texting Link and Chaz, and now he hurried to knot his tie exactly right at his throat. He hadn't cleaned up in the kitchen either, and Mitch hated coming home to a messy house. But there was nothing to be done for it now.

He reached over to the dresser and picked up his cowboy hat, settling it easily on his head. Even though he didn't work the ranch or wrangle cattle or even do so much as feed chickens, he sure liked wearing his cowboy hat. He'd been wearing one since he came to Three Rivers as a ten-year-old, and he'd even dusted it off and worn it on dates in Virginia as well.

Every man and some women would be wearing their cowboy hats for today's wedding, and Mitch's was the one he'd worn to Link and Misty's wedding several years ago.

His heartbeat pinched through his veins because his cousin and best friend had so many things that Mitch now realized were missing from his life—an adoring wife, two kids with a third on the way, and a new addition going on the Top Cottage in the woods at Shiloh Ridge Ranch.

Mitch told himself that he had a very good life here on the property that he'd purchased as well, and that having an amazing home and a dream about to come true was nothing to be upset about.

He simply wanted more.

As a sigh slipped up his throat and passed his lips, he felt the hot frustration of it. It was also quiet and seethed some-where inside him he couldn't quite soothe, and Mitch wondered what to do about it. He told Lacy he'd pick her up at ten-thirty and lights started to flash from his phone, his reminder that he needed to go, and go now.

A fleeting thought that Mitch should say a prayer before he left his bedroom crossed his mind, but he reached for his phone to turn off the alarm instead. He'd already been distracted by chatting with his cousin and brother, and he didn't have time to talk to a God who wouldn't talk back.

With the alarm off, he shoved his phone in his pocket and turned around to face his dog. He gestured toward the door, and Champ got up to open it. Mitch beat him there, though, and he ended up pulling open the door that exited his converted apartment on the second floor. He usually turned right and went down the stairs to the first floor, where he had an administrative office in one of the bedrooms, and where he and Lacy shared the kitchen and dining room.

The master suite sat on the first level as well, but Mitch had converted it into a conference room, where he and Lacy had been doing their business meetings with contractors, conducting their interviews via video, and anything else related to the academy they were trying to open.

Today, he looked left and up the stairs to the third floor where Lacy's apartment sat. He took in a deep breath, expanding his lungs as far as they would go, looking down at Champ. *This is our big moment, bud*, he said. *Let's go.*

The dog didn't know sign language, at least not ASL, but Mitch could direct him with hand signals and other hearing dog signs, so he grinned at his pupper and pointed up the steps. Champ seemed to grin back before he turned and went upstairs.

Mitch followed, his boots feeling heavy and sluggish against the plush carpet. The landing on the third floor was hardwood, just like his, and vibrations moved through the heels of his boots and up his legs when he stepped there.

Champ sat outside the door and looked up at Mitch, waiting for his next instruction. He'd forgotten the dog's tuxedo, and his mind honestly felt like it had been severed from his body. He stared at the door as if he didn't know what to do now that he realized she didn't actually have a doorbell. He'd had Uncle Bishop come and frame in the doorways that led to the second and third floor to make their apartments in the first place.

As he stood there, his mind blitzed from topic to topic. He probably should ask Lacy how things were going for her here, if she was happy or if she'd rather live somewhere else. She'd never said anything, and in all of their "wellness interviews," as Mitch liked to call them, she'd told him how much she loved the job, wanted to be there, and couldn't wait to open his academy.

She also always called it *his* academy, while Mitch knew he couldn't have done anything without her.

He finally knocked, flinching and falling back a step immediately. He patted his leg, and Champ came to his side as well. He fiddled with his tie and then straightened his collar, suddenly more anxious than before.

The familiar war began within him, with part of him

screaming, *Leave, go! Lacy has a car; she can make her own way to the wedding.*

Another part of him bounced in excitement that this was finally happening. Whatever *this* was, Mitch didn't know, and a third combatant entered the raging unrest inside of him. No, he didn't know what this was, but he really wanted to find out.

And that meant he had to stay right here until Lacy opened the door.

Chapter Four

Lacy still wasn't sure about the blue dress she'd managed to zip up by herself, but a knock sounded on the door, and she didn't really have a choice after that. The breath left her lungs, and she sucked in another one, trying to find some semblance of peace, and if not that, something that told her she shouldn't be going on this date with Mitch.

No such thought entered her mind, so Lacy took another deep breath, shook her hands out, and moved down the hall to answer the door. She didn't particularly enjoy dating and never had, and after Landon's death, she certainly hadn't wanted to jump right back into that shark-infested pool.

Moving to Three Rivers had been amazing in so many ways, and the fact that the dating scene wasn't very lively was just one of those.

Of course, she couldn't escape the handsome cowboy

she lived in the same house with, and as the months had passed, she realized she didn't *want* to avoid Mitch. What he'd said in the kitchen a couple of hours ago had cemented itself in her mind.

Two out of three isn't bad, right?

No, it wasn't bad, but it wasn't good either, and Lacy didn't want a near-failing grade with him.

She also didn't want to lose him as a friend, and she absolutely couldn't lose her job here. She'd fallen in love with this academy, with this town, and she couldn't imagine being able to stay if something happened between her and Mitch that left either one of them brokenhearted or angry at the other. She'd fled San Antonio just to get away from the bad things that had happened there, and she could see herself doing the same thing again if she had to.

Lacy had been mad at God for a long time now, but she found herself hitching all of her defenses into place, straightening her shoulders, and saying a fast prayer of simply *Please*, as she reached for the doorknob.

When it wouldn't turn and she'd already started to pull, foolishness ran through her as she realized the door was locked. She fumbled to open it, heat filling her face in a single second. Then the door swung open and a cowboy god in human form stood on her landing.

Mitchell Glover.

Hey, he said, his eyes locked on hers. They released and swept down her body, and Lacy felt every inch of her five-foot-four frame as he drank it in. She couldn't simply say hi back, because he wasn't looking at her and wouldn't be able to hear her. So she waited, forcing her hands to stay at their sides instead of brushing nervously at the sleeve that felt too tight against her bicep or her hair as it floated past her cheek.

Mitch finally looked at her again, and she couldn't believe it, but he carried a hint of redness in his face now. *You look amazing,* he said. *I am going to be the luckiest cowboy at the wedding.*

He grinned that easygoing, trademark grin he had, and Lacy found herself returning the smile easier than ever.

Thank you, she said.

While he'd dragged his gaze over her, she'd had a chance to take in his dark suit too. *You clean up nice too, cowboy.*

He laughed, the sound rich and full and deep, and one of the only sounds Mitch ever made, which simply made it more special.

Thanks, he said, reaching up to press his hat further down. *This hat is from Link's wedding.*

It's very black, she said, which was a strange compliment but what she had on the tip of her tongue nonetheless.

He nodded down to her shoes. *Are those your dancing shoes?*

She stepped out of her apartment and brought the door closed behind her, noting how perfectly still and silent Champ waited for Mitch.

Yep, she said. *These are my dancing shoes.*

She had chosen a pair of silver strappy sandals to go with her deep-blue-sky dress. She tipped up onto one toe and watched the gems glimmer in the overhead light. "I think they'll do." She smiled at Mitch, and he returned the gesture.

Then he reached for her hand, and Lacy easily slid hers into the safety of his, glad for the warm anchor in her life. She felt like she'd been tossed to and fro in recent years, that the storm still raged around her in an almost violent way, sometimes pitching left and right in the same moment, threatening to drown her with a simple thought of the life she thought she'd have.

The stairwell wasn't exactly wide enough for both of them to go down hand-in-hand, but Mitch refused to release her hand as he led her downstairs. He simply let his arm trail behind him, his fingers clasped surely around hers. When they reached the bottom level and the space opened up, Lacy moved to his side, suddenly feeling shy and scared at the same time.

He told Champ to open the door, and the dog trotted ahead to do that. Mitch swiped his keys off the side table where he kept them without breaking stride. Lacy smiled at him when his eyes came to hers again. They said nothing as they went outside and passed the bench where Mitch liked to sit whenever anything troubled him.

He led her to the passenger side of his big king cab, Texas edition truck, and he opened the back door and the front door at the same time, releasing her hand to do so. Champ jumped up into the back while Mitch turned toward her, blocking her entrance to the vehicle. He slid one hand along her waist and leaned in close, taking a deep breath of...her.

Lacy had never felt so cherished in all her life, and she stood very still in the circle of Mitch's presence, his one hand carefully resting on the small of her back, the weight of his arm along her hip, the only points of contact between them. She closed her eyes and breathed in the clean, crisp scent of his cologne as well. Somehow, everything in the world felt exactly right, and so much brighter than yesterday.

He stepped back. *I forgot something inside,* he said. *Let me get the truck started, and I'll go grab it.*

She nodded, and he went one way while she went the other. She climbed up into the truck while he jogged around the front of it. He leaned in and started the vehicle, indicated the dashboard in front of her, and ran back toward the house. She took his gesture to mean, *Adjust the temperature however you want,* and she did. She realized that the back door had not been closed, and she glanced up to see Mitch flying into the house.

She wondered what he'd forgotten as she twisted to get out of the car and close the back door. That done, she got back in her seat and had just buckled her seatbelt when Mitch came rushing back out of the house. He carried a black leash studded with diamonds and what looked to be a piece of black fabric. As he quick-stepped down from the porch, she realized it was a tuxedo for Champ.

"Of course it is," she whispered to herself with a giggle. Mitch couldn't attend a Glover family wedding without Champ dressed appropriately. He vaulted into the truck and put the things between them.

We can get him dressed when we get there, he said quickly. *We're already so late*. Then he put the truck in drive and drove around the circle in front of the house and back onto the lane that led to the road. He buckled as he went, and Lacy settled into the silence for the drive to town.

It was hard to talk while Mitch drove. Since she'd spent a lifetime working with Hard of Hearing and Deaf individuals, Lacy had become very good friends with silence. She reached over and tapped his elbow. He looked at her, and she indicated the radio. *Do you mind if I turn it on?*

He reached over and did it himself, sweeping his hand along the bottom where the pre-programmed stations were listed. Country rock blared through the speakers, and Lacy flinched, then hurried to turn down the volume. With it at an acceptable level, she smiled at Mitch. Feeling brave and bold and all the things Lacy had not been for many years, she reached over and took his hand in hers.

She wondered how he would present them to his family. Before, she'd always been a friend, his interpreter, or the woman he worked with at the academy. They had not held hands, nor danced or snuggled into a pew in a church. Today would be a very difficult day for Mitch, because it was always a struggle for him to communicate in a large group, and the dinner table syndrome would be very real today.

She watched the road in front of them, almost expecting a sinkhole to open up in the asphalt and swallow them whole. So many new things seemed to be unfurling around her, and Lacy had no control over any of them. Memories of her own wedding streamed through her mind, making her throat tight as her emotions rose and rose and rose.

She had withdrawn into herself since Landon's death, and she had not attended anything more than the two or three family parties that Mitch had brought her to as his interpreter.

Weddings are joyous occasions, she told herself. She turned and looked out the passenger window, seeing her faint reflection in the glass there. She smiled, and surprise ran through her when she realized she looked...*happy*. "So try to have fun," she whispered to herself. "Try to enjoy today for what it is."

She looked over to Mitch, and concern rode in his expression as he asked, *Okay?*

She nodded, her smile only growing. *Yeah*, she said. *I'm totally okay.*

He smiled too, a faint version of the megawatt one she knew he possessed, and squeezed her hand. Lacy's stomach clenched too, but as she looked out the windshield again, she didn't imagine sinkholes swallowing them up. Instead, the summer sunshine streamed in, lighting the parts of herself that had become dark over the years. Today felt like a new beginning, and while Lacy worried about some of the steps along the way and if her heart was whole enough to attempt to love again, she decided it was definitely time to try.

Chapter Five

C onrad Walker watched as his daddy ducked out of the groom's room. He knew what that meant: Grams would be coming in to lead their family in prayer before he needed to get down the aisle to the altar. He honestly couldn't believe that today had arrived, the day when he would marry Glory Rose Glover and they would become a family together with his four-year-old daughter, Sarina.

He turned away from the door and nearly collided with his mother. "Oh," he said, his nerves rioting through him. "I'm so nervous."

She reached up and brushed both hands across the top of his suit jacket. "Of course you are," she said. "It's your wedding day, and you're marrying a beautiful woman."

She smiled and pulled him into a tight hug. "But she loves you, Conrad, and you love her, and you've already been through some hard things together."

He held his momma close and nodded. "You're right."

She pulled away, grinning at him. "I usually am."

He chuckled, shook his head, and said, "Eighty percent, Momma," referencing their joke where she was right eighty percent of the time. Conrad and his triplet siblings lived for the twenty percent where Momma was wrong, and even she could laugh now when she was mistaken about something. Conrad loved his parents immensely, beyond grateful for all the things that they'd given him.

Momma moved to the side, and JJ took her place. Easton joined him, and they both smiled.

"What's going on here?" Conrad asked, grinning back at the pair of them.

"Austin's getting the fastener," JJ said, and he reached up to Conrad's lapel to put on his flower. They'd advanced past pins that never seemed to hold the weight of a bud, thankfully. Austin arrived with a magnet that JJ expertly put on the back of Conrad's collar and held the peachy-pink rose in place.

"Ward gave me this," Easton said, holding out his hand. Conrad put his palm up, and his brother gave him a tie tack. "He said he wore it when he and Dot got married."

"Oh sure," Conrad said, because he'd asked Ward for this adornment. He gazed at the tie tack—a bright silver slip of metal with a pair of horses trotting along it.

Ward had said it represented two people traveling through life together, and Conrad had liked that. He slid it onto his tie—a bright blue that went with the softer peach-pink flowers. Glory Rose had added a beige to their color scheme, and Conrad liked the softness and brightness of them all together.

He couldn't wait to see Glory Rose, though he suspected that her dress and this wedding would be far more traditional than the two others the Walker family had experienced. Tate Reynolds and Clara Jean had been married at Seven Sons in a simple outdoor ceremony with a big family party on the back lawn.

JJ and Ruby had been married in the backyard too, but theirs had been an elaborate outdoor wedding that had transformed the ranch into a beautiful facility ripe with flowers that Ruby had paraded through in a gorgeous red dress.

Glory Rose had originally wanted to be married in the Glover family barn, True Blue, but had quickly changed her mind to the church here on the south side of town that they both attended. She had asked her aunt *and* her uncle to perform the ceremony, and Conrad had no idea what that meant. He knew Glory Rose and her momma had been here since early this morning, and he knew he'd gone up to True Blue last night to help set up tables and chairs for their wedding luncheon, which they would host there.

He and Glory Rose would be making the drive to Amarillo this afternoon, where they'd stay tonight before they boarded a plane destined for Puerto Rico. From there, they'd get on a cruise ship and sail around the Caribbean. Conrad wasn't much for vacations, but he figured he only wanted to get married once, and he better celebrate it appropriately. He'd never traveled much and neither had Glory Rose, and the same quiet excitement that he'd been harboring since he'd asked Glory Rose to be his wife came bubbling to the surface.

Behind him, the door opened, and Grams appeared on Daddy's elbow. He didn't let her get too far, and she walked fairly unsteadily in her heeled church shoes as she approached. Conrad went to greet her, hugging her tightly and then taking her other elbow.

"We're ready, everyone," Daddy called.

The men in the room turned from their conversations, their final fixes of cufflinks and bow ties and cowboy hats, and came over to circle up around Conrad and Grams. Momma stepped closer to him and said, "I'm going to go check and make sure Sari is ready."

Conrad swallowed and found his throat so dry, but he managed to nod. She hurried away, her heels clicking against the tile floor, leaving Grams as the only female in the room. Conrad met his father's eyes over her head, and Daddy raised his eyebrows.

"Oh, right," Conrad said. "I was gonna say something."

He glanced around the room at everyone there, a wave of gratitude overcoming him. "Thank you all for being here," he said, and he couldn't imagine if one of them wasn't. His younger brothers, Easton and Austin, though they seemed cut from two completely different bolts of cloth, they'd always been each other's best friend. JJ and Jason, the only males in Uncle Jeremiah's family. Oliver, Isaac, and Tate. Wyatt's sons—Warren, Cole, and Harry. Skyler's boys, Sawyer and Gideon, and Micah's, Trap and Jensen.

And of course, Daddy and all of his brothers. Oh, how Conrad loved his uncles. They'd all given him the perfect example to follow in different ways, and he looked up to each one of them for separate reasons.

They all gazed at him with equal expressions of love and support, and Conrad didn't have to hide his face from anyone anymore. "Grams is going to say the prayer," he said, his throat tight. He reached up to remove his cowboy hat as others in the room did the same.

"Dear Lord," Grams said, her voice shaking. She'd been old before, but she had gotten so much older in the past year. Conrad truly felt like she'd been holding on just to make it to this day, so he wouldn't have to be alone in the farmhouse where they'd been living together for the past several years.

"We're grateful for Thy loving hand of mercy in our lives," Grams said. "We're grateful that we have the opportunity to speak with Thee and feel Thee in our lives, and we ask for an increase of faith in each of the young men's lives who stand in this circle today, that whatever questions they have can be answered, and wherever they need to go, Thou will lead them. Bless Conrad and Glory Rose as they start their new life together, that they will be patient and kind to one another, and that they will put each other first in all things."

She paused, and Conrad felt the calmest he'd been in weeks. He did need to have more faith, and he could always ask God what He wanted him to do, where He wanted him to go, what he should say.

"Amen," Grams said, her voice a mere whisper in the

room. She sagged against Daddy's side as others echoed the end of her prayer. Conrad didn't say it, but he put his cowboy hat on and watched as Daddy held up his mother. Praying seemed to have sapped her strength, and Conrad stepped back as Uncle Jeremiah came to her side as well.

"Come on, Momma," he said. "Let's get you out to your seat." He nodded to Daddy, and then Conrad, and said, "All right, you lot, let's go."

Conrad and Glory Rose had discussed having a full family parade for their wedding party. She could have all of her aunts and uncles walk down the aisle, and he could have all of his, and it would be nearly twenty couples. They'd laughed about it as they lay in the barn and watched the stars. In the end, they'd decided to have their wedding party be their immediate-family siblings.

So Conrad's two brothers stayed back with him as everyone else left. Glory Rose had two brothers as well, which left Elaine as the lone bridesmaid. Glory Rose had asked her cousins, Fawn and Pearl Jo, whom she'd lived with for years, to be in the wedding party, and that had left just Easton without someone to walk with.

He'd actually come up with the idea that he could carry Sarina down the aisle, and that way, they didn't have to have a bridesmaid that wasn't part of the family and he wouldn't have to find a date for the wedding. As far as Conrad knew, none of the wedding party had brought a date. Elaine had been dating quite a bit in the past year, but she didn't currently have a boyfriend, and Conrad didn't think she'd bring him to such a circus, even if she did.

The door opened again, and Momma said, "He's right there, Sarina. Go grab him. East."

Easton laughed and laughed as the little girl ran toward him, and he scooped her up into his arms. She squealed, and he settled her in the crook of his elbow as Momma followed and fixed her dress to cover her up properly.

Conrad couldn't help but grin widely at his beautiful daughter. "Daddy, we go get marry-ed today," she said, and Conrad moved over to give her a kiss.

"We sure are, baby doll," he said. "You smile big for everyone, okay?"

"I smile so big, Daddy. Everyone see me." She cheesed it up for him, and Conrad chuckled.

"Everyone will see you, all right."

He nodded at Easton, and he followed their mother out of the room. Austin went next, and they found Silver and Flint in the hallway waiting for them. Conrad smiled and nodded at them, and they moved down the hall. At the corner, they met Fawn, Pearl Jo, and Elaine, and Conrad hurried to follow his sister. He'd enter the chapel after them and have to make the long trip to the altar alone.

The event started with twinkling, happy music filling the air as the wedding party moved forward. Elaine waited at Silver's side, her palm tapping mildly against her outer thigh. *Six, seven, eight, nine, ten*, then she took a step. Conrad had to do the same—wait ten beats, and then step out. He wasn't sure why it mattered, as all eyes in the congregation had already come to him. He bore their gaze decently well—at least better than he had in the past.

When it was time, he stepped out and moved down the aisle.

The altar sat up on the stage where Willa Glover and Patrick Knowlton usually preached from. Today their podium had been lowered and extended and covered with a snowy white blanket with classic diamond-shaped patterns, a silver gem positioned perfectly in the middle of each intersection.

It was classic and simple, and exactly what Conrad figured Glory Rose would do. She'd draped white tulle from the ceilings as well, and lights had been hung there, creating a magical, fairy-like atmosphere. The end of every row of pews had been decorated with the same peachy pink roses that Conrad wore on his lapel, and a three-foot-tall lantern added light to the space, making the old church feel new and warm and special.

He arrived at the altar, where Willa Glover hugged him, and he shook Judge Glover's hand, thankful he didn't have to stand there alone for too long. He clasped his hands in front of him and stood next to them as he turned to face the top of the aisle. Several long seconds passed until the music changed, and Conrad expected to hear the organ piping out the wedding march. Instead, his favorite song from Alan Taylor piped through the building.

"Oh, holy cow," he said right out loud as Glory Rose appeared in the opposite doorway from where he'd come down. Her daddy stepped into the doorway where he'd been, but Conrad couldn't look away from his bride-to-be.

She wore the classic white wedding dress, and sleeves

hugged her upper arms and blended into her bodice, leaving her shoulders bare. The dress swung down in a curve, in and then out, and then flared finally at the knee. He'd heard Elaine call this type of dress a *mermaid gown*, and he could see why.

Glory Rose wore a white cowgirl hat, and Conrad watched, mesmerized, as she took two steps by herself and then took JJ's hand as he rose from the end of a bench where Conrad hadn't even seen him. He balanced her as she went up steps to a platform that had been built over the benches.

Conrad had not even seen it until that moment, and then Ward Glover did the same thing on his side. They met in the middle where Glory Rose leaned into her daddy's kiss against her cheek, and the two of them faced Conrad. The aisle now came right down the middle of the room to the raised stage where he stood waiting.

It seemed to take forever and no time at all for Glory Rose to arrive, and when she did, Conrad received her into his arms and pressed a kiss to her other cheek. "Wow," he murmured. "You are exquisite. I can't believe I get to be yours."

She smiled at him, and they faced one another with the altar between them and Judge and Willa. Conrad told himself to hang on for fifteen or twenty more minutes, to be present, to listen, because he knew her aunt and uncle would have amazing things to say, and he didn't want to miss a moment of his love—and life—with Glory Rose.

Chapter Six

Willa Glover loved weddings. None of her own children had gotten married yet. In fact, this union between Conrad Walker and Glory Rose was only the second wedding for the Glover family. Link and Misty had been married for several years now, and her eyes flitted to where they sat in the second row with their two boys, Misty's hand protectively on her pregnant belly and Link's arm around her. He'd seemed to settle into himself and to his place in the family quite nicely, and Willa, once again, found herself praying for the same thing for the son she'd brought to her marriage with Cactus Glover, and ultimately, the Glover family at large.

She worried over Mitch constantly, as she hadn't seen him in church in over a year. And any time she tried to talk to him about anything faith-based, religious, or having to do with God or Jesus Christ, he shot her down quickly. She'd spent many nights on her knees weeping and begging the Lord to know what to do for her son, and for now, He'd told her to wait.

If only waiting weren't the hardest thing God asked people to do.

"Welcome to this joyous occasion," Judge said, and Willa blinked out of her thoughts and back to the present. She had a job to do, and she didn't want to let Glory Rose or Conrad—or anyone in the congregation—down.

She could stress-bake while she stewed over her son, and she could talk with Cactus and he would calm her down again, the way he had several times before.

She was thrilled that this wedding had brought all of her children back to Three Rivers as their lives had taken them in different directions.

She found Mitch sitting next to Link on his left and Lacy on his right, both of them seated near the middle, where he would have the best view to see her sign. She remembered then that she needed to sign what Judge said as well, and her hands flew into motion. She knew Mitch did not like the large family gatherings because he was always left out of the conversations.

A lot of people in the Glover family had learned sign language, but their abilities ranged from fluent to barely functional, and she didn't blame her son for how he felt in a large group. Heck, she could hear, and sometimes *she* didn't want to attend the Glover family parties.

Thankfully, everyone had a pretty thick skin, and they knew that whatever was said that might hurt their feelings was not malicious or intentional. They'd all had to learn various degrees of forgiveness over the years, that was for sure.

"Today we're joining two amazing families," Judge said. "Into one unit." He smiled at Glory Rose, and then Conrad. "And it's always a miracle, in my opinion, when the Lord brings together two people and commands them to be one. Even if they're from the same place, and even if they have the same values, it is difficult to blend into one."

That sure was the truth, but Willa kept her smile hitched in place as she signed what he'd said.

"Today, I'm going to give a little bit of advice for how to treat your spouse," Judge said. "And then I'm going to turn the time over to Willa. She'll say whatever she wants."

He smiled at her, and Willa returned the gesture. Glory Rose had asked her to "do whatever she did," and she always liked what she had to say. And so Willa had been planning to do that. Sometimes she wrote out her sermons, but more often than not, they simply came from her heart in the moment, and she couldn't wait to hear what God had to say to Conrad and Glory Rose.

"I've heard advice given before," Judge said. "To not go to bed angry with one another, and to always make sure you say your prayers together. But I've actually found that that doesn't work for every couple. So my best advice to you today is to figure out what *does* work for you. Perhaps you need a few minutes—or an hour—apart, or some time to sleep on something before you can have a rational conversation about it with your partner. Perhaps it's okay to have your own personal prayer before you share one with your spouse. Maybe you'll need to walk around the ranch to blow off some steam and try to see things from the other's perspective before you open your mouth."

He smiled out to the congregation and then switched his gaze to Conrad. "Now I've heard Conrad doesn't have a whole lot to say, and so I urge you, Glory Rose, to listen to what he *does* say and to pick up on any unspoken things that he might be trying to tell you."

She nodded soberly. Judge looked at Conrad. "I encourage you, Conrad, to say what's in your heart, to not be afraid of what Glory Rose might say or think. A team means that you *both* bring something to the task, and you work together to accomplish it, be that building a barn, fixing a fence, raising a family, or being in a marriage."

He looked over to Willa, who was still signing what he'd said, her hands moving at a leisurely pace, and her facial expressions really adding to the narrative. Judge stepped to the side, and she moved into his spot.

"Marrying people is the best part of my job," she said. "Because I get to stand close to the couple and see how much they love each other. It comes off of them in waves, and it's beautiful."

She let her hands catch up, and she let her feelings settle down into her stomach. "I feel impressed to say that God loves each person sitting in this room."

Her eyes landed on her son, and from her raised position on the stage, she could see that he held Lacy's hand. She had not seen him do that before, and she wondered when they had started a romantic relationship. She lost her train of thought for a moment, and then, like a quiet whisper in a silent room, she heard the voice of God telling her that her son was thirty-four years old, and he didn't require a babysitter.

She smiled at the thought, hoping it looked like a marriage smile and not something else. "God loves weddings," she said. "He loves it when we put another person's needs above our own, and He loves it when we work hard to stay together and when we forgive each other."

She drew a breath. "I'm not sure who needed to hear that, perhaps only me. Sometimes we as humans have a strange way of showing each other that we care. And you know what? God is the same. The way He shows *you* that He cares about you is different than the way He shows me. I usually feel it way down in my chest and in my gut. But I know somebody else who doesn't feel that, but knows that God loves him because of the people that He sends into his life. And I know another person who feels God's love by looking at nature and seeing the beautiful things around her. Sometimes we can feel it when we hear another person say, 'God loves you,' and sometimes we can't. But I hope that you'll look for the way that God communicates with you, and that you'll feel that love in your life."

Her words ran out, and so Willa clapped her hands together, startling herself for a moment. She chuckled into the microphone. "Whoops. It's time to get married. I believe Conrad and Glory Rose have written vows for each other."

Glory Rose nodded and cleared her throat. Willa stepped back, because this was not her show.

"Conrad, from the moment I met you, I saw a strength and kindness in you that drew me in. It took us a while to get to that first date, but I would wait forever to be with you." She drew in a breath, and Willa wished she sat with Cactus, the love of her life, to witness such sweet words.

"Today, I stand here, ready to join my life with yours, not just as your partner, but as a family with Sarina. I promise to love and support you in all that you do, to be there in the joyful moments and the challenging ones, and to cherish every memory we create together on our farm.

"As we build our lives together, I promise to stand by your side, to share in your dreams, and to always hold our family close to my heart. With all the love I have, forever and always, I am yours."

She nodded, and Willa noticed her mother reaching up to dab at her tears. Willa loved Dot like a sister, as all the ranch wives contributed so much to the Glover family—and Shiloh Ridge Ranch—and Willa personally.

"Glory Rose," Conrad said, his deeper voice filling the chapel a little easier. Still, Judge moved to hold the microphone closer to his mouth.

"I am the luckiest man alive to be standing here with you. You have brought light and laughter into my life and given me a love I never thought possible. I promise to be your steady rock, to support you in all your endeavors, and to cherish you every day of our lives together.

"As we become a family with Sarina, I vow to be the

husband and father that both you and she deserve. I promise to protect you, to love you fiercely, and to always make our home a place of warmth and happiness. With you by my side, I know that together we can face anything that comes our way. I give you my heart, my soul, and my life, today and always."

Willa's smile finally settled into something pure and genuine, where she wasn't thinking about anyone or anything else. Just the love of this young couple.

Judge came to her side, and Willa looked at him, and then back to the couple. Then they said together, "We now pronounce you husband and wife. Conrad, you may kiss your bride."

As Conrad gathered Glory Rose into his arms, both of them laughing, the congregation surged to their feet, the applause starting. Willa added her own clapping to the noise around her. The Glovers, combined with the Walkers, certainly could raise the roof, and the yeehaws and whoops filled the chapel in a way that sent love pouring through it like Willa had never felt before.

The party would now move up to Shiloh Ridge and True Blue, and as Willa watched the smiling face of her son, and then as he looped his arm around Lacy's waist and pulled her close to him, she decided she would try to sit by them and find out what was going on.

Chapter Seven

Mitch couldn't seem to let go of Lacy's hand no matter how hard he tried. He'd held it all through the wedding, and he'd ignored both Link and Chaz when they'd seen him and raised their eyebrows. He didn't have to answer to them. He was older than both of them, and they knew he'd dated a lot in the past. Maybe not so much since he'd returned to Three Rivers, but he was an adult, and Lacy had agreed to go out with him.

It didn't take a genius to figure out how they'd met and what was going on, and he figured he didn't need to answer their questions. Holding her hand seemed to do that just fine on its own. Link had told him that he would save him a spot at True Blue, which set his mind at ease as he made the drive from the chapel in town up into the hills where the ranch sat.

Lacy carried a healthy pink flush in her cheeks, and her

smile was quick and easy for anyone who looked her way. She spoke effortlessly with them, signing everything she said to include him in the conversation. He loved that about her, that she never spoke without making sure that he was included. Even during their business meetings, she would cut off another person to make sure that his voice got heard. And Mitch could admit that was one of the reasons he liked Lacy so much. She treated him like he had value, and not only that, but she *believed* that he really did.

He wanted to live up to who she thought he was, and he wanted to be the smart, capable man she acted like he was. *Croaking frogs*, he thought, as he turned the corner after going underneath the arch that welcomed them to Shiloh Ridge Ranch.

Trucks and cars had already started to pile up, and Glory Rose's brothers, Silver and Flint, acted as parking ushers. They waved Mitch down past True Blue and into the grassy area behind it. He pulled in where Gunnison, another cousin, told him to, and then he put the truck in park.

He looked over to Lacy. *You ready for this?*

Her smile radiated throughout the truck. *So ready*, she said.

She started to unbuckle, and Mitch reached out and touched her hand. She stopped and looked at him.

What are we going to tell people? he asked.

What do you mean?

I mean, Chaz and Link were both looking at me funny at the church, and I know my momma saw us holding hands.

Right, Lacy said, that cute confusion pulling down her left brow more than her right in a sweet, lopsided frown that Mitch found so adorable. *We're on a date, Mitch. We're just going to tell them we're dating.*

Are we? he asked.

I thought that's what you wanted. Lacy's hands flapped a little bit, indicating her frustration, and Mitch wished he could take both of her hands in his, pull her toward him and press his cheek to hers to calm her and reassure her.

I do. Absolutely. That's what I want, he said, and then added with a grin. *Dating means more than one date. Would you go out with me again?*

Her frown disappeared as her lips tipped upward. *Asking me out on a second date before the first is even over? Wow, that's bold.* She shook her head, and Mitch basked in the happiness that poured from her as she laughed.

Instead of insisting she answer him, Mitch turned and dropped from the truck and went to get her door. He held her hand on the way in, grateful for the blessed kiss of air conditioning as they entered the back door of the barn. Lacy gave no indication that it might be loud, and she stayed glued to his side. As Mitch rounded the corner, he paused to take in the scene before him.

His eyes worked overtime, flooding from person to person and marveling at the sheer number of tables they'd managed to squeeze into True Blue.

They'd held many family weddings, birthday parties, anniversary parties, and Christmas gatherings here. They'd hosted Thanksgiving dinner for their family and anyone else they'd heard of who didn't have anyone to celebrate with.

They'd organized supplies and food during natural disasters from True Blue.

And somehow, today, the number of people in the space topped all of those. Of course, the Walkers weren't a small family, and Mitch found his daddy standing shoulder to shoulder with Wyatt Walker and Micah Walker, the three of them laughing and talking about something.

He had no idea where Link was, and he felt as out of place as some of the young adults and older teenagers who were hanging on the sidelines as well.

Lacy tugged on his hand and nodded to her right. She took a step that way as Mitch looked, and he found Chaz standing with Melissa. They were his half-siblings and full biological children of Momma and Cactus Glover. They'd also adopted three other children as Mitch was growing up, and Cameron, Kyle, and Lynn had all come home for the wedding. Mitch knew they didn't feel like they belonged in the Glover family, and they didn't come to very much at the ranch.

Cameron had graduated from college several years ago and worked as a human resources manager for a company in Amarillo. Kyle had moved to southern Oklahoma and worked a ranch there, and Lynn had moved south to Corpus Christi, and Mitch honestly didn't know what she was doing down there. He was twelve or thirteen years older than her, and she could barely speak sign language, so it wasn't like he called her up and they had long, deep conversations about their lives.

"There you are," Chaz said, both with his hands and his mouth, as Mitch and Lacy approached. "One of Link's boys got stung by a bee," he said. "He took him home for a minute."

"Misty thought that she could have the kids sit with Heather, but now she wants to sit together," Melissa said. "So let's find a table." She smiled over to Lacy and extended her hand. "Hey, how are you? I'm Melissa. I don't think we've met."

Mitch quickly stepped forward. *Oh, sorry, this is Lacy Hayes,* he said, his heart pounding in his chest. He nodded to Chaz. *You've met Chaz, but Melissa is my baby sister.*

He grinned at her and put one arm around her as he moved to her side. He looked back at Lacy and signed, *Guys, this is Lacy, and we just started dating.*

Lacy dropped her chin in a shy gesture, but when she raised it, her blue eyes blazed with that semi-green fire he liked. "It's nice to meet you, Melissa," she said, and she shook his sister's hand. "Chaz, good to see you again."

Chaz had sat by them at the wedding too, so it wasn't like this introduction really needed to be made. Mitch did want to sit with sign language-friendly people, and he turned to scope out the seating choices. The table closest to them already had four chairs tipped up, so they could definitely sit there and take up the other half of the table. But Mitch didn't know who had taken those seats, so he stepped past those chairs to a table where Aunt Charlie sat alone.

Are these places taken? he asked. Chaz voiced the question for him, and Charlie smiled and shook her head. "Nope, just for me and Preacher. I don't know where our kids are."

They had three, and if Mitch took four of the seats, they wouldn't be able to all sit together. He said as much, and Chaz relayed the message.

"It's fine," Charlie said.

Uncle Preacher arrived, and he grabbed onto Mitch and gave him a big healthy hug, clapping him on the back as he did. He stepped back, and he was better at sign language because he'd been a foreman as Mitch had grown up, and he'd had to work with Mitch plenty. "Are you going to sit with us?"

If there's room, Mitch said. *I don't want to take a spot from one of your kids.*

"Oh, Daisy's gonna sit with Willow and Linden," Preacher said, glancing over his shoulder. "Betty and Hank might be with us, and we should save them a couple of seats, but the other four are free."

Mitch liked Uncle Preacher a whole lot, and he pulled out a chair for Lacy so that she could sit. Everyone settled down, including Preacher, and Mitch met his eye again.

You guys remember Lacy Hayes, he said. *She works with me, and this is our first date.*

Lacy nudged him with her elbow, and he glanced over to her. *What?* he asked. *It is.*

She just shook her head and turned her attention back to Charlie. "I emailed you about coming to do a chemistry demonstration for our students in our first semester," she said, signing as she spoke.

"Oh, sure," Charlie said. "Didn't I respond to that?"

She exchanged a glance with Uncle Preacher, who tipped his head back and started to laugh. Mitch smiled, though he wasn't sure what the joke was about.

Betty and Hank arrived, and Charlie got up and hugged them both, as they didn't live at home anymore, and they sat down at the table too. Shiloh and April, Aunt Arizona's oldest daughters, came over and started talking. But Mitch hadn't introduced Lacy to everyone, and she couldn't possibly sign everything everyone said. Mitch swallowed the pinch of missing out flowing through him freely.

He hated this most about groups. They all knew he couldn't hear, couldn't participate in the conversation, and there was no way he could read that many mouths, even if he wanted to. Lip reading was the worst way for a deaf person to get the information that they needed. And though Lacy's hands flew, and he tried to keep up, he finally put his hand over hers and shook his head.

She wore a look of discomfort, and her face turned red for a different reason now than before. All at once, everyone at the table started to laugh, and Mitch hated that more than anything. He loved having a good time, but he hated parties. He turned to Chaz and asked, *What's so funny?*

Still chuckling, Chaz waved him off and said, *I'll tell you later.*

Mitch hated that with a passion. He was here *right now.*

Chaz got to know what was funny *right now. Everyone* at the table got to know except for him.

Forget it, he said, but Chaz wasn't even looking at him anymore.

Intellectually, Mitch knew his brother didn't want to hurt him. His brother wasn't leaving him out on purpose, and yet the hurt still spiraled through him as if someone was whisking it into his blood and making sure that he felt every ounce of it.

He got to his feet, his chair barely sliding back to give him room, and signed wildly. *I want to leave.*

Lacy stood up too, and that brought more eyes to them. "Whoa, whoa," she said, and her mouth moved, which meant she'd said it out loud, and that meant everyone could hear her. *We don't need to go.*

She glanced over to Shiloh and April, and Preacher and Charlie, and Betty and Hank. "It's fine. One of the girls— I'm sorry, I don't know their names." She glanced apologetically to them, and Shiloh must have said her name, because Lacy nodded and smiled and looked back at Mitch.

"Shiloh said that there's never a dull moment in the Glover family, and that your Uncle Ace had bought a case of silly string, but Ward would be mad about that, and that no one wanted to clean that up out of the barn, and so all of your brothers...*their* brothers—"

Lacy looked over to Shiloh again for help, and Mitch lowered his head and glared in that direction too. He still stood in front of his chair as if he would walk out at any moment.

"All the brothers and uncles intercepted the case, and they emptied every can on Ace's truck, and he's pretty mad about it." Lacy smiled, and Mitch could see why everyone would laugh at that. He didn't feel like laughing, though. He felt like he just caused a scene, and yet he didn't feel that bad about it. He nodded and sat back down.

Chaz touched his arm, and Mitch barely turned his head enough to see him. *I'm sorry*, Chaz said. *I should have just told you.*

I hate parties, Mitch said.

Chaz wore worry in his eyes, and he nodded. *I know. I'm sorry. I didn't mean to leave you out.*

Mitch knew that too, and he nodded his forgiveness. He looked over to Lacy and found her talking to the several people over on her side of the table, including his aunt and uncle. She wasn't talking to him, and yet, she signed everything she said. It was a habit she'd admitted to him, and he found her saying, *It's not fair for us to leave him out. He's not stupid, and he wants to belong as much as any of us do. So I know it might be a little awkward, but until I figure out who all of you are, and I can keep track of who said what and keep him looped in, it would be great if you could tell me your name when you came over to us.*

Mitch ducked his head, because he didn't want to see his family's reactions to her request. He hadn't had time to introduce everyone to her, which was irritating in its own right, and he didn't want Lacy pointing at everyone as she tried to keep up with the busy conversation.

A slip of humiliation burned inside of him for only a

moment, but it quickly got replaced by admiration for Lacy. She was an interpreter, and she wouldn't want to leave him out.

She touched his leg under the table, and he tilted his head in her direction. She gave him a small, timid smile, and Mitch grabbed onto her chair and pulled it closer to his, so they were sitting practically hip to hip again.

He pressed his lips to the side of her face, hoping the message of his gratitude would be conveyed. No, he didn't want to be there. Yes, he was going to miss out on a lot of conversations today, and as much as he wished it wouldn't, the familiar resentment began to fill him and fill him and fill him.

He would have to deal with it eventually, but in that moment, the bride and groom arrived, and everyone jumped to their feet and started clapping. Mitch couldn't hear their voices whooping or catcalling or whistling, but he definitely felt the incredible energy as it soared through the room.

Conrad and Glory Rose entered the barn hand in hand, and Conrad lifted their arms up into the air. Glory Rose had changed out of her wedding dress into a pretty blue party gown, and he bowed while she curtsied—and then Uncle Ward stepped to their side with a microphone in his hand.

Mitch didn't care what he said. Probably something about the food and how to get it. But in this case, Mitch could simply be a sheep and follow the herd, and he had eyes that worked and functioning taste buds to know if he would like the food or not.

When hats started to come off, he copied, knowing it

would be for a prayer. In the past, he used to say his own prayers in his head. Today, he simply stood there with his hat pressed to his chest, watching those around him with their heads bowed and their eyes closed, their hearts uniting at this wedding luncheon prayer.

His heart felt cold in that moment, and then his eyes met his mother's. A bolt of lightning moved through him, and he quickly closed his eyes and bowed his head so that he wouldn't have to hold her powerful gaze. But he knew in his heart he needed to go talk to her about a great many things.

Soon, he told himself as Lacy tapped his arm, signaling the end of the prayer. He brought his head up and stuffed his cowboy hat back on, pressing it down low and tight, so he wouldn't have to look at his mother until he was ready to talk to her.

Chapter Eight

L acy felt like she was floating as she drove down the road and made the turn to go to her brother's apartment. Jacob had moved to Three Rivers several months ago, where he worked at Mitch's academy as a groundskeeper. He'd left a few hours ago, at the end of his shift, to cook for Lacy.

Her brother possessed mad skills in the kitchen, and she wasn't sure what it was about deaf people that made them such good cooks. Of course, that was a stereotype, as surely there were some deaf people who couldn't cook too. But a lot of the ones Lacy had known seemed to produce amazing food.

Lacy had thought about inviting Mitch to dinner tonight, but then she'd have to explain something to her brother, and she suddenly understood why Mitch had asked her how to introduce her at the family wedding last week.

He'd done a fine job, in Lacy's opinion, though they hadn't stayed very long at the luncheon. Not even long enough to dance.

She hadn't questioned him about it, because the meal had started off awkwardly, and she knew how difficult it was for him to participate in large groups.

They'd been working together all week, and while he'd teased about asking her out on a second date, he hadn't actually done it yet. Lacy told herself not to worry, but she held a PhD in Fretting Over Things She Couldn't Control.

So her stomach vibrated as she pulled into a parking spot in front of her brother's apartment building. He lived around the back on the first floor, and she reached over to the passenger seat and grabbed the peanut butter chocolate chip cookies she'd made and headed in that direction.

His birthday was coming up next month, and she needed to scope out what he didn't have in his apartment that she could provide. He was usually good for some sort of kitchen gadget, but Lacy wanted to get him something perhaps a little more personal.

She didn't bother knocking, because Jacob wouldn't be able to hear it anyway, and she simply entered the apartment to the fanfare of flashing lights.

Jacob turned from where he worked in the tiny kitchen at the back of the apartment, his smile blooming across his face only a moment later. She wasn't sure why, but seeing her brother always made her heart happy. Perhaps it was because she didn't have to be dressed right, and he didn't care if her hair was messy. He wouldn't be asking her any questions or her opinion on anything. Lacy loved her job, but sometimes the decision fatigue became overwhelming.

Hey, she said, lifting the paper plate laden with treats. *I brought your favorite cookies.*

This is why you're my favorite sister, he said with a laugh. Jacob spoke pretty well, as he'd learned sign language from birth, as well as attended a school where ASL and spoken language was taught. He still signed everything he said, and sometimes he opted not to speak at all.

Lacy was his *only* sister, but she slid the cookies onto the counter and drew her brother into a hug. He smelled like soap and garlic, and as Lacy drew back, she took in the array of food on the counter.

What did you make?

Your favorite, he said. *Ham and cheese pinwheels.*

He picked up a whisk and stirred the Alfredo sauce next to the perfectly golden buns in the casserole dish.

Wow, she said, her mouth watering. *This looks amazing.*

I know, right? Jacob had everything out and ready, and he picked up a plate and slid a spatula under the ham and cheese pinwheel in the corner. He put it on a plate and handed it to her before nodding down to the bowl of salad beside the casserole dish.

Lacy picked up the pair of scissors there and opened the packet of dressing. She mixed up the salad and then put a healthy tong-ful on her plate. She sat down at his tiny table for two, and he joined her.

How's work? he asked.

Oh, it's work, she said. *You know how it is.*

79

Jacob nodded. *Mitch wants to schedule me for a wellness interview.* His eyebrows went up as he sliced into his pinwheel. *What does that mean?*

Lacy smiled at the thoughtfulness of her boss. *He does them periodically*, she said, and she thought Mitch was actually a little bit behind on doing Jacob's first wellness interview. *About every six months or so. It's ten or fifteen minutes of him asking you how you're doing, if you like your job, and what he can do to make it better.*

Wow, really? Jacob asked.

Lacy forked off a bite of the ham and cheese pinwheel, the gooey Swiss melting out when she cut into the bun. *Yep*, she said. She swiped the bite through a puddle of Alfredo sauce and put the whole thing in her mouth. Instant saltiness and breadiness and goodness filled her mouth. She moaned as her eyes rolled back in her head. She nodded at Jacob as she chewed, and he grinned.

Good? he asked.

So *good.*

Lacy was accustomed to signing everything she said, and she especially did it for Jacob as he'd learned how to speak by matching others' mouth movements. Mitch said he could read lips too, but it wasn't a great way to communicate, and Lacy didn't want him to have to rely on that, not when talking to her.

Listen, she said. *I have to tell you something.*

Yeah, all right, Jacob said, keeping his eyes on his food, and while Lacy had gotten down that first bite, she now cut off another chunk of pinwheel but couldn't put it in her mouth. Once she told Jacob that she and Mitch were seeing one another, there would be all kinds of questions. Maybe then she'd be able to breathe, though.

You're freaking me out, Jacob said. *Just tell me. Am I going to lose my job? Is it Momma or Daddy? What's going on?*

Lacy shook her head and waved her hand. *No, no, she* said. *It's none of those things. It's...well, I started seeing someone.*

Jacob started to cough and choke, and Lacy rolled her eyes again. She waited until he looked at her and wasn't about to pass out. *It's not that shocking, is it?*

It's a little shocking, he said. *I mean, you and Landon....* His eyebrows went up, and so much was said in a facial expression that he didn't have to continue.

I know, Lacy said. She studied her plate and the perfectly brown bake on the pinwheels. She looked up again. *It's Mitch.*

Jacob had not taken another bite of food, and this time he fell back against the back of his chair. *You're kidding.*

He wore no humor on his face, no teasing in his expression.

I'm not kidding, Lacy said. *He asked me out over a year ago, and I told him no, but I can't stop thinking about him. We went to his cousin's wedding as a couple.*

Jacob blinked once, then twice. Finally, he said, *Wow.*

Lacy nodded, because that summed up so many things. Her dating again, her dating someone she worked with, her dating her boss, oh, and *her dating again*. He knocked on the table, and she looked up at him.

I hope it goes well, Jacob said, with a sense of pure genuineness in his expression. *I mean it, Lace. I really hope it goes well for you. I really like Mitch. He's a great guy.*

Lacy managed a small smile. *Yeah*, she said. *He is.*

She pierced her bite of pinwheel and slathered it in Alfredo sauce. *Enough about that*, she said. *Let's just enjoy these pinwheels.*

She beamed a smile at him that she hoped would reassure him, though so many things inside her still quaked and ached. She did like Mitch. He was a good man. He took good care of everything around him, and she could only hope that he would do the same with her.

Lacy laid the single printout with the top five names for the academy that she and Mitch had previously brainstormed in front of his chair. He hadn't arrived in the conference room yet, and Lacy settled into her usual spot on one side of the triangular table.

She was never late, something that had been ingrained in her as she'd studied interpreting. Mitch, on the other hand, rarely arrived on time. He always had a reason, and it almost always included a conversation that he'd gotten swept up in, usually with Link or his daddy. Sometimes Chaz.

The time of their meeting, eleven a.m., came and went,

and Lacy wasn't that surprised that Mitch didn't show up. She simply sat on her phone and checked her email, running through a few things that needed to be answered or filed.

When Mitch came bustling in several minutes later, he said, *Sorry, sorry. I got caught up talking to the webmaster. They're gonna have all those changes done by the end of the day, so we'll be able to launch on Tuesday as planned.*

Lacy beamed at him because she expected no less from Mitch. *That's great,* she said. *I just got a confirmation from the state interpreting office in San Antonio. They said they would put the academy on their website as well.*

You're kidding. Mitch pulled out his chair and sat down, ignoring the paper in front of him completely. *That's great news.*

Lacy nodded. *Yes. They just need to know what the name of this place is.* She nodded to the paper, and Mitch scrambled to pick it up.

Right, right, he said, and he studied the list.

When he looked up, Lacy said, *These are your top five choices. We have to pick one today, Mitch. I have to put in the order for the signage. We need to order our pamphlets and our other printables, and it has to go on the website.*

A flurry of activity would happen as soon as a name was decided upon, and she couldn't believe this hadn't been part of Mitch's dream.

Okay, he said, glancing over to where she had an identical paper in front of her. *You've got one too?*

She held up the paper. *Yes.*

I think we should circle our top one and see if they match.

Lacy wanted to tell him that this was *his* academy, and hers didn't have to match his at all. He could simply do what he wanted. She'd told him all of this before, so she saw no reason to reiterate it. Mitch could be as stubborn as he was handsome, so she simply reached for a pen from the container sitting in the middle of the table. She hesitated, hoping to catch a glimpse of what Mitch would circle, so that she could match it. She thought all of the names on the list would do just fine, though, of course, she did prefer one over the others.

He laid his forearm on the table in front of his paper, gave her a glare that said, *I know what you're doing,* and reached for a pen with his other hand.

Lacy ducked her head and waited until she heard the scratch of pen on paper before she made her choice. She folded her paper in half quickly and handed it to him, her chin raised slightly, a silent reminder that he owned this Academy, he was her boss, and he could make this decision without her.

He simply wouldn't.

She admired the way he got input on everything, as much as it sometimes annoyed her. He hadn't folded his paper and now, he turned it toward her, almost aggressively. He'd circled *Signs for Success,* and all the air whooshed out of Lacy's lungs. She grinned and met Mitch's eyes as he tilted his head in that adorable canine-like way.

She nodded to her paper. He flicked it open, and it only

took him a moment to find that she had circled the same name as him, and his laughter filled their conference room, filled Lacy's heart with hope, filled her whole life with happiness.

As he sobered, he looked at her and said, *I'm glad we picked the same one. I guess we're going to name this place Signs for Success.*

I guess so, she said, and before she could tell him that he could have done this without her, he dropped her paper and covered both of her hands with his.

Thank you, Lacy, he said. *What are you doing tonight?*

Her heartbeat fell to the soles of her shoes. *Nothing*, she said.

He ducked his head and reached up as if he wore a cowboy hat, but he didn't. *Maybe we could go to dinner.* His hand that he'd signed with landed back on hers, and when he looked at her, Lacy felt made of diamonds and stardust and other shiny things.

Finally, she thought. But she said, *Yes. I'd like that.*

Chapter Nine

M itch sat on the edge of his bed, texts flying between him and Chaz.

She's really great, Chaz said. *I'm glad that you're dating again. It's been a while for you.*

They'd been talking about Lacy for at least the past half-hour, and Chaz was the type of texter who would stop abruptly and then come back to a conversation hours later. Another text came in, this time from Lacy:

I'll be waiting downstairs on the front porch, she said, and his adrenaline spiked as he tapped over to her message, sure he'd read it wrong.

But nope. He'd read her message correctly. His first thought was that he was late. He often got absorbed into conversations, sometimes via text and sometimes via video, that left him running late and making apologies. A quick glance at the clock at the top of his screen told him he still had fifteen minutes until he'd promised to be standing outside Lacy's apartment.

He felt slightly better, but only for a moment—because he only had fifteen minutes to finish getting ready, and he currently sat on his bed with his shower towel around his waist. Chaz texted again and then again and then again, and Mitch hurried to tap over to his brother's messages.

Hey, I have to go, he said. *I'm picking Lacy up for our first date in fifteen minutes.*

I thought you already had your first date, Chaz said before Mitch could even navigate away from the text string.

A family wedding with one hundred people is not a real date, he said.

Then he, for real, stashed his phone face-down on the dresser, so that he could finish getting ready—or rather, so he could start.

Mitch didn't mean to run late, just like he didn't mean to forget something every time he left the house. The forgetfulness came because he was always rushing, and today, he told himself everything would be fine. Once he had his jeans on and his belt in place and his shirt tucked properly, he could find his cowboy hat, and his wallet, and his keys and everything would be fine.

And a leash, he reminded himself, because they had to take Champ with them to a restaurant, and most places wanted dogs on leashes.

He made sure he had everything he needed before he stepped out the front door. He found Lacy sitting in the thinking seat, wearing a pretty pale pink blouse and a denim-colored maxi skirt. Mitch loved denim and was known to wear it from head to toe on special occasions—or any occasion really—though tonight, he'd chosen a brown, orange, and beige plaid shirt for their first date.

She looked over to him and got to her feet. *There you are,* she said.

I'm only five minutes late, he said. *I was chatting with Chaz.*

I figured, she said.

Mitch tilted his head. *Really? You thought I was talking to Chaz?*

I figured you were talking to someone. She put her hands in the pockets of her skirt, and Mitch didn't think he'd ever met a prettier woman than Lacy Hayes. She definitely made his heart beat with desire, and he reached for her hand.

Where do you want to eat tonight?

You didn't pick somewhere? she asked.

I thought you might like to pick.

Lacy didn't say anything as he led her to the truck parked in front of the house. He opened her passenger door, and she got in, and Mitch went around to get behind the wheel. She never offered to drive for him, which Mitch really appreciated. The number one question he got once people learned he was deaf was if he could drive or not, and Mitch honestly didn't understand it. Did hearing people drive with their ears?

He supposed there were certain aspects of driving that would require hearing, but he'd managed for thirty-four years just fine, and it was not a requirement to be able to hear to get a driver's license.

Mitch's truck would vibrate when he got too close to leaving the lane, or if a car was in his blind spot. His rearview mirrors were also equipped with safety lights to indicate the same, and honestly, the only thing that Mitch couldn't hear while driving was someone honking at him or an ambulance siren. But he'd never been in an accident, and he had functioning eyes, so he could see ambulances anyway.

In fact, deaf people were statistically better drivers than hearing people. He had no distractions, and his peripheral vision and reaction to motion was faster than hearing people.

Not only that, but Champ had been trained to alert him anytime there was a siren. When he drove alone, Champ rode in the passenger seat. He assumed Lacy knew that she should alert him should she hear a siren or something else he needed to know.

Lacy still didn't say where she wanted to eat, though she had reached for the radio and switched it on. When he reached the end of the lane, he turned to look at her.

Where to? he asked.

She held up her phone. *There's a new place in town. It's Mediterranean. Does that sound good?*

I love a good chicken kebab, he said, with a smile.

Lacy grinned and faced the front again. *Let's go there then.* She turned her phone toward him and set it in the console. *It's called The Olive Pit, and it's kind of on the north side of town.*

Mitch studied her phone for a moment. *I know where it is*, he said, and he made the right turn onto the highway. Sometimes he turned left and jogged down about a half mile before turning right to go across the southern highway, which bordered Golden Hour Ranch on the left and Seven Sons on the right.

Once he reached the T-junction past Seven Sons, he could turn left and go to Shiloh Ridge, or go right and head into Three Rivers. This western highway would take them up north and curve them almost to where The Olive Pit sat.

Mitch never had to worry about small talk while driving, but that didn't mean his thoughts didn't storm through his head like an anxious army about to meet their enemy. He reminded himself over and over that he'd known Lacy for a year and a half. They'd talked about many things, and he knew some personal details of her life. She only had one brother, and he was Deaf.

Jacob had inspired Lacy to learn sign language at a young age and go into Deaf Studies and become an interpreter as an adult. He was seven years younger than her, and her parents had no other children. They were still married, and they lived in San Antonio, where Lacy once had too. She'd been a full-time interpreter there, and she'd owned a house with rose bushes lining the front.

Lacy loved rose bushes, and it was the main reason Mitch had chosen to put them in front of the dormitory buildings at the academy. Of course, he hadn't told her that yet, as the landscaping company wouldn't be coming until next week to lay the sod and plant the bushes and trees and flowers that Mitch had ordered. He hoped she'd be happy with them, and that she might even tend to them herself, as she claimed she liked doing.

He had a huge garden space behind the house, and once he'd learned that she liked roses, he'd told her she could plant anything she wanted in it.

She said she'd actually plant tulips. *All the colors*, she'd said with a smile. *They're so...happy, while roses are... beautiful.*

Plant both, he'd told her.

But she hadn't planted anything, and Mitch understood why. One, it wasn't truly her land, no matter what he said, and Lacy wasn't the kind of woman who would pretend like it was. And two, she worked more than he did on bringing the dream of Signs for Success to life.

Mitch smiled at the thought of the new name for the academy, as he thought it fit so well with Deaf culture, Deaf education, and as a community resource for understanding and helping those who were Hard of Hearing or couldn't hear at all.

He navigated them to The Olive Pit with success and parked the truck by backing it into a spot way down on the end, away from other cars. He turned to look at Lacy and said, *Wait right there.* She smiled and nodded, and Mitch grabbed the leash for Champ and slid from the truck. He got Champ out on his side of the truck first and took him around to get Lacy.

When he opened her door, he found her holding Champ's service dog vest, and Mitch chuckled and shook his head. Of course, he'd forgotten something. She smiled and let him help her to the ground before she bent and put the vest on Champ.

She didn't try to take the leash from Mitch. No one ever did, because Champ was his hearing dog, and he was the one who was supposed to handle him. Mitch reached for Lacy's hand with his free one and wanted to tell her about the dogs he had coming to the academy, but both of his hands were occupied.

While familiar frustration filled him that he couldn't talk right now, he headed for the restaurant, telling himself not to be grumpy and that he had plenty of time to talk to Lacy over dinner about anything he wanted.

Inside, the restaurant seemed to hold a vibe in the air that spoke of music and laughter and bottles and glasses clinking. The scent of hummus, garlic, and roasted meat filled the air, and Mitch took a deep breath of it while he waited for their turn at the hostess station. He held up two fingers, and the woman picked up two menus and said something, probably "Follow me."

He let Lacy go first, and then he followed with Champ behind her. This place was more of a bistro than anything else, with the tables crowded close together and the path between them narrow. The hostess twisted and said something over her shoulder, and Lacy answered her. She took them to the back of the restaurant and then turned left, where even more tables sat along a wall of windows.

Mitch would much prefer a booth, as it would give Champ more room to lay down out of the way, and he found Lacy pointing to one a little further back than the table where the hostess had stopped. She nodded and continued there.

Lacy smiled as she slid into the booth, facing him, and Mitch nodded to the woman as she set their menus on the table and said something. He pointed to the bench seat, and Champ jumped up, went all the way against the wall, turned around, and laid down. Mitch squeezed in beside him, the comforting weight of his dog's head on his thigh enough to prompt Mitch to relax. He picked up the menus and handed one to Lacy before he buried himself behind the one in his hand.

Only a few seconds passed before Lacy put her hand on the menu and pushed it down. She wore concern on her face. *Are you okay?*

Mitch hated being asked if he was okay, and he wanted to nod curtly, growl, and go back to the menu. He told himself not to be so grouchy and not to let every little thing bother him. Who cared if Lacy got them to the table that he wanted? Just the fact that she knew him well enough to do that should make him happy, not irate. He swallowed hard and nodded.

I'm okay.

Why are you upset? she asked.

I'm not upset, he said back, his frown deepening.

You look *upset*, she said, and she took his menu from him and laid it on top of hers. *You* seem *upset. You're glaring.*

The fight inside Mitch tensed so tight he felt like he couldn't breathe.

Did you not want to sit in a booth? Lacy asked, pressing the issue. *I thought it would have more room for Champ, and I—*

He reached over and covered her hands as she continued to talk. She silenced, her eyes wide. Mitch could admit that he'd just been pretty rude by cutting her off mid-sign, and he honestly didn't know what to say to her. He slid to the end of the bench, easing out from under Champ's weight, and rounded the table to sit by her.

Lacy looked at him, pure shock on her face, only realizing he was going to sit down, whether she moved over or not, at the last moment. She managed to slide over, and Mitch crammed himself into the small booth on her side only a moment later. He put his arm around her and drew her into his chest, taking a deep breath with the scent of her hair. She smelled like vanilla and orange and honey, and Mitch wanted more and more and more of it.

He threaded his fingers through hers on the table in front of them, liking how her fairer skin stood out against his darker, more tanned tone. Then he released her hand and told himself to keep his hands as calm as possible.

I sometimes get upset by simple things, he said. *And I just need five minutes to let them go. It's no big deal.*

Okay, she said. He had no idea if she spoke the word or just signed it, because she'd tucked her head against his chest, making him feel strong and capable and like he could protect her and take care of her.

I don't like that I can't tell her what kind of table I want, he said. *I don't like that I can't talk to her. I don't like that you have to do it for me.*

She raised her head, and with only a foot between them, she looked him straight in the eye. *I won't do it if you don't want me to.*

It's not that I don't want you to, he said. *I just need a minute.*

Okay. She nodded to his side of the table and picked up his menu. *Go take your minute, cowboy.*

He took the menu, but he didn't stand up. He pulled her close and leaned down. His mouth hovered dangerously close to her ear, and he pressed a kiss right along the side of her face, then against her cheek, then up on her temple.

By then, everything had settled inside of him, and Mitch took his menu, returned to his side of the table, and hid behind the Mediterranean restaurant's offerings.

Yeah, he needed a minute all right, but now it was to cool down before he started kissing Lacy in public. He wanted to kiss her, but not where everyone else could see, and definitely not after he'd just admitted that little simple things irritated him to the point of needing a break.

He found a kebab plate that included beef and chicken, and he flipped the menu over to find out his side choices, since he got two. Once he decided on French fries and the Greek salad, he put his menu down and looked at Lacy.

She looked up from the menu, which she was not hiding behind, and smiled at him.

Thank you for giving me my minute, he said.

You can have as many as you want, she said. *Anytime you want them.*

Mitch fell a little bit more in love with her with these simple words, and he reached down and stroked Champ's head just as the waiter arrived to get their drink orders. This was something else that Mitch couldn't do very well, but Lacy did not order for him.

Since they'd never been out before, he kind of expected her to do so. Instead, she gave her order and then looked across the table to him, her expression open and unassuming, and Mitch knew that he would have to ask her to order for him if that was what he wanted her to do.

He slipped and slid as he fell even more, because, yes, Lacy was kind and compassionate and smart and knowledgeable, but she wasn't going to be Mitch's crutch, and she wasn't going to do anything that would make him feel less-than.

He tilted his menu and pointed to the icon of Diet Coke, and then he signed to Lacy, *Will you ask him if they have lemon?*

She did, and the man nodded, looked right at Mitch, and said, "Diet Coke with lemon. You got it, bud."

Mitch half expected him to clap him on the shoulder as he left, but he didn't. He simply went away, and Mitch looked across the table to Lacy.

Thank you, he said, reaching for her hands. He looked down at them instead of at her, finding he needed another minute to let his emotions roam through him and figure out what they were. Of course, he knew he liked Lacy more and more with every moment he got to spend with her, and that scared him quite a bit. He didn't want to talk about work, and his mind blanked as to what else they could possibly speak about.

Mitch found himself doing something that he thought he'd given up a while ago.

He prayed.

Chapter Ten

Lacy considered herself exceptionally skilled at conversing with people. It didn't matter if she didn't know them. She could ask them all kinds of things about themselves and generally make it through any small talk unscathed. When Mitch just sat there, she tapped the back of his hand and said, *You haven't told me about the dogs.*

She put the warmest smile on her face that she could muster, hoping that the awkwardness between them could be bridged quickly. Thankfully, his face brightened too, and Mitch said, *The dogs are great. At least they will be once they get here. I had another video call with them yesterday afternoon, and I think they're going to be perfect.*

When do they arrive? she asked.

Next weekend, he said. *My daddy and Uncle Bishop are coming to help me finish the pens. I've got all the food ordered, and that means all I have left is name plates.*

Of course, Mitch would want to have name plates for his dogs. *How many are you getting again?* she asked, though Lacy knew he was getting three.

Three, he said. *Though I'll tell you there was a fourth, and Titan tempted me mightily.*

He laughed, and just like that, all of the awkwardness between them dissipated.

I have no doubt you'll get your fourth dog soon enough, Lacy said. *Probably even next weekend.*

He shook his head as he continued to chuckle. *No, I'm really not going to get a fourth one,* he said. *It would be unfair to both me and the dogs. I can't train that many at once.*

Their drinks arrived, and Lacy paused the conversation while Brett-the-waiter set down her Diet Coke without lemon and Mitch's Diet Coke with lemon. She knew Mitch would not sacrifice his time and energy for anything he couldn't do one hundred percent correctly. She unwrapped her straw while Brett asked, "Are you two ready to order?"

He looked at her and then over to Mitch, just as another woman arrived at his side. To Lacy's great surprise, she signed to Mitch. *Hello, I can help you with your order.*

She wasn't sure if Mitch would like that or not, but something warm and satisfying grew inside her own stomach. Brett had seen Mitch sign for five seconds, and he'd found someone to come take his order. That was some good service.

She watched as Mitch's eyes widened in surprise, then he nodded and signed to the interpreter that he wanted the combo kebab plate with beef and chicken. He put in his side orders, and Lacy ordered her salmon power bowl with a side of the chickpea salad, and Brett and his serving friend left.

Wow, Lacy said. *They got you an interpreter to take your order.*

I'm kind of surprised, Mitch said. *I didn't know there were other people in town who knew sign language.*

You didn't know her? Lacy asked.

No. Mitch twisted and looked over his shoulder, around the corner of the booth. He turned back to her. *Do you think we hired her already?*

You haven't hired anyone, Lacy said, raising her eyebrows. *Have you?*

I mean, I've set up a lot of interviews.

He grinned at her, something so playful and boyish about that lopsided smile. *You're going to have to start hiring people*, she said. *If you want to open in three months.*

We're not talking about work tonight, Mitch said good-naturedly.

We were just talking about the dogs, she said.

Well, I don't want to talk about work now. He sobered and said, *Tell me something about your life in San Antonio, or your life before I knew you. Did you date a lot?*

Mitch had no way of knowing that he literally just stabbed an ice pick in her jugular. She swirled her straw through her drink, watching the ice cubes clink around together and against the sides of the glass. She took a drink, the words inside her mind in another language, one that she wouldn't be able to speak coherently.

How could she tell him about Landon? How could she not?

Lacy cleared her throat and looked up into Mitch's waiting, expectant expression. *I haven't dated for a while....* She trailed off, her hands held in midair, as if her mind had gone blank and that had transferred to her fingers.

Mitch blinked, and he breathed, but of course, he didn't speak, and he didn't pressure her, and he didn't wave away his question. He lived life with purpose and with intensity, and Lacy wanted to do the same thing.

I haven't dated for years, she said again. *Mostly because I was married for a few years before my husband died. So it's been a while since I've done anything like this.* She gestured between the two of them and let her hands fall to the table in front of her.

Mitch's eyes widened, and his tongue darted out to wet his lips. *You've been married?*

She nodded and looked away, sudden tears pressing into her eyes. She wished Mitch would come sit by her again so that she could fold herself into the warm safety of his embrace and not have to look at him. He knocked on the table, and Lacy thought it would be rude to ignore him. She took an extra moment and then switched her gaze back to his.

He passed away?

She nodded again, everything that had happened suddenly there piled up into a large cinder cone that was ready to explode. *He got in a car accident,* she said. *He broke both legs, but his other injuries weren't that bad—or so we* thought. *Turns out, he had a collapsed lung, and it got infected. He got sepsis—it's where your body overreacts to the infection, and...they couldn't save him in time. It was so dumb and so senseless.*

She reached up when she felt a tear curling out of the corner of her eye. Embarrassed, she wiped at it quickly. *You think people don't die of infections in the hospital anymore, but they do.*

Kind of, but still. The infection had caused the sepsis, and Lacy couldn't separate the two.

I'm so sorry, Mitch said. He covered one of her hands with his and continued with, *How long ago was this?*

A couple of years now, Lacy said.

You moved here right after that?

About eight months after, she said. *I just couldn't handle the way all of my friends looked at me with such sad faces.* She sighed, her resolve for leaving San Antonio behind strong and sure. *My mom asked me all the time if I was okay or not.*

She reached for her napkin and dabbed at her eyes, finding some of her black makeup on it. She took a deep breath and steeled everything behind a heavy metal door. *I came here, and it was so freeing. No one asked me any questions about Landon.* She realized she'd used the sign that Jacob had created for Landon's name, and she quickly spelled it out for Mitch.

No one was asking me if I needed something to eat, she said. *No one brought food over. I didn't have to answer my door and see the way my mom looked sadly at the sweat-*

pants that I wore. It was really nice and just what I needed.

I feel really bad, Mitch said, and he wore a pained look on his face. *I would have taken better care of you had I known.*

You take great care of me, Lacy said. *You're always feeding me, and you bought the creamer I like, and I didn't even have to ask.*

Her emotions wavered and her voice broke, though he couldn't hear that. She knew, and she took another moment to steady everything inside herself. *Coming to Three Rivers, coming to work with you, has been a huge blessing in my life.*

He gave her a small smile and nodded just once. *I guess I don't need to do your wellness interview then.*

For some reason, that tickled Lacy's funny bone, and she tipped her head back and laughed. Mitch didn't join her, but he wore a wide, satisfied smile on his face when she looked at him again.

I like it when you laugh, he said. *You look so happy.*

I am happy, she said, recognizing it and accepting it in her life. *Are you happy, Mitch?*

I'm enough, he said.

Well, that's not good enough, she said.

I'm stressed about the academy, he said. *And I know myself well enough to know that as soon as we open, there will be something else that I'm not pleased with, and I'll just have to keep working. My daddy says I have to learn how to figure out how to be happy with where I am right now, with the process of what I'm doing, that there's no ulti-*

mate thing that will happen that will suddenly make me happy.

He shrugged one shoulder and finally reached for a straw to put in his cola.

Your daddy's right, Lacy said. *Though it's a lot harder than he makes it sound.*

Mitch balled up the straw wrapper and tossed it next his glass. *Yeah. He lived out on the edge of Shiloh Ridge for a long time by himself. He said he wouldn't talk to anybody, and only Uncle Bishop and Uncle Bear could go to his house. He barked everyone else off of his property.*

Wow, Lacy said, smiling. *How did he meet your momma then?*

Well, my momma is a saint, Mitch said with a chuckle. *She can tame the hardest of hearts and the grumpiest of cowboys.*

Mitch looked away, his throat moving as he swallowed. *I need to go see her.*

Lacy wanted to ask him why, but he didn't look at her, and she let him have his minute. She took the moment to wipe her eyes again and make sure that she wouldn't be embarrassed when the waiters returned with their food.

Mitch looked at her again. *Let's talk about something lighter,* he said. *Though I'm really sorry about Landon.* He used the same custom sign that she had for her husband's name, and that made Lacy's heart glow like a warm coal on a cold evening.

You never planted anything in the back garden, he said.

I felt too busy, Lacy said. *Maybe next year.*

She heard the promise in her voice, the one that said she would be at the academy next year, that she would still live on the third floor above Mitch next year, that they would still be working together next year.

She didn't know if that was really true, but she sure hoped it was. *What about you?* she asked. *You've only talked about work.*

Nothing heavy, he said.

Nothing heavy, she promised.

He stayed silent and still for several long moments, and then he rolled his eyes, and then his whole head as he stretched his neck. *Heck, my whole life is heavy*, he said. *I haven't been to church in forever, and I know my momma wants to talk to me about it, and I'm avoiding her.*

I've been talking a lot with Chaz, but Link's been irritating me lately, and I know I need to go talk to him too. I just don't want to do any of it.

Surprise filled Lacy, because Link was Mitch's best friend. *Link's been irritating you? Why?*

He'd never said anything about that, though, of course, Mitch and Lacy usually talked about work while they were at work, and she realized she needed to bring more of their personal private lives to the forefront, even though they lived and worked together.

Oh, it's just something stupid Link said, Mitch said. *It'll be fine.*

He looked down again, and Lacy recognized that he didn't want to tell her what Link had really said. The need to know burned inside her, and she squeezed his hand to make him look up.

Was it about us? she asked.

Mitch's jaw tightened, and that was all the answer that Lacy needed. Still, he nodded and said, *Yes, and he has no right to make judgments about anything. He pined after his wife for months and months after she ended things with him the first time, and I was right there on every video call telling him to just wait, just give her some time, to try again.*

His hands moved in large arcs, his anger flowing freely from his eyes, in every expression and move he made.

And he did, and look at him now. Married, almost three beautiful kids, healthy, happy, a new house—and he's gonna tell me who I can and can't go out with?

He shook his head. *I told him it was none of his business. We haven't spoken much since.*

Lacy offered him a small smile. *You sound a little prickly, like your daddy. You've said he was hard-headed like this too.*

I'm not hard-headed, Mitch said.

Lacy raised her eyebrows and tilted her head slightly. Mitch softened instantly, actually smiled, and then gave a laugh that didn't sound exactly happy.

All right, he said. *I can be a little stubborn.*

Just a little, she said, her grin wide so he would know she was teasing him good-naturedly. *Link's your best friend,* she said as she sobered. *When are you going to talk to him?*

I don't know, Mitch said. *Chaz says he feels real bad, and that just irritates me too. If Link feels bad, he can call me and talk to me about it. He doesn't need to be telling my brother and my daddy.*

He told your daddy?

Oh, he's called me a million times too, Mitch said. *I just pretend like I can't see it.* He grinned at her, and Lacy shook her head even as she giggled.

So you're avoiding your momma, and *your daddy,* and *Link.*

Yeah, that's about right, Mitch said. *It was a lot easier when I lived in Virginia.*

Am I going to have to stage an intervention? Lacy asked.

Absolutely not. His jaw clenched again. *Though I have to get out to Shiloh Ridge soon, or one or all three of them will show up at the academy.*

That would be embarrassing, Lacy teased, and she looked up at the same time Champ did. Their food arrived, and Brett said what hers was, though she'd ordered it and could remember just fine. At the same time, the waitress set Mitch's plate down and signed to him what he'd ordered.

Anything else I can get for you? she asked.

Mitch surveyed his plate and then looked up. *Yeah, can I have a side of guacamole and sour cream?* He looked across to Lacy. *You need anything, sweetheart?*

She took in the deliciousness of her salmon bowl with the pickled cabbage and spiced white rice. "Yes, can I have some tartar sauce?" She signed and spoke, looking up at the waitress who could speak ASL.

Tartar sauce coming up, the woman said, and she grinned at Mitch as both waitstaff left.

Mitch seemed to be bursting with pride, and Lacy loved that he'd gotten to take the lead and ask her if she needed anything. He was as masculine and protective as they came, and she knew he wanted to take good care of her. He'd shown it many times in the small and simple things he'd done for months—for over a year—as they'd lived and worked together. She thought about what he'd said as she picked up her fork and flaked off the corner of her perfectly grilled salmon filet.

Sweetheart.

I wish I would have known. I would have taken better care of you.

She had no idea what that would have looked like from Mitch Glover, but oh, how she wanted to find out.

Chapter Eleven

Mitch opened his door on the second-floor landing and tossed the leash inside after Champ. Then he took one step and pulled the door closed again, leaving himself alone to follow Lacy up to the third-floor landing. He wasn't sure what was going to happen up there or why he didn't want Champ to witness it.

He knew what he *wanted* to do, and that was to kiss Lacy goodnight, hold her close, and go out with her again for breakfast. He didn't think any of that would happen, as he had a phone call at seven-thirty with the webmaster to go over any last-minute items before the weekend and their launch on Tuesday.

Lacy had gone ahead of him, so she already had her door open when he arrived. She turned in the doorway and asked, *Do you want to come see my place?*

Mitch nodded, his throat so dry. He'd drunk three colas at the restaurant, and still, he needed more. *Sure,* he said. *I can compare it to what I did with my unit.*

He grinned at her and let her lead him into the third-floor apartment he'd prepared for her. A hallway ran down the middle, leading off the wider foyer area that had once been part of the landing. He knew a bathroom sat through the first door on the left, but Lacy opened it and showed him that she had decorated with pale blue, yellow, and gray in terms of bath mats and shower curtains and even a picture of a lemon on the wall.

Bathroom, she said.

The room across from that was a bedroom, but it didn't hold a bed. It had a bookcase and a folding table in it, and Mitch could just picture Lacy sitting there, doing some work for the academy after hours. Two stacks of about ten boxes sat against the wall, and she indicated them.

Stuff I brought from San Antonio that I'm not sure I really need—Christmas decorations, other house decor, stuff like that.

He noticed one of the boxes read "Landon's Stuff," and he reached for Lacy's hand. He'd had no idea that she'd been married before. She had never once mentioned it, not through any of the interviews, and not at all when he talked to her about her family or personal life. Of course, after he'd asked her out fifteen months ago, she'd shut down on him completely, and they'd only talked about work for six months after that.

Mitch wished he'd dug a little bit more into her, because he wanted Lacy to be nothing but happy and comfortable and taken care of, and he would do anything and everything in his power to do that. Of course, he knew better than most that he couldn't *take* a person's pain from them. But he believed that another person could ease their burden enough to make it carry-able. And Mitch wanted to be that person for Lacy.

He recognized his momma's teachings in his thoughts, because she often preached that God rarely sent help in the way that we wanted it as human beings. He didn't give us a million dollars when we needed money to pay our bills; he put a person in our life to offer us a job.

He didn't take away the concern or insecurity, like Mitch's deafness once was, or Momma's limp. He provided people to help carry the burden, like Cactus, who'd been Momma's constant support for twenty-five years now; or Lacy, who could read Mitch and speak with him better than anyone he'd ever met.

Mitch really needed to go see his mother and had been putting it off for almost a week. He wondered how long she'd allow him to do that, and he knew he only had a few more days before something would upend his life.

He preferred to be in control of when that conversation happened. He tried to think through his schedule for tomorrow. He couldn't quite do it, because Lacy had just opened the door in the far corner and said, *This is my bedroom.*

She didn't move inside, and Mitch certainly wasn't

going to. She had a beautiful all-wood furniture bedroom set with matching nightstand, dresser, and bed frame. Mitch had actually seen all of this before because he'd helped her bring it up three floors to the apartment.

This is nice, he said, noting the thick comforter on the bed and how she'd made it that morning. She would die if she saw his place, where he never made his bed, and he dropped his clothes wherever they happened to land, and he couldn't remember the last towel he'd hung up after a shower. No, Mitch wasn't the cleanest man alive, and it was just one more thing where he and Lacy differed.

She was always on time. He ran late. She could keep a cool head. He lost his temper at the slightest of things. She'd been committed enough to a man to be married, and Mitch had never had a relationship that lasted longer than four months.

He swallowed hard, wondering what he was doing here in Lacy's apartment, holding her hand, taking her on dates, thinking about kissing her.

This is my rec room. She opened the door to the third bedroom. *I have a little dining room table in here and a mini fridge, a microwave, and my TV and couches.*

She'd used the biggest of the three bedrooms for that, and Mitch hadn't realized that she didn't use the kitchen every time she needed something to eat.

Worry shot through him. *You don't have to have a mini kitchen up here*, he said. *Am I taking up too much room in the kitchen?*

No, she said. *No, of course not.*

He looked at her, still full of questions that surely showed in his eyes.

I didn't know you when I moved here, she said. *And I didn't know if I would want to go downstairs and share a kitchen or eating space with you.* She indicated the fridge. *Landon had these at his office, and I just brought them with me.*

What did he do? Mitch asked.

She smiled, no tears in sight, for which Mitch was thankful. Watching her cry at the restaurant had been excruciating, and he'd wanted nothing more but to take his spot next to her on the bench and comfort her. Something in Lacy's body language had told him not to, though, and Mitch was extraordinarily good at reading other people.

He was a veterinary assistant, she said. *He ran a lot of tests and did scheduling and helped with vaccinations.*

Oh, that's great, Mitch said. *Did you guys ever have any kids?*

She shook her head. *No. We were only married for about two years before he died.*

I see. Mitch put his arm around her and held her right at his side. *Thank you for telling me about him.*

Lacy nodded but didn't say anything else, and she indicated the coffee maker that sat on top of the microwave. *Do you want coffee?*

He shook his head. *No, it's too late, and I should go.* He backed up a step and looked at her. He cradled her face in one hand and gazed at her. *I really liked going out with you.*

Her whole countenance brightened, and she smiled. *I had a great time too.*

When can we go out again? Tomorrow?

She ducked her head even as she nodded. *I have a call in the morning,* he said. *And I think I better go up to Shiloh Ridge tomorrow too, but let's plan on dinner and a movie.*

She shook her head, obviously laughing as her shoulders shook. Mitch dropped his hands to her shoulder and reveled in the vibrations there.

No sir, she said. *No movies for you. I'm not signing through the whole thing.*

I'll find us something to do, he said with a grin, and he forced himself to back up another step. He wanted to kiss her, but something told him he shouldn't, that perhaps she needed more time, that she'd told him some very hard things about a man she loved, and he could wait.

Mitch had spent his life waiting, and he turned and walked down the hall and off the third floor without looking back.

He found Champ waiting for him just inside the door, and he bent down and scrubbed his dog real good, so glad he didn't have to come home to an empty apartment. He thought of Lacy having to do that and how lonely she must have been all this time that she'd been in Three Rivers. As he straightened and toed his door closed, he told himself she would never have to be lonely again. He would make sure of it, even if they broke up.

Then he pulled out his phone, and as he sauntered

down the hall to his bedroom so he could kick off his boots and step out of his jeans, he texted his momma.

What are you doing tomorrow for lunch? Can I bring you something from The Pennsylvania so we can talk?

* * *

Mitch's nerves went into full riot mode the moment he turned onto Shiloh Ridge Ranch. When he'd first come to the ranch as a ten-year-old boy, none of the buildings which currently stood on either side of the road had existed. Now Uncle Bishop and Uncle Mister lived down here, along with six cowboy cabins full of men.

They had huge equipment sheds and barns and a new stable that had just gone in last year, and the teeming, thriving ranch atmosphere started from the highway now, instead of the top of the hill, where the arch still sat, welcoming everyone to Shiloh Ridge Ranch. Mitch wondered if Uncle Bear and Uncle Ranger would ever move it, but they weren't in charge of the ranch anymore. Now, Link and Wilder ran the ranch together, and Uncle Ward had finally moved into full retirement as well.

Mitch had been told many times that he could have a place on Shiloh Ridge anytime he wanted it, but it had never been something that teemed inside him the way it did Link or Wilder or even Gunnison. Pearl Jo loved the ranch too, as did Hank and Smiles and Rock. Rock had not left for college and, in fact, had moved right into a cowboy cabin and started working with the horses at Shiloh Ridge.

He trained them to round up cattle and cut cows out of the herd, and he managed all of their breeding and cattle sales now. Mitch actually wondered what Smiles would do when he returned to the ranch once he finished college, but he had another year to go.

He eased under the arch, and he usually turned left and went past True Blue, Uncle Bishop and Uncle Ace's house, and up the hill again to Link's house. Link had always been Mitch's safe person, and he couldn't believe he'd let a few comments about who he dated come between them.

Of course, Mitch had let a lot of things irritate him in recent years, including anything religious, most family things, and anyone who didn't seem to understand Deaf culture as well as he did. He knew he needed to soften up on some of those things. He simply didn't know how.

You're taking the first step, he told himself as he turned right and went past the huge homestead where Uncle Ranger lived with Aunt Oakley. Bull House sat next to that, where Uncle Ward and Aunt Dot had raised their family. Barns and stables sat across the street from them, and Uncle Ward had also put in an enormous picnic area with gravel and tables and plenty of places to sit around the fire so that anyone who wanted to roast marshmallows, or hot dogs, or Starburst could come any time, day or night.

At the end of the road, the Ranch House sat, all of the Christmas decorations gone for the year, though Uncle Judge would probably start pulling them out in only another couple of months. He and Aunt June still had a couple of kids at home, and Mitch rounded the corner to the beautiful view of Aunt Etta's house.

He loved Aunt Etta with his whole heart, and she never let a week go by where she didn't see him in person, usually with one of his favorite treats, or where she didn't call him. She'd done it every week, even when he lived in Virginia, even when he was so busy he could barely sleep.

She loved him endlessly and unconditionally, and Mitch's throat tightened at the mere thought of her. Her front door bore a bright yellow wreath of tulips that made him smile—and think of Lacy.

The road turned left, and that led to a row of cowboy cabins, but Mitch kept going straight. Uncle Bear and Aunt Sammy's house came up on the right next, and he kept rumbling past that.

He'd grown up in the Edge Cabin, sleeping in the barn for the last five years that he lived at Shiloh Ridge. His parents had added on to the cabin, but it had taken a couple of years to get it all done after they had adopted Cameron, Kyle, and Lynn, who were full siblings, and had no one to take care of them.

Mitch had given up his bedroom when Melissa was born, a baby he'd been extremely angry about, because his momma was not well physically. Even to this day, she walked with a limp, and she existed with pain through her hip and back almost all the time. She had done physical therapy and treatments, and she took painkillers and anti-inflammatories when she had to. Both of her pregnancies had been extremely, extremely difficult for her, and Mitch had been very upset when she'd gotten pregnant with Melissa.

So maybe he'd always been a bit of a hothead, and a touch temperamental, and a tad opinionated. He honestly wasn't sure why his mother was surprised at anything he did, even now as an adult.

She's probably not, he thought. *She probably just wants to know what's going on with you.* He could admit that he did not keep her in the loop very often. He talked to his father a lot more than his mother, and he wasn't even sure why.

He took a breath as the road jogged around and then curved back toward the Edge Cabin. He'd driven this path so many times, and he'd only been this nervous once—when he'd come home to tell his parents he was moving to Virginia.

As he pulled up behind the house and parked next to his mother's SUV, he knew exactly why he talked to his daddy more than his momma. She was a pastor in town, and she honestly couldn't help herself from giving advice, and it was advice that Mitch *didn't* want.

He didn't want to be lectured about his lack of faith, or that he needed to read the scriptures more, or that he should just trust in God and everything would work out.

He hated platitudes like that; in fact, and he'd stopped going to church years ago. He loved God, and he knew God loved him. He simply wasn't sure he believed in divine power, for he'd never really seen it work in his life. *He* worked and *he* got the job done, and if he were being completely honest with himself, he didn't want to give any of that credit to God.

Surely his mother knew he had arrived, and to her credit, she did not come to the door and gesture for him to come in. Mitch sat there wrestling with his feelings, wrestling with his beliefs, wrestling with his faith.

And when he couldn't stand it anymore, he got out of the car and went to go talk to his mother.

Chapter Twelve

C actus Glover growled low in his throat. "What is taking him so long?"

"We're lucky he's here at all," Willa said. "Don't go rushing out there, Charles."

She'd been cooking all morning for this lunch, though Mitch had offered to *bring* them the meal. The man had plenty of money, Cactus knew that, and yet Willa calmed herself by baking and putting together casseroles and sandwiches and salads. They had enough food to feed Mitch for a month, and she'd probably try to send him home with all of it too.

Cactus knew Mitch had not been talking to Willa as much as him, and he tried not to make a big deal out of it. He didn't want his wife to feel bad, or to change who she was—or what she said to Mitch. She was exceptionally skilled at listening to the spirit and acting on it, and if she felt like she should say something to him about anything in his life, be that the women he dated, the job he'd chosen, or what he should have for lunch, she did it.

But what she'd been truly worried about for many months now was Mitch's relationship with the Lord. Cactus had tried to tell her over and over that those relationships were personal and that she could not force such a thing onto another person. He knew; he'd lived for years in this very cabin by himself, shutting everyone out, including God.

He'd had to come to church and religion in his own way, and half the time, Cactus still didn't want to attend services. He'd taken jobs on the ranch on Sundays to get out of it, even after he and Willa had gotten married and he felt reconciled to the Lord.

Not everyone loved to listen to sermons for an hour, or loved to sing hymns, and yet they could still be perfectly good Christians. He hoped Willa would remember that—and that she would listen to the spirit and say what she felt like she needed to. He simply prayed that God would provide a way for Mitch to feel loved *and* for Willa to feel heard.

There had to be a dovetail there somewhere, and Cactus offered another silent prayer just as the back door opened. The tension in the air cracked like a whip as Mitch stepped inside, his cowboy boots thudding against the floor. Cactus stayed right where he was—seated in the recliner in the living room. Willa stepped away from the stove and wiped her hands on her apron.

She signed to him, and Mitch smiled and said, *Hullo,*

Momma. He stepped into her and gave her a hug that felt and looked awkward to Cactus. Their eyes met, and Mitch's grin widened into something a little more real and quite a bit happier.

Cactus raised his hand and said, *Hello, son.*

Howdy, Mitch said, and he surveyed the counter laden with food. *Momma, did you make all this?* He looked at her with surprise running through his eyes. *I told you I would bring lunch. What time did you get up this morning?*

She waved him away and said, *I wanted to make it.*

Mitch wore a dubious expression on his face, and Cactus wished he could tell Willa that things like this didn't bring Mitch closer; they only made him feel worse.

I made enough that you can take some home for you and Lacy, she said.

Mitch looked at her out of the corner of his eye. *Me and Lacy. Is that what you want to talk about?*

Yes, Willa said. *That's one of the things.*

Mitch sighed, and Cactus swore he could hear the irritation in it from twenty feet away.

Let me go say hi to Daddy, he said, and he came into the living room. Cactus got to his feet, a twinge in his back telling him he wasn't as young as he'd once been.

Hey, boy, he said, and he drew Mitch right into his chest for a tight hug. He wished he could whisper in his ear about how hard his momma had worked for him and how much she loved him. When he pulled back, he told him all the same. *Just try to listen,* he said. *She's really worried about you. We both are.*

I know, Mitch said. *I don't know why. As you can see, I'm healthy as a horse; alive, doing well. We open our registration on Tuesday.*

Yeah, we know the surface stuff, Cactus said. *We know the work stuff. We want the* personal *stuff.*

Mitch's jaw tightened, but he didn't argue back, and Cactus counted that as a win. Champ alerted when Willa said, "Mitch," and he turned back to his mother.

Come get something to eat, she said. *I made that braided pizza bread that you love and the caramel apple salad.*

He turned away from Cactus as he spoke, so Cactus wasn't sure what he said in response. It didn't matter. It sure felt good to have their boy home again. And while Mitch came to the ranch to visit regularly, it didn't feel like he ever really *showed up.*

Cactus only wanted the best for all of his children, but he could admit that he had a special place in his heart for Mitch. Life was not fair, that was for certain, but he still wanted it to be *good* for his son.

He joined Willa and Mitch in the kitchen and put together a plate of food for himself as well. They all sat down at the kitchen table, and Willa said, *Tell us when you started dating Lacy.*

The wedding was our first date, Mitch said. *I mean, I made a fool of myself over a year ago, asking her out. She shot me down pretty fast.* He grinned, and Cactus joined him.

She's great. I really like her, Mitch said, and he signed honestly, his expression matching his hands. *I didn't know this until yesterday, but she's been married before, and her husband died right before she came to Three Rivers, so it makes sense that she was a little standoffish last year.*

Oh, well, that's too bad, Willa said. *What happened? Was he ill?*

One thing about Willa, she really cared about people, and she wasn't asking just to be nice—or to be nosy. Mitch explained that Lacy's husband had been in a car accident and then gotten an infection that had ultimately ended his life.

Cactus had seen a lot of strange things in his life too, mostly with cattle and horses, and he nodded sympathetically. *That's too bad, son.*

Anyway, Mitch said. *She's a little closed off. But, I mean, I guess I am too.*

Are you? Cactus asked.

I mean, I don't even really know how to have a long-term relationship, he said.

Sure, you do, Cactus said. *You've had a long-term relationship with us. You've been best friends with Link for years.*

Mitch's expression hardened. *I'm kind of mad at Link right now. Can we talk about that?*

You're mad at Link? Willa asked, shooting a look in Cactus's direction. *Why?*

He said some stupid stuff about Lacy, he said.

Willa smiled. *So I shouldn't say anything stupid about her...like what, so that I know?*

Link said...he was questioning whether I should be dating her or not. I had to remind him I'm older than him and that I can live my own life the way I want.

It's a great reminder, Cactus said, looking over to his wife. Their eyes met for the briefest of moments, and then Willa went right back to Mitch.

I can admit I was a little bit surprised, she said. *But you two seem cute together.*

You saw us for ten minutes, Mitch said. *How would you know?*

And ah, there was that bluntness that Mitch had developed when he'd moved to Virginia. Cactus did his best to hide his smile behind a bite of pasta salad.

Anyway, he made it seem like we shouldn't be together or that I didn't know what I was doing. Mitch shook his head. *I kind of told him off. I'm gonna go see him this afternoon and apologize.*

Probably a good idea, Willa said. *We always have to work on forgiving those around us—and ourselves.*

Mitch gave her a wary look. *I know, Momma.*

Cactus thought she might stop there, but he knew Willa better than that.

I haven't seen you at church in a long time.

He shook his head. *I don't like going to church.*

Why not? she asked.

Mitch filled his mouth with food and glared at her as he chewed it. The temperature in the room went right back up again, but Cactus knew better than to say something.

They all waited for Mitch, as a conversation with him was different than with anyone else.

It feels fake, Mitch finally said. *Okay? It doesn't feel real. It feels like I'm playing pretend, and I don't like it.*

Willa nodded, and she glanced over to Cactus again.

I'm a good person, Mitch said. *I work hard. I take care of my business. I'm kind...ish to others.*

You're kind, Cactus said. *You just don't like being told what to do.*

You don't like being questioned, Willa said.

No, Mitch said. *I don't like either of those things, and it's because people have treated me like I'm dumb my whole life. I'm not dumb.*

No one thinks you're dumb, son, Cactus said.

No one here, Mitch said. He glared over to his momma. *At least I didn't think so.*

Of course, I don't think you're dumb, Willa said, her fingers flying as she punctuated the words with the same bite that existed in her tone. She frowned. *Why would I think that? You hold a PhD, for crying out loud, and you've never given me any reason not to be proud of you.*

Except I don't go to church, Mitch said.

I worry about you, Willa said, and Cactus could hear the kindness and genuineness in his wife's voice. She put her hand on Mitch's arm. *I love you dearly. I will do whatever you need. I'm here to support you and love you, and I feel like you've closed the door on me.*

Mitch put his head down, and Willa sniffled and swallowed while he wasn't watching. He looked up again and said, *Maybe I have.*

You talk to your daddy more than me, and I don't know. She glanced over to Cactus, but didn't really meet his eyes. *I guess I'm jealous.* She reached up and wiped her eyes. *I guess if you have to talk to someone who's not me, Daddy's okay.*

Cactus put his hand on his wife's knee under the table, and she looked at him. He nodded, and she did too.

I'm sorry, Mitch said. *I don't mean to upset you. I just don't want to be lectured, and Daddy just...lets me be.*

I know, Willa said. *I know that, and I'm going to do my best not to lecture you.*

Mitch nodded, and Cactus was exceptionally good at knowing what to say and when to say it. But in that moment, he looked at his beautiful wife, who he loved and adored, and his beautiful son that had come into his life right when Cactus had needed a son to take care of.

What do you need from us, Mitch? he asked. *We're here for you, and we'll do anything you need.*

Mitch sniffled and reached up and wiped his eyes too. *I need to learn how to not be so hot-headed,* he said. *Or so grumpy. I'm afraid if I can't figure that out, I might lose Lacy.*

He glanced over to his mother. *And not just as a girl-friend, but as my director, and I need her at Signs for Success.*

Signs for Success, Willa said, her face brightening. *Is that what you're going to name the academy? That's amazing.*

Cactus smiled and nodded too. *I love that,* he said.

Mitch's whole countenance brightened. *Yeah, Signs for Success.* He looked down at his plate, which he'd mostly emptied, and then back up at Cactus. *I also don't want to be the grouchy headmaster when the academy opens. You used to be really prickly.* He smiled in that kind way he had. *And now you're not. How do I do that?*

He's not really prickly, Willa said with a laugh. *But you should steer clear of him before he has coffee.*

Cactus chuckled good-naturedly, but he had a feeling that Mitch was asking a serious question. He looked at his son and cocked his eyebrows. *I don't think you'll like this answer.*

Give it to me anyway, Mitch said.

Cactus drew a deep breath and held it, and he looked at Willa. He tried to find a different answer, a different way to tell his son to de-prickle, but there was no other answer.

I prayed for help, he said, practically throwing his hands around. *And I relied on those around me to tell me when I was being stubborn or mean or ridiculous. A lot of times, that job fell to your mother, sometimes Aunt Sammy, and then you kids.* You, Mitch.

The younger man nodded and swiped up his last bite of pepperoni pizza braid. *All right,* he said. *I'll work on it.*

That's all we can be expected to do, Willa said. *We just work to try to be better today than we were yesterday.*

Mitch nodded, and she patted his arm and looked at Cactus again. He didn't know what she wanted him to say, and all of his words had run out. He said a silent prayer for Mitch as they finished up lunch, and he knew that Mitch, just like all of his children, were in God's hands.

Yes, he had to learn to trust God to take care of them and lead them where they needed to be, and that included carefully bringing Mitch back into His fold.

Chapter Thirteen

Lacy sat back in her chair as the number in front of her flipped from forty-nine to fifty. She couldn't believe it. Registration for Signs for Success had opened that morning—less than four hours ago.

She and Mitch had made a launch video over the weekend announcing the academy, their goals, and their vision—what would be available for students, teenagers, and adults alike. They had not discussed goals. Neither one of them had known how many people would sign up for an academy like theirs.

Three Rivers sat in the Texas Panhandle, an hour away from a major airport. Yes, the town had grown in recent years, with a population almost at thirty thousand now. Yes, she'd reached out to everyone she knew and so had Mitch. Yes, they had an amazing facility and curriculum here—and it was all showcased on a beautiful and professional website. But she still hadn't known what to anticipate in terms of enrollment.

The number flipped to fifty-one and then fifty-two, and Lacy pushed away from her makeshift office on the third floor and headed for the landing. She had no idea where Mitch was. Perhaps he sat watching the enrollment numbers tick up the same way she did.

She thought through all the things she needed to do now that they had real students: sort them by age for classes, hire teachers, sort them by who would live on-site versus those who would live in town, and hire Resident Assistants.

She would also have to make room assignments and send out roommate questionnaires for those who signed up solo but wanted to live with someone. Her heart pounded as she ran downstairs, stopped at Mitch's door, and banged loudly with the side of her fist.

She waited, practically dancing on the landing for him to answer. "Mitch!" she yelled, because Champ should alert him at his name. The dog should alert at a knock too, but if Mitch wasn't home, Champ wouldn't alert to the pounding, but he would to the name. "Mitch!" she called again as she ran downstairs.

His office sat down the hall toward the conference room, and he appeared in the doorway as she hurried toward it.

"We have fifty-two people registered for Signs for Success!" she said, speaking and signing in her excitement.

His eyes widened, and he reached up and took off the

cowboy hat he wore. She didn't see him wear one often, but every now and then he exhibited the country boy who existed inside of him.

You're kidding, he said.

He turned around and strode back into the office, and Lacy practically jogged in behind him.

"I'm not kidding," she said out loud to his back, glee filling her from top to bottom. How many more people had registered in the few minutes it had taken her to come downstairs and find him? Lacy's hopes felt tied to an enormous bunch of helium balloons, and they kept rising and rising and rising. She tried to grab onto them and pull them back to Earth, because she knew she'd be sorely disappointed eventually.

Mitch sat in front of his desk. *I had no idea what to expect.*

We didn't set any goals for enrollment, Lacy said, too keyed up to sit in one of the chairs in front of his desk.

Do we even have enough room for fifty people? He glanced up, and Lacy laughed.

Mitch, you built two huge buildings for people to live in, she said. *Four stories each. Remember? We can house one hundred and sixty students.*

Right, right, he said. *Twenty on each floor.*

And besides, not all of them will be on-site residents anyway.

Mitch nodded and swallowed, his nerves so adorable. He returned his attention to his computer, where he clicked and moved his mouse around until he found what he was looking for.

Fifty-six, he said. He stared at the screen and clicked again. He looked up at Lacy. *It says fifty-six.*

She laughed again. *It's fifty-six then.* She rounded the desk and stood at his shoulder. *Look how many views our video has gotten.* She wasn't sure if he'd seen her sign, but she pointed to the video. It had been watched thirty-five-hundred times in only four hours. Lacy honestly didn't know if that was good or bad, but thirty-five-hundred was more than zero.

Mitch clicked on the video for some reason, and Lacy heard her own voice say, "Hi there. I'm Lacy Hayes, the Educational Director for Signs for Success, and I'm sitting here with its founder, Mitchell Glover." She signed everything she said, of course, and Mitch shone like a new penny. He looked downright wholesome in his cowboy hat, plaid shirt, and jeans, and she was his complete opposite in a pair of navy blue slacks and a blouse the color and texture of clouds.

He paused the video and sat back in his chair. *This is unbelievable*, he said. He reached for her hand, and before Lacy knew it, he tugged her forward and around the arm of the chair, and right into his lap. Lacy had not been this close to a man in a long time, and adrenaline pumped through her stronger than ever. Everything Mitch did felt normal and natural and easy, and he curled one hand around her waist while he reached for his mouse with the other one. He made a couple of clicks and pointed at the screen.

Lacy leaned forward slightly, feeling a bit off balance now. He'd clicked over to the waiting list and the interest forms. Of course, the waitlist was zero, as they were not full, but the interest form had over one hundred entries.

"Holy cow," Lacy breathed, the words barely leaving her mouth. She turned toward Mitch as awe ran through her. *We have a lot of emails to reply to,* she said.

He laughed, the deep, rich sound of it reaching up toward the ceilings of his house. *You set up the automation, remember?* He grinned and grinned. *Who's forgetting things now?*

Lacy pushed playfully against his shoulder, though she didn't mind being teased—not by him. She stood up and reached for his hand. *Let's go make a cake.*

A cake?

She turned and towed him out of the office and into the kitchen. "I can't sit still," she said. *We have fifty-six people registered, and we need a cake to celebrate.* She opened the fridge to get out the butter and eggs. *Surely, you have a cake recipe.*

Do I? he asked, and he'd barely taken two steps into the kitchen.

Yes, Mister, she said. *Get over here and help me.*

He got over there, but he didn't do anything to help her. *I think we should go to lunch,* he said. *And dinner. We can get cake and cheesecake and cookies and ice cream there.*

He wrapped her in a one-armed embrace and gazed down at her. *You really want to make a cake?*

Lacy's mind blitzed around, and she honestly didn't

know what she wanted. *I feel jumpy,* she said. *If we go out, we have to get something and go to the park, somewhere where I don't have to sit and be proper in a restaurant.*

She looked up at him, hoping he would understand. *Somewhere where we don't have the Internet, so I can't check every thirty seconds how many more people have registered.*

He smiled down at her and leaned closer. Lacy's heartbeat misfired, thinking he might kiss her right there in the kitchen. Did she want him to do that? Did she want their first kiss to be in the house, this kitchen that they shared?

She wasn't sure, and pure indecision raged through her even as her eyes drifted closed, her body and her mind two completely separate beings in this moment.

Mitch turned his head at the last moment and looked down. Lacy followed his gaze. She found Champ with both paws up on Mitch's thigh; he had alerted. Mitch pulled away, stepped back, and watched as Champ dropped to his feet and trotted out of the kitchen.

I think someone's here, he said. He moved to follow his dog into the living room and to the front door. Lacy walked on wooden legs after them, pausing in the doorway between the kitchen and the living room. Champ already had the front door open, and, sure enough, a deliveryman stood there.

He said something to Mitch that Mitch waved away. He pulled out his phone and started typing. He showed it to the man. He simply held up his tablet and the pen; Mitch had to sign for something, which he did. The man smiled, reached down, patted Champ, and turned to leave the porch.

Mitch stepped out and picked up the package that sat there. Lacy had no idea what it was. He ordered things all the time online, and she did plenty of web ordering herself.

Is it for me or you? she asked.

Me, he said. *I have no idea what it is; I haven't ordered anything.*

She'd ordered plenty of items in his name for the academy, but now that they had a name for it, she would use that. But until then, she had no way of knowing if the package was for him personally or for work.

He took it into the kitchen and slid it onto the counter. Lacy looked at the butter and eggs that she'd pulled out of the fridge, and now that her adrenaline had gone down slightly, she realized she did not want to make a cake. If she could get Mitch to take her to lunch, that would be a much better celebration.

Mitch sliced open the top of the box and lifted the flaps. A grin burst onto his face, and he lifted out what looked to be a license plate. He turned it toward her, and Lacy read the name *Sunshine.*

It's the nameplates for the dogs, he said, and she loved that such simple things made him so happy. They made her happy too. Lacy took the Sunshine nameplate from him so he could pull out the next one. He showed her *Maven* and *William,* and then he took them all from her.

She edged in close to him, initiating contact in a rare move. *Will you really take me to lunch?* she asked, curling her hand up the back of his bicep to his shoulder. He looked at her, and she realized how close she'd pressed in.

He nodded, and Lacy tipped up onto her toes and brushed a kiss across his cheek. *Great,* she said. *Let me just go grab my phone and check the enrollment one last time, and I'll meet you down here in five minutes.*

Chapter Fourteen

Lincoln Glover made the turn onto Mitch's lane. His throat suddenly felt too dry and too narrow. He could barely get any air down, but he'd put this off for a week longer than he should have.

Chaz had told him that Mitch would be stopping by last week, but he'd never come. Link had stopped talking to Chaz about Mitch because he knew Mitch wouldn't like it. Heck, Link wouldn't have liked it if he had been in Mitch's place. The Glover family was simply too big and too nosy to indulge in gossip.

Link had tried to apologize multiple times over the past several days since the wedding. He'd finally gone to his father after church on Sunday and confessed everything he'd said to Mitch about his new girlfriend, Lacy. It didn't really matter what Link thought. It didn't matter if he didn't think Mitch should be dating someone he worked so closely with and on whom he relied for so much.

He hadn't truly meant to comment on it at all. He'd been surprised, sure, and tired after a night of almost no sleep with a sick wife, frustrated and irritated after his son had gotten stung by a bee. It was still no excuse for passing judgment, and Daddy had told him about a time when he'd bought a car for Aunt Willa while she and Uncle Cactus were dating.

"Boy, Uncle Cactus sure was mad," Daddy had said with a chuckle. "Took a swing at me and everything, and then he wouldn't talk to me for weeks. I called, I texted, I went out to the Edge Cabin, and nothing. That man can hold a grudge." Daddy could grin about such things now, but Link sure hadn't. "He's stubborn, but he's my brother, and I love him."

Daddy had not told Link exactly what to do, but Link heard all he needed to know. Mitch was stubborn and head-strong too. He had a quick temper that fired easily and hotly, and while Link had called and texted, he had not gone to see Mitch.

Until today.

He had his small ranch owners meeting in about an hour, but he would miss it if he had to. He would do what-ever it took to make things right with Mitch.

Link swallowed again, hoping his pride was completely gone so that he could talk to his cousin—his best friend besides Misty—and make things right.

He pulled up to the house where both Mitch's truck and

Lacy's SUV sat. "So they're here," he whispered as he put his car in park. Yes, they were here, and the moment Link knocked on the door, Champ would tell them.

He reached for the cinnamon raisin bread that Misty had made last night and heaved himself out of the truck. He took the steps two at a time and didn't hesitate as he rang the doorbell, then knocked, and then opened the door.

"Mitch," he called, his voice sounding like he'd swallowed rusty nails and his vocal cords had been punctured.

Link stood in the silent living room, praying with everything he had that Mitch and Lacy were not in a meeting. Mitch had texted earlier this week when the enrollment for his academy had opened. He and Lacy had seen eighty-two registrations on the first day, and everyone in the Glover family had celebrated with them with words and emojis and sentiments of congratulations.

Please, dear God, Link thought. *Bless his heart to be open and forgiving. Bless him to forgive me.*

"Mitch?" he called again.

The sound of footsteps came toward him—cowboy boots on hardwood, which had to be Mitch. Champ preceded him by only a stride or two, and then Mitch entered the living room. He paused when he saw Link standing there, and the two of them faced each other silently.

Surprise drove through Link when he realized Mitch was wearing his cowboy hat and looked every bit like he could step onto Shiloh Ridge, take over one of their chores, manage their stables, or lead the cattle roundup. Of course he could. Mitch had grown up on the ranch, same as Link.

Just because a cowboy left a ranch didn't mean the cowboy way left him.

Link held up the bread. *I am* so *sorry for everything I said about you and Lacy, and I can't go another sleepless night.* His guilt was too much for him.

Mitch's dark hazel eyes stormed, and then he dropped his head as his shoulders loosened. Link set the bread on the couch and moved over to Mitch. His cousin looked up, and Link signed everything he'd already said.

I'm miserable, because I hurt you. This week has been terrible, because we don't talk about the silliest things, and I miss it—I miss you, he said. *Please forgive me. I'm so sorry.*

Mitch shook his head, waved, and said, *There's nothing to forgive, brother.* He grabbed onto Link and pulled him into his chest in a tight hug. He clapped him on the back good-naturedly, but Link simply held onto Mitch with every ounce of strength he had, reveling in the sweet sensation of reconciliation.

He stepped back as Mitch asked, *Is that cinnamon raisin bread? Did Misty make it?* A small smile started across his face.

Link nodded before he turned to get the bread. When he faced Mitch, he held it up. *Do you want me to toast some for you right now?*

For sure, Mitch said. *Can you stay for a minute?*

Yeah, Link said. *It's the small ranch owner's meeting today, and I think you should come.*

Mitch tilted his head, his smile faltering. *Why would I do that? I don't own a ranch.*

You have just the same type of operation as Alex or Finn, Link said. *You have a lot of land and a lot of buildings, and just because you're not looking after horses or experimenting with guineafowl doesn't mean you don't have a lot of the same concerns as the rest of us.*

You think so? Mitch asked. *Do you think they'd care if I came?*

They ask about you every time, Link said. He nodded his wide-brimmed cowboy hat toward the kitchen. *Let's go make toast. I'll tell you what this month's topic is, and you can decide if you want to come or not.*

He led the way into the kitchen, and Mitch pulled the toaster out of a cupboard while Link got a knife from the block. *Misty wants you to come for dinner,* he said. *You and Lacy.*

I don't know, Mitch said.

Why not? Link asked.

We're still really new, Mitch said. *And I'd rather wait until we're more serious.*

But if you end up together, Link said. *Me and you—and Lacy and Misty—will do a lot together. So you'll have to come sooner or later.* He sliced off the butt of the bread and handed it to Mitch. *So you might as well just come sooner.*

Are you gonna let this go? Mitch asked.

You've met my wife, right? Link asked. *Even if I let it go, she won't. She loves you. She's been so mad at me since the wedding that I haven't been able to get all the details on you and Lacy.* He grinned and went back to slicing bread.

Mitch chuckled, and when their eyes met again, he said,

There are no details. We've been out a few times, but boy, I really like her. His smile testified of that too.

Mitch ducked his head, but his hands kept moving. *I've liked her for a long time. I asked her out fifteen months ago, and she told me no.*

Wow, Link said. *That is a long time.*

And especially for Mitch.

But Link had known Mitch for twenty-five years, and the man had intense passions and things he cared a lot about. And when he found that thing, he bit on like a pit bull and would not let go.

And if that thing was Lacy Hayes, Link definitely better get them to come to dinner *way* sooner rather than later.

Chapter Fifteen

F inn Ackerman brought his truck to a stop just as his phone started to ring. It blared through the console, cutting off the country song he'd been listening to.

He parked down on the end, next to Dawson Rhine-hart's truck, and reached to answer the call. "What's up, Daddy?"

"Where are you right now, son?"

Finn's brain computed many things at once. One, the serious nature of his father's tone. Two, the fact that he had not said hello. And three, why did he need to know where Finn was?

The human brain was a marvelous organ, as he thought about his mother and what she was doing that day—and his sister, and what she and Rusty might be doing—both of his brothers—and then Edith, and their three children.

And yet, only two seconds had passed before Finn said,

"I just got to Alex's. We're having our ranch owner's meeting. What's going on?"

"Have you got a minute?" Daddy asked.

"Yes," Finn said, though he'd been running late. He had to be one of the last people to arrive—if Brandon Rhinehart was already here.

"We just got news about Tyson Greene," he said, and on his end of the line, something slammed closed.

"I'm going to put them in the basement, Squire," Finn's momma said, her voice barely coming through the line. "They'll have everything they need down there, and they can come and go as they please."

"Absolutely," Daddy said followed by a big sigh.

"What's goin' on with Tyson Greene?" Finn asked. The last he'd heard, Ty had been on the pro rodeo circuit and doing very well. He competed in team roping, as well as bronc riding, and he'd traveled all over Texas, the Western United States, and up into Canada to compete.

Finn had grown up with Tyson, though he was probably a decade older than him. Ty's daddy had worked at Three Rivers Ranch for a long time, and his momma owned Bowman's Breeds, the horse training facility right next to the homestead where Finn had grown up. She trained horses for bronc riding, roping, and barrel racing—and she herself had been a champion barrel racer. His daddy had been a bull rider, and Ty's path to the rodeo had been paved with gold.

"He got thrown during a training exercise," Daddy said. "He's in the hospital in Calgary right now, and Ethan and

Brynn are making their way up to see him and find out what's really going on."

"That's not good," Finn said, his heart settling somewhere near his tailbone.

"No," Daddy said. "Ty's girlfriend called Bowman's Breeds and talked to the secretary there. They've tried calling back, but they haven't been able to get through to anyone."

"Did they say what happened?"

"Just that he got thrown during a training exercise, but we don't know if it was from a bull or a horse," Daddy said. "There was something about a broken leg and some broken ribs, and maybe even a collapsed lung."

"Oh, no," Finn said. He hadn't spoken to Ty in years, but that didn't mean his human compassion couldn't be activated. "Do you guys need help on the ranch?"

"Your momma is making an apartment for them in the basement," he said. "What with them working out here and all."

Finn nodded and looked at the beautiful ranch house where Alex lived with his wife and family. The land could seem so serene sometimes, with horses that swished their tails back and forth to swat off the flies, and chickens that clucked as they laid eggs, and sheep as puffy as white clouds on a summer day.

But wild animals were still wild, and horses still got spooked, and farms and ranches had to be treated with respect, or they could claim a man's life.

"I can come help feed horses," he said. "Theo and Bubba are getting pretty good at it."

"I told Brynn I'd go over and see what was going on at her place," Daddy said. "I'll let you know."

Finn watched as another truck arrived, this time carrying Link and Mitch Glover, so he wasn't the last to arrive.

"I have a lot of friends," Finn said. "They'd all be willing to come help."

"They've got ranches of their own," Daddy said.

"Yeah, and so do you," Finn said. "And every time there's been a flood or a tornado or anything else that's happened, you were right there helping out the Glovers or the Bellamores or the Walkers, and they'll come help too," Finn said. "We *want* to do it, Daddy; you can't deny us that."

His father chuckled, and Finn could just see him shaking his head in acceptance. "I'll keep you informed. You have a pretty good network of young men, and some of them, I imagine, are Ty's age."

"Yeah, I reckon so," Finn said. "I'll let them know at our meeting today, and I'm sure they'll come if he needs help."

"All right," Daddy said. "Keep him and Brynn and Ethan and their family in your prayers."

"Will do," Finn said, and the call ended. With a slightly heavier heart, he got out of the truck and headed into Alex's farmhouse. The man sure could put good food together, and while sometimes they met at the IFA and didn't cater food, they also sometimes met on someone's ranch or farm. Today,

Alex had provided lunch—complete with a Texas sheet cake, a huge bowl of cheesy popcorn, and pulled pork sliders.

Finn closed the door behind him as he took in everyone who had arrived. Henry, Finn's cousin, handed his wife a plate full of food and turned back to the bar to get some for himself. Angel sat next to Nikki at the long, golden-wood picnic table that Alex and Nikki used as a family dining table. They just had the two boys, twins, who were six years old and in kindergarten now. Nikki worked alongside Alex on the ranch, and she did all of the gardening and landscaping around the house, as she had a real green thumb.

Finn and Edith spent a lot of time with Alex and Nikki, because Alex was Edith's brother, and she had lived in this house once upon a time. Link and Mitch had joined the group at the counter to get food, where Dawson and Brandon Rhinehart were just leaving. They moved over to the table and took seats across from Nikki and Angel. Another group of young men laughed, and Wilder Glover scooped up a plastic cup of popcorn as he added something to whatever JJ and Conrad Walker were already chorting about.

The door opened behind him, and Finn quickly sidestepped out of the way as Rusty and Libby entered the house.

"Oh, good," his sister said. "We're not late."

"Looks like they just started," Rusty said.

"I just got here too," Finn said, drawing their attention to him.

"Did you hear about Ty?" Libby asked, and she moved right over to Finn and hugged him. She was a tough woman when she had to be, but Libby's heart was as soft as they came. "Momma's making an apartment for them in the basement."

"I heard," Finn said as he held his sister tight. "Do you have an update?"

"We got a little bit more information out of Tiffany," she said. "She said the woman who called—she couldn't remember her name—was Ty's girlfriend. Ethan says her name is Jenn, and she said that his leg had been broken in four places."

"Which one?" Finn asked.

"Left side," Libby said. "Everything on the left side is apparently crushed—ribs, lungs, everything." She wore a look of pure worry when she stepped back, and she took Nora from Rusty as the little girl started to fuss. "I'm going to go see if I can lay her down in Nikki's bedroom," she said. She bustled off to do that, and Rusty stuck by Finn's side as they moved toward the bar.

"Howdy, brother," Alex said, and he shook Finn's hand and pulled him into a hug. "What is eating at you?" He pulled back, his gaze serious. Of course, Alex was always a little bit serious, even when laughing.

"I'll save it for news," Finn said. "I only want to say it once."

"It's not good news?" Alex asked.

Finn shook his head and picked up a plate. He handed it to Rusty, who had really come into his own in the past year.

He and Libby ran Three Rivers Ranch and had been doing it for eighteen months now, and Finn loved his brother-in-law. They moved through the line and got their lunch and sat down at the end of the table just as Libby returned.

Alex stood at the head of the table. "All right, everyone, let's go around and do news, and then we're going to talk about applying for small business and agricultural grants, and keep up with some new ranching policies that have been introduced into the state."

It wasn't the most glamorous of topics, but in the end, Finn did run a business. He happened to live on the land where he raised his cattle that he sold to feed his family. He did have to keep up with policies and regulations—they all did—whether he liked it or not. And as he took a bite of his pulled pork sandwich, Alex said, "I'll start with the news," but he didn't go on.

That caused Finn to look up, and he found his usually stoic, strong, and fairly silent brother-in-law swallowing hard as he reached for his wife's hand. She rose to her feet too.

"Nikki and I just found out," he said. "That she's going to have another baby."

A gasp went through the men and women sitting at the table, Finn's included. Alex and Nikki had struggled mightily to get their twins, and they'd had to go through a fertility clinic to do it.

"That's amazing," Libby said, the first to speak. "Congratulations!" She stood up and hurried down the long row to both Alex and Nikki to hug them.

Angel did the same, and Finn finally found his voice to say, "Congratulations, brother."

He wondered if Edith knew, and he met Alex's eye, who shook his head. Finn quickly pulled out his phone to text his wife. She could come to these meetings, but they still had two little kids at home, and while she helped on the farm, she certainly didn't run it. She'd much rather attend couples' nights or family game evenings that Finn helped to organize with all of his friends than what she called "boring ranch stuff."

He grinned and grinned, because he didn't exactly blame her. He also knew she'd be here within a half-hour so that she could congratulate Nikki as well.

YOU'RE KIDDING. Her text came in all caps. *How long will this meeting last?*

They're usually about an hour, he texted. *Alex has pulled pork sliders and popcorn.*

I'll be there with the kids in twenty minutes.

Finn expected no less, and he tuned back into the news as Paul said, "There must be babies in the air, or good luck, or just God's blessings, because Brielle is finally pregnant too."

"What?" Henry roared. "And I'm hearing about it at a *ranch owner's meeting?*" He planted both palms on the table and half-stood. "You are supposed to text me before this."

Paul laughed and shook his head, then reached up and wiped his eyes. "She's four months along. This is the first pregnancy that's lasted this long," he said, looking at his brother with a hint of iciness in his eyes. "So we didn't tell anyone. It's so much easier to grieve when it's just two of you."

"Is it, though?" Henry challenged, always the outspoken, hot-headed one. "You shouldn't have to go through something like that alone."

"Well, after *you* have to tell people *four times* that your wife has lost a baby, I'm sure you'll think differently," Paul said coolly.

"All right," Alex said. "This is *good* news. We don't need to fight about it." Angel put her hand on Henry's arm, and he sat back down.

"Sorry," he said. "We don't have any pregnancy news." He shot a look at Angel, and she merely smiled at him.

"Do you have anything else?" Alex asked.

"I got a new cat," Angel said, almost with a question mark on the end.

Alex chuckled. "That's good news too—if it's a good mouser."

"Does it have to be good news?" Libby asked, and Finn realized he might not have to tell them about Tyson.

"Not exactly," Alex said, his eyes roaming back to Finn. "We can talk about job needs too, remember?"

"Well, I want to welcome Mitch," Conrad said. "He doesn't exactly run a farm the way we all do, but I imagine he has a lot of the same challenges."

"Yeah," Finn said. "Let's welcome Mitch. He hasn't been here in a while." Everyone signed "hello" to Mitch, and he beamed back at them and waved.

"He has some good news," Link said. "Do you want to

tell them?" He smiled at his cousin, but Mitch's eyebrows drew down, and Link laughed as his cousin signed to him. "He asked what his good news was."

They all twittered a little bit, and then Link said, "He and Lacy Hayes—" He cut off when Mitch's hand clamped down on his arm. He looked at it, and then Mitch, and oh, something was going on there.

Finn didn't know what, and Link signed a few more things without saying them out loud. Relief painted itself across Mitch's features, and he nodded.

Link faced the group again. "He and Lacy Hayes opened their enrollment for their Deaf academy," he said. "They named it Signs for Success, and they had almost one hundred people register on the first day."

"Wow," Brandon said, holding onto the word. "That's amazing." Applause went around, and Link showed them how to do it in sign language, and they switched to that silent version of celebration. Mitch actually ducked his head and blushed, and Finn hoped that he would come more often.

"I don't think we have much news at Shiloh Ridge," Link said. "Do we, Wilder?"

"Does it have to be ranch news?" Wilder said. He grinned around at everyone. "Well, since Glory Rose got married, all any of us can talk about at Shiloh Ridge is who we want to go out with. So if y'all need to be set up with someone, there's a lot of single women about my age at Shiloh Ridge." He chuckled, and once Link had signed it for Mitch, he tipped his head back and laughed.

"Yeah, how's married life?" Finn asked Conrad.

"It's great," he said. "Glory Rose is all moved into the farmhouse now. She's talking about setting up a daycare. I might build her a building just on the other side of my donkey pasture, then she can take the kids out there to feed them."

Murmurs of appreciation went around the group, and Finn looked at Brandon.

"What about you, brother?" he asked. "You seein' anyone new?"

"I have given up on dating," Brandon said. "And I'm not joking. I don't want to be set up with anyone at Shiloh Ridge. I don't want to be set up anywhere. I'm ordering all my groceries online—and everything else I can get delivered to the ranch. I'm going to become a hermit." He looked over to Mitch. "Like your daddy."

Mitch laughed and tipped his head back and signed something.

"He doesn't recommend it," Link said, and that caused another round of laughter to go around the table.

"I should have said this earlier," Dawson said. "Caroline's gonna have another baby."

"Already?" Link asked. "She just had a baby girl last year."

Dawson leaned down the table to look at him. "Joy is eighteen months old," he said. "And we're not getting any younger. This will probably be it for us."

Link nodded, his smile wide and easy. "Congratulations."

"You got any names for your baby?" Angel asked Link.

"Oh, yeah," he said. "Misty has a whole list of them, but she won't show it to me or anyone else." He chuckled.

"Well, I'm sure the aunts all know," Wilder said. "You're telling me she hasn't told your momma, and she hasn't told everyone else?" Wilder scoffed and shook his head. "I don't believe that for a single second. In fact, I'm pretty sure I heard my mother and yours talking about baby names just the other day."

A look of surprise crossed Link's face. "If my momma and all the aunts at Shiloh Ridge know the name of my baby before I do, there's going to be something to be said." That caused another round of laughter to pass through the group, and Finn found himself smiling and feeling so comfortable with everyone here.

Alex said into the twitters at the end, "Anything else? Or should we move on?"

They all looked around at one another, and Finn sure did love this group of men and women who came together, some of them his cousins, like Paul and Henry, and his siblings, Libby, and then some just friends that he'd really come to love and appreciate over the years, like Link and Mitch and Wilder Glover from Shiloh Ridge, and Dawson and Brandon Rhinehart from their family ranch, which was technically called Hidden Hills, and JJ and Conrad Walker from Seven Sons.

"I have one thing," he said. "Before we move on to policies. Is there anyone else who needs to be invited to these meetings?"

"I still have news," Libby said. "After we talk about that."

"I was thinking we should invite Colt Franklin," Alex said. "Nikki knows his family pretty well." He switched his gaze to his wife. "They own the apple orchards, and he just took over from his momma."

"Oh, sure, Colt," Brandon said. "I know him. He's got to be close to my age."

"I actually think he's closer to mine," Link said. "Early thirties. He just got divorced."

"His wife—well, ex-wife now—worked with Caroline at the wildlife office," Dawson said. "Her name's Ivy. They got married just before me and Caroline."

"Great," Finn said. "Who wants to reach out to him? Seems like a few of you know him."

Brandon, Dawson, and Link looked around at one another, but it was Nikki who raised her hand. "I'll text him and tell him about the meetings. He'd probably really benefit from them. I know he's been drowning since he took over the orchard and his wife left."

"Do they have any kids?" Libby asked.

"Just one," Nikki said. "A little boy. He's two or three, and I don't know if Ivy took him or not."

Finn nodded, his heart heavy all over again. Sometimes the world held so much sadness and so much heartbreak, and he didn't know what to do with all of it.

"We have news out of Three Rivers," Libby said. "Most of you know Ty, Ethan, and Brynn Greene. They train the rodeo horses at Bowman's Breeds."

Murmurs and nods of assent went around the group.

"Their oldest son got in a pretty bad accident," Libby said. "He's in a hospital in Calgary, and they're going to be bringing him back to the ranch as soon as they can. They'll be living at the homestead with my momma and daddy, and they could use our prayers."

Brandon ducked his head right then, as if saying a silent prayer for Tyson and his family. When Libby didn't seem like she would say much more, Finn added, "They might need our help. And I told my daddy that he could call on any of us to go help feed or exercise horses anytime at Bowman's Breeds."

"Yeah, of course," Paul said.

"Absolutely," Angel and Henry said as one, while others nodded. Mitch raised his hand, and everyone looked at him.

"I can come help," Link said. "Or rather, Mitch can. He wants to, if necessary. He doesn't get to work with many horses lately, and—" He blinked, then grinned slowly at his cousin. "And he's decided he has some news too."

"Do tell," Alex said.

"He wants everyone to know that he and Lacy Hayes are dating." Link grinned around at the group as Wilder got to his feet.

"Mitch is *dating?*" he demanded. "Fine, he's off the list for available Glovers." He waved both hands above his head, and then he started to laugh—and Finn joined him, because Mitch's face bore no redness at all.

Mm, yes, he liked this Lacy Hayes a whole lot—and he wasn't even embarrassed about it.

Chapter Sixteen

"I still think we should have told them," Henry Marshall said to Angel as he climbed into bed beside her.

"I'm only three weeks along," she said, giving him a glare. "We're not going to tell all of your friends that I'm pregnant when I've done two tests—and one of them was negative."

"Oh, all right." Henry wasn't really mad, and he grinned as he laid his head on his wife's belly. "I really think you are, though."

He hoped she was. He *prayed* for it, because the single joy in his life was being her husband and Wrangler's daddy. "I hope it's another boy."

Angel ran her fingers through his hair, and the whole world slowed down to just the two of them. They'd put Wrangler to bed an hour ago, and Henry had finished cleaning up in the kitchen before walking the farm to make sure everything had been locked up tightly for the evening.

They lived right on the edge of the woods, and coyotes and foxes and other small game predators came in and tried to take their chickens and ducks. They'd been extremely busy at Lone Star lately, and Henry had thought he wouldn't be able to get away for the meeting that had happened yesterday. In the end, he'd simply walked out of a job and left it for someone else to do, something he'd never done before.

But sometimes his world got really loud and really violent, and he needed a way to slow down. Angel had always been that way.

He lifted his head to look at her. "You want a girl, don't you?" He grinned at her and slid up to lay his head on her chest, her heart beating in a strong, steady rhythm.

"I wouldn't mind a girl," she said. "We're not that bad."

Henry grinned and let his fingertips trace down her arm. "No, you're not that bad."

"Just because your family only has boys," she said.

"I'll admit we don't know what to do with girls." He chuckled, because he only had brothers, and none of them had children yet. Only him and Angel—and they'd had a boy.

"I didn't want to say anything over Paul and Brielle either," Angel said. "They need to have their happy moment. We've already had ours."

"I know," Henry said. "You're right."

"So we're not telling them tomorrow at dinner either," she said.

Henry pressed his teeth together. "Fine," he said. "But it's at *our* house. I feel like we should be able to do whatever we want."

"We can," she said. "Just not that. Everyone's coming. John's going to have his new girlfriend. We don't need to cause a big circus."

"It won't be a circus to announce a baby," he said.

"Have you met your mother?" Angel argued back. "She's already going to be bawling about Brielle's pregnancy. I don't need that spotlight on me."

True, Angel did not like it when eyes came to her, but Henry couldn't help being excited about another baby in his life. *His* baby.

Let this go. The words came into his mind, and Henry recognized they came from the Lord. "They haven't told Momma and Daddy?" he asked.

"No," Angel said. "I called Brielle yesterday, and she said they haven't told anyone."

"I don't even know how that's possible," Henry said. "They live right next door to them, and I guarantee you, Paul's been out there bawling."

"You would be too," Angel said. "Don't act like you wouldn't be crying if you'd been trying for four long years to have a baby and you finally got one."

Henry couldn't deny it. In fact, he'd teared up when Angel had told him a few days ago that she'd missed her period and thought she might be pregnant. "When will you know for sure?" he asked.

"I have a doctor's appointment next week," she said. "They'll do the blood test, and then we'll know."

"Are you worried?" he asked.

"Yes," she whispered. "How am I going to run Lone Star with two babies?"

"Well, Wrangler is almost three," he said.

"He is not," Angel argued back. "He turned two a few months ago; he won't be three until next year."

"Well, it's already June," Henry said.

Angel scoffed, but she didn't continue the argument. They weren't really arguing anyway; this banter back and forth between them was familiar and comfortable, and Henry loved that he could say whatever he wanted, and so could she.

"She already knows what they're having," Angel said. "They've done so many tests and ultrasounds, so they know."

"Wow." Henry sat up further and met his wife's eyes. "Did she tell you?"

She shook her head. "They want to do it tomorrow when they tell your momma and daddy. This is their big moment, baby. We can't ruin it for them."

"I *know*," Henry said. "I won't, I promise."

"And John is bringing home a girl."

"I know." Henry pressed his lips softly to his wife's. "I won't say a word." He kissed her deeper then, fully satisfied with his life. Well, if he didn't have to work fourteen hours a day and worry so much about what Angel would do when she'd wanted to be a mother but also ran a major horse boarding operation that had been in her family for generations. An idea wiggled around in the back of his mind, but he didn't bring it forward yet.

Angel's momma had died a couple of years ago, after quite the struggle with several health problems. Her daddy was still kicking, and she had an older brother. He did quite well around Lone Star as well.

What they simply needed to do was hire another foreman who acted as a manager the way Angel did. She had resisted the idea when she was pregnant with their first, and Henry had supported her however possible, be that conducting interviews, making schedules, working longer hours, whatever it took.

But he felt at his limit right now too, with the small family farm they owned, as well as their two-year-old and all of the horses and clients and employees at Lone Star.

She would see it. She'd have to, and Henry would bring it up at a more appropriate time.

The following afternoon, he carried a bowl of sweet pea salad out to the deck. "Momma and Daddy just got here," he said to Paul, and his brother got to his feet.

"Really?"

"Them and Rich," Henry said. "And we still haven't seen John."

"I can see John on the map," Brielle said. "He just passed the mechanic shop south of town. He's probably fifteen minutes out." She wore an oversized T-shirt that day, and because Henry knew to look, he could see the baby bump.

His momma was a very observant woman, and he still didn't understand how Paul and Brielle had kept this news from the mighty Chelsea Marshall. Growing up, Henry could never get away with anything, and even if Daddy never found out, Momma *always* knew.

"We're here," she called from inside the house, and Henry turned to take from her whatever she'd brought. Angel had coordinated all the food, and his stomach roared when he found his mother carrying a large tray of oatmeal carmelitas.

"Oh, I love these things," he said as he took the tray. He slid them onto the dining room table and then took his momma into a hug. "I love you, Momma."

"How are you, my boy?" she asked. And while Henry had given them the most trouble growing up, he had settled into himself quite nicely as an adult. Daddy's loud laugh filled the house as he swooped Wrangler into his arms.

"How's my baby cowboy?" he boomed, because Daddy never said anything quietly. Wrangler started babbling in two-year-old language that no one understood, but Daddy carried on a full conversation with him. He came over and hugged Henry from the side and slid Wrangler into Momma's arms.

"Are we leaving desserts in here, so they don't melt?" he asked.

"We've got fans and misters outside," Henry said. "But we can leave them in here until later."

"Nope, I want all the food outside," Angel said. "Pick it up, cowboy, and take it outside."

"Yes, ma'am." Henry gave her a smile and did as she asked. She came out last and left the door open. She positioned a fan in it to blow out onto their screened porch. They'd had all the windows open until only a few minutes ago, so the heat of the Texas sun had not been baking the sunroom.

Now everything sat closed tight, and both fans in the ceiling ran while a mister introduced cool air from the side of the house. Henry had installed that himself, and a slip of pride moved through him at his own handiness.

"Has anyone met John's girlfriend?" Momma asked.

"Oh, we're not playing that game," Henry said with a chuckle.

Rich gave her a glare. "You seriously think we would tell you if we had? I value my life."

"Oh, come on," Momma said. "I don't have to be the first to meet her."

"Yes, you do," Henry said. "And we all know it. So even if John had invited me to meet Virginia, I wouldn't have gone, because I value my life too."

Momma gave him a glare and picked up a chunk of cheese to feed to Wrangler.

"He seems to really like her," Brielle said.

"First woman he's brought home," Paul agreed. "So, yeah, I think he must really like her."

"Any news on Tyson?" Henry asked, trying to keep the conversation away from too much speculation about John's girlfriend. Paul put his arm around Brielle and drew her close to his chest. He'd always been touchy-feely with his wife, but Henry also didn't want Momma and Daddy to pick up on any hints about their pregnancy quite yet.

John already felt a little left out of the family because he didn't live in Three Rivers like everyone else. He'd gone to school at Baylor, and he'd gotten a job with a horse trailer company out of San Antonio. He lived and worked there, and though Henry had told him many times that he would always be welcome at home, John had claimed that ranching wasn't the strongest gene in his blood.

Henry had told him he couldn't feel left out then, but John still did. Henry understood that too, because sometimes the human psyche didn't make sense, and a person felt things, whether they wanted to or not.

"Yeah, we got a little bit more information," Daddy said. "Ethan and Brynn are in Calgary now, and Tyson's leg is shattered—broken in four places, two in the tibia and two in the fibula. He got thrown from a bull and then trampled. It's really bad. They don't know if he'll be able to keep the leg at this point, and even if he does, he might not be able to walk again."

"Oh no," Brielle said. "That is so sad."

"It's not great," Momma said. "He's definitely out of the rodeo, and it's the only thing he's ever done."

Daddy nodded along soberly. "He broke six ribs on his left side. Both of his lungs are collapsed, and right now he's actually paralyzed all up and down his left side."

Henry sat there, completely still, trying to imagine how a life could change so suddenly—a single moment of time, and everything he'd known was now gone, completely wiped out, changed, different.

"Wow," he said. "I don't even know what to do with that."

"It gets worse," Momma said. "Jenn broke up with him. Said she has no idea what to do with someone as broken as he is. She's already left Calgary."

"You have got to be kidding me," Angel said, her tone filled with disgust. "What a coward."

Henry reached over and took her hand. "We don't know her, baby."

"I don't *want* to know her," Angel muttered.

"When are they going to be able to bring him home?" Rich asked.

"He can't travel right now," Momma said. "Not with his lungs like they are. They're hoping to get the ribs and lungs healed up a little bit first. They've got an apartment there at the hospital. They'll probably be there a couple of months."

"We can come help with the horses," Henry said.

"Uncle Squire is setting up a rotation right now," Momma said. "We've been managing with the cowboys who live at Three Rivers, but it's summertime, and those horses need to be worked and trained, or at least exercised."

"They have to be fed a couple of times a day, and they have medical needs too," Daddy said.

"Make sure you put all of us on the schedule," Paul said. "And you've got Finn and Alex and Link and Wilder and all the cowboys at Seven Sons."

"Squire has been texting everyone," Momma said. "We're going to make sure they're taken care of."

Henry nodded, his stomach growling again. "Where is John?" he grumbled.

"John is right here," his brother said, and everyone swept their attention to the doorway. He nudged the fan out of the way and stepped out onto the screened porch with a pretty brunette trailing in his wake. He grinned around at them. "Hey, everyone. We made it."

"Yes, you did." Momma passed Wrangler to Daddy and jumped to her feet. She hugged John close and then stood at his side and said, "Introduce me."

Henry tried not to chuckle, but he failed.

"Momma," John said dutifully, "This is Virginia Switz. We've been dating—oh, I don't know, eight or nine months." He smiled at her with all the power of gravity. "I really like her, so it would be great if you could not scare her off with the first question you ask."

"Who says I'm going to ask her a question?" Momma asked.

"*That* was a question," John said dryly. "Ginny, this is my momma. I've told you all the things that she's going to ask you." He nodded over to Daddy. "That's my daddy. He's holding Henry's son, Wrangler. This is Henry and Angel right here."

Henry raised his hand.

"My younger brother, Rich, and my oldest brother, Paul, and his wife, Brielle."

Howdys and hellos went all around. And then Momma linked her arm through Virginia's and said, "So tell me. Where are you from?"

And the questioning began.

"Momma," Paul interrupted before things could get too far—before Ginny could even answer Momma. "Brielle and I have an announcement."

Only the sound of the fan and a tiny ticking noise from the mister filled the air. He looked at Brielle, who had started to cry, and Momma pulled in a breath.

"Paul Franklin, you tell me right now what's going on," she said.

He lifted his wife's hand to his lips and placed a gentle kiss to her wrist. "Brielle and I are going to have a baby boy the week before Thanksgiving," he said, and he grinned as wide as the sky and as bright as the sun.

Henry whooped, his natural reaction. He swept his cowboy hat right up off his head and threw it into the air as his loud voice started the cheering and congratulations for Paul and Brielle.

Fine, his wife was right. They deserved this moment, and he would never be the one to take it from them.

Momma sobbed and sobbed as she got up and went around the table to give a simultaneous hug to both Paul and

Brielle, and Henry took in the shell-shocked look on Virginia's face.

"We're not usually this exciting," he said. "Today is just a big event. They've been married for years."

"They've been trying for a baby for a long time," John said.

"This is great news," Ginny said. "I'm happy for them. Look how happy they are."

Daddy took his turn hugging Paul and Brielle while Momma wiped her face. Then Daddy clapped his big hands together. "Is it all right if I say our family prayer over lunch?" he asked, looking at Henry and Angel.

"Of course, Daddy," Henry said, because he did love listening to his daddy pray.

"Let's do that now," Angel said. "Then we can keep talking while we eat."

Henry had already tossed his cowboy hat, so all he had to do was duck his head and close his eyes. He did that, reaching for Angel's hand under the table, so he could slow down and solidify himself in this moment.

Daddy helped even more as he said, "Dear God, Thou art so good, and we are so blessed. We are so grateful that Thou hast seen fit to send another baby to our family."

Angel's hand tightened in his, and Henry leaned over and pressed a simple kiss to her temple, because God *was* good, and they *were* so blessed.

Chapter Seventeen

Mitch held up his hand in a fist, and Sunshine, Maven, and William all dropped into a sit. He loved dogs with his whole soul, and right now he was training a yellow lab—Sunshine—a chocolate lab—Maven—and a golden retriever—William.

In his head, he'd already started calling William "Willie," and the thought made him smile. He pointed at the ground, and Maven and William settled into a lay. It took Sunshine a moment, and she glanced over to her canine pals before she did it.

Mitch had carefully selected these dogs based on their temperament and intelligence. They were all friendly, alert, and ready to work whenever they saw him. He'd bought the dogs from trained and registered breeders when they were eight weeks old, and then he'd put them through an eight-week puppy training program in Amarillo with a specialized trainer who taught them all of the hand signals that he wanted them to know before they came to see him.

The puppies had been well socialized there, and Maven and William especially had extreme focus in various environments and situations. Sunshine struggled still, but Mitch felt in his heart that she would be an excellent hearing dog.

He'd had them since Saturday, and he'd hauled their kennels up onto the back porch last night only mere minutes before it had started to rain, and boy, had it rained and rained and *rained*. The lane and yard had flooded, but it was starting to dry out now.

Mitch always started his training sessions with basic obedience commands such as sit, stay, come, go back, lay down, and bark. Getting a generally agreeable dog who rarely used its voice to bark was a feat in and of itself.

Today, he wanted all the dogs to bark, and he'd put on his sound detection watch. It was an alert device that he'd learned about at Whispering Paws.

Basically, a deaf person could wear a bracelet or a watch, and it would vibrate to alert the wearer of sounds detected by his smartphone app. He knew some people who used them when they drove if their cars didn't have the more advanced safety features as his truck did.

Today, he tapped to open the app, because it would register the sound of a bark, and that would cause the watch on his wrist to vibrate, telling him that the dog had done what Mitch had commanded it to do.

He could usually tell when a dog barked simply by

watching it, but Mitch liked gadgets, and he didn't have to stick to a budget.

He held up his left hand, palm out, in the canine sign for *stay*. He separated William from the other two dogs by pointing to the right, indicating William should come with him. He moved him away about ten feet and turned his back on the other two dogs. They should stay where they were until he told them to come.

But Sunshine came over and nosed the back of his calf. Mitch turned around and backed her up physically and told her to lay back down, all using his hands and body language. She obeyed, and he held out his palm again, mentally commanding her to *stay*. *Stay*.

He turned his back on her again and took a couple of steps away until he stood right in front of William again. He held up his right hand this time, palm out, and he brought his thumb and finger together, almost like a bird chirping. He did it one, two, three times, and then he brought all his fingers down on his thumb. With this sign, he expected William to bark.

If he could get the dog to bark, then he could train the dog to alert when the doorbell rang instead of with the hand signal, or when an alarm clock went off instead of with the hand signal. And then he could move from barking—something hearing people could alert to—to a silent alert for a deaf person.

Deaf people could see the movement in their dog when they barked, but he would move them from a bark to a silent alert against a person's leg—or their face if the dog needed to wake them when their alarm went off.

William sat up, but he didn't bark. Mitch gave him the signal again, three taps of his pointer finger to the pad of his thumb, and then he brought all of his fingers together.

William barked.

Mitch laughed as he crouched down and showered the dog with love. He scratched behind his ears and right down his spine, running his hands through the dog's gloriously golden fur. Then he reached in his pocket and pulled out a bite of hot dog and gave it to William.

He held up his hand to stay, and he separated Maven from the other two dogs simply by backing her up in the pen where he worked with them. She laid down again, and he brought her back to a sitting position.

The dogs should be able to bark from any position, but Mitch realized that sitting would be easier than lying down. He gave her the signal, and she barked the first time. Mitch rewarded her with love and hot dogs and moved back over to Sunshine.

He gave her a hot dog right out of the gate, because she had stayed right where he had told her to stay. She licked his face, and Mitch shook his head and held up his hand again. Some dogs were simply more loving than others, and some dogs loved to lick, but Mitch didn't want a hearing dog that licked, because not all people wanted their dog to lick them.

He gave her the signal to bark, and she turned around in a circle. Mitch shook his head and had her lay down and then sit up again. He wished he could tell her, "Bark. *Bark*," because, according to the texts he'd read, dogs responded really well to short, simple commands in a strong tone of voice.

They were exceptionally smart at reading hand signals as well, and Mitch felt a great connection to them because he had to communicate through his hands too.

He gave her the signal again, and she still didn't bark. He reached into his pocket and pulled out a piece of hot dog and held it up. Sunshine wanted that, he could tell, and he transferred it to his left hand and held it down by his waist. She didn't look away from it for a single moment, and he raised his right hand again and waited until she looked at him.

He should reward her for that, but he held the hot dog firmly and gave her the signal to bark again—*one, two, three taps, all fingers closed.*

She didn't bark.

She did stand up and put her nose on his knee, and Mitch looked down at her, wondering what in the world she was doing. Then Lacy touched his arm, and he dang near jumped out of his skin. He yelped as he danced away from her, his heartbeat stuck in the back of his throat and spiking through his body.

Lacy held up both hands. *Sorry,* she said. *I thought—* she cut off because, of course, she couldn't say, "I thought you'd heard me."

He realized in that moment that Sunshine had alerted him that something was happening, and he'd ignored her.

He fed her the hot dog and stroked his hand over her

head before he faced Lacy again. *She won't bark*, he said. *It's frustrating.*

What's the sign for bark? Lacy asked.

Mitch called all of the dogs over by lifting the whistle around his neck and giving it a quick puff of air. They gathered around him, and he held up his fist so they'd sit as he let the whistle hang back against his chest.

They should bark, he said. *When I give them this signal.* He made the signal, and the watch vibrated against Mitch's wrist, because both William and Maven barked.

Pure joy filled him when his watch vibrated again, and he looked over to Sunshine and found her barking also. She stood up and barked and barked and *barked*, and Mitch waved his hand and commanded her to sit back down. She did, and when he looked over to Lacy, he found her laughing.

She knows how to bark, she said.

He couldn't help smiling too. *She's gonna be the hardest one*, Mitch said. *But I'll use William to teach her what she doesn't do.*

It looks like it's going well, Lacy said.

I love them so much, Mitch said.

What are they learning today? she asked.

I want them to be obedient in all commands, he said. *I want them to move where I want them to move, and I want them to stay where I put them. So we've been working on that since I got them.*

She nodded and reached down and stroked William's

face. Then she straightened. *Oh, sorry. Was I not supposed to pet him?*

You can, he said. *We're going to go for an off-leash walk, and I'm going to expect them to stay right at my side. I'll leave one of them behind and force them to stay until I call them forward again.*

She touched the whistle against his chest. *And you do that with this?*

Yeah, he said. *But if we're not back in an hour, I suppose you better send out a search party.* He chuckled and reached for her hand. *Did they bark last night when I brought them up onto the porch?*

She shook her head, a hint of a blush seeping into her cheeks. *No,* she said, *I didn't hear a peep all night.*

Mitch nodded. *That's good. They're really good dogs, and I'm so excited to have them here.*

Who do you think you'll train with Champ first? she asked.

I think probably William, he said. *He's really smart, and he's very eager to please.*

He's the most handsome one too, Lacy said, beaming down at the dog. *I just like goldens better than labradors.*

I love a chocolate lab, Mitch said as he admired Maven.

Anyway, Lacy said. *I just came out to tell you that we reached one-hundred students today.* Mitch shook his head, still marveling at how much they had accomplished and how many people knew about their academy. They'd gone live last Tuesday, only eight days ago.

One hundred students, he said. *That's amazing.*

I've been sorting and categorizing them, she said. *Only about half of them will live on-site, so we still have plenty of room in the dorms, and about thirty percent of them are adults.*

She paused and glanced down at her phone, where she'd typed up some notes. *Our third biggest group is teens in the fifteen and sixteen-year age range.*

Do we have any fourteen-year-olds? he asked.

Lacy shook her head. *No, so we might only have to do ninth, tenth, eleventh, and twelfth grade courses, and those will probably be combined anyway.* She looked up at him. *We have a* lot *of requests for younger students. Tons in the 'more information' form.*

Mitch nodded, his mind, which had once been clear while working with the dogs, now started to buzz with all the administrative tasks he had to do.

I really think we should hire Selma, he said. *She's going to be the best one for math and science. She knows all the technical signs.*

I agree, Lacy said. *I've started to put together her job offer and contract, and I just need you to approve it when you get back to the office.*

Okay, he said. *Who are you thinking for our adult beginning sign language classes?*

Do you really want to know? she asked.

I just asked you, didn't I? He tilted his head at her.

She grinned, despite his bluntness. *You, Mitchell. I think you should teach the adult beginning sign language class.*

He fell back a step, though Lacy's face shone with sunshine. *Me?*

Who knows more about sign language than you do? she asked.

Well, you do, he said.

She shook her head, her pretty smile tucked into place. *Not true. You have a PhD. You have studied across multiple areas, including politics, government, science, and the medical industry. You should be teaching that basic class. In fact, you should be teaching all of our adult classes. But I know you won't have time to run the academy and train your dogs if you do that.*

Irritation fired through Mitch because no, he would not have time to do all of that. *I thought you were going to do some of the adult classes too.*

I think we should each do one, Lacy said. *You can do the basic one, and I will test them and move them into different groups based on what they're interested in. And then I will do those.*

Sounds good.

We're still going to need people who can do math, English, she said, *The various branches of science.*

Yeah, I know, he said.

And with fifty people who want to live on-site, she said. *We need ten resident assistants.*

Well, we have a short list that we can pull from, he said.

Yes, she said. *I'm just wondering when you would like to start hiring.*

Mitch knew he'd been holding back, and he knew he

couldn't do it for much longer. *Let's make sure we get everyone finalized that we know we want this week, and we'll make job offers on Monday,* he said. *I can set up calls. I want to talk to them in person via video.*

Lacy nodded. *All right. I only have one more thing.*

She turned suddenly in that moment, and Mitch followed her gaze to find Jacob running toward them, waving both arms above his head, clearly calling for help. Mitch started toward him instantly, Lacy hot on his heels.

Jacob said something else, and thankfully, he started to sign. *There's a broken pipe along the side of the road, and it's flooding everything.*

He stopped a few paces away from Mitch, gestured for them to follow him, and took off running back the way he'd come. Mitch picked up the pace and broke into a jog, because they'd already had too much rain, and the last thing he needed was a broken pipe to be washing away all of their hard work.

Chapter Eighteen

L acy almost tripped in her ballet flats as she ran after Jacob and Mitch. She had no idea what she could possibly do with a broken sprinkler pipe, but she couldn't just stay in the dog pen either. Her brother had been working around the grounds for several months and was in far better shape than Lacy. And Mitch, hot cowboy god that he was, seemed to be able to run as if he'd been training for marathons.

They both disappeared around the corner of the house at least ten yards ahead of Lacy. She pushed herself on, recognizing the way her feet sank into the soggy lawn, since it had rained all night. As Lacy hurried down the side of the house, she definitely heard the gushing of water.

"This is so not good," she panted.

The landscaping company had just started last week, and she'd fielded the calls from them this morning to say they were going to give the Panhandle a chance to dry out before they returned. Since it was only the first week of June, Lacy had seen no reason to panic that their grounds weren't quite done.

Of course, she and Mitch wanted to do some virtual tours of the grounds, including some drone shots, and they couldn't do that until the sod was all laid, the bushes all planted, and the trees standing up tall.

She had gone over the blueprints for the landscaping with the architect, but Mitch had done all of the ordering. Mitch's house sat at the end of a long lane like a Southern plantation manor commanding all of the land around it. He had a circle drive in front of his house where they parked, and a detached garage off to the right that they never used.

Lacy had gone in there once and found it stuffed full of packed boxes. She'd felt so much better about the eight or ten that she kept in her spare bedroom after that. But on the west side of the house, Mitch had planted grass all the way down the length of the lane. He'd left the trees over there too, and Lacy had put in hundreds of wildflower seeds. They had bloomed this year, but summer had already arrived, and they were gone now.

On the east side of the lane sat the dormitories and the academy campus. To Lacy's great relief, the broken pipe was on the side with only the grass. Still, it gushed straight up out of the ground in a five-foot column that reminded her of the way Old Faithful went off at Yellowstone National Park.

As she watched, Mitch arrived, skidding on his knees as he literally dove headfirst into the geyser.

This wasn't a situation that a deaf person could handle very well, because he couldn't yell for help and he couldn't call for tools. She jogged toward them, finally kicking off her shoes as they continued to flap and slow her down.

Mitch tried to slow the tide of water with his bare hands, and his cowboy hat went flying as he pulled them back and the water shot upward again. He tried a different tactic by picking up the pipe and turning it toward the fence. He could only move it so far, though, because metal weighed a lot and metal filled with water weighed more.

Lacy arrived and tapped his shoulder. *We need to call for help*, she said.

Call my uncle Preacher, he said, and he thrust his phone at Lacy. *Tell him to bring all the tools that he can.* He turned to Jacob. *I have a toolbox in the garage. Will you go grab it? It's on the shelf on the left, third or fourth one up, right inside the door.*

Sure. Jacob turned and ran off.

Lacy had Preacher dialed, and he took his sweet cowboy time before he answered with a "Howdy, Mitch."

"Hey, it's Lacy," she said, her voice bordering on the edge of panic. "I'm with Mitch at his place, and there's a pipe gushing water everywhere. He said you might have some tools and could come help us?"

"We're on the way," Preacher said, and the call ended. At least when cowboys needed to act, they did.

Lacy didn't know what to do with Mitch's phone, and she watched as a couple of drips of water fell off the bottom corner of it. She stuffed it in her back pocket and turned to help him.

What are we going to do? She took a step forward while Mitch reached down into the hole where the pipe had originated from, sloppy, muddy water going all the way up to his shoulder as he leaned all the way into the ground.

She took another step, and her foot sank. She slipped, and the next thing Lacy knew, her hip and then her shoulder hit the ground. She cried out as the stench of mud hit her nose and the wickedly cold temperature of the water stung her skin.

She gasped the air out of her lungs and struggled to breathe after that. She couldn't get her bearings, and she flopped around, trying to find a flat place so that she could push herself up and away from this muck and mess.

In the next moment, Mitch grabbed her hand and pulled her up, his other hand sliding along to her back and heaving her out of the mire she'd fallen into. But as he did that, he slipped and fell hard, landing on his backside with a horrible grunt.

We've got to get out of here, Lacy said. "What are we doing?" She tried to help Mitch and ended up on the ground next to him. He looked at her, absolute angry frustration in his eyes. And though she felt like crying, what actually happened was a laugh came out of her mouth and filled the sky with joy.

We have to laugh or cry, she told him. *I'm choosing to laugh.* And Mitch's expression lightened by degrees until a smile formed on his face too.

You got a little bit of mud here, he said, as he reached out and pushed back her hair that had been plastered to her face with grimy gunk.

Just a little? she asked.

Mitch's mega smile appeared on his face. *Don't worry,* he said. *You're still beautiful.* His hand lingered around the back of her ear and slid down the column of her neck. The moment between them turned tight and tense and oh-so-delicious. Lacy's eyes dropped to Mitch's mouth, and she reached up and curled her hand around the back of his neck too.

She had no idea what it would be like to kiss a man like him after so long of being starved for touch and compassion and love. She knew she didn't want to wait another moment to find out, and she brought him toward her, her heart breaking free of the cage she'd put it in when Landon had died and thundering through her veins like the hooves of a thousand wild horses.

Mitch put his other hand on the back of her shoulder a mere moment before Lacy closed her eyes, taut and ready for a kiss from the cowboy she'd been dreaming about for months.

His lips touched hers, and the intensity of the sun seemed to increase tenfold. Lacy pressed into him eagerly, as she'd refused to recognize how much she wanted this until now. Mitch explored tentatively at first, his touch gentle and soft.

He pulled away for a half a second, and Lacy whim-pered, needing and wanting so much more. He growled somewhere in his chest, and then matched his mouth to hers again and kissed her and kissed her and kissed her.

Lacy floated almost outside of her body while struggling to maintain some semblance of reality. She didn't want to miss out on this, the most exciting kiss of her life, and yet, the pure pleasure of it almost had her detached from reality.

Somewhere in the back of her mind, she knew she should pull away. Her brother would be returning with the tools soon, and Preacher would arrive from Shiloh Ridge, and she couldn't have Mitch's muddy kiss-prints all over her face.

He broke the kiss in almost a violent way, immediately moving his mouth along her jaw to her neck and up to her ear. Oh, how she liked how he touched her, both inside and out, and Lacy knew that she had been changed forever simply by Mitch's presence in her life.

With him, she would never be lonely again. And without him, the world would only exist in black and white, shades of gray. She would be miserable navigating the rest of her life alone.

She gently guided his mouth back to hers, where she poured everything she had into their third kiss that hope-fully would lead to many, many more.

Chapter Nineteen

Mitch's hunger for Lacy would never be satiated. He knew he should stop, pull away, keep his hands to himself, and yet he couldn't. He only wanted Lacy closer and then closer again, and then even closer.

She understood him more than anyone else in the world. And while he'd thought about kissing her a lot in the past year and a half, it had never been this good, this sensual, or this *loud*.

Everything inside Mitch seemed to scream—from his mind, telling him to pull her onto his lap and keep kissing her, to the way his heart reverberated through his chest and down to his toes and up to the top of his head.

He'd lost all reason, and Lacy sure didn't seem to mind. She kissed him back in a needful, powerful way that flipped every switch inside Mitch to on.

Lacy sighed into him as he kissed her, her body turning

to butter, melting into his and forming to whatever he wanted.

After what felt like a long time and not nearly long enough, Lacy gently broke the kiss between them and cradled his face in her hands. He opened his eyes, the sunshine dancing so brightly around him.

Mitch had gone completely inside himself, shutting everything else out, so that he could focus on exactly what he wanted—and that was Lacy.

She looked at him soberly, her eyes searching his, and oh, how he hoped and prayed that she'd enjoyed that kiss. Her cheeks bore mud on the outside and a blush from within, and Mitch finally ducked his head to touch his forehead to hers. He took one of her hands from the side of his face and signed *Okay?* into it. She nodded, and they simply breathed in and out together.

Mitch wanted every moment of his life to be filled with this feeling of acceptance, of love, of being kissed so completely by the woman of his dreams. Lacy pulled away a moment later and turned to look over her shoulder. Jacob came back toward them, struggling under the weight of the enormous red toolbox.

The chill of the water seeped into Mitch now that he wasn't kissing Lacy, and he turned onto his hands and knees and pushed himself up. He helped her to her feet too, both of them dripping with mud and muck and water, and he held her hand tightly as they navigated out of the swamp that the lawn had become.

Let's just wait for my uncle, he said, and he took the

toolbox from Jacob and set it on the side of the road. *Thanks, man. It's crazy out there, slippery, and really cold.*

Jacob looked from Mitch to Lacy. *Yeah. Looked like it,* he said. Mitch simply blinked, but a smile exploded onto Lacy's face.

She seemed to be laughing as she pushed her brother in the chest. *Stop it. Were you spying on us?*

You were kissing out in the open, he said. *What was I supposed to do?*

Turn your back, Lacy said.

Mitch grinned too. Since he didn't have to answer to Jacob about anything in his life, including dating his sister, he figured he didn't have anything to be embarrassed about. He did need to get this plumbing issue taken care of, and then he needed to keep working with his dogs. After that, he and Lacy had about fifteen thousand tasks they needed to complete before the end of the day.

Any other time, Mitch would have been made of irritation by now, ready to snap and bark at anything that came his way, but with Lacy's hand still secured in his, he felt like a superhero, like he could take on the world and win, like this was just water and they'd get it fixed and move on with their lives.

A truck came around the corner, and Mitch waved his free arm above his head, as if his uncle wouldn't be able to see him. Preacher pulled up with Uncle August and two cowhands from the ranch, a man named Nathan and one named Brady.

"What have we got here?" Preacher asked as he got out.

Mitch nodded to Jacob, who went to talk to his uncle. He towed Lacy along beside him at a slower pace, as Uncle Preacher pulled a toolbox twice as big as Mitch's out of the back of the truck, and all four cowboys waded right into the watery mess.

Preacher had fixed a thousand pipes in his lifetime, and Mitch finally went back into the quagmire to watch what he was doing, so that he could do it himself next time. He turned and gestured Lacy forward because he needed someone to interpret for him, and he touched Preacher's shoulder and asked Jacob, *Can you ask him to tell Lacy what he's doing so that I can learn?*

Lacy actually repeated the request for Uncle Preacher, and he nodded, a smile on his face. He clapped Mitch on the shoulder. "Sure thing, bud. So the thing with pipes is they have these joints, right? These connectors, and sometimes they fail, especially when we get a lot of rain."

Mitch followed, his attention between what Uncle Preacher did with his hands and Lacy's interpretation so that he could try to keep up. In the end, he fitted the new connector around the joint in the pipe that had failed and tightened it. Then he watched as the last of the water dripped from the pipe and no more came out.

He sat back on his haunches, a bit surprised he'd been able to do it, despite Uncle Preacher's tutelage. *Thank you,* he said, and he threw one arm around Uncle Preacher and gave him a quick shoulder hug.

Uncle Preacher recoiled violently from him, and Lacy

said, "He says you're cold and wet and muddy, and he doesn't want that on him."

Mitch tipped his head back and laughed much the way Lacy had done after they'd both found themselves flat on the ground in this disgusting mess. He had no idea what had possessed him to kiss her in that moment, only that he'd wanted to. And it had felt right.

Uncle August extended his hand and pulled Mitch to his feet. "I texted Etta on the way here," he said. "And she invited you guys for dinner." He looked over to Lacy and Jacob. "All three of you. We know what it's like to have a burst pipe and how you don't want to do anything but shower and wear sweats for the rest of the day."

He grinned, and Mitch watched as Lacy did too. She nodded, though her lower jaw had started to shake. She stood in ankle-deep, icy-cold water, and Mitch wanted nothing more than to get her out of the situation. And hey, if he didn't have to cook tonight, all the better.

Yeah, we'll come, he said. *What time?*

"We usually eat around six," August said. "Just at our house."

"We'll be there." Lacy thanked Preacher, August, Brady, and Nathan, shaking their hands. "Thank you. Thanks to all of you."

The cowboys from Mitch's family ranch turned to leave, and Mitch lunged toward Lacy and scooped her up into his arms. Surprise bolted across her face, she scrambled to clutch her arms around his shoulders, and the buzzing of his watch told him she'd made a noise.

She looked at him and blinked, her eyes so deep and wonderful and beautiful. *What are you doing?*

Holding her, he couldn't sign, so he simply smiled at her and started in the direction of the house. He wished he could leave everyone and everything behind, because he simply wanted to be with Lacy. He wanted to be the man who provided everything for her, the man who comforted her when she was sad and helped her when she didn't know what to do, and lifted her into his arms so that she didn't have to stand in cold water.

She relaxed in his arms and even laid her head against his shoulder as he continued toward the house. Once his boots didn't squelch through an inch of soggy ground, he paused and set Lacy on her feet.

Why don't you go shower? he said. *I'm gonna go take care of the dogs and put them away, and then I'll come in and get cleaned up too.*

All right, she said. *You didn't get your full training session with them.*

I can go back out when I'm not covered in grossness. He looked down at his clothes, which were soaking wet and covered in smears of muddy grass.

She nodded. *We can go over all of our notes and hiring packets in the morning.*

We might have some time today, he said, and Lacy simply smiled and did the most magical thing that only *she* could do to make Mitch's life better.

She put one hand on his chest and fisted his shirt in her fingers as she steadied herself against him, tipping up to touch her mouth to his in a sweet, silent kiss that told him so much. She didn't carry on for much longer than a breath before she settled back onto her feet, smiled, and turned to go in the house.

A few moments later, Mitch felt the ground at his feet vibrate slightly. He turned around as Uncle Preacher drove his truck around the circle drive and stopped. Uncle August rode in the passenger seat, and he rolled down the window. He didn't speak but he signed for Uncle Preacher, who leaned toward him and asked, "Did you just kiss that woman?"

Mitch tipped his head back and laughed. *Catch up, Uncle Preacher*, he said. *We're dating.*

Uncle August laughed as he repeated what Mitch had said for everyone in the truck, and then he waved to them and turned to go back into the backyard. He could work with the dogs after he changed into some dry clothes, but he needed to make sure that they got put away properly first.

His dogs meant a great deal to him, and Mitch's heart stopped when he reached the backyard and realized that the door to their training enclosure was wide open.

He couldn't see Sunshine, Maven, or William anywhere, and he broke into a jog for the second time that day, reaching for the whistle still hanging around his neck. He put it in his mouth and blew hard, praying with everything he had that his dogs had not gone far. He'd been dealing with the sprinkler for at least a half-hour, and they could be anywhere by now.

He blew again, this time giving an internal voice to his prayer. *Please, God,* he prayed. *Help me find my dogs.*

They'd only been here for four days, and Mitch had never let them get more than five feet from him. They lived in their kennels, and they worked in the training enclosure, and that was it. He simply had to find them.

Please, dear Lord, he thought. *Open my mind and eyes and give me an idea of where they are.*

Chapter Twenty

L acy had just entered the kitchen when she heard Mitch's whistle peal through the air, and she hurried toward the back door, where the sound had come from. She'd made it into the main bathroom, dripping mud and water everywhere, where she'd taken a towel and cleaned herself up enough not to track so much muck through the house.

That was when she'd remembered Mitch's phone in her back pocket, and she planned to take it out to him, because he hated being without his device. He relied on it so much to communicate, and she didn't want to make him wait through her shower to have it.

The whistle sounded again, and Lacy pushed out onto the back deck to find Mitch racing toward the dog enclosure —but there were no dogs.

He blew the whistle a third time, and movement came

on Lacy's right side. William, the marvelous golden retriever puppy that Mitch had gotten, ran toward Mitch at a full sprint, with Maven and Sunshine hot on his heels.

Mitch, of course, couldn't hear them, and he had his back mostly turned toward them as he looked out across the pastures in front of him and to his left. Then William arrived, and Mitch fell to his knees, his arms open as he received all three puppies. His laughter filled the sky and burrowed right into Lacy's heart.

And she knew—she was falling fast for her cowboy boss.

She hurried down the steps and across the lawn to give him his phone.

Oh, thanks, he said when she held it out to him.

She held up a towel she'd used to dry her feet and legs. *I'll leave this for you on the back porch too.*

He nodded and indicated the door. *They got out,* he said. *I thought I'd lost them.*

She nodded and reached out to tap the whistle against his breastbone. *Good thing you trained them with this,* she said, and Mitch nodded. *I'm going to go shower.*

She turned away from him before the smile fell from her face, because she didn't want him to know about the teeming turmoil that had started inside her the moment she'd been separated from him.

She almost felt a sense of...disloyalty to Landon, and she didn't even know why. It had just been a busy few days with a culminating event that had ended with her soaking wet and muddy. She found herself stomping upstairs, getting angrier and angrier with every step.

Her feelings made no sense. She should be *thrilled* with what had happened today. They'd taken big steps in the academy, from getting their dogs to hitting one hundred registrations. Mitch had even committed to hiring people, something Lacy had been stewing about for several days now.

She entered her apartment, went down the hall to the master bedroom, which she used as her living room and kitchen, and right on into the bathroom. She closed and locked every door behind her, including the one in the bathroom, and stood in front of the mirror, her chest heaving.

Her hair hung in muddy clumps around her face, sending horror washing through her like ocean waves that just kept coming and coming and *coming*. She had streaks of dried mud on her face, and her blouse, which had once been the color of pale lemon curd, and would never come clean.

She stripped off her clothes and made it into the warm shower before she started crying. Thankfully, Lacy's tears always dried up quickly, and she found a way to scrub herself clean and find some relaxing relief in the hot water.

Once finished, she wrapped herself in a dark purple puffy robe and went into the bedroom where she slept. As she moved over to her dresser to get out new undergarments, her eyes caught on a framed photograph of her and Landon.

It had been taken on his birthday when she'd surprised him at work with a fresh set of clothes and a reservation at his favorite fondue restaurant. She'd asked the waitress to take it, and she barely recognized herself in the photo, as she'd lost about fifteen pounds since then, and she'd cut her hair to include bangs.

Landon looked exactly the same. Everything about him, bright and normal and oh-so-accusatory. She picked up the picture and stared at it.

"I'm angry," she told him. "I'm angry that you died."

She let herself feel that powerfully for a moment, and then, as if she still stood in the shower, the feelings washed away, swirled down the drain, like they didn't exist anymore.

"I'm seeing someone new," she said. "His name is Mitch, and I think if you were still here, you would be friends with him."

Her emotions settled. Then Lacy took her husband's picture to the edge of the bed and sat down, cradling it in her hands. "What do I need to do, Landon?" she asked. "I have a new life in Three Rivers. I have a really good job I love." She tried to come up with more blessings in her life, more good things. Finally, she whisper-added, "And I have Mitch now."

It still didn't feel like enough, and Lacy honestly wondered how much more she could take on. She thought of the little blue house she and Landon had bought in San Antonio, with the rose bushes out front and the carport on the side. Their life had been simple there, but good. She'd always been a little intense, and he'd balanced her. Mitch had as much intensity as her, and an inkling of doubt started to creep its way through her chest.

"When in doubt," she started to repeat something that her momma had said hundreds of times while Lacy grew up.

She couldn't get herself to say the words out loud, but they streamed through her head. *When in doubt, get down on your knees.*

Lacy could not remember the last time she'd knelt beside her bed and prayed, nor the last time she'd been to church, nor the last time that she'd involved God in anything in her life at all. She expected her anger to come roaring back, because she had been angry with the Lord for so long.

Instead, a small, quiet voice seemed to fill her whole soul. *Try again,* it said.

Lacy closed her eyes and tried to hear her husband saying those words, but she'd lost the sound of his voice a long time ago. While she sat there meditating, in the still silence of the third floor, the answer to what she needed to do came to her—and oh, she did not like it.

Lacy rode in the truck with two Deaf men, the silence suffocating her. It normally didn't bother her, but tonight, Mitch drove them onward toward his aunt's house while her skin itched for someone to talk to.

She'd been up to Shiloh Ridge on a couple of previous occasions, but Mitch had never given her a tour of the place. She knew his Uncle Ranger used to be one of the foremen and lived in the big main homestead. And Uncle Bear had once lived there with him before he'd built another house somewhere on the ranch.

They went past barns and stables, picnic areas and

grassy lawns. Another house sat on the corner, and Mitch followed the road and kept on going past it. Fenced pastures sat on her left, with some open land on the right, before it sloped down the hill and toward town.

A big two-story house came into view on the left, and Mitch turned down the short jog of a road that led to the driveway. He parked beside another truck and behind a red sedan and killed the engine.

He looked at her. *Etta promised me it would just be her family*, he said. *So you won't have to meet everyone.*

I'm fine to meet everyone, Lacy told him. She cut a look back to Jacob. *Let's go in.*

She turned to open her own door and get out of the truck, because it wasn't like she and Mitch were on a date. She'd never brought her brother along for one of those, that was for sure.

Mitch met her at the front bumper and took her hand. *Aunt Etta is fluent in ASL*, he said. *So it should be a fun night.*

Your uncle seemed to know it as well, she said.

Mitch nodded, his jaw jumping for just a single moment. *Aunt Etta made sure everyone in her family knew, so that if Link or my parents weren't around, I had someone I could communicate with.*

That's so sweet, Lacy said, her heart expanding a couple of sizes for this aunt she'd probably only met cursorily.

Mitch pressed the doorbell and then walked right into the house. The scent of frying oil and fresh vegetables met Lacy's nose, and she smiled at the homey decor in the entryway. A formal living room sat on the right, and it held a piano and two short love seats, both upholstered in bright pink, furry fabric.

Lacy blinked at them and said, *Wow. Look at those.* She looked over to Mitch, but he hadn't realized she'd spoken.

He let go of her hand and jogged the last couple of steps to a pretty, petite woman who wrapped him up in a tight hug, a joyful expression on her face. Lacy watched their exchange with fondness, because she wanted only good people in Mitch's life—those who loved him and cared for him and worried about him.

He stepped back and took his aunt's hand to face Lacy and Jacob. *Guys, this is my aunt,* he said. *Etta. And you guys met August earlier today.*

"He's out on the grill," Etta said, her hands moving as her mouth did. "You must be Lacy and Jacob. Mitch has told me all about you."

Lacy raised her eyebrows at her boyfriend, who simply shrugged one shoulder, his grin so wide and so beautiful. His face held a different kind of smile, and Lacy had learned that Mitch had many inside of him. This one was almost childlike, giddy like a little boy on Christmas morning when he discovered Santa had brought him exactly what he'd asked for.

"Come on in," Etta said.

"Where did you get these couches?" Lacy asked as she stepped forward.

"Those were my mother's," she said. "She kept one for me and one for my twin, but Ida thinks they're hideous."

Etta trilled out a laugh while Mitch said, *I agree with Aunt Ida.*

"I love them," Lacy said, simply adding to the list of differences between her and Mitch. She didn't mind them so much, because he was so good in so many other ways, and whether he liked a pink couch or not didn't matter to her.

"This is my brother, Jacob," Lacy said. "He works with us at Signs for Success."

"Yes, welcome," Etta said, and she linked her arm through Jacob's and turned to go back into the kitchen. "My twins are here, Nash and Nellie, though I imagine you're quite a bit older than them."

I'm twenty-eight, Jacob said.

"I've got another son, Joey," Etta said, as Lacy moved back to Mitch's side. She searched his face, a sense of wonder on hers. *She's wonderful.*

Being able to communicate meant so much—it showed she cared—and Lacy liked Etta simply because she'd done something amazing for Mitch.

He leaned down and touched his lips to hers in a brief kiss. *She's my favorite aunt.*

"And then we've got a daughter, Hailey," Etta was saying from the kitchen. "She's thirty-one, and she got called in on an extra shift tonight at the restaurant she manages, so we probably won't see her."

Lacy tucked her hand into Mitch's and followed his aunt into the kitchen, where a Caesar salad sat on the counter, along with a tray of freshly baked rolls and one of twice-baked potatoes doused in cheese, green onions, and bacon.

Lacy's mouth watered, and her attention got diverted over to the sliding glass door as it opened. August entered carrying a plate laden with golden, brown, sizzling steaks, and Mitch moved to take them from him.

"Do you need any help with anything?" Lacy asked. "This all looks so great."

"We're all ready," Etta said. "Nellie, will you get the sweet tea off the back porch?"

A teenager rose from the couch where Lacy hadn't even seen her slouching. She flashed her a smile that wasn't entirely friendly and ducked out onto the back deck with her daddy. Etta moved back toward the front door, stalling in front of the staircase that went up to the second floor.

"Nash, dinner," she called up the stairs. "If you miss the prayer, you miss the meal!" She turned around and shook her head. "He probably won't care to eat anyway." She bustled back into the kitchen and opened a drawer, where she pulled out silverware. She spread them on the counter next to the plates, and it was clear they would be going buffet style down the row of food before they sat at the table.

"Can someone open this door a little bit more?" Nellie griped, and Lacy hurried to do that. She pulled it open, and Nellie struggled inside with the heavy jar of sweet tea.

"Right there on the end," Etta said, as if her teenager's attitude didn't bother her.

Lacy smiled at the younger woman. "I'm Lacy," she said. "Mitch and I are dating."

"It's great to meet you," Nellie said, and she signed too.

"Oh, do you know sign language?" she asked.

"Momma taught us all," Nellie said. "So Mitch can understand everyone. I'm not as good as her or Daddy, but I do okay."

You do great, Mitch said, as he threw his arm around his cousin. *How's summer school?*

Nellie groaned mightily and rolled her eyes. "I hate it," she said.

"Well, maybe you should pass your chemistry class the first time," Etta barked to her. "And then you wouldn't have to do summer school."

"I've already graduated," Nellie said, turning her eye roll toward her mother.

"But if you can pass that test next month," Etta said as she turned back to the fridge and opened it. She pulled out condiments and set them on the counter. "You can test out of chemistry in college. And trust me, you want to do that."

"I barely want to go to college at all, Momma."

"Then don't go," Etta said, and then she held up one hand. "We're not talking about this tonight. Mitch is here with his girlfriend, Lacy, and her brother Jacob, and we're going to have a nice evening."

Nellie looked over to Jacob and nodded at him. She looked back at her mother and said, "Yes, ma'am," and then stepped over to Lacy's brother and started conversing with him.

August came back inside, this time with hamburgers and hot dogs and toasted buns. He slid everything onto the counter next to the rest of the food and looked around. "Are we all here?"

"Your son is still upstairs," Etta said, and August didn't hesitate before he walked over to the stairs and clapped loudly with an open palm against the wall—once, twice, three times.

"Nash!" he bellowed. "We're eating in thirty seconds!"

He turned around, and Lacy smiled at him. Mitch came to her side and said, *You remember Lacy from earlier today? We're dating. She's my educational director at Signs for Success.*

"Yeah, it's great to have you in our home," August said. "And Jacob's your brother?"

Lacy nodded. "Yep, he's my only sibling. He's several years younger than me."

"Where are your parents at?" August asked.

"San Antonio," Lacy said. "My daddy works as a marine biologist there."

"Oh, that's incredible," Etta said. She looked toward the stairs as rapid footsteps came thumping down. "There's Nash," she said, and when her son entered the kitchen, she added, "Finally," in a somewhat salty tone.

"Sorry, Momma," he said good-naturedly, his smile wide and a really bright personality hitting Lacy straight in the chest. "I was talkin' to Smiles and Gun."

"You were?" Etta asked. "Pray tell, what could you three possibly be *talking* about?" Nash ignored her and stepped over to Mitch.

"Hey, brother." He grabbed onto Mitch, and they did some cousin-bro-handshake-thing, and then Nash hugged him, slapping him heartily on the back.

"We got steaks and burgers tonight?" he asked as he stepped back. "Thanks, Daddy." He stepped over to August and hugged him, which caused the older man to chuckle, and Lacy knew instantly why Nash always seemed to get his way. He had more personality in him than Lacy had seen in someone in a long time, and she grinned at him while Mitch said, *Nash, this is my girlfriend Lacy and her brother, Jacob.*

"Yeah, Momma said you guys were coming tonight." He moved over to Lacy and swept a kiss along her cheek, and then shook Jacob's hand. "Thanks for coming, so we get double meat. I'm always asking my daddy for extra protein."

"You get plenty of protein," Etta said.

"Trying to build my muscles," Nash said, and he flexed his somewhat skinny arms. He did have broad shoulders, and Lacy couldn't help laughing with him.

"Me and Nellie are twins," he said. "In case you haven't worked it out. We just graduated from high school this spring, and we're going to Amarillo State in the fall."

"Is that right?" Lacy asked. "What do you want to do?"

"Not go to college," Nellie said, clearly the grumpy one of the pair.

"I'm going to do robotics," Nash said. "Or maybe computer science, or maybe something with graphic design. I haven't really decided yet." He picked up a plate and looked at his momma. "We haven't prayed, have we?"

"We're always waiting on you, son," she said dryly. "Put that plate down and say grace for us."

Nash grinned at her and did what she said, and Mitch swept his cowboy hat off his head at the same time August did. He bowed his head and closed his eyes, and Lacy did the same. When Nash started his prayer with, "Dear Heavenly Father, we're so grateful for this *amazing* summer day," she grinned and edged closer to Mitch.

She simply liked being around him, and he'd told her his family was loud and somewhat obnoxious, and it could be a lot for him to handle, and that he'd introduce her around one by one. She was glad she got to see a different side of him with his family, and see his relationships with his cousins, and simply learn more about him and spend more time with him.

Something sharp wiggled into her soft heart, reminding her that she had so many things to make right that she should probably get up on Sunday morning and get herself dressed and get to church. She resisted the idea, replacing it with the memories of hurt feelings and how abandoned and lost she'd felt after Landon's death.

The pin in her heart softened too, and Lacy had a new thought enter her mind: maybe God had removed her from one path only so that she could find a better one...here in Three Rivers.

She didn't know what to do with that, but she let it sit there, determined to keep it close until she could figure it all out.

Chapter Twenty-One

Mitch got up from the thinking seat as the big dump truck pulled around the corner and onto his property. Things had finally dried enough for the landscaping company to come lay the sod. They'd been here for a couple of days this week already, leveling the land, putting down sand, and putting in the concrete edges that would go in front of the building.

They'd planted roses in the front and the back and other amazing bushes that made Mitch smile every time he walked out onto the front porch. He and Lacy had fed them cupcakes for Jacob's birthday, and everything would finally come together with the sod.

Mitch quick-stepped down to the sidewalk that led between two emerald green patches of grass in his front yard to the circle drive.

A flatbed followed the dump truck, and there was his

pristine sod. He'd paid a pretty penny for that, and he paused when his boots met gravel to pull out his phone. Once they had sod, he and Lacy could do their virtual tour videos and get their drone shots for the website.

He wanted to show off Signs for Success to the whole world, and right now, they only had indoor dormitory videos for people to look at. He'd hired a company to make a time-lapse video of the construction of the buildings, and they had that up, but the pristine final academy shot still wasn't in place.

A sense of overwhelm hit Mitch right in the gut as he scrolled down in his contacts to try to find Jared Daniels, who would come do the drone shots. Those had to be scheduled as there were FAA regulations with drones that Mitch didn't understand. That was why he hired somebody.

He finally found Jared's name and sent the man a text: *Getting our sod laid today. Tell me when you can come do the aerial shots and the virtual tour for the campus.*

Jared cost him a lot of money too, but Mitch had prioritized certain things that he could use over and over as promotional items for the academy—and good video and good landscaping and excellent facilities all qualified.

Jared didn't answer right away, and Mitch tapped over to his amplification app, which would alert him if someone spoke by vibrating the watch on his wrist. With that open, he tucked his phone into his back pocket and headed toward the dormitories. They would lay sod in the front, and back, and all across the quad, and Mitch expected the landscaping guys to be here for the rest of the week.

He shouldn't have been surprised to see Lacy come out of the front doors of the administration building, and yet, somehow he still was. She wore a white pair of beach pants with a bright blue blouse with tiny pink flowers all over it. She screamed professional and stylish at the same time, and Mitch liked her so, so much.

He liked slow mornings with her, where they drank coffee together in the thinking seat. He liked meetings with her, where she made sure his concerns and questions were heard and answered, and he liked working with her. She had a quick mind and spoke with professionalism and knowledge, and she knew every detail of Signs for Success, some Mitch didn't even know.

He picked up his pace, so he didn't miss too much of the conversation, and he found Lacy shaking one man's hand and then talking to another. The ease with which she handled herself in every situation never ceased to amaze him, and she glanced over to him as he stepped up onto the sidewalk.

"Oh, Mitch is right here," she said, starting to sign. "He'll want to know all of this too." She smiled at him, and Mitch moved right over to her side. He wanted to sweep her into a hug and kiss her, but he reminded himself that they did have professional boundaries they should probably maintain. So he didn't. He simply stepped to her side and shook the man's hand in front of him.

Howdy, Mike, he said, and Lacy repeated it for him. *Tell me what we've got going on today.*

"Well, we've got your sod," Mike said, and he indicated

the flatbed trailer behind them. Mitch eyed it too, as well as the four or five other men that Mike had brought with him. He frowned as something pinched in his gut that told him this wasn't exactly right.

"Mitch," Lacy said, and Champ nosed his leg. He didn't look down at his dog because he'd seen her sign, and his watch had vibrated.

"They were just telling me that this is only half the sod," she said. "They want to know where you want to start."

Only half the sod? Mitch asked, immediately irritated. *Why is it only half the sod?*

She repeated the question as the tension on the sidewalk pivoted up. "It's all we could get right now," Mike said, and he didn't seem too concerned about it. Mitch certainly was, because he'd already waited an extra week to get this sod here.

When will you have the rest of it? Mitch asked.

"I got my guys calling around," Mike said, and Mitch got the gist before Lacy signed it for him.

That's not good enough, he said. *You were supposed to have all my sod last week, and now we're a week late and we still don't have it. Where is it?*

Mike's expression turned a tad harder, but Mitch didn't care.

I need it done. We've got things that we're waiting on the sod to do.

"You and everyone else," Mike said, which was the exact wrong thing to say to Mitch. His fingers curled into fists as his irritation combined with frustration. He started signing rapidly—not very nice things, either—and Lacy stepped in front of him and faced him.

Her pretty eyes fired ire at him. *I am not going to say that to him.*

Yes, he said, *You are.*

She shook her head. *He can't do anything about it, Mitch, and yelling at him isn't going to get the sod here any faster.*

I just texted our drone guy, he said, his signs a little bit too wide, indicating his anger. *I'm sick of these stupid delays. We need our academy to fill up, or we can't pay our bills. Ask him when the sod is going to be here. Right now. Ask him.*

I already know when the sod is going to be here, Lacy said. *And you cannot talk to me like this.*

Mitch blinked at her. *What?* Lacy had never refused to interpret for him, and they'd been in plenty of tense meetings with contractors just like Mike.

You are being incredibly rude and unprofessional right now, both to me and to them, and I am not going to say those things that you signed. She put one hand against his chest and pushed him back.

Mitch did not like that. His interpreter's job was to say what he said, not *their* interpretation of it.

Tell him I'm not happy, he said.

He already knows you're not happy. She glared at him and stepped back to his side. She took a deep breath and said, "We're understandably upset that there's not enough sod. Can you guarantee us that there will be a second load of sod to finish our quad on Monday morning next week?"

Mike looked from her to Mitch and held his gaze. "Yes," he said. "You'll have your second load on Monday."

Without Lacy willing to argue back—and nothing more Mitch could do—he grunted, turned, and walked away, leaving Lacy to handle the rest of the situation. He stalked to the shady side of the northern dormitory building, needing to go see his dogs. He'd put benches there, bordered by hedges, and he sat down and ran his hands along Champ's head to calm himself before he took his angry energy to the puppies.

Several minutes later, his dog alerted him, and Mitch looked over to the corner of the building, expecting to see Lacy. Now, Lacy he did see, but she was more like Hurricane Lacy as she came storming toward him, a look of extreme displeasure on her face.

Why'd you walk away like that? she asked.

I was mad, he said. *You told me you wouldn't say what I wanted to say. What's the point in staying?*

The point in staying, Mister Glover, she said, as she came to a stop in front of him. *Is that you own this academy, and you're the one in charge. You left me out there by myself.*

You seemed to know what you were doing, he said. *You refused to interpret for me and said whatever you wanted anyway. So...*

She wouldn't say what he'd wanted her to say. He honestly didn't understand why he'd needed to stay.

Lacy's shoulders stood all boxed up by her ears, and as she exhaled, they went down. She gestured back toward the corner in a universal sign of *whatever had just happened over there.*

That is not okay, she said. *You do not get to treat other people like that just because you're upset. And I can understand you yelling at him. I don't understand you yelling at* me.

Mitch blinked at her as his pride deflated and his humiliation kicked in. *I'm sorry,* he said.

You should be sorry. She sank onto the bench next to him and folded her hands in her lap. That was Lacy-speak for, *I don't want to talk to you right now.*

Mitch gave her a few seconds, and then he reached over and tried to take her hand. She glared at him for a moment, and then grudgingly let him press his palm to hers.

You weren't even expecting me to meet with the landscapers today, were you? he finally asked.

She shook her head, her jaw still tight.

Then why are you so mad?

It took her a moment to look at him, and when she did, she wore fierce determination in her gaze, along with that hint of vulnerability that he found so sexy.

My husband used to treat me like that, she said. *And I hated it.*

Like what? Mitch really needed to know so that he didn't do it again. His heartbeat bobbed somewhere in the middle of his chest, feeling off-kilter and all wrong. He did not want to make Lacy's life harder, and he didn't want to lose her over an argument about sod.

Like— She paused for a moment, her hands hanging in

mid-air. *Like, he would go off half-cocked at something that upset him and leave me to deal with the aftermath of it. And it wasn't fun, and I hated it, and I don't want to do that with us.*

Mitch squeezed her hand and lifted it to his lips. He pressed a kiss on her thumb joint and then her first knuckle. *I'm sorry*, he said again.

Landon was very opinionated, she said. *A little bit like you, but different, and he alienated a lot of people.*

Do I do that? Mitch asked.

No, Lacy said. *I know it's different. You being mad about the sod and him calling my brother stupid, but it felt the same, and I didn't like it.*

I'm so sorry, Mitch said. *Please don't be mad at me. I can't stand it when you're mad at me.* He offered her a smile when she gave him a wry look.

How would you know? she asked. *I've never been mad at you.*

He chuckled and tugged on her hand. *Yes, you have. You think I don't know how upset you were about how indecisive I am about who to hire, but I do.*

Lacy just shook her head, but a smile appeared on her face now too.

Or naming this place, he said. *That irritated you too.*

Because I needed to make the signs and pamphlets, Lacy said.

Come sit with me, he said, pulling on her hand harder. She got up and settled herself in his arms, on his lap, and

Mitch gazed at her. *You're my favorite person in the whole world*, he said. *Please forgive me.*

I do, she said. She traced her hand down the side of his face, the moment between them sober and wonderful.

Your husband thought your brother was dumb?

Lacy looked away, her jaw tight, and Mitch recognized that as her wanting to say something and trying to keep the words in.

He thought all deaf people were a little bit dumb, she said. *It was a very sore spot between us.*

Did you have a lot of others? He reached up and turned her face toward him. *Did you have a lot of other sore spots?* Mitch would never say this, but it didn't sound like Landon was a very nice guy, and he wondered how he'd gotten Lacy —someone so good, so pure, so wonderful, and so dedicated to helping others—to fall in love with him.

A few, she said, and Mitch decided not to press her any further.

He nodded and said, *I've been working on my temper for a while, and I'll do better. I promise.*

She nodded, and Mitch took her face in his hands and brought her close. He wanted to tell her he was falling in love with her, and the way she loved purple, and the way she handled tense situations, and the way she was always right where he needed her to be.

Since he loved holding her face in his hands, and he didn't want to let go so that he could talk, he simply matched his mouth to hers and hoped the message would be conveyed all the same.

Chapter Twenty-Two

Lacy felt like a criminal as she snuck out of the house on Sunday morning. She'd never had to account to Mitch for what she did in her time off, and she certainly hadn't told him that she was going to church this morning.

The broken pipe—and Lacy's near-mental break-down—had happened ten days ago now, and while she knew she needed to try going to church again, she had resisted last week. She'd barely been able to sleep last night, and she figured she could put in the time for one sermon to get her guilt to go away.

By this afternoon, she'd be napping well, and no one would have to know that she'd been in the chapel. She'd deliberately left late so that she would arrive after the service had started. She wasn't even planning to find a seat. Most churches had a speaker that played in another part of the building for mothers with fussy babies or late-goers like her.

She didn't need to see the pastor, especially if it was Mitch's mother, and she hoped that her long hours here at Signs for Success meant that no one in town would recognize her.

She pulled into the full church parking lot twenty minutes later and drove up and down aisles until she found somewhere to park. She got out and moved toward the front doors of the church before she realized that she could hear the sermon right now, or at least someone talking.

Curiosity drove her onward, and Lacy found a bright yellow arrow taped to the door of the church. It pointed to the left, and she went down the sidewalk that way. Upon gaining the corner, she realized that the service had been moved outside.

Huge white tents had been set up, and the sound of Willa Glover's voice carried better here. Lacy went down the sidewalk, wondering if Three Rivers held their church services outside very often. In mid-June, that didn't seem like the wisest move, and Lacy quickly realized that she would not be able to stay for long in the outdoor heat.

As she approached the back of one of the tents, a man rose and handed her a battery-powered, personal fan, a wide smile on his face. Lacy did not recognize him, but she took the fan and moved into the shade, where someone had set up misters as well. It was at least fifteen degrees cooler inside than outside, and relief rushed through Lacy as she found a seat and sat down.

Willa stood probably fifty yards away on a raised platform that couldn't be more than five by five feet wide. She sat today, and Lacy's heart immediately softened toward her. Mitch had told her of his mother's physical impairments, and she'd met the woman a couple of times now.

"Life can be so busy," Willa said. "I know this better than anyone. I raised six children, and they each came with their own set of needs that pulled me in several different directions, seemingly at the same time."

She spoke in an easy cadence, and Lacy could admit she could listen to this woman tell stories for a while.

"Singing is quite important to me," she said. "And I've run the choir here at church for many years now. Maintaining family relationships is important to me, as is being a good friend, and providing a good sermon for you—all of these things are important to me. Over the years, I've had various interests and hobbies and even a career, as I'm sure all of you have as well."

Lacy had no idea where Willa was going with this sermon, and she didn't know how much she'd missed. She would never want to be a preacher, what with all those eyes on her and having to come up with something amazing to say.

Yes, she had people looking at her as an interpreter, but she simply said what someone else did. She became their voice. She didn't have to have one of her own. Perhaps that was why she liked working with Mitch so much. He wanted her to have a voice, and he gave her space to do it.

"Yes, life can be busy," Willa said. "It's extremely overwhelming, even at the best of times. And so today, my dear friends, I'm going to urge you to do one simple thing that will make your life easier."

Lacy perked up at the joyous sound of her voice, because who didn't want their life to be easier?

"Focus first on Jesus Christ," Willa said. "He can't be an afterthought. He must come before everything else. This is why I read my scriptures first thing in the morning, and I pray before I leave my bedroom.

"There are so many other good and worthy endeavors that we can choose to do as human beings on this earth. They mean a lot personally to you, and some of them may even advance the work of God, but they cannot come *before* the Lord.

"Your career, your family, and anything else that you care about so deeply, God will make time and room in your life for those things, and He will bless your efforts as you work at them, but *He* must come first."

She said it with a smile, like this was great news. Lacy's heart started to prick at her, because this didn't sound like great news to her. This sounded like more work, like she was being condemned for the things she didn't do first.

"He loves you," Willa said next, but Lacy could barely hear her through all the blood rushing through her ears. "And He has given you a secular work to do on this earth. He wants you to find a balance between it and Him, and He will help you do it."

Tears started to stream down Lacy's face. She wasn't sure if they were angry or repentant—what she knew was that she couldn't stay there any longer, couldn't listen to another word, and she got to her feet. She'd had to go past a man and his wife to find her seat, and now she stumbled across them to get out.

"Sorry," she said right out loud, which only drew more attention to her. So many eyes, so many faces, turned her way. Lacy didn't even see them as she finally gained the aisle and rushed out.

Focus first on Christ, she thought as she fled the scene, once again feeling like she'd been somewhere she shouldn't have been and had gotten caught. Would she ever find somewhere to belong? Would she ever feel whole again?

She made it back to her SUV, her breath coming in great sobs. "I tried," she gasped out, resting both hands on the steering wheel and then putting her forehead on the backs of her knuckles. She focused on breathing in, her mind scattering thoughts everywhere.

"Dear God, I tried."

Willa had just said that the Lord would bless her efforts, and yet, Lacy felt further from God than ever.

Chapter Twenty-Three

Mitch looked down at his phone as it vibrated against the desk and flashed lights at him. Link's name came up on it, and he tilted his head to read the text: *Are you at church today?*

Mitch scoffed and picked up his phone. *No,* he sent back to Link, wanting to add something grouchy, like, *Why would I be?*

Instead, he left it at the one word and found his cousin already starting to type a reply. The three dots at the bottom of the screen continued to blip by over and over, and then a message popped up.

We just saw Lacy run out crying. Misty went after her, but she came back and said she couldn't find her. And I thought maybe you two had come together.

Mitch got to his feet as he reread the text. Lacy had run out of church crying? He looked up as if she would walk through his office door. He hadn't seen her yet that morning, and of course, he couldn't hear if she left the house.

He walked out to the front porch and looked down to where he parked his truck. She usually parked right beside him, and her SUV was gone.

How long ago was this? he asked Link.

Ten minutes or so, Link said. *I guess she could still be here.*

Thanks, Mitch said. *I'll watch for her to get back to make sure she's okay.*

All right, Link said. *I hope she is.*

Mitch moved over to his thinking seat and sat down, his mind positively boiling with ideas about what to do. Should he get in the truck and head over to the church? Would Lacy even come back if she was crying? And if she wouldn't, where would she go?

Mitch knew she liked lists, and she loved gelato, and she liked eating dessert first when they went out to eat. She never ate her full meal, but she liked sitting on the back steps and watching him work with Sunshine, Maven, and William.

She loved her job, and her brother, and flowers. Mitch tapped to get to the delivery app on his phone. The local grocer, Wilde & Organic, would deliver flowers, and he quickly tapped in an order for a bright bouquet of multicolored tulips. They would be there within the hour, and Mitch looked up, praying Lacy would be too.

He took a deep breath and closed his eyes, trying to slow down and think rationally. *Help me to know what to do,* he prayed, as Mitch had been doing a lot more since the pipe had burst and his dogs had gotten loose.

When he didn't know how to get Sunshine to do something, he would pause and pray, saying, *Open my mind, soften my heart, and give me an idea that I can use to help her, please.*

He had given real voice to his thoughts, and Mitch could admit that he felt a little bit closer to God because of it. He still didn't want to attend church, but he wanted to be a good person, a good dog trainer, and a good boyfriend.

He looked back at his phone and quickly tapped out a text to Lacy. *Hey, where are you right now? I want to show you something.*

Surely God would forgive him for the little white lie if he could spare Lacy's feelings and find out where she was at the same time.

Are you in your office? she asked.

Yes, he said, because he could get there in twenty seconds or less.

I'll be there in fifteen minutes, she said. *I had to run to town for something.*

Mitch looked up from his phone, a stinging sensation in his lungs and stomach. She didn't want him to know she'd gone to church, and Mitch didn't know how he felt about that. She hadn't exactly lied. She *had* gone to town for something, but he didn't want there to be anything between them.

He got up from the thinking seat and moved into the house, holding the door for Champ. Then he sat in the recliner that faced the window, so he could see Lacy when she arrived, without her seeing him.

She pulled down the lane only four or five minutes later, not fifteen, and she didn't come all the way to the house and park in the circle drive. Instead, she veered into the parking lot in front of the academy building, pulled up to the curb, and got out.

Mitch stood and pressed his nose to the window so he could see better, but from this distance and angle, he couldn't tell if Lacy had been crying or not. *She has been,* he told himself. *Link saw her.*

She didn't enter the building but went down the skinny sidewalk that stretched between the classroom building and the northern dormitory. Mitch patted his leg and headed for the front door. Champ came along with him, and together they went down the front steps and across the lawn. Mitch's heart pounded with every step he took, and he told himself not to be accusatory, but to be kind and comforting.

Behind the building sat a square where he imagined students would hang out in between classes. The landscape architect had put a fountain there, and the work on the grounds surrounding these buildings had come a long way since the rainstorm a couple of weeks ago. Mitch made it down the sidewalk that Lacy had walked on, and he paused in the shadows. She sat on the wall of the fountain with her back to him and her feet in the water as it splashed merrily into the pool.

Mitch swallowed and forced himself to stay still. *Do I go talk to her, Lord? What will I even say?*

Hey, sorry, but my cousin ratted you out, and I've been worried about you.

He shook his head to get that thought out, because he would not be saying that.

He did start across the cement toward her, and he knew the moment she heard his footsteps, because she raised her head and twisted to look behind her. A jolt of surprise crossed her eyes, and then it settled into resolution.

She turned away from him again, and Mitch took precious seconds to pull off his cowboy boots and socks and roll up his jeans, then he stepped into the shin-deep water and sat beside her. The water was cool and soothing, and he tucked his jeans up under his knees.

He'd never navigated relationship terrain like this before, but it felt natural to reach over and take her hand in his, so he did that. She seemed a little resistant, and Mitch turned and pressed his knees into hers.

You've been crying, he said. *What's going on?*

She shook her head, even as her bottom lip shook, and tears leaked out of her left eye. Mitch reached over with his free hand and wiped them away.

Tell me, he said, hoping it didn't come across as too pushy, but...gently insistent. *Maybe I can help you.*

She looked at him with spikes in her eyes, their gazes locked for only a moment before she looked away.

You planted rose bushes along the back of this building, she said.

Mitch blinked and turned to look. *Well, I didn't,* he said with a smile.

Lacy's gaze flickered to his face and then away again. He held his hand out, so she could see as he said, *The landscaping guys did it.*

You ordered the roses. He loved the way her delicate hands spoke and moved and brought him so much comfort.

Yes, he said. *You love roses, and I want you to be happy here.*

I am happy here, she said, pulling her hand away from his. *At least I thought I was.* She lifted her hands into the air and then let them fall back to her lap.

I went to church, she said. *I've been feeling like I should, and it was awful.*

Was it my uncle or my momma? Mitch asked, because neither one of them gave "awful" sermons, though Uncle Patrick could be a little bit more boring than Momma.

Your mom, she said. *She actually said wonderful things. Do they have church outside very often?*

Mitch struggled to keep up with the conversation, as she had jumped from one thing to another. *The service was outside?* He shook his head. *No, that's not normal. There must be something wrong with the building.*

There was a note on the door, Lacy said. *But I didn't read it.*

Mitch swiped on his phone to show her Link's texts. He handed her the phone, and she read them quickly and then looked at him.

Why did you leave crying? I'm worried about you, and I just want you to be okay. What can I do to make it okay?

She simply shook her head, and Mitch leaned down and

pressed his cheek to hers to break their eye contact. Sometimes it was so hard to tell someone something while he looked them straight in the face, and yet that was how he had to communicate.

Today, he slid over to his notes app, and he opened a new one and made it purple, one of Lacy's favorite colors.

What did my momma talk about?

He passed her the phone, and she started to type into it. She did a lot on her phone, the same as he did. So it didn't take long until she handed him the device back. *She talked about putting God first,* she said. *In all things, and that if we would put Him first, that He would bless our efforts and everything else that was important to us.*

Mitch told himself not to look at Lacy. She'd already told him that it was awful, so she clearly didn't like the message.

That doesn't sound that bad, he typed out.

She took the phone from him and hunkered over it again. Her fingers flew, and several seconds later, she shoved the phone back at him.

Mitch glanced at her without truly making eye contact while he righted the phone in his hand. He read the message, and his heart pinched.

It's not bad; it's amazing. I just don't feel like God puts me first, and He certainly didn't put Landon first, and it feels really unfair that He now expects me to move Him to the top of my list.

He pressed the power button on his phone and set it face down on the cement bench next to him. Then he lifted his arm around Lacy's shoulders and guided her into his chest. She only resisted for a moment, and then she sagged into him, the hotness of her breath and tears seeping through his T-shirt.

I'm sorry, sweetheart, he said. *Sometimes life is really unfair.* He simply let time tick by, and Lacy quieted quickly.

I came here, she said. *Because Landon and I used to love going to these gardens outside San Antonio, and they were filled with fountains. I made sure I brought a whole roll of nickels, so that we could make as many wishes as we wanted. There's something about the water as it bubbles up through the fountain and chats to different parts of itself that really soothes me.*

I'm glad we have a fountain here then, Mitch said.

Lacy's sigh covered his arm, and then she straightened and looked at him, her expression filled with that usual boldness he was used to. *If you had to do one thing—and it has to be small—to try to put God first in your life, what would you do?*

Mitch swallowed, feeling very out of his element. *I don't know*, he said. His momma would know exactly what to say to Lacy, but Mitch had no idea.

Yes, you do, she said, her hands hanging in the air as she thought. *What would your momma tell you to do?* She wore such an open, questioning expression, and Mitch's heart expanded for her.

He smiled and chuckled. *Well, I know what my momma would say.* He tucked his head and looked up at her. *Are you sure you want to hear this?*

She nodded, and Mitch decided there was nothing he could do but tell her. He waited another moment and another, begging God silently. *Please tell me if I should say this or not. If I shouldn't, make my arms numb and my hands unable to sign.*

His body continued to function normally, and still, Mitch prolonged the moment until he couldn't put it off any longer.

Momma would say...you can't eat an elephant in one bite. You have to cut it into a lot of little pieces, a lot of little bites, he said. *And over time, if you do them every day, soon enough, you've eaten the whole elephant.*

Lacy nodded, and Mitch hoped that the metaphor made sense. *So if I wanted to put God first in my life, my momma would say: start with something small. That might be that you commit to read a scripture on your phone before you get out of bed or part of your morning routine is kneeling down to pray, because you'll never be fully dressed if you're not wearing the armor of God, and you can't wear the armor of God if you don't pray and read the scriptures.*

Mitch watched the water swirl around his feet, popping and jumping as new parts of it fell from above. *That's what she would say. Start with something small that will bring you closer to God, until you're so close that all those little things you've done are just part of you and part of Him, and you're one.*

Mitch let his hands fall to his knees, where he rested his forearms on his knees and continued to watch the water. Lacy reached over and took his hand, carefully and blissfully sliding her fingers between his, and he looked at her again, barely able to see her past the brim of his cowboy hat.

Thank you, baby, she said, and she leaned forward, clearly wanting to kiss him. Mitch wanted to do that as much as possible, and he straightened to meet her halfway.

He wanted to tell her how sorry he was that she hadn't enjoyed church and how brave she was for going at all, but he kept his hand in hers.

Instead, he kissed her sweetly and held her close and vowed to tell her how amazing she was later.

Chapter Twenty-Four

There is a pair of swans out here on this pond. Lacy sent the text to Mitch and then spread out the blanket she'd brought with her for their picnic today. Her brother's car wouldn't start earlier, and Mitch had gone to get him and take him to the mechanic shop on the south side of town.

They'd called, and Lacy had driven Jacob back to the shop to pick up his car, and then she'd gotten lunch. This idea for an impromptu picnic had entered her mind in a moment and stuck.

She wore a far more sensible pair of shoes to be out wandering the grounds today, and she'd even changed into a pair of capris and a light tank top. Now that the calendar marched toward July, the heat in Texas wasn't going to get any softer.

She set the picnic basket on the edge of the blanket and

knelt down in front of it, her attention out on the swans. The pond had been on the property when Mitch had bought it, but he'd dug around it to make it safer and cleared a few trees that had fallen and swept across the surface. He wanted the students to be able to enjoy the grounds, maybe even use the pond for biology class.

Her phone chimed, and she looked at it.

You'll never guess what happened, Mitch said.

Lacy smiled, because she knew exactly what had happened. Mitch hadn't been able to take Jacob to pick up his car, because he had gone to see his parents at Shiloh Ridge this morning.

You got swallowed by a horde of grasshoppers, she said, giggling to herself. *Wait, I know. There was an alien at the Edge Cabin, and he abducted all of you, and you're on your way to Mars right now.* She burst out laughing and sent the appropriate emojis to mimic her behavior.

Oh, I know what happened, she said. *You got stuck talking to your daddy, and now you're running late.*

It's almost like an alien invasion, Mitch said, and he sent back her laughing emojis.

How are your momma and daddy? she asked.

We'll talk about it when I get there, he said. *I'm only twenty minutes away.*

Lacy set her phone down, a soft, contented sigh slipping out of her mouth. After he'd found her crying on the wall of the fountain, she'd decided to do one small thing each day to try to put God first in her life.

She'd written down a list of things that she could do that

would make sense for her life and her personality. She'd realized she always had these little pockets of time while she waited for Mitch to show up for something, and she could easily read a scripture, go over notes from a sermon, or simply meditate to clear her mind and focus it on the Lord.

She didn't like reading on her phone, so today, she navigated to a podcast that she'd found called Mindful Living. It wasn't entirely religious-focused, but sometimes the host quoted the Bible or spoke about an inspirational journey toward a higher power. Lacy had been listening to the "shorts," which were three-minute or less daily reminders.

She tapped to open the site and scrolled down to the fifth one, finding it called "Harvest Time."

Lacy had not grown up on a farm or a ranch, and she'd never really worked one either, but she understood the concept of the harvest, and she tapped to listen to the short

"Welcome to Mindful Living," a soothing female voice said. "I'm Shanna Shane, your host, on your journey toward a more peaceful existence with yourself, those around you, and God Above."

Pause. "Today's short is about the harvest. I grew up on a large family farm that grew only tomatoes."

"We were responsible for supplying two local roadside stands that we needed to sell produce from in order to pay our bills. I remember my father worrying over early frost and when to move the tomato plants out of the greenhouse and into the ground, and exactly how much water to give them.

"He'd study weather charts religiously, and he lovingly

put together his organic pest control paste that he then watered down and sprayed throughout the fields.

"When I was old enough, my daddy took me out in the field and showed me how to pick the tomatoes and put them in the cartons exactly right. If the tomatoes were not the right size or the right color, we couldn't use them. And I asked my dad one day why everything had to be so perfect.

"He said it was because people expected a certain product from Shane Farms, and he would not compromise on his standards. It felt like such a waste to me, and when I said as much to my father, he said, 'Don't worry, those tomatoes won't go to waste.'

"But sometimes a tomato would be mushy when I went to pick it, and it would smash and I would toss it to the ground and leave it behind. We did put together batches of misshapen and miscolored tomatoes and sold those for a discount. But since this was how we paid our bills, and so much emphasis was put on growing and cultivating the exact right crop, I still wondered about those tomatoes that didn't seem to respond to our loving care and attention to their growth.

"At the end of the season, the tomato vines withered, and it was obvious how much of the fruit we had actually lost. And then I stood on one of the platforms in the fields one day as my father tilled under the field to be ready for next season, and it was then that I realized that the ruined tomatoes were not a waste. They were actually contributing to the quality of our soil in a way that was much needed.

"No matter how hard we worked on the fields or

contributed to keeping the pests out, or continually checked the chicken wire to make sure raccoons didn't get in and steal our crops, we never had a perfect harvest until we tilled everything back into the earth, where it would continue to provide for us. God perfected that harvest by allowing us a way to have organic matter in our soil that didn't cost us anything.

"So, though there may be things in your life that feel like a waste, and you don't understand why something that you've cared for and poured your whole heart and soul and energy into has fallen by the wayside, I urge you to remember that God does not forget about those squishy tomatoes, and He will perfect the work that you do in His name."

Lacy breathed out into the silence, and then Shanna said, "That's it for our harvest short today. I hope these few minutes have brought a ray of sunshine to your soul, and I'll see you tomorrow."

The podcast ended when Lacy reached out to stop it from going to the next one. She gathered her hair at the nape of her neck and re-fixed her hat, her thoughts wiggling around. She tried to sort through them and fit them together, the way she would a puzzle.

She lay back and looked up into the sky. She closed her eyes and whispered, "Help me to understand and accept Thy will." That was one thing she really needed to work on, and it felt small enough that she could do it in manageable bites.

She let the serenity and peace of being away from the

office, away from the house, away from her phone, seep into her. She heard something, a rustle through the grass maybe, and she opened her eyes. It came closer and got louder, and there was definitely more than one animal moving around.

Then she heard the panting.

She barely had time to sit up before William and Sunshine were upon her, and she trilled out a laugh as William rubbed along her like a cat, and Sunshine started licking her face. Maven arrived, and she put her hands on Lacy's shoulder, as if she needed to be alerted of her presence.

With the puppies, came Mitch.

He laughed too, the sound glorious and rich, and Lacy knew in that moment she needed it every day in her life. He gave one short *breep!* of the whistle, and the dogs went right back to him. He moved them to the edge of the blanket and told them to stay with only his hands before he dropped to the ground beside her.

Hey, cowboy, she said. *Did they like your dogs?*

Daddy wanted to keep all of them. He grinned and grinned. *My daddy loves dogs.*

Lacy had heard that before, and she simply basked in the warmth from Mitch's body as he sat at her hip.

They're doing good, he said. *It's good to go see them. I'm glad I'm doing that more.*

She picked up her phone and put it back down, the screen still dark. *I listened to my podcast,* she said.

Yeah? What was it about today? he asked.

How God perfects the harvest, she said.

Mitch's eyebrows went up, but he didn't ask another question.

It's just...growing something is a lot of work. The conditions have to be exactly right, and you need enough sunshine and enough food and enough water. The temperature has to be just right.

He nodded and pushed her hair gently over her shoulder. He hummed in the back of his throat and pressed his lips to the hollow of her neck. She couldn't talk to him while he kissed her, and she waited until he looked at her again.

And it doesn't always go right, so sometimes you get stuff that's not as big as others, or it's not the right color, or it's rotten. But God knows all those things. He knows us, and He will bless our works when we put Him first.

Mitch grinned. *I'm glad you like the podcasts.*

Lacy grinned, even as she gave a simple shrug with one shoulder. *They're all right*, she said. She knew they were a gateway to really getting back into the scriptures, which she hadn't fully done yet, but she believed that God was happy with baby steps, and baby steps were all Lacy had to offer right now.

I have good news, Mitch said, and he lay back on the blanket, pulling her down with him. She snuggled into his side, enjoying the way he put his strong arm around her and held her close to his body. She raised one arm up above them so he could see and asked, *Did you want to eat first?*

No, he said, making his signs in the sky above them too. *But we had four more RAs accept their hiring offers this morning.*

Lacy pushed herself up onto her elbow and gazed down at Mitch. *You're kidding,* she said. He grinned at her, and oh, she wanted to kiss that cocky, lopsided smile right off his face. She leaned down to do just that, feeling more content and happier than ever.

She'd known coming to Three Rivers was the right thing for her, but she'd had no idea how many good things the Lord would provide for her—not only with an amazing place to live and an amazing work to do, but that He could open the door to her heart and let this tall, handsome, amazing man inside.

He chuckled as she kissed him, which caused her to giggle along with him. She loved the way they laughed together, and the way everything seemed so easy with Mitch.

I got turkey BLTs from the deli, she said, and a smile spread across his face. He pulled her closer to his side, making no move to get the food that she'd brought for lunch.

He looked up into the sky, a sigh softening through his shoulders and chest as he relaxed beside her. Mitch didn't relax very often, and Lacy liked that they could exist in this place together and be so comfortable. The sky didn't hold a single cloud, and today felt pretty perfect.

Mitch raised his arm and said, *You have a pretty voice.*

She only smiled, because he couldn't hear her voice.

It matches your pretty hair, and your pretty face, and your pretty personality. I think you're pretty great.

Lacy loved that they'd found this way to talk to one another, that they didn't have to have such strong eye contact. She raised her hand and twined her fingers with his and squeezed, and then let go.

I think you're pretty amazing, too. Then she dropped her hand to his chest and slid it all the way across his torso, so that she could be as close to him as possible.

She only moved her eyes when he started to talk again. *Do you want kids, sweetheart?*

Her heartbeat came to a standstill, and she reminded herself that she could tell Mitch the truth. He'd insisted on it. After she'd gone to church and hadn't told him, and then said she'd had to run to town for something, he'd given her a couple of days and then he'd told her, *I don't like how you didn't tell me the real truth.*

They'd agreed that they'd be honest with one another, so she raised her hand up and said, *Yes, I want kids.*

You and Landon didn't have any, he said.

Landon didn't want kids, she said.

And that was okay with you? Mitch asked.

Lacy swallowed, and he turned his head toward her. He couldn't have felt the movement in her throat; Mitch was simply very good at picking up on feelings in the air.

She tucked herself further against his chest, because she didn't want to look at him. *It upset me,* she said. *But I loved him, and he loved me, and I thought that it might be okay.*

Was it? Mitch asked.

I don't think I really got the chance to find out. Like you said, we weren't married very long, and most people don't expect you to start having kids on your wedding night.

Mitch burst out laughing, but Lacy didn't think she'd

said anything funny. She once again pushed herself up to look at him, and while he threw out a fresh round of laughter, he also said, *You haven't met the Glovers then.*

Lacy grinned at him. Someone *won't take me home to meet them all*, she said.

Mitch reached out and grabbed her wrist, suddenly sobering, his dark eyes glinting with sunshine and happiness and also something a tiny bit dangerous. *You want to go home and meet my family as my girlfriend?*

Yes. She rotated her wrist, capturing Mitch's with her fingers. *Yes, I want you to take me home as your very serious girlfriend and introduce me to everyone.*

You don't know what you're asking for, he said.

I'm not afraid, she said.

He grinned at her wickedly and rolled her gently so that she was on her back, and he hovered above her. *You should be*, he said, right before he lowered his head and kissed her like his life depended on having his mouth against hers.

Chapter Twenty-Five

E laine Walker finished primping her dark hair, making it curl and wave nicely over her shoulders. She'd painted her lips a dark red, and she looked like a million bucks. She still didn't want to go out tonight as a seventh wheel, but she told herself that Austin and Easton were not a couple. They only *seemed* like it because they were twins, inseparable, and Elaine was the third part of their triplet who never seemed to fit in.

She was the only girl in her family, but now that Conrad and Glory Rose were married, Elaine had another woman to pal around with.

Glory Rose had been kind in including Elaine in everything with Sari, Conrad's daughter. She still called Elaine to come help with her hair and paint her nails, and Elaine had feared that she would lose that time with her niece once Glory Rose and Conrad got married.

She tried to be extra gracious and grateful whenever Glory Rose invited her to do anything with her and Sari or her, Conrad, and Sari.

"Like tonight," she muttered to herself as she ran her hands down the black sweater dress she'd chosen to wear.

She'd inherited some curves from her momma, and she'd gotten them early in life, so she had plenty of experience in dealing with boys and men looking at her and judging her. She didn't care at all what they thought. She loved her size-twelve frame, and the only thing she'd ever asked God for was another couple of inches. She hadn't gotten them, but she didn't hold a grudge.

Her phone chimed, not just once but several times, and Elaine swiped it up from the bathroom counter.

We're here, Conrad said. *Are you ready?*

We're waiting in your front driveway, Glory Rose said. *Are you chickening out on coming? It's cousin night, Elaine!*

Instead of answering them, Elaine hurried out of her bathroom and down the hall to the living room. She grabbed her purse, a cute little orange quilted bag that she could carry in one hand, and headed for the front door.

She'd gone out several times with her siblings over the years for siblings' nights, but they'd expanded that to include JJ and Ruby and Clara Jean and Tate. And Elaine realized in that moment that she wasn't just a seventh wheel. She was a *ninth*.

Austin and Easton never brought up the fact that they were single, and Elaine didn't want to be a party pooper, so she kept her thoughts to herself.

Of course, Easton and Austin hadn't tried dating at all this year, and Elaine felt like she went out with someone new every other week. She'd had two boyfriends since last July, and she was currently single, though she did have a date with someone new on Saturday.

She tried to keep an open mind, but Elaine hated first dates, and she could admit that she put too much stock in her initial impression of a man. She had a very short list of males that she would like to ask her out, but she didn't know how to get them to do it. She'd seen some people make love connections on TwoCents, but that had never been her vibe. She didn't want to meet someone online before she met them in person.

But working at HealNow as a secretary in the Small Claims Department didn't offer her a lot of opportunities to meet anyone interesting. The people she usually saw were already married, too young for her, too old for her, or irate about something. She didn't want that to be her first meeting story, anyway.

Fine, Elaine could admit that she romanticized things a little bit.

She pushed out the front door just as her phone rang. She waved her orange purse and pulled the door closed behind her. "Sorry," she said, as she boosted herself up into Conrad's back seat. "I was in my bathroom, which is a little bit of a dead zone for my service. How long have you guys been waiting?"

She felt breathless as she pulled her dress across her knees the right way.

"Forever," Conrad deadpanned at the same time Glory Rose said, "Not that long."

They looked at one another, their smiles so cute, and their inside jokes sickenly sweet. Elaine had hated being around Clara Jean and Tate while they were engaged, but they'd gotten far more tolerable. Conrad kept private things private, and he and Glory Rose were just so stinking cute that Elaine could never be upset with either one of them.

"We're gonna be the last ones there now," Conrad said. "You know that, right?"

"I hope we are," Elaine bickered back to her older brother. "Then I won't have to slide into the middle of the table, and I'll be able to go to the bathroom if I need to."

They were going to a sports bar tonight, where Elaine loved the buffalo wings, but she didn't love the bar top tables or the booths, and that was all they had there. The bar tops only held four, which meant their party of nine would one hundred percent be seated in a booth, and Elaine had found herself trapped in the middle of it more than once on cousin nights.

No, thank you, she thought, as she looked out the window.

Conrad navigated them to The Salty Saloon, and in they went. He'd apparently gotten the text from Austin as to the location of their booth, and he led them through the maze of sports watchers, waitresses, and appetizers to a booth in the corner. Elaine brought up the rear, having worn a cute pair of ankle boots with her dress that didn't allow her to walk as fast as she might have normally.

She didn't mind, because that meant she got to sit on the end, and that was where she wanted to be—hopefully next to Easton, because he wouldn't ask her who she was dating or suggest ten different apps she could try.

Glory Rose didn't do that either, but JJ and Conrad and Tate all seemed to have an idea of how Elaine should live her life—at least when it came to men. Conrad claimed to be playing the "older brother role," so that he could protect her and keep her safe, which Elaine certainly didn't mind. She simply didn't want to talk about it tonight.

"Elaine?" She turned to her left as she heard her name in a deep voice. Only a moment later, the gorgeous sight of Cavalry Stone met her eyes.

"Cav," she said, and she detoured toward him. She hugged him lightly and put an enormous smile on her face, for Cav sat on the short list of men Elaine wished would ask her out.

She'd met him at a church linger longer several weeks ago, and she'd flirted the best she knew how. He'd even gotten her number and texted a few times, but only about the fish and chips place that had gone in up north and then once about how to file email—both things Elaine had claimed to be an expert at: knowing where to eat and knowing how to get to Inbox Zero.

As she stepped back, she prayed mightily that she had more skills than that to hold a man's attention. But when it came to Cav, she sure didn't think so. He would have texted again if she had, wouldn't he?

She hated these questions the most about dating. She

just wanted to feel good about herself. She wanted to feel smart and beautiful, and dating made her feel the opposite of both.

"How are you?" Cav asked. "I haven't seen you in forever."

"Still here," Elaine said, doing a mini-curtsy. "Same as always. What about you?" She glanced to the woman next to him, her heart falling all the way to the tips of her ankle boots.

"This is my sister," Cav said, his eyes flickering to the woman too. "She's in town for a few days, so I finally left the house." He chuckled and brought the woman to his side. "Hannah, this is Elaine Walker."

"It's great to meet you," Hannah said, and Elaine smiled widely.

His sister, perfect.

"You too," she said, quickly switching her attention back to Cav. "You haven't been leaving the house?" she asked, realizing that she had probably drawn the attention of all eight people at the booth waiting for her.

JJ would grump about having to wait to put in their orders, and she glanced over her shoulder to find all of them looking at her. *Great.*

"Listen, I'm out with my brothers and my cousins," she said. "You've got my number." She stepped in a little bit closer. "You could use it more often, you know." And with that, she turned and walked away from Cav and his sister.

She felt his gaze on her back, and she maybe added an extra

sway to her hips as she went. But she tried not to be too obvious, because she'd have to answer about that to everyone at the table as well. She slid into the seat, feeling a bit breathless and sweaty.

"Sorry," she said. "I met a friend."

"A *friend?*" JJ asked.

"Yeah," Elaine said, setting her glare on him. "Do you guys know Cav Stone?"

"Cav Stone?" Conrad repeated, and he might as well put ten question marks at the end of the man's name. "That is not his name." He chuckled, and Austin downright laughed.

"That *is* his name," Easton said, ever the serious one. "I've met Cav. He's a good guy."

"Cav?" Tate asked. "Like a *calf*—like a cow?"

"No, his name is Cavalry," Elaine said, pushing her hair back off her neck to try to get some air. "It's a totally normal name." She looked at Glory Rose for help, and then Clara Jean.

"Cav comes shopping for his mom," Clara Jean said. "He's a good guy."

"Yeah, leave Elaine alone," Glory Rose said. "She can't help what the man's name is." She smiled at Elaine and patted her hand. "Have you been out with him?"

"I wish," Elaine said, sort of muttering the words, so that her brothers wouldn't hear.

"Oh, you *like* this Cav Stone?" Conrad asked, and he half rose in the booth and looked over her head. "Did he ask you out?"

"No," Elaine said. "Do you not understand what 'I wish' means?"

"But you like him." Conrad settled down and looked at her again, only some of the teasing still lingering in his expression.

"I mean, I would say yes if he asked me out," Elaine said.

"Where'd you meet him?" JJ asked.

Elaine saw no reason not to tell him, so she said, "Church linger longer. Why?"

"He lives out east of town," JJ said. "On a *homestead*."

"Oh, boy," Easton said, laughing over the words. "You know what that means, don't you, Laney?"

"No water," Austin said. "No electricity. There's no way you'd survive out there, Laney."

"Stop telling me what I can and can't do," Elaine said. She glanced over her shoulder to the table where Cav sat with his sister. His eyes were stuck to the TV in the corner, and then he glanced over to her.

Feeling wild and a bit out of control, Elaine pushed out of the booth.

"Hey, don't go," Conrad said. "We won't talk about him anymore," he yelled.

As Elaine walked away, she heard other people in her family chattering behind her, but she kept on toward Cav.

"Hey," she said as she approached.

Cav dropped from the chair and reached up to press his cowboy hat to his head. "Hey. Is everything okay?"

"Sort of," she said, and Elaine couldn't believe what she was about to do. "Look, I liked you when I met you, and I gave you my number, hoping you'd ask me out, and then you never did."

At the table, Hannah started to snicker.

"Yeah," he said.

"Why?" Elaine asked. "Did you not like me too? Not even enough to try a first date?"

"No, I did," he said.

Elaine waited for him to give a further explanation, and when he didn't, she drew in a deep breath. "Would you like to go out with me?"

"Right now?" he asked.

"No, silly," Hannah said. "She's out with her cousins and brothers. She wants to know if you'll take her to dinner another night." She shook her head, and Elaine smiled at her, and then looked at Cav with her eyebrows raised.

"Well, what do you think?"

He had to be at least five years older than her, and while that wasn't really old enough for Elaine, she wanted a date with this man, and why couldn't she ask him?

"All right," Cav said, a smile crossing his face. "What are you doing on Saturday?"

"Oh, well, Saturday's not going to work," she said. "But what about Monday after work? We can just do something casual, so you can decide if you really like me enough to ask me out." She leaned in closer and put her hand against his chest. "Because next time, cowboy, *you're* going to have to ask *me*."

"Yes, ma'am," he said.

She moved back, a smile on her face. "Great. Text me and we'll set up a time on Monday."

"All right." He grinned at her, and Elaine ducked her head, suddenly feeling shy though she'd literally marched over to the man and demanded to know why he hadn't asked her out.

She returned to the booth with her head held high and sat down feeling like she'd just run a marathon.

"Can we order now?" JJ asked.

"What just happened over there?" Glory Rose said, leaning closer. "He is *staring* at you, and he has *not* looked away."

Good, Elaine thought. Then she said, "We have a date on Monday night."

Chapter Twenty-Six

Wilder Glover tucked in his shirt, wondering if he should go with plaid or not. Surely some of the cowboys at the Fourth of July dance would wear plain colors, wouldn't they? He still lived in the homestead at Shiloh Ridge because he'd taken over as foreman and saw no reason to move out. The house was centrally located, and he had an entire wing to himself. His parents had even put in a kitchenette, and Wilder only had to go down the stairs and out the front door to escape them.

He'd sat down with his parents to discuss his living arrangements, and they'd agreed not to ask him where he was going and what time he would be home. He was twenty-six years old and ran the ranch, for crying out loud. If they couldn't trust him past that, he didn't know what he was doing there.

He liked his little sanctuary, and he loved Shiloh Ridge,

but he did want someone special in his life. He'd started dating more, but he hadn't found anyone to stick yet. So he'd had a string of first dates where either he didn't want a second one or the woman he went out with didn't.

A door in his wing slammed, and Wilder turned from the mirror where he had been making sure his belt buckle sat right in the middle of his body.

"What?" he managed to say before Uncle Ace flew into the room. "This is my house," Wilder said.

"Your daddy says this window has the best view of the road off the ranch," Uncle Ace said, as if that was an explanation. He moved right past Wilder to the window that, yes, overlooked the road coming up the hill to the ranch.

"All right," Wilder said, still confused. "What's going on?"

"I'm pretty sure my son is lying to me," Uncle Ace said with a hint of disgust in his voice.

"Which one?" Wilder asked. He'd had plans to go to the food truck fair and summer dance tonight with Smiles, Rock, and Gun, but Gunnison had canceled last minute. Wilder knew why, but Uncle Ace had *two* sons, and it could have just as well been Ashton telling a little white lie to his father.

"Gunnison," Ace said. "Oh, my heck, there he is." He slapped one hand against the window. "He is leaving the ranch *right now*, that little sneak. He told me he was sick." He whipped around to face Wilder.

He started to laugh. "He told you he was sick?" Wilder asked. "That's not what I heard."

Uncle Ace took one step toward him almost menacingly. "What did he tell you?"

"He told me he has a date," Wilder said, really hitting the T hard. Ace's mouth fished open, as if he didn't know what a date was. "Uncle Ace, the man is twenty-four years old. He can go out with a woman if he wants to."

"Yeah, I mean, of course he can," Ace said. "I just don't get why he didn't tell me about it."

"I wish I'd taken a video of what just happened," Wilder said. "That would tell you why he didn't tell you about it.'

Uncle Ace's face settled into a grumpy expression, and he folded his arms. "Who's he going out with?"

"You think I'm going to tell you who he's going out with?" Wilder asked. "Oh, man, listen, Uncle Ace, Gun is one of my best friends. I don't want him to be upset with me. Maybe you should just ask him about it."

"I'm gonna ask him about it," Uncle Ace said.

"Great," Wilder said. "So that's settled."

"You don't have to tell me. You can just nod or shake your head or—or blink. One blink for yes, two for no."

"Oh, my word," Wilder said.

"Is it Camila Walker?"

Against his will, Wilder blinked just once. Uncle Ace whooped and pumped his fist in the air. "I knew it. I *knew* he was going out with her." He stepped over to Wilder and slapped him on the shoulder. "You've been incredibly helpful tonight, Wilder. What are you doing?" He glanced down to his boots. "Are *you* going out with someone?"

"We're going to the summer dance, sir," Wilder said.

"And you will not, under any circumstances, tell Gun that *I* told you he's going out with Camila."

"So he is going out with her."

"I can neither confirm nor deny such a thing," Wilder said, though Gun was totally going out with Camila Walker, and in fact, tonight was probably their fourth or fifth date. Gun lived in a cowboy cabin over on the side of the ranch with the guineafowl, and he clearly wanted to keep the relationship to himself for a little bit longer.

Wilder wasn't sure why. According to Gun, he and Camila had hit it off after a concert in the park only a couple of weeks ago, and he'd kissed her that very night.

Life seemed a little unfair to Wilder in that moment, because he'd been trying to find someone to date and was really open about it. Gun had accidentally showed up at a concert, because his momma had conned him into going along and helping with the catering and he met someone?

Not only that, but they'd known Camila Walker their whole lives.

Uncle Ace left Wilder's suite, and he told himself, "You should be glad your cousin is going out with someone he's known his whole life. Maybe you can find someone like that too."

He picked up his cowboy hat and put it on his head. "Maybe tonight at the summer dance."

Then he pulled out his phone and sent a text to Gun. *Your daddy barged into my place and saw you driving off the ranch. Thought you'd want to know he knows you're not "sick."*

That done, Wilder headed downstairs to his truck, because he had to get around the bend in the ranch to pick up Smiles and Rock for their summer evening of wild cowboy fun.

* * *

Wilder finally found a parking spot about two blocks away from the park where the dance and food truck fair had been set up. "All right, fellas," he said, as he put the truck in park. "Smiles, you are not going to outshine me tonight." He grinned at his cousin and best friend.

Smiles smiled back at him. "I never outshine you," he said good-naturedly.

"You so do," Rock said from the back seat in his usual gruff manner. He'd definitely gotten more of Uncle Bear's genes than Aunt Sammy's, and he never said more than necessary, and almost always in a growly voice that Wilder could barely hear.

Smiles twisted and looked at his younger brother. "How dare you?" he said. "I hooked you up with Alyssa."

"First off," Rock said, as he ran his hand down his face and shaped his beard just right. Rock was dark from head to toe, including his eyes and his hair, and the fact that he'd worn a black cowboy hat with a black shirt for a Fourth of July celebration about summed the man right up.

Wilder grinned at him because Rock had earned his nickname by being stubborn as a child, and he played right into it as an adult, being grumpy and grouchy even when he really wasn't.

"I did not *hook up* with Alyssa," he said. "Do you even know what that means, Smiles?" He glanced over to Wilder. "Second, she was all wrong for me, and that date was one of the worst nights of my life. You *tortured* me, brother, so no, I will not be thanking you."

Smiles burst out laughing. "Torture? Going out with a pretty woman is *torture.*"

"She wore pink from head to toe," Rock said. "Her toenails were painted pink, her sandals were pink, and she wore a pink bow in her hair like a Texas cheerleader." He folded his arms. "No, thank you. I don't even want to be at this dance."

"Hey, this is a fun night," Wilder said. "It's tacos from a truck and really big ice cream cones and country music. If you don't want to dance, don't dance."

"I'm not asking anyone," Rock said. "And I don't need anyone needling me to do it."

"Deal," Wilder said. He raised his eyebrows as he looked over at Smiles. "Are you going to make a deal with the man or not?"

"So I can't force Rock to ask anyone to dance," Smiles said. "And I can't outshine you."

"That's right," Wilder said.

"What *can* I do?" Smiles said.

"Stand at my side and be a good wingman." Wilder grinned at his cousin. "I mean, Gun's got Camila now, and that means I've got Mister Grumpy Secret Service cowboy over here at my side. I *need* you, Smiles." He looked out the windshield at another couple walking by, this time a man and a woman hand-in-hand. "I'm gonna hang back, scope things out, and hope someone comes over to me."

"You're not going to ask anyone to dance?" Smiles seemed surprised by that, and Wilder latched onto the idea.

"I'm gonna play it by ear," he said. "I need a good wingman to talk me up, you know?"

"All right," Smiles said. "Let's do this." He unbuckled his seat belt like he was loading a rifle, and the three of them spilled from the truck.

Wilder moved to Rock's side, but he barely stood as tall as the man, and Smiles stood taller than them all. He always stuck out in a crowd, and though he'd been going to school at Amarillo State for the past three years, he still seemed to know everyone in town.

They'd probably get stopped five times just on the way to the park, and Wilder would be lucky if he saw Smiles after that. He shone like a pot of gold at the end of a rainbow, and people acted like they'd found such a thing every time they saw him.

Rock would remain steady and share Wilder's side, but he sometimes made little grunts and sighs like it was very hard for him to put up with the young adult conversation Wilder needed to have with a woman before he could get her phone number.

"Do we really have to have tacos tonight?" Rock said.

"They have steak," Wilder said.

"I just want a really big burger," Rock said.

"They'll have burgers."

Smiles bent down and picked up a pamphlet that had been lying on the ground. "This is a list of all the vendors. Why don't you just pick, and we'll go there?"

Wilder would be down for that, and so he left Rock to figure out how to walk and study a vendor list at the same time while he tried to get his mental game together to find a date.

They arrived in the park to an atmosphere of high energy, with the street closed and food trucks lining both sides of it for a couple of blocks. Wilder definitely wanted to eat first and deal with the dancing second, which took place on the other end of the park, where they laid down a hard floor over the grass. Cowboys and cowgirls needed somewhere to stomp their boots, after all, and Wilder could admit he liked a good line dance as much as the next red-blooded Texan.

Rock had indeed found them a burger truck to visit, and they joined the short line that had queued up there.

"They've got truffle fries," he said, reading from the board. "And rosemary fries and cheese fries."

Someone turned away from the pickup window with an order of French fries, and Rock whistled. "Holy cow. Is that how big they are? We could share."

"I don't like the truffle ones, but either of the others is fine," Smiles said.

Wilder looked at Rock, and Rock looked back at him. "That cheese looks fake," Rock said. "I ain't eating that."

Wilder grinned at him. "Rosemary or plain, then."

"Yeah, all right," Rock said, but he didn't say what kind he wanted. They put their orders in, Rock taking a complicatedly long time to make sure that his burger wouldn't have onions but would have avocado and bacon. In the end, he ordered plain fries and joined Smiles and Wilder in the pickup area.

"You always do such complicated orders," Smiles said. "I don't get why. You can't just pick the onions off?"

"I don't want the onions," Rock said. "They should save them for someone who does." He made no apology for his complicated order, and Wilder simply prayed that it would come out right. He didn't like Rock being upset on a good day, and a hungry, upset Rock was definitely not in Wilder's plan for the evening.

He and Rock had graduated from high school at the same time, and Rock had put in his year in the cowboy cabins and then moved into the stable manager position at Shiloh Ridge Ranch. He had zero interest in book learning or college, but he knew a heck of a lot about horses and how to care for them. He took care of all thirty-two equines at the ranch, including all the personal family horses.

"What we really need is a new vet," Wilder said.

"No," Smiles said. "We are not talking about work."

"Don't you want to be a vet?" Wilder asked. "It's only five more years of school." He grinned over to his cousin, who simply smiled, of course, and shook his head. He didn't deny it, and Wilder wouldn't be surprised if Smiles did decide to continue on to veterinary school.

Shiloh Ridge did need a full-time vet. Heck, they probably needed two, and right now they were getting by with a couple of family members with vet tech degrees and Uncle Cactus, who had technically retired, but somehow still went to work every day.

The woman in the food truck called Smiles's name, and he went to get their order. Rock went with and inspected every piece of it before allowing Smiles to move away from the window.

"Dude, you're so embarrassing," Wilder said. "You could have done that at a table." He led them out of the street and under the trees where a plethora of picnic tables had been set up. He found one in the shade and sat down with Smiles sliding the tray of food onto the table a moment later.

"I want my order to be right," Rock said. "I paid for that."

"Yeah, like you can't afford to pay for it again," Smiles said.

"They wouldn't make you repay anyway," Wilder said.

"It would be wasteful," Rock growled as he sat down.

"You and your care of the environment," Smiles teased. "The man can't even throw onions away." He laughed, and Wilder grinned, and Rock took their ribbing pretty well.

He'd just dunked a French fry in ketchup and stuck the whole thing in his mouth when a woman said, "Russell."

All eyes turned to the female voice who'd used Rock's real name. Wilder found a pretty blonde woman standing there, and she turned to the two others she was with and said, "I'll catch up to you guys."

They looked at her, then surveyed the three cowboys

sitting at the table, then walked away. By then, she'd looked back at Rock.

So did Smiles, and his eyebrows went up. "Russell?"

"It is my name," Rock said. He got to his feet and went around to the woman, "How are you, Clover?" He swept his lips along both of her cheeks, and that, more than anything, caused Wilder to sit back and gape.

Of course he expected Rock to be a Texas gentleman. Aunt Sammy had raised her boys well. He'd just never seen it in action.

"I didn't know you were coming tonight," Clover said, clearly flirting with him. She didn't even look at Smiles or Wilder.

"Yeah," Rock said. "It's the Fourth of July."

She slid her hand up the buttons on his black shirt. "Yeah, you sure look dressed for it, cowboy."

He laughed, and a scoff fell out of Wilder's mouth, for he had never heard Rock make a sound like *that*.

"Yeah, well, I don't own any red, white, and blue."

Clover had dressed to the nines in the patriotic colors, but she didn't have a cheerleader bow in her hair. Wilder thought she was pretty cute in her American flag tank top and blue denim cutoffs.

"Are you going to the dance later?" she asked.

"Yeah," Rock said. "Sure am." He indicated Smiles and Wilder. "You know my older brother Smiles, and my cousin Wilder?"

"No, I don't think we've met," she said. "I'm Clover Broadbent."

"Nice to meet you, ma'am," Smiles said, half standing up. Wilder likewise shook her hand, and when she moved back to Rock, she settled very, very close to him.

She leaned in, and he ducked his head down. "Will you ask me to dance tonight, cowboy?"

Wilder actually found himself leaning closer, so he could hear Rock's answer, thinking of how not twenty minutes ago, Rock had declared that he would *not* be asking anyone to dance. Absolutely not. No way.

"Yeah, all right," Rock said, and with that, Clover slid her hand along his forearm to his elbow. She squeezed there and stepped away. Rock turned his head and watched her go, but Wilder couldn't look away from his cousin.

"Come sit down," Smiles hissed to Rock. "You're staring."

Rock flinched and did what his brother said.

Wilder opened his mouth, but Rock blurted out, "I'm not talking about her." He picked up his hamburger, his face flaming red.

"Are you going to ask her to dance?" Wilder said. "You just vowed you wouldn't ask anyone to dance tonight."

Rock glared at him and said, "If you ask someone to dance, I'll ask Clover."

Wilder blinked. "I'm just scoping out the scene tonight," he said.

"Then I'm going to be Mister Secret Service Cowboy at your side," Rock said, his dark eyes glittering with something dangerous. "You need a wingman. How can I possibly dance with her?"

Wilder grinned and grinned and grinned. Then he looked over at Smiles. "Smiles, will you dance with me tonight?"

"Sure thing, brother," Smiles said, and Wilder nodded at Rock.

"There you go. You have to ask Clover."

"That so doesn't count," Rock grumbled, and then he simply took another bite of his hamburger.

Wilder did hope that he could find someone else to dance with besides his cousin, but if he couldn't, he'd just keep trying. There had to be someone in this town that was for him. God wouldn't be that cruel to put him here and not lead her here too.

Would He?

Chapter Twenty-Seven

Brandon Rhinehart sat in his truck parked in the hardware store parking lot, the air conditioning blasting to keep him cool. He'd texted on the family string about his whereabouts.

Dawson's wife, Caroline, was pregnant again, and still in the first trimester, so she'd been quite ill. When Brandon had told everyone that he would be in town that afternoon and to send him a list of anything they needed, Caroline had requested ginger ale, raspberry Jell-O, and caramel rice cakes.

Brandon still had to get to the grocery store, and thankfully no one in his family had asked on the group text what he was doing down in Three Rivers. His family ranch sat forty minutes south of town, which was why he'd texted everyone that he would be there that day. They didn't always make it to town, and his daddy really loved creamer in his coffee.

He'd asked for two bottles of that—*plain vanilla, none of that fangled flavored creamer*. Brandon grinned just thinking about his daddy's grumpiness.

He looked out of the windshield, the smile retreating. "And he somehow got two women to fall in love with him."

Brandon's daddy had been married previously, and he and his first wife had had Duke. Then his wife had passed away. Daddy had remarried only a couple of years later to Brandon's momma, and they'd had Dawson and then him. He'd turned thirty-six this past spring, and he had yet to be married once.

It's fine, he told himself as his phone vibrated with another text. He glanced down at it to see his sister-in-law, Arizona, with a whole list of things that she needed from the grocery store. She'd included a few items from the hardware store as well, and Brandon quickly copied them over to his list.

She'd asked him off the family string why he was going to town, as had Dawson. Brandon thought about giving them two different answers just to see what would happen— or the same answer that wasn't true at all. In the end, no one ever thought Brandon's jokes were as funny as he did, and he'd simply told them that he'd come down to interview as a ranch hand for the Davies.

That had prompted both Dawson and Arizona to call him, and a wave of exhaustion moved through him at the very thought. He'd talked to both of them, and he'd explained how he felt. It wasn't anything new anyway, and he talked about it with both of them previously.

He looked out the side window and then back at his phone. *Last call*, he said. *I'm putting in the grocery order and heading into the hardware store now, and then I'll be on my way back.*

We're good, Caroline said. *Thank you, Brandon.*

All good here too, Momma said.

You got my list? Arizona said. *That's everything.*

I got it, he confirmed. He quickly added her groceries to the order at Wilde & Organic and sent that off to be fulfilled.

With the list of items he needed from the hardware store in front of him, Brandon got out of the air-conditioned truck and dropped into the July Texas heat. Why he lived here, he had no idea—and that was only another reason why he had to get off of Hidden Hills Ranch and out into the world.

The Davies place sat about an hour southeast of Three Rivers in another small Texas town called Boulder Creek. Brandon had never gone to college, but he knew how to be a cowboy—and a really good one at that—but his family ranch didn't need him.

Duke was still working hard and had another decade in him before he'd slow down, and he had two girls and two boys, and *they* all still worked the ranch.

Dawson and Caroline had just started their family. They had a little boy and a baby girl, with another on the way. Dawson worked the ranch full-time too. They didn't need Brandon.

No one seemed to need Brandon.

That's not true, he told himself as he went inside, the blessed kiss of air conditioning brushing across the back of his neck. "Howdy, Jean," he said to the woman who always stood at the register.

"Hey-you, Brandon," she called back. Jean was not dating material. She was two decades older than Brandon and had been married three times.

He'd been out with over a dozen women in Three Rivers, and he simply didn't see any prospects here. Dawson told him new people were moving to town all the time and to be patient, but Brandon felt like he'd put in his dues when it came to patience.

He grabbed a little shopping cart and started to push it down the narrow aisles of the hardware store. He had collected the super glue and the box of screws that Arizona needed before he moved into the aisle with the space heaters and portable air conditioning units. He still lived in the cabin he'd once shared with Dawson, and while it had central heating and air and running water, the air conditioner had been acting up this summer.

Brandon did not want to wake up in the middle of the night covered in sweat one more time. He only had a little fan that he could use, and blowing around hot air still meant it was mighty hot.

He started examining the air conditioning units, and he kept his head down and his thoughts focused as people moved around him. He used to crave times out like this, because he could meet women at the hardware store or the grocery store—but now he didn't want to do that at all. He felt like everyone in town was talking about him, and not in a good way.

If he could just get a job somewhere else, even for a little while, he felt certain he would be happier.

A text popped up at the top of his screen and said his order at Wilde & Organic had been canceled. Brandon frowned and tapped over to it. "Canceled?" he muttered. The grocery delivery app showed that his payment method had not gone through, and then his phone rang.

He swiped on the call and said, "Hey."

"This is Brandon Rhinehart?" a perky female voice asked.

"Yes," he growled.

"We just tried to run your card here at Wilde & Organic, and it didn't go through."

"Yeah, I just got a notification that my order has been canceled."

"Yeah, that's our system default," she said. "This is Clara Jean Reynolds."

"Oh, hi, Clara Jean," he said, as her husband and brother and cousin all came to the same small ranch owners meeting that Brandon attended. His heart died a little and flopped in his chest when he realized he wouldn't be in town for those meetings if he got another job.

"If you want, you can pay when you come to pick it up," Clara Jean said. "Or I can take a number over the phone."

Brandon glanced down to the end of the aisle where a man walked by. If he had to go inside and pay, that meant he had to...go inside and pay. He'd have to mingle with the public, possibly women.

"I'll just give you a card," he grumbled, and he reached into his back pocket to pull out his wallet.

He gave Clara Jean the number, and waited a few moments until she said, "Yep, that one's just fine. It's ready for you whenever you are."

"Thanks," Brandon said. "I'll be there in a few minutes." The call ended, and he resumed his studying of the air conditioning units. In the end, he selected a tall tower, one that would oscillate the cold air back and forth, at least enough to keep a bedroom cool so he could sleep. Just for good measure, he picked up a second one, because he really only spent time in his bedroom or the living room, and these would do until he could get someone out to the ranch to look at the air conditioning.

He could probably ask one of Arizona's siblings or cousins to come do it. "Heck," he said, as he started to push his cart down the aisle. "I think Link fixed his air conditioner; maybe he could come look at yours."

He went around the corner just as an enormous clattering sound filled the hardware store. A tall wire display rack of screwdrivers had just been knocked over. Brandon saw the end of someone's cart and the flash of golden hair right before the woman went down. His heartbeat leaped into the back of his throat, and he abandoned his cart as he stepped toward her.

"Are you okay?"

He was so focused on her that he didn't pay attention to

the fact that screwdrivers had been scattered everywhere. And if there was one thing that his daddy had taught him, it was that screwdrivers roll. He'd bellowed at Brandon plenty to equip them with rubber on the handle so that he could set one down and have it stay where he put it.

None of these screwdrivers had that extra tape on the handle, and when Brandon's slick cowboy boot came down on one of them, he lost his balance—and his feet went out from under him.

No, no, no, shouted through his head, and he flung his arms out, as if he might be able to grab onto something. He did—a shelving unit full of kitty litter. And with gravity and his weight pulling on the shelves, it ripped right off the wall.

Brandon landed hard on his tailbone, pain shooting up his back as he curled into himself and covered his head with his hands as plastic bottles of kitty litter rained down on him. The pellets in the plastic bottles made a horrific crash-ing-grating-shaking sound all around him that seemed to go on for several long seconds, and then finally, everything silenced.

He found himself sitting in the hardware store, the scent of rocky kitty litter wafting through the air, screwdrivers laying at haphazard angles all over the floor, and the most beautiful woman he'd ever laid eyes on only a few feet from him.

Their eyes met, and Brandon only had time to recognize that she'd been crying before she wiped her tears away, and someone said, "Nuts and bolts, are you guys all right?"

People converged on them then, and Brandon accepted

the help to get back to his feet. Someone righted the screw-driver rack, and Brandon started picking up the tools that had spilled.

"Brandon, are you all right?" Jean asked.

"Yeah, I'm fine," he said. "Just a little spill. Sorry about the kitty litter. You can put it in my cart." He looked around for his cart and didn't find it anywhere. "I had a cart..." he said. "It had some glue and stuff in it, couple air conditioning units...."

His voice trailed off when he saw the pretty blonde poke her head around the corner, way down at the end of the hardware store. She stood next to a cart with Brandon's two air conditioning units in it, and every cell in his body came alive.

"I'm okay, Jean," he said. "Thank you. Sorry about the mess."

"It's just kitty litter," she said. "It's no big deal."

He nodded, and though his tailbone smarted with every step he took, he headed for the blonde who had taken his air conditioning units.

Along the way, he coached himself silently. *You will not ask for her number. You are not dating. You are not going to stay in Three Rivers. You're looking for another job. Just get your air conditioners and go.*

Chapter Twenty-Eight

L enore Sawyer saw the handsome cowboy head her way, and she ducked back around the end of the aisle. She had no idea why she'd grabbed his cart and ran away from the scene. It was a simple accident, not a crime, that she'd tipped over a screwdriver display rack.

She'd driven her cart right into it, and apparently, in her distress to find the right aisle with the replacement parts she needed for the generator at the homestead, she had enough force to knock over an entire rack of screwdrivers.

Then she'd rammed her stomach into the handle of the shopping cart, and that had taken her breath and caused her to fall to her knees. From there, she'd started to cry, and honestly, Lenore cried at everything these days.

In fact, tears welled up in her eyes right now, and she brushed angrily at them, wondering if there would ever be a day when she didn't feel so overwhelmed, so sad, and so out of her league.

She didn't know the tall, sandy-haired cowboy who came around the corner. He wore a neat beard and a dark brown cowboy hat, along with a blue and white plaid shirt, jeans, and cowboy boots. Those boots had betrayed him when he'd stepped on a screwdriver, and man, she'd never seen anyone pull kitty litter off the shelf the way he had.

She'd been far enough away that only a few errant pebbles had hit her. And yet in his presence, she felt where they'd stung against her forearm. She wiped absently there as he said, "Hey, you rescued my cart."

He'd probably sing tenor in the choir, and Lenore longed for the days when her biggest worry was making it to choir practice on time and getting her math homework done. Those days were long gone, as Lenore had quit college to return home to the homestead after her daddy had fallen and hurt himself. He hadn't been able to keep up with the chores after that. Though Lenore had been helping for a decade, she could not maintain a homestead by herself.

Momma and Daddy were gone now, but Lenore could not simply walk away from what they had spent their lives building.

Building, right, scoffed through her mind, because no one would call the Sawyer homestead something worth keeping, and yet Lenore could not let it go. Her parents were buried there, and she was determined to revitalize it and bring it back to life.

Starting with the generator, she thought.

Brandon blinked at her. "Are you okay?" he asked. "Did you hit your head?"

She shook her head, and his hand fell back to his side.

"I've asked you several questions," he said. "And you haven't answered."

She blinked, trying to stay in the present. "I just need a part for my generator," she said. "Do you happen to know where I could find one of those?"

"Yeah," he said. "They're right over here." He took his cart and went around the other side of the aisle.

Lenore pushed hers behind him, being careful to give clearance around the racks at the ends of each aisle. "What kind of generator you got?" he asked, and Lenore panicked. She had no idea what kind of generator she had. Brandon cut a look over to her out of the corner of his eye, and what Lenore really wanted to do was ask him to come home with her.

She'd come to town not only for the generator, but to find out how to put a job listing on TwoCents, the Three Rivers community app that had grown from a recommendation tool to so much more. She desperately needed cowboys at the homestead, and she had a little bit of money left from Momma and Daddy's savings. She could pay three or four people to come work for a couple of weeks, and maybe they could get everything back to the place where she could then maintain it.

She didn't get too close to Brandon, because she hadn't showered in a long time. That was a hazard of living on a homestead without running water. She quickly pulled out her phone. "I took a picture of it," she said, navigating to the shot. She held her phone out to him, and he looked at it.

"Oh, you've got a Thompson," he said. "Those are down here." He went further down the aisle, and Lenore pulled her cart after her as she followed him.

"Do you work around here?" she asked.

"Yeah, our place is south of town," he said. "You?"

"I'm northeast," she said.

Brandon nodded, and he indicated the wall of Thompson supplies in front of her. "What's wrong with the generator?"

"Pull cord snapped," she said, and Brandon reached out and plucked another one from the hanger. "Looked like this?"

"Had a red handle," she said. "But yeah, close enough." She took the part from him and accidentally met his eyes. The chaotic nature of the hardware store, with people coming and going and asking questions, and the general smell of metal and plastic faded into nothing. All that existed was this hot, handsome, helpful cowboy, and Lenore's nerves and emotions once again quivered on the edge of a knife.

"You got your own place?" she asked.

"It's my family ranch," Brandon said, and he looked away. "You?"

"It's my parents' homestead," she said.

Brandon nodded and gave her a tight smile. "Well, that should do it for the generator."

"Thanks," she said, and he nodded and turned away.

She watched him go, and Lenore wondered how she was ever going to hire anyone and allow them to come to the homestead.

She sighed and turned her back on the direction that Brandon had gone. She hadn't asked him if he needed a job or if he could come help, because she was embarrassed that then he would see the current condition she lived in. She put the part in her cart, found the rest of the items on her list, and got the heck out of there.

Three Rivers had just put in a new truck stop on the eastern highway, and Lenore stopped there next and grabbed her shower bag. She stayed in the hot spray for a full half-hour, and then took her time blowing out her hair with the electricity that just flowed so freely from the walls.

She stocked up on a few groceries from the truck stop: all the meat and cheese she could afford, hot dogs, and a few cans of chili and soup. She added as much yeast as she could find and checked out.

Then, she headed northeast into the hills outside of Three Rivers. Her grandparents had dreamed of living off-grid, and they'd found what they'd called "the perfect piece of land."

It actually had two houses on it, both built by her grandfather, a master carpenter. When her daddy had taken over the homestead, his dream had been to raise a milk cow for milk, and beef cattle for beef, as well as chickens, turkeys, and goats.

Her parents had tried digging a well three separate times, and had not been able to find water. One whole room of the cabin that Lenore lived in was filled with batteries that she charged with the strong Texas sun. But she didn't have a good system, nor was it sophisticated, and she lost as much energy as she gathered.

A heaviness descended over her the moment she made the turn from the highway onto the dirt road that led back to the homestead. She had to travel five miles off the main highway, and it took her fifteen minutes to drive. Then the road branched to the right again, and Lenore finally arrived back on her own property.

Signs of neglect existed everywhere, from the trees that needed to be cut back from the road, to the way the porch held so much stuff, to the way chickens pecked around in the front yard when they should be contained behind fences.

Lenore didn't know how to fix a fence properly enough to keep the chickens in, and every time she tried, they simply got out again. They were the only animals that she had on the homestead right now, and she lost more to hawks and a rare fox with every day that passed.

She parked in front of the house, a fresh round of tears pressing into her eyes. "Dear Lord," she said right out loud. "I need help, and I need help badly."

She wished she'd thought to get that cowboy's name and number, but she hadn't. He hadn't asked for hers, either, and Lenore sighed as she got out of her truck.

"Probably because you smell like the sewer," she muttered to herself as she went to the back to get the things that she had bought that day. She now knew how to put a job listing on TwoCents, and once she had this generator fixed, she'd have enough energy in her phone—and in her body—to get that done.

She looked up into the sky, which was gloriously blue and filled with heat waves from the summer sun. "Lord, I want to keep this place," she said. "Please, bless me to be humble enough to allow someone to come here and see what this has become, and give them the skills to help me fix it."

She went up the steps, still talking to herself. "I'm willing to learn, but I need to have someone good to learn from. Please, bless me that there's someone out there looking for a job just like this." She glanced over to the other cabin. "And who is willing to come here and live in this squalor."

Lenore entered the cabin, which smelled a little bit like rotting vegetables. She hadn't been able to find the source of the smell, and the one thing she had going for the homestead was that she could garden.

She ate mostly eggs and produce, and as she quickly put all the meat that she'd bought at the convenience store in the fridge, she added, "I just need two weeks. Lord, please, just send me someone good for two weeks."

Two weeks wasn't too much to ask for, was it?

She turned back to the counter to get the milk, something in the back of her head telling her that something wasn't quite right. She opened the fridge again and set the milk inside, realizing that it wasn't as cold as it should have been. Her lungs felt like someone had filled them with cement. "Great," she said. "Now the fridge is out."

She reminded herself that fridges ran on electricity and

her generator had gone out, so she unbagged the new pull cord and went to solve that problem, hoping that it would solve this new one.

Deep in her heart, she simply knew that a good pair of cowboy hands could solve *all* of her problems. As she fought with the generator to install the new pull cord, she prayed that God would please, please, just bless her with one good pair of cowboy hands.

Chapter Twenty-Nine

Mitch sent Finn a *Happy Birthday, brother!* text, glad he'd set the reminder weeks ago. He'd learned to set reminders on his phone for everything while in college, and the habit had saved him multiple times.

He really liked Finn, and he'd enjoyed going to his birthday party in the past, but Mitch didn't see how he could get away from Signs for Success right now. Tomorrow marked the first day of August—and also the first day his contracted advisors and faculty would be arriving at the academy.

The Resident Assistants and three faculty members would be moving in, and Mitch had told them that he would have a dozen cowboys here between the hours of eight a.m. and noon to help.

He and Lacy had not furnished anything in the faculty apartments or Resident Advisors dormitories. The student dorms came with beds, a desk and dresser, a dining table and chairs, a full kitchen with appliances, and two full-length couches per unit. They'd have to share a laundry room with everyone on the floor, and each floor could house twenty people in either a private apartment or a two-person shared situation.

Extra-small appliances like blenders or toasters had to be brought in by their owners, and Mitch was not providing any dishes, silverware, linens, or towels. He did have two utility closets per floor that had a vacuum cleaner, a mop and a bucket, and an ironing board.

Otherwise, he expected students to bring their own cleaning supplies and Resident Assistants to maintain their cleaning checks once a month. Students began arriving in ten days, only a weekend before classes began.

Mitch couldn't believe that this time had finally arrived. His attention felt pulled in a dozen different directions, and he smiled as Finn responded with a cowboy emoji and the words, *We'll just have to go horseback riding once you're settled.*

Mitch loved horseback riding, and he didn't do it nearly as often as he would like. He sent a thumbs-up and flipped his phone over, so he could focus on the other items on his to-do list.

He and Lacy had sent the directions to arrive at the academy from Amarillo, as well as from Oklahoma City, as well as from the south. They had people coming from all over the United States to work at Signs for Success, and

Mitch flipped open the blue folder that Lacy had put on his desk since the last time he'd been in his office.

It held a map of the faculty facilities, including what apartments had been assigned out, as well as their classrooms and offices. She was currently working on a packet for each person with final assignments.

Mitch clicked around on his computer to get to his email to see when the key cards would be delivered. He'd been promised they'd be here by today, and if they weren't, then no one would be able to get into their apartments and offices. Of the ten faculty members they'd hired, only three had wanted to live on site, and that made things pretty easy.

They all needed offices, though, and classrooms, and Mitch found an email that said his keycards had been delivered to his mailbox.

Perfect, he thought, and he went back to the folder. He turned the page to find a staff briefing already typed up. Almost everyone had confirmed that they would be there in the morning. It really was the best time to do anything in the Texas Panhandle in the summer, and Mitch had planned to cater lunch and then dedicate the afternoon to the staff briefing. He wanted everyone to know upfront what was expected of them and how things ran at Signs for Success.

Lacy had warned him not to be too rigid in his expectations and schedule, because they were brand new, no one had ever worked here before, and they had never had a faculty or staff before. Intellectually, he knew she was right, but he still wanted everything to be perfect.

He scanned the meeting agenda, which included emergency procedures, orientation materials distribution, maintenance needs, and available materials. He'd just closed the folder when both William and Champ alerted, one dog on either side of him. His heart soared with happiness, because William had come so far in the six or eight weeks that he'd been under Mitch's training. He learned the fastest, worked hard, and he had been palling around with Champ now for a couple of weeks.

He reached down and stroked the golden retriever's head as he looked over to the doorway. Lacy walked toward him, and today she didn't wear her normal office attire, but a pair of dark blue shorts that went almost to her knee and a T-shirt that said *Three Rivers* on the front of it.

You know what we should get? he asked. *T-shirts—Signs for Success.* He spread his hands as if he could see a marquee in front of him, and he grinned at Lacy.

She did not smile back. *You are not putting more work on my plate right now, Mister Glover,* she said, her hands moving crisply and concisely. She stood on the other side of the desk and consulted her clipboard.

We need to go through all of the physical final inspections, she said. *The housekeeping team just left, and Jacob says every room is ready, from the dorms to the faculty apartments to the offices to the classrooms to all the bathrooms and laundry facilities.*

She handed him a clipboard that Mitch frowned at. *But we need to go through it personally and make all the checks.* She pointed to something and waited for him to look back to her.

Jacob will go through the same checklist after us, and I want to make sure there's adequate toilet paper and cleaning supplies on every floor for our students and faculty, as well as in our educational building.

He nodded, because Lacy clearly had a lot to say, and Mitch didn't need to delay her.

I called the Wi-Fi company, she said. *And June said she'd send someone out, because that Wi-Fi does not reach all the way into the main hall at the back of the building.*

He nodded, and he trusted that Aunt June would take care of him. She owned an internet service company in Three Rivers, and Mitch had never had a problem with his Wi-Fi here at the house.

Then we need to stage all the common area furniture, she continued. *Both inside and out. I have Jacob unwrapping the patio furniture right now, and then I want to put up our banners, decorations, and prep the signage, so that everyone knows right where to go to check in when they get here tomorrow morning.*

She consulted something on her own clipboard, and Mitch simply relaxed back into his chair.

How many people are coming tomorrow morning? she asked, looking so sexy with her pen poised just so, waiting for his answer.

All my uncles, Mitch said, schooling his thoughts. *And my daddy. I'll be here, and so will Jacob. Link is going to leave the ranch with Wilder and a skeleton crew and bring down Gunner, Smiles, Rock, Chaz, Birch, Hank Bell, and Robbie. Oh, Ollie's coming too.*

Mitch smiled at her Very Serious Expression—and he knew not to tease her when she wore such a look. *And some of my female cousins said they'd bring down pancake-wrapped sausages and coffee.*

Lacy blinked, and Mitch understood, because his family could be a lot. *I told you we wouldn't need to hire help.* He grinned at her. *The Glovers got it covered.* He did a faux family-gang sign, and Lacy simply blinked at him.

I'll say, she said, and she made a mark on her clipboard. *Did you get lunch ordered?*

Yes, ma'am, he said. He twisted in his chair to get a printout from the printer, and he handed it to her. She scanned down the list of Italian food that he had ordered for tomorrow, figuring everyone liked pasta and garlic bread, and tucked the sheet onto her clipboard.

This looks great, Mitch, she said, and she handed him another piece of paper. He looked at the columns of names, quickly realizing that she had typed everything out. They had a faculty of twelve arriving, twenty Resident Advisors, and seventy-one people, ages fourteen to twenty-five, about to be living at Signs for Success.

She'd listed them all out by first and last name, with their assignments and locations. He set the paper down and looked at her. *Great, thanks.*

Her eyebrows went up. *Great? Thanks?* She repeated back what he'd said to her, but her facial expression gave away her displeasure and the fact that she'd turned those two words into questions.

What? he asked.

You need to memorize those names, she said, nodding to the discarded paper. *And where their offices are.*

The air left his lungs as disbelief rushed in. *Why do I need to do that?*

This is your *academy, Mitch,* she said, growing more animated. *Knowing someone's name and how to find them goes a long way.*

He glanced down at the list and back to her. *There's going to be over one hundred people here.*

Only thirty-two of them are coming tomorrow, she said. *We will be doing name tags, and of course, during our orientation meeting, we'll be learning all their name signs as well. But it would be great if you at least had an idea of who they were.*

I already know who they are, he said. *We've done multiple video interviews with everyone.*

Some of them you haven't spoken to in at least a month, she said. *And last time I heard, we're still waiting on three confirmations from people saying they'll even be here tomorrow. Have you followed up on that?*

Not yet, Mitch said, feeling a bit defensive. *It's on my to-do list. I'm going through the folders right now.*

You spent too long outside with the dogs, she said.

I did not, Mitch argued back. *I spent the same amount of time out there with them today that I do every day.*

But today is not like every other day, Lacy said. *We're very busy today.*

You think I don't know how busy we are? he shot at her. *I just texted one of my best friends that I can't come to his birthday party tonight. I know how busy we are.* His signs got bigger as his irritation grew. *What about the packets?*

That was next on my list to tell you about. She looked away from him, and Mitch's gut seethed. Nothing good could come after that avoidance. Sure enough, when she met his eye again, she said, *They're not ready.*

So not okay, but Mitch tried to still his hands and give himself a moment to settle down before he spoke. *Okay,* he finally said. *When will they be ready?*

I don't know. She lifted her head. *They said they might be done by tonight, but no matter what, we would have them by eight a.m. in the morning.*

Eight o'clock tomorrow? he repeated, his own facial expression now mirroring a question mark. *How is that going to work? We need them here so that we can assemble everything into packets for people who are arriving at eight a.m.*

I know what time everyone is arriving, she said. *I have no control over this.*

Well, we need to call them. They need to deliver when they said they would, and they told us five p.m. today.

I've already spoken to them, Mitch, she said.

Call them again, he said. *Call them every hour. I don't want them sitting down on the job.*

They're not sitting down on the job, she said.

You don't know that.

I know calling them and interrupting them while they try to do their job isn't going to help.

Mitch turned away from her and reached up to swipe

his cowboy hat off his head. He did not want to argue with her about this, not today. He patted his outer thighs, and both dogs came to his side.

He saw Lacy sign out of the corner of his eye, but he didn't look at her. That only caused her to dart in front of him.

Where do you think you're going? she asked.

I've got to get out of this office, he said. *I've been trapped in here for three hours working through things we already know, reminding myself of names of people that I've already been on video calls with. I'm gonna walk down to the end of the lane and get the mail. Is that okay with you?*

She frowned, and her eyes revealed a pinch of hurt. Mitch instantly regretted what he'd said, but he really did need to get out of the office, and his key cards had been delivered.

Lacy fell to the side, and Mitch walked out. He told himself with every step that Lacy couldn't control a printer —and that he couldn't either.

She was right. Calling and yelling wouldn't do any good. He could still be irritated about the situation, and he didn't have to apologize for that.

A blast of hot air hit him in the face as he exited the house, but he kept on down the sidewalk and then down the gravel drive. Along the way, he sent a text to everyone at Shiloh Ridge who'd said they would come help him, simply asking for confirmations.

He reminded them that he had thirty-two people coming for lunch and twenty-three to move in, and if there was any food being prepared, to please account for those numbers, and that he would have enough food to feed all of them as well.

Texts started pouring in from his family, and Mitch suddenly felt more supported than he had a few moments ago. No, not everything was going to go exactly right tomorrow. There would be hiccups and missed turns and problems, and Mitch reminded himself that the staff briefing was not at eight a.m., and he could ask for help with the printed materials.

His family knew how to collate and staple and slide things into folders, and everything would be just fine.

He blew out his breath, finally feeling the tension in his shoulders and lungs release, but everything came roaring back, tightening and latching with sharp teeth when Lacy came to his side.

He glanced over to her, but she looked steadfastly forward. She didn't slide her hand into his as she had so many times before. She was mad too, and Mitch told himself she was allowed to feel like that.

He decided to wait for her to say something first, and they simply continued down the road toward the mailbox together.

Chapter Thirty

L acy felt like the clipboard in her hand had become a permanent extension of her arm. She never went anywhere without it, and hadn't for the past ten days, as she'd been steadily working toward opening Signs for Success. With faculty and Resident Advisors arriving tomorrow and daily meetings during the workweek scheduled, Lacy felt at capacity in her life—so the last thing she needed was Mitch's attitude.

She simply didn't know how to bring up what she wanted to talk about. This summer had definitely been eye-opening for her, first as she explored this new romantic relationship with Mitch, who was the first man she dated since Landon's death.

They'd shared meals together around the house, gone out to the pond and watched the clouds drift through the sky, talked about his time in Virginia and her experience in college and then with the interpreting office.

All of that was easy and fun, and she loved getting to know him as more than her boss. In the evenings, she retreated to the third floor and looked at pictures of her late husband, feeling more and more detached from him with every passing day.

Not only that, but she'd realized how complacent in her relationship she had been. They went where Landon wanted to eat. They saw movies that Landon wanted to see. He didn't want children? No problem; they wouldn't have children. *Her* wants and desires and dreams had never been considered, and Lacy had not even realized that until the day Mitch had held her hand and asked her if she wanted kids.

She felt a little bit more like herself every day—sometimes on an hourly basis—and like watching a bruise go from deep purple to greenish-yellow back to full healthy skin, Lacy could see how much she had healed and grown this summer. They reached the curve in the road that turned toward the highway; only another hundred feet, and they'd reach the mailbox.

Lacy prayed with each step she took that she'd be able to find a way to order the words inside her and then be brave enough to say them to Mitch. She'd never found that courage with Landon, and she hadn't even realized some of her own unhappiness inside that marriage until this summer.

She'd been thinking about going to church again, but this time, she didn't want to go alone. She didn't want to hide her attendance, and she wanted Mitch to go with her. She wasn't sure he would ever do that, and now Lacy had to decide what she would do if he said no. Go by herself? Was she strong enough to do that?

They reached the mailbox, and Mitch wrenched it open, creating a loud screeching sound of metal on metal. She flinched away from it, but of course, Mitch didn't react at all. He started pulling things out, and Lacy sucked in a breath when she saw the bright white commercial envelope.

She snatched it away from him and held it up, a smile on her face. *Do you know what these are?* she asked.

Yes, he said, still grumpy.

They're the key cards for our faculty offices and classrooms. She grinned at him. *Something came through right, Mitch.*

He simply slammed closed the mailbox and turned to go back the way he'd come.

Oh, Lacy was not having this. She did not like watching Mitch walk away from her, and she jogged to get in front of him, grateful she'd worn more casual clothes today, as they still had to go through the two dormitory buildings and complete their physical facilities checklist. She stopped in front of him and slapped the envelope against his chest.

Okay, enough with the grumpy cowboy.

She released the envelope, and Mitch bobbled everything in his arms and still managed to catch it. Of course.

I just want to say something, she said. *And then you can decide what you want to do with it.*

Mitch nodded, and though she didn't have everything perfectly ordered, she figured she might as well speak from the heart.

I really love this academy, she said. *I love Three Rivers. And while I'd never thought of myself as living in the Texas Panhandle, I love it here. I am happier every day that I'm here than I ever was in San Antonio, and part of that reason is because of you.*

Her chest shook as she breathed in, but she forced herself to go on. *I am falling in love with you, and I think we work really well together, and that we could both be married and have an amazing life on one hand, and also run this academy together incredibly well on the other. I understand that we think differently about some things, and I don't mind our discussions, even though some people might call them arguments—but I really don't like being dismissed the way that you dismiss me.*

Mitch's eyes seemed to blaze with fire, and the frown between them deepened.

Landon did that too, she said. *And I let him. He called my brother names, and I let him. He said we wouldn't have children, and I went along. Well, I don't want that again. I want a partner who believes in me, who thinks my voice has value, who thinks I'm smart and listens to what I say, even if he doesn't agree. I don't want someone who's just going to walk away to get the mail when we have something important to talk about.*

Mitch nodded just once. *I get to feel how I want to feel too*, he said.

Absolutely, she said. *I'm irritated about the printing delay as well. But don't you trust me to handle it?*

He looked like she'd hit him with the envelope again, this time in the nose. *Of course I do*, he said. *And I listen to you too.*

Yes, she acknowledged. *Sometimes. But when you get mad, I can see a switch inside you, and it flips. And no matter what I say, you're going to do what you want.*

He nodded, a swallow moving tightly down his throat. *I'm sorry.*

You get to feel how you want to, she said. *I acknowledge that sometimes things irritate me for no reason, and I want to be able to feel irritated.* I totally get that, and I knew you'd be mad about the printing, but I had already handled it, and I don't need you to tell me what to do on top of that.

You're right, he said, and he took a slow step toward the house. Lacy moved back to his side and took some of the mail so that he didn't have to carry it all.

I've realized I was not very happy in my marriage with Landon.

I'm sorry, Mitch said.

I want us to be different, she said, keeping her gaze forward. The road arced, and the academy and the house, with its pretty fountain out front, came into view.

I want that too, Mitch said. *I want to make you so happy, Lacy. It's all I think about.*

She smiled and looked up at him. *All you think about?*

She hoped her expression made the question teasing and not confrontational.

He met her eyes, that intensity with which he lived his life buzzing in his. He nodded, and then took the mail from her and tossed it on the side of the road. He edged her back, and she almost tripped as her shoes went from gravel to grass.

Shade covered them as they moved under the tree branches, and Mitch caged her against the trunk with one hand on the side of her face, and the other along her hip. She imagined a whole host of wonderful things he would say to her in that moment.

I'm falling in love with you, too.

I've been thinking about what our life would be like if we were married and had a family and still ran Signs for Success.

I think you're gorgeous and smart and wonderful.

Mitch curled his fingers into the hair at the back of her neck and leaned down and kissed her, and all the things that he hadn't said, but which she had made up, came true. While Lacy had told him she was falling in love with him, Mitch had just *shown* her that he was falling for her too.

Lacy wanted nothing more than to step into a cold shower and get all the sweat off her body. She, Mitch, and Jacob had just finished going through the two dormitory buildings and the administration building for the last time, checking box after box after box for supplies, working outlets, projectors in classrooms, and needed furniture.

June had sent somebody to fix the Wi-Fi, and it worked great in the classroom where it had been malfunctioning earlier.

They'd arranged couches and end tables, TVs and stands, in all the common areas on each dormitory floor, so the same work getting done eight times. The outdoor accommodations were just as spectacular, with built-in benches around the quad, where the grass glittered like emeralds now that the sod had been down for several weeks.

They'd attached the huge welcome sign that ran from dorm to dorm over the top of the admin building, and all the signs for where their staff briefing would be, where the offices were, and where lunch would be served. Lacy would simply need to put them out in the morning, and they'd be ready to go.

The only thing she needed now were their printed materials for the faculty members and Resident Assistants. She followed Mitch up the steps to the front porch, and instead of going through the front door, he detoured over to the thinking seat. Lacy glanced at her phone and found the clock sitting just past five-thirty.

She knew Three Trees Printing was open until six, and she pressed her eyes closed as she prayed for a small miracle. She'd seen several in her life this summer, and she knew more than ever that she needed to get back to church.

She could make a phone call without disturbing Mitch, so she moved over and sat next to him. He lifted his arm around her shoulders as she tapped to dial the printer as she snuggled into his side. She put it on speaker and then tilted the phone toward him so that he could see who she was calling.

He nodded, and Lacy's nerves kicked into another gear as the line rang. The last thing she wanted was to run to town and get the printing, but it would make their morning better.

Mitch tilted his phone toward her, and he'd typed, *I'm going to order dinner*. She nodded just as someone picked up the line and said, "Three Trees."

"Hi," she said. "It's Lacy Hayes, and I—"

"Oh, Miss Hayes, I just sent Magnolia your way. We got everything done, and she left about five minutes ago. I was just about to call you."

Lacy's heart beat faster, pumping warm blood through her body, which suddenly felt numb. "The printing is done?" she asked.

"It's done," the man said jovially. "And it's on its way to you—delivery free of charge, because we couldn't make our deadline."

"Wow," Lacy said. "Thank you so much."

"Let me know if she doesn't show up in the next fifteen minutes or so," he said. "She should be there by then."

"Okay, great," Lacy said. "Thanks."

The call ended, and she looked over to what Mitch was ordering. It looked like something from Supa-Fresh, where Lacy had told him she loved their salads. She covered his phone with her hand, which caused him to look at her. She felt shiny and new and refreshed, though it had been a very long day, and tomorrow would be even longer.

You should order dessert, cowboy, she said. *We have something to celebrate.*

We do?

On second thought, she said as her stomach growled. *Lots of food, lots of dessert, and lots of coffee, because the printing is done, and it'll be here in fifteen minutes.*

His eyebrows went up, and Lacy laughed. *And that means me and you are not done for the day.*

He grinned too and took her hand into both of his. *Doesn't even feel like work when I'm with you.*

With those words, Lacy melted into his side and let him hold her close to his heartbeat. He picked up his phone again and held it in front of them, tilting it toward her in a silent question whenever he landed on something he thought she might want. She nodded yes to all of it, and Mitch put in their dinner order and set his phone down again.

I can't wait for this time tomorrow, he said. *We should go out to celebrate our first move-in day. Just me and you.*

And the dogs, she added, to which Mitch laughed.

It's always going to be me, you, and the dogs, isn't it?

She straightened and looked at him. *I hope more than that one day,* she said. *Do you want kids, Mitch?*

He seemed to trace every line of her face with his eyes

before he brought his back to hers. *With you?* he asked, his eyebrows going up. *Desperately.*

Lacy smiled and let Mitch kiss her until she heard the crunch of tires on gravel. Then she got up, excitement flowing through her veins at the sight of the van with *Three Trees Printing* emblazoned on the side.

Let's go, cowboy, she said. *We've got work to do.*

Chapter Thirty-One

Mitch rose with the sun, which for the beginning of August came really early, and bustled into the kitchen to make coffee. His family wouldn't be there for hours yet, but Mitch had found he couldn't sleep any longer.

The faculty and RAs would move in today, and they'd have their first meeting, and tomorrow, he and Lacy had planned meetings before lunch as well. He moved around the kitchen, putting together something to eat as the coffee started to brew, and he definitely wanted to get lunch tomorrow for everyone as well.

Then they would have the rest of the afternoon and the whole weekend to get settled into their apartments, become familiar with the town of Three Rivers, explore their class-rooms, and set up their offices.

They had a couple of full weeks of work on campus before the students would start arriving. Move-in for them would happen on Friday and Saturday, and also gave students a weekend on campus to get settled into their dorms and for others to move to the area before classes started on the seventeenth.

Mitch couldn't even imagine standing up in front of a group of students again and teaching, though he'd done it for years in Virginia. Teaching was a skill, and when he didn't do it very often, he lost the ability. He'd tried to get out of teaching the adult sign language classes twice now, and Lacy simply wouldn't hear it.

He didn't truly want to pass on the task, though. He did want to spend most of his time with the dogs and, of course, with Lacy. He'd never run an institution like this before, and he hoped that his twice-weekly class would not be a burden. It had been scheduled in the evenings, as adults had jobs and needed to be able to work as well as take their classes.

Mitch told himself it was two hours a week out of the one hundred sixty-eight that God gave him, he could do it— and he would do it gladly—because he didn't want to make Lacy's life any worse than it already was.

He honestly couldn't believe she was still here with him, still laboring to get Signs for Success open, and that she cared about it as much as he did. But she sure seemed to.

He'd just put a pan on the stove and lit the burner under it when Champ alerted. William's nose touched his bare calf a moment later, and Mitch flinched away from it. He looked down at the dogs to find them watching the left exit of the kitchen, the one that ran closer to the hallways and up the stairs than the one that went toward the front door.

He found Lacy standing there wearing a bright, puffy, purple bathrobe, her hair in curlers and a look of extreme displeasure on her face.

Do you know what time it is? she asked, immediately folding her arms afterward.

Mitch knew the neighborhood of what time it was, but he wasn't looking straight at a clock.

You were being so noisy, she said. *Slamming cupboards, blasting the radio, banging pans down on stovetops. She* came over to him and lifted the pan and set it back down. Of course, Mitch couldn't hear it.

He couldn't hear any of that, and he grinned as he said, *I'm so sorry. I forget things make noise.*

She looked at him sternly for only another moment before her smile dissolved all of that away. *I had just finally gotten to sleep,* she said, as she moved over to the radio and switched it off. *Are you nervous?*

Absolutely, he said. *You've been to one of my all-family things, right?*

They're going to be great, she said. *They're going to line up where you tell them to, and when someone comes and says, 'I need help moving in,' we're going to send two or three people with them, so the job gets done fast and it's not hard for anyone.*

She nodded toward the pan. *That butter is really sizzling.*

Mitch smelled it in the next moment, and he flicked off the burner. *Do you want eggs?* he asked. *I'll make some for you.*

It's five-ten *in the morning,* she said, grimacing afterward. *I'm going back to bed, and* you're *going to be quiet for at least another hour and a half.* She grinned at him and pressed into his chest. *Do you hear me?*

He hooked his arm around her waist and held her against him. *I hear you. I'm sorry.*

She left the kitchen smiling, and Mitch watched her go in her bare feet, finding her so sexy and so wonderful. He didn't exactly know how to be quiet, so he simply poured himself a cup of coffee and grabbed a protein shake out of the fridge before he retreated from the house, taking his dogs with him.

They always soothed him, and Mitch moved out into the training enclosure and released Maven and Sunshine from their posts. They slept together in the same house, but they lived on different ropes, which still allowed them plenty of freedom around the yard.

Neither one of them liked seeing William free when they were tied up, and the moment they could, they ran over to him and started sniffing and welcoming him back to their pack. Mitch wanted all of them at his side that day, as they would bring him comfort and show others that he was a good dog trainer.

He squashed the pride rising through him, and instead, moved to the edge of the fence and looked into the eastern sky, where the sun had barely started to lighten the day.

Dear God, he prayed. *I know I can't ask for perfection, but I would like today to go as smoothly as possible. If Thou can bless my efforts and Lacy's efforts and everyone's efforts who's labored to get here today, I would really appreciate it.*

He sipped his coffee and looked down at his hounds. He hadn't brought out the vibration bracelet that day, and he decided he didn't need it. He plucked the whistle from where he hung it on the post, and he opened the gate and let them all out. He gave one short blow on the whistle, and all four dogs fell into line beside him.

Maven had really matured, and she would definitely be the next dog Mitch moved to work with Champ and William. Sunshine still let her nose get away from her sometimes, but as they walked out to the pond and all the way around it, she didn't deviate once.

He glanced at his phone as he went back inside—six-thirty. So he fed his dogs on the back porch and started making breakfast, assuming Lacy would be downstairs in the next half-hour.

He made himself some sunny-side-up eggs and ate them with a couple of pieces of sourdough toast before returning to the stove to crack her eggs. She liked her yolks broken and cooked hard. He got the job done and slid her breakfast onto a plate. He'd just pulled out his phone to text her when Champ nosed him.

Is this for me? Lacy asked.

Right on time, he said, and instead of simply giving her the plate of eggs, he swept her into his arms and held her against his chest. He loved holding her and being with her and talking to her. She'd told him yesterday that she was falling in love with him, and that had been the best thing that someone had ever said to Mitch.

He'd never been in love before, but the way he felt about Lacy had to be really close. He touched his mouth to her earlobe, and then her neck, and finally slid his lips against hers. Then he stepped back and smiled. *Good morning. Were you able to go back to sleep?*

She smiled up at him, almost dreamily. *Yes. For a few minutes.*

I'll pour your coffee, he said. *Do you want the hazelnut creamer?*

Yep, thank you. She took the plate of eggs around the counter and sat down while Mitch poured her coffee and served it to her. They had all of the employee packets ready to go in his office, the signs had been filled with the right papers and simply waited for them to put them in the right place, and their lunch order had been confirmed for a twelve-thirty delivery.

Lights flashed from his phone on the countertop, and Mitch reached to pick it up. He read the text and then looked at Lacy. *My momma and daddy just left*, he said. *They'll be here in twenty minutes.*

Perfect timing, she said. *We'll have everything ready for them.*

He looked back at his phone as it vibrated in his hands, and lights flashed up from where he held it. He grinned over to Lacy. *My momma made cinnamon rolls. We're going to want to make sure we get that tray here in the house and not set out for anyone else.*

He laughed, glad when Lacy joined him. He loved the joy that lived in her expression whenever she laughed, and when she looked to him again, he said, *I'm gonna go get everything ready to go. I'll meet you out on the porch when you're ready.*

She nodded, and Mitch hurried into his office, where he had put all of the employee folders into a bin. The key cards had been laid on top of them, and Mitch simply stood at his desk wondering what else they needed to do that day. Surely they'd done enough, though Mitch knew he'd probably also forgotten something, and he would fall down several times in this endeavor to bring Deaf education to more people.

He picked up the tote and carried it out to the porch, where Lacy joined him only a few seconds later. They made their way over to the administration building, where Lacy set out the signs while Mitch went to get a folding table.

He set it up in the foyer and put three chairs behind it, one for him, one for Lacy, and one for Jacob. They'd split up the Resident Assistants and faculty members so that each of them had ten or eleven, and he laid out the packets in front of the chairs and set up the signs that Lacy had printed indicating which line people should get in.

He looked toward the door as it opened, and his daddy walked in. Everything in Mitch's life suddenly shook, as if God had sent an earthquake to the Texas Panhandle. At that moment, he feared to take a step lest the ground would crack and swallow him whole.

He realized now where he'd learned to tilt his head and ask a silent question. His father did it from ten feet away as he'd come to a stop, seen Mitch and whatever showed on his face, and tilted his head to the side.

What's wrong? he asked.

I'm suddenly so nervous, Mitch said from the opposite side of the table. *What am I doing? This is* insane. *There are going to be fourteen-year-olds living here, and I'm responsible for them.*

Panic moved through him in a quick clip now, his hands matching the way his heartbeat had gone wild. All of the things that he and Lacy had been over—that there was literally one adult for every four people living on site, and some of those were adults—that they'd gotten all of the legal permissions to have kids that young there, but their parents knew and were willingly bringing them—that they had a curriculum in place—it all flew out of his head.

Hey, it's okay, Daddy said, and he moved toward Mitch. He went right around the table and took him by the shoulders. *You have been working on this for* two years. *You're ready. It's incredible.*

I'm just one man, he said. *A cowboy.*

One man can do incredible things, Daddy said. *And cowboys are the best men of all.* He hugged Mitch and held him tightly, and the weight and pressure against Mitch's chest and back calmed him enough to find a rational line of thought.

Daddy stepped back and said, *Okay?* his expression mirroring his concern.

I'm okay, Mitch said. *Where's Momma?*

They're setting up a tent outside, Daddy said. *Melissa,*

Heather, and Sunnie have been baking for two days, and they've got muffins, cinnamon rolls, caramel pecan buns, and more outside.

You're kidding, Mitch said.

I think there's enough to feed all of us and everyone who's coming twice over. Daddy laughed.

Well, I ordered lunch too, Mitch said, realizing how grumpy he seemed a moment after he'd spoken. *I mean, it's fine. It's food, right? There are plenty of people who will eat it.*

Daddy blinked at him, a smile slowly painting over his face. *Wow, son, you've come a long way.* His attention got turned to the door as Momma came through it, and Mitch wondered what he meant while his momma, in all of her golden glory and smiles, limped toward him.

You have done it, son, she said. *And you've got cowboys gathering out here who would like some directions.*

Is Lacy not out there? Mitch asked.

He couldn't just walk past his momma without giving her a hug, and he pulled her into his chest and held her tightly. *I love you so much,* he said when he stepped back. *Thank you for always supporting me.*

Of course. Momma glowed with the familiar radiance Mitch had seen as she preached from the pulpit, and he realized that the best thing that he could have done was invite his parents.

Momma loved people, and people loved her, and she would tell every faculty member and every Resident Assistant who came that day how amazing Mitch was, and how awesome Lacy was, and how much this academy meant to them. She would basically start building the team before Mitch and Lacy even had their first meeting, and he couldn't be more grateful.

He stepped out into the morning sunshine, another reason to be grateful streaming through him. Good weather, a perfect day, and a dozen cowboys standing on the sidewalk waiting for instructions. He waved his arms above his head, and Lacy said, "Mitch is ready for you," and pointed toward him.

Thank you so much for coming, he said. *We're going to be doing all the checking-in inside, in the air conditioning. The buildings are all connected, and Lacy, Jacob, or I will tell you which building and what floor to help speed the process.*

Please be careful and as helpful as much as possible. We've got a ton of food here for breakfast.

He glanced over to the two tents that had been set up on the front lawn, and he had no idea where those tables had come from.

Probably True Blue, he thought just before he went on. *And lunch will be here at twelve-thirty. Again, we'll be eating inside, because no one should be outside more than they have to be today. And I really appreciate all of your help.*

Lacy had moved to his side during his speech, and she added, "We have four coolers of drinks inside—waters and sodas. No one should be thirsty today. We don't want any injuries or problems. Okay?"

Heads nodded and mouths moved, and Mitch grinned

at his family. He looked at Lacy and said, *Tell them I want a group hug.*

She blinked. *A group hug? Do they know what that means?*

Mitch grinned and grinned. *Just tell them.*

She looked toward his mess of uncles and cousins, and he wasn't surprised to see Aunt Sammy there, or Aunt Etta standing with Aunt Oakley, and Aunt Arizona next to Aunt Montana, though he didn't expect them to carry furniture or boxes today.

"Mitch wants a group hug," Lacy said, and he opened his arms wide and let the Glovers engulf him.

He'd never felt as loved and as accepted as he did when standing among family, and he knew that no matter what happened that day, it would be blessed by the hand of God.

Chapter Thirty-Two

Lacy went downstairs about an hour before she needed to leave for church. She wanted to give Mitch the opportunity to get ready and come with her—if he wanted to.

The past couple of days with new residents on the property had brought renewed energy to the land and academy. Lacy loved seeing cars in the parking lot and an occasional person walking down the sidewalk.

She and Mitch had sat on the front porch on Saturday morning, holding hands and sipping coffee while they watched the RAs and faculty members come and go. It had been wonderful and beautiful and serene.

Her anxiety reached a new height as she approached Mitch's office. Then a ruckus drew her attention to the kitchen. The man had no concept of noise, and Lacy normally didn't mind. She could always follow the thudding or whistling to find him.

She just didn't want to hear him slamming doors and cast iron skillets at five o'clock in the morning. Mitch wasn't a night owl, so his noisiness wasn't a problem in the evenings, but Lacy woke to his radio blasting from the kitchen almost every morning.

The sound of dishes clattering in the sink welcomed her to the kitchen. Mitch turned from the running water in the sink, a giant bowl of liquid sloshing in his hands. He moved over to the area where he fed his dogs, and today, he had all four of them in the house with him.

Lacy paused to take in the simpleness of the situation. The majesty of it.

Mitch sure loved his dogs, and he took impeccable care of them. Four big dogs in the house was a lot of canine, but Lacy didn't mind. The house itself had a lot of square footage, and it would take a bunch more dogs to make it feel too cramped.

Two of them immediately started lapping at the bowl of water, while Sunshine and William followed Mitch back into the kitchen, where he had four food bowls sitting on the island.

He caught her eye, and Lacy raised her hand in a wave of *Good morning, cowboy.*

He scanned her down to her heels and said, *Don't you look as pretty as a picture?*

She smiled at him and moved toward him. As he came closer to her, he eased her into his arms with practiced grace, and Lacy loved being this close to him. She inhaled the scent of his skin and the sunshine from his shirt, and tipped her head back to get her kiss. She fell and fell and fell as she stood in the kitchen with Mitch and kissed him.

When a dog squished between her shins and his, he stepped backward and looked at William. The dog put his front paws up on the counter and whined at his phone.

Mitch picked it up while Lacy's heartbeat settled back to normal after such an amazing greeting.

It's Link, he said. *He and Misty* really *want to have us for dinner.*

We should go, Lacy said. *We're always going to be busy. We could go today.*

Mitch looked over to her. *You're going to church.*

She nodded, her throat tight. *Yes*, she said. *And I was wondering if you would like to come with me.*

She watched him for his reaction, and he didn't reject her immediately, but after a few moments of consideration, he shook his head. *I don't know about that.*

What are you worried about? she asked.

I'm not worried about anything, he said. *I just don't like going to church.*

He turned back to the food bowls and started opening cans to pour over the dry food that he had already dished out. She watched him work as he added water and then split a can of green beans between two bowls. He mixed it all up with a rubber spatula and fed each dog before he returned his attention to her.

Do you think this will be a problem between us? he asked. *If you want to go to church and I don't?*

Lacy swallowed, suddenly unsure. *I don't know*, she said honestly. *I think life would be easier if we lived it on the same page, but I don't think it's a deal breaker.*

Did Landon go to church? he asked.

Lacy shook her head. *He said we could study at home, which we did on Sundays*, she said. *We had discussions about the scriptures and stuff like that.*

So he kind of acted like a pastor, Mitch said.

Something flitted across his expression that Lacy didn't understand before it disappeared. *Something like that.*

She'd opened up to Mitch a lot about Landon, but he'd never said anything too terrible about him or what he thought of him. She didn't think he would. Mitch hadn't known him and could hardly pass judgment.

Lacy had found a journal from the time that she'd dated Landon and the first couple of months of their marriage. She hadn't made it all the way to the end yet, because she could see and hear her own pain in the entries.

She hadn't realized it, but she'd used writing in the journal as a form of therapy to deal with the things in her relationship that she didn't like. She didn't have very many more entries to get through, but sometimes she was too tired to read one, and other times, she simply didn't want to have the negativity in her life.

She'd loved her husband, and no, their lives had not been perfect. He was not perfect, and there were definitely things about a romantic relationship that Lacy would like to be different this time around. She was older now, wiser, and just because things with Landon hadn't been perfect didn't mean they were bad.

What are you making for breakfast for us humans? she asked.

Oh, now I have to make your breakfast? His eyes crinkled as he teased her.

Well, you're hogging the kitchen, she said.

He tipped his head back and laughed and grabbed onto her. He slow danced with her as he sobered, and Lacy could do this for a good long time. After a couple of minutes, he stepped back and said, *I'll make you whatever you want, sweetheart. Quiche, frittata, those hockey pucks you like.*

He grinned at her, and Lacy shook her head. *I think I'll just have yogurt and sit in the thinking seat. Last time I went to church, I had a panic attack, and this time I'd like things to be a lot different.*

He nodded, suddenly serious. *You could sit by Link and Misty if you want*, he said. *They go every week, unless one of them is sick or their kids are too sick to go.* He lifted his phone. *I could text them.*

Lacy thought about his offer for a good long minute, really considering it. It had been very difficult for her to go to church several weeks ago, and she'd gone already in a heightened state of nervousness. She didn't feel like that today when she ended up shaking her head.

I want to do it myself, she said. *I think I can. The only person I would want to go with me is you.*

His jaw tightened, and he nodded. *Okay. You want coffee?*

I always want coffee, she said, with a smile.

He fixed a cup for her, handed it to her, and then pulled out the package of eggs. *I'll come sit by you when I'm done making breakfast.*

She took that as her cue to leave, and she retreated to the thinking seat on the porch. Church didn't start until ten o'clock, and the wicked summer sun had already heated the air. The roof kept the porch nice and shady, and she flipped on the switch that would start the fan above it. At least it moved the air around, and it was better than nothing.

She sighed into the seat, grateful for such good things in her life. "Thank you so much for helping us get this academy open," she murmured. "Thank you for leading me to Three Rivers, and thank you for giving me the strength and skills to work with Mitchell Glover."

Her momma and daddy had taught her to pray for the things she was grateful for first, saving the things she wanted to ask for until last. She wasn't sure why it mattered, because she'd also been taught that God knew her heart and He knew her—and if God knew what she wanted and what she was grateful for, why did she have to say it out loud?

She took a slow sip of her coffee and enjoyed the breeze as it danced across the porch and ruffled her hair.

"I'm so grateful for this second chance," she said. "Not only in my career, but at a family and a husband. I'm grateful that Mitch loves his dogs, and I'm grateful that I have such a nice place to stay, and that the air conditioning works so well in all the buildings."

She thought of Jacob then, as his air conditioner had been on the fritz. She pulled out her phone to send him a text.

You should come over after church, she said. *Our air conditioning works great here. How hot is it in your place today?*

You're going to church? Jacob asked. *What time does that start?*

Ten, she said. *You're welcome to come with me. I go to a little building here on the south side of town. Mitch's momma is one of the pastors, and his uncle is the other one.*

I'm already hiking out in the Valley of the Gods, he said. *I won't make it back by ten, but I'm totally going to take you up on that afternoon air conditioning. My unit really struggles when it gets really hot.*

Are they gonna come look at it? she asked.

Said they would on Monday.

You can sleep at my place too.

Thanks, Jacob said. *I'll think about it.*

She thought of him hiking out in this Texas heat, and she prayed, "Please bless him, that he'll be safe and that he brought enough water."

Her thoughts then moved toward the things that she needed to be blessed with. "I really just want to have a good experience at church today," she said. "Doesn't have to be earth-shattering or life-changing. I just want to...."

She trailed off and paused, her thoughts suddenly off the

tracks. What did she want from church? Why did she feel such a strong need to go? Was it in the simple act of getting up and getting ready and putting God first, or was there a message that would be said there that she needed to hear?

"I want to feel like I belong there," she said. "I want to feel comfortable in Thy presence, and I want to feel safe and loved, and I want all the hectic things in my life to slow down and go away."

To her, that was the beauty of the Sabbath Day. She didn't have to work. She didn't have endless to-do lists and dozens of emails that all needed to be answered by nine a.m. She could simply *be* and have room and space in her life to feel the Lord's presence and acknowledge His hand.

Mitch never joined her on the porch, and Lacy took her empty coffee cup back inside and rinsed it out in the sink. She set it in the dish drainer, noting the scent of fried eggs and cinnamon raisin toast, two of Mitch's favorite foods.

The dog bowls sat empty, and none of them had come to greet her. Mitch would get mad at them even if they did, and he'd used her to help train the dogs several times. Someone had to ring the doorbell, so that he could get them to alert and answer the door. Someone had to be able to vocalize certain words, as Mitch couldn't do that by himself either.

What he could do with those dogs with only hand signals and a whistle was absolutely incredible. Lacy could admit to more than one morning of standing on the back porch watching him from afar and falling a little bit more in love with him each time she did.

She opened the coat closet on the short wall between

the kitchen and the living room and lifted her purse from the hook inside. Today's drive to church happened in calm silence as Lacy kept the radio off and her thoughts centered on God.

She didn't worry about who she'd see there, or what they'd say to her, and she'd already told Mitch she was going, so she didn't feel like she was running from phantoms and secrets.

She pulled up to the church ten minutes before services began, which seemed to be about the same time as everyone else in town. She did manage to find a spot far closer than she had last time, and she joined the others walking into the building.

Her family had always sat in the same place—middle center pew, four back. Since Lacy had never been here before, she didn't want to take someone else's regular spot. Her heartbeat thudded a few extra times, and her fight-or-flight response told her to leave, that she didn't belong there, that if she sat in the wrong place, there would be too many eyes on her.

She scanned left and right as there were side benches down the edges of the chapel. Since she was alone, she figured she'd take one of those. A family had just started past her, and she waited until they'd gone, and then she took the first step.

"Hey, Lacy," someone whispered, and she turned her attention to the woman.

She was dark-haired and pink-cheeked, and Lacy had no idea who she was. She paused, her confusion showing in her facial expression she was sure, as she let everything show there, a habit of her interpreting.

The woman rose and smiled. "You may not know me. I'm Clara Jean Reynolds. I go to the small ranch owners' meetings with Mitch."

"Oh, sure," Lacy said. "He's mentioned you."

"I knew it was you, because I looked up your website, and most people don't have a profile picture that looks just like them, but you do."

"Mitch had us get new pictures this summer," Lacy said with a smile.

"Listen, I wanted to ask you about something," Clara Jean said, and Lacy looked left and right, thinking, *Right here at church?*

No one seemed to care about the whispered conversation happening in the aisle, and people could still get past her. She met Clara Jean's eye again and said, "Okay."

"Finn put me in charge of organizing this month's ranch owners' meeting," she said. "Any topic I want, and I wondered if you and your brother would be willing to talk to us about physical facilities management. Mitch said he does all the maintenance at the academy."

Her eyebrows went up, and Lacy nodded. "Yes," she said, her chest filling with a balloon of pride. "We manage a lot of physical facilities at the academy."

"I think most of the farm owners and ranchers have to do the same," she said. "Barns and stables, houses and pens. Heck, I have to deal with fruit stands and an entire grocery store, and it would be great if we could get some maintenance tips or talk about concerns. Maybe make a short list of people that we rely on and trust to call when we need help with something. I thought you guys might be a good resource for that."

Lacy smiled at Clara Jean. "I think your meetings are on the third Thursday?"

"Yes," Clara Jean said. "Does that work for you guys, or will you be too busy with the start of school?"

"Our students will be here next weekend," Lacy said. "But school doesn't start until the nineteenth. Is your meeting before that—on the fifteenth, since the first was Thursday?"

Clara Jean nodded. "If that works, that would be awesome. We're having the meeting at Wilde & Organic, upstairs on the second floor in our administration offices. But we can come to Signs for Success if that's easier."

"Any place is fine," Lacy said. "I'll talk to Jacob. I mean —what are you looking for? A little presentation?"

"Sometimes we just ask questions and have people answer them," Clara Jean said. "But maybe fifteen or twenty minutes on what it takes to maintain buildings? And like I said, that resource list—that would be great."

"Okay," Lacy said.

"I'll text you more details," Clara Jean said as the piano started to play louder than it had been before. She sat back down, and Lacy felt totally disoriented as she faced the rest of the rows.

The organ joined in, and she knew the choir would be

coming down the aisle any moment. She needed to find a seat. Fast.

She hurried down several rows on the left side and slid onto the end of a row where another couple sat against the wall. Three or four more people could fit here easily, and Lacy gave them a tight smile just as choir members filed in from the left and right sides of the stage, and voices sounded from behind her.

Others clapped along with the song, but Lacy didn't. She simply wanted to exist in the space and find her place there, and she prayed once again that she would find the room to belong.

The choir congregated on the stage and moved from a more rousing number into one that was much more reverent. Lacy's heartbeat settled as well, and all of her anxiety seeped away, seemingly into the lyrics of the song about the beauty of God's creations.

The song ended and the choir sat. Mitch's mother rose to her feet and approached the microphone, and Lacy smiled at the familiar face.

She knew Willa much better now, though Mitch still had not taken her home to meet his parents officially as his girlfriend, nor to eat dinner with Link and Misty, nor for anything else on the ranch, really. His uncle had once again had a giant birthday party in July, and Mitch had gone by himself for thirty minutes before he'd returned to the academy. He did not like big groups, and Lacy was not going to push him on the matter.

"Good morning, my brothers and sisters," Willa said. "My friends."

In that moment, Lacy truly felt like every person in that chapel was a friend. She may not know them yet, but she could call on them for anything, and they would be there—the way friends did.

The tightness in her body melted away, and she sagged back against the bench. A moment later, someone tapped her shoulder, and her adrenaline flew to the back of her mouth. She looked up to find Mitch standing there. He gestured for her to move over, and Lacy quickly slid down the bench to make room for him.

He sat next to her, draped his arms across his legs, and let his hands hang between his knees as he ducked his head as well.

He wore an enormous cowboy hat, and by putting his head down, he'd effectively cut off being able to see his momma. Willa wasn't signing, and Lacy threaded her arm through his and asked with only her hands, *Do you want me to tell you what she's saying?*

Mitch shook his head just once and curled his fingers through hers. He tilted his head enough for their eyes to meet and signed with his free hand. *I just want to be here with you.*

Warmth filled Lacy from top to bottom, because Mitch had changed into a pair of slacks and a white shirt. He wore a tie covered in blue paisleys, and that sexy cowboy hat. And though he hadn't wanted to come to church, he had.

For her, he had come.

Chapter Thirty-Three

Mitch could hardly believe that he sat on the hard pew in the chapel he knew so well. Lacy's hand in his felt like absolute perfection, but Mitch still hadn't been able to lift his eyes to meet his mother's.

Her sermon would be fabulous, he knew, and Lacy would sign it for him down low, so that no one else could see. Otherwise, Momma would have to be facing straight at him the whole time, which she wouldn't do.

Knowing her, she'd seen him practically run down the aisle to Lacy's side, and she'd start signing if he looked up. That would also draw attention to him, and Mitch simply didn't need it.

At the same time, something jiggled in the back of his mind and finally worked itself loose. There were now definitely several more Deaf people and Hard of Hearing people and people who knew sign language living in Three

Rivers. He had twenty-three of them living on his property, and another ten faculty members in town who knew ASL. That fact gave him the bravery he needed to squeeze Lacy's hand and look up to his mother.

She currently looked to her left when Mitch sat on her right, and she possessed her usual angelic glow as she spoke. The chapel was mostly full when Mitch had arrived, and the choir had already been on the stage, and he wasn't surprised by any of it. Momma and Uncle Patrick truly had a gift for speaking God's word, and they'd created a thriving community here in Three Rivers.

Her attention swung toward the middle of the congregation, and Mitch could see her mouth moving now. Lacy reached over with her other hand and encapsulated his. He ducked his head, and she pressed her lips to his cheek. He took that as a silent question of, *Do you want me to interpret?*

He shook his head and turned to sweep a kiss along her cheek too. He didn't mind people knowing they were together, but he certainly didn't need to put on a show at church, either. He faced his mother again, just as she turned to the right.

Their eyes met, and it felt like God throwing thunderbolts and lightning through the chapel. Surprise crossed Momma's face, and she actually stopped speaking. Mitch blinked, sure his presence at church wasn't *that* big of a shock.

He'd been dating Lacy all summer, so it couldn't be the

fact that they'd come together. Mitch frowned, and that seemed to thaw her.

Momma reached up and wiped her eyes and continued her sermon. She did start to sign, and after a moment, Mitch noticed several people turn toward the back of the chapel. They must have heard something, and when he looked over to Lacy, she said, *Someone just called out from the back, thanking her for signing her words.*

She wore joy in her eyes, and Mitch felt it move through his whole body.

He didn't want to change the world. He didn't think one simple cowboy from Three Rivers, Texas, could do that anyway, no matter what his father said. But he did want to make life better for those he could, and he'd been praying for years that his academy could be that change for just one person—fine, maybe two or maybe two hundred—because Mitch knew what it was like to be completely isolated because of his inability to communicate, and he didn't want anyone to suffer through the same loneliness that he had.

He turned back to his mother and found her talking about the Savior. Momma was very good at including Christ in all of her sermons, and it took him several moments to realize that she spoke about the parable of the ten lepers.

He was familiar with all the scriptures as he'd studied the Holy Bible growing up, and even in his own spare time as an adult. He wasn't adverse to religion, and he wasn't sure what had kept him from attending church and studying as much as he once had.

Perhaps general overwhelm? He'd let life's busyness get in the way? He wasn't sure.

He did feel restless by the end of the sermon, and he was glad when they finally got to stand and sing. He put his arm around Lacy and kept her close, hoping they could make a quick escape once the meeting ended.

He should have known better.

The group hug the Glovers had given him just a few days ago should've acted as a warning.

The moment the choir finished and the closing prayer ended, no less than eight Glovers converged on their pew. Uncle Bear had apparently been sitting the closest to them, and he and Aunt Sammy grabbed onto Mitch and hugged him.

Irritation drove through him, because they'd stolen him from Lacy, and he simply wanted to be at her side on this slow, easy Sabbath Day.

It's good to see you, son, Uncle Bear said, and he knew enough sign language to sign it.

Thanks, Mitch said, not sure what else he was supposed to say. They'd apparently all texted one another, and he had to give Uncle Judge and Aunt Etta, Aunt Sammy and Aunt Oakley, and both Bishop and Montana a hug before he could even exit the bench. That had given his father enough time to arrive in the aisle, once again blocking Mitch's escape.

What are you guys doing for lunch? he asked, his gaze flitting over to Lacy. *You should come out to the Edge Cabin. Momma's made a whole mess of food to send home with Chaz and Melissa when they return to campus this week.*

Then it's for Chaz and Melissa, Mitch said.

Lacy slipped her arm through his and squeezed his elbow against her body. She looked up at him, and Mitch had a silent conversation with her—the first one he'd ever had with a woman. He knew then that he'd just fallen all the way in love with Lacy Hayes, and he prayed harder than ever that he could become the man she deserved.

I'd love to go to lunch at your family's house, she said.

Mitch ducked his head and raised his eyebrows in a silent *Really?*

She nodded. *You've been hiding me for a long time.*

He wanted to argue back, but didn't feel like this conversation was private enough for that. After all, his father and a lot of his aunts and uncles could speak sign language just fine.

Mitch looked at his father, feeling backed into a corner. He'd felt the same way when he'd seen Lacy sitting in the thinking seat, and he'd retreated to his office instead of joining her. He'd paced in front of the window there, trying to decide if he could really get dressed and go to church with her. By the time he decided he could—and should—she'd already left.

He didn't like feeling trapped or like he was being forced to do something he didn't want to do. As he stood there in a silent battle of wills with himself, a very peaceful feeling settled over his shoulders, almost like God had arrived with a warm blanket, and the thought of, *Your parents would love to get to know her more, and you have been keeping her from them.*

They'd been extraordinarily busy at Signs for Success, and Mitch had made a pledge to go see his parents twice a month at the Edge Cabin. He'd kept that schedule, but he had not taken Lacy one time. His heart softened into a big puddle of marshmallow, and he nodded.

All right, we'll come to lunch, but I have to go get the dogs. I only brought Champ with me to church. I want you to see how they're doing, and it would be great to train them up there in an unfamiliar environment.

He'd taken William up to Shiloh Ridge a couple of times, and the golden retriever had done well in a new place. He could only imagine what Sunshine would do with the rabbits that lived in the big pine trees on the edge of Shiloh Ridge Ranch, and he actually smiled, thinking about it.

Daddy's grin matched his. *Yes, Momma will be a few minutes here, as always. We were planning to eat around one.*

That was a couple of hours from now, and Mitch glanced over his father's shoulder as Link and Misty arrived. He'd been putting off his best friend and cousin as well, and now he stepped over to them and drew them both into his arms. Link's chest shook as he laughed, and he clapped Mitch on the back. When they parted, he looked at him with questions in his crinkled eyes and said, "What's going on with you?"

Lacy and I would love to come to dinner one day this week, he said.

Misty's eyes widened, but she didn't hesitate as she said, "How about Wednesday?" easily accepting his unspoken apology and inviting him to their home. "I'm getting pretty good at the sourdough bread, and I'll make you a couple of extra loaves."

I love your bread, Mitch said with a grin. *Wednesday sounds great. I'll make sure Lacy puts it on our calendar.*

The chapel had started to empty, even some of the Glovers going, and Mitch looked back at his father.

I don't want it to be a whole family thing. Those are really hard for me, Daddy.

I know that, he said. *It's Melissa and Chaz and me and your mother.* He looked over to Lacy and drew her into a one-armed hug. *And you and Lacy. It's six people, and we all know sign language.*

Mitch nodded, his jaw tight and his teeth aching. He released the pressure there. *I don't want Momma making anything that she hasn't already made. It makes me feel stupid.*

I'll tell her, Daddy said. *But you know I can't control your mother.* He grinned at Mitch, who tipped his head back and laughed.

Just tell her we won't come if she does, Mitch said. *That ought to do it.* He glanced toward the back door, thinking of a better plan. *In fact, I'll tell her myself right now.*

He reached for Lacy's hand and towed her up the aisle and out into the lobby. Momma stood out there and talked to the parishioners as they left the building.

Uncle Patrick stood with her, and she shook hands and

hugged old ladies as radiant and vibrant as ever. When she saw Mitch, she burst into tears, and that only added to the guilt Mitch carried in his gut. She opened her arms to him, and Mitch stepped into them.

An instant wave of relief flowed through him, erasing the weight in his body that came from guilt and shame. He imagined this was what it would feel like to be welcomed into God's presence, and he clung to his mother and reveled in this feeling of love and acceptance.

He stepped back and said, *Lacy and I will come for lunch today. I'm bringing all four dogs, and I told Daddy that if you made even one extra thing between now and one o'clock, that we wouldn't come.*

He raised his eyebrows. *So what's it gonna be? Are we gonna come, or are you going to freak out in the kitchen?*

She looked over to Patrick, who laughed and laughed and laughed. She wiped her eyes again as she looked back at Mitch. *I will not make one single thing between now and one o'clock.*

She reached over and squeezed Lacy's hand, and Lacy shone like all the stars in the sky. Mitch's mind opened then, and he realized for maybe the first time that Lacy had no family here. He had so many of them that he'd completely forgotten that she and Jacob had been separated from their parents. He'd felt alone, like an island, in Virginia, and he'd always appreciated when he got to spend time with other people's parents. He swept a kiss along both of his mother's cheeks, and then reached for Lacy again.

We'll see you at one then, Momma. Thank you.

He left the building, and though he had no idea where Lacy had parked, he walked down the sidewalk to the shade of the trees on the west side of the building. He turned back to her and said, *I'm really sorry that I've been keeping you from my family. I just....*

He stopped, not quite sure how to go on. He gestured back to the chapel. *I just had the strangest thought that perhaps you might be missing your mom, and my momma might be a great comfort to you here, and I'm really sorry that I haven't let you get to know her and have that relationship.*

Lacy pressed her teeth together as her bottom lip and chin started to shake. She looked away from him, but her gaze came back quickly. *I do miss my mother,* she said. *Before we started dating, I hadn't hugged or touched another human being in months, so I may have been a little clingy.*

He chuckled and shook his head. *Oh, sweetheart. Out of the two of us, I'm definitely the clingiest one.*

They laughed together, because Lacy had told him a couple of times this summer to just give her a *little* space.

He always wanted to be right on top of her, to be close to her. Mitch could admit that he liked being physical; he liked holding her hand and putting his arm around her and feeling her breathe. He liked touching her hair and kissing her and tracing her fingertips with his.

Let's go change, she said. *And we'll get the dogs and go up to the ranch.*

I set up dinner with Link and Misty on Wednesday night, he said. *Hope that's okay.*

It's fine, she said. *I set up a small ranch owners' meeting where Jacob and I are going to talk about physical facilities and maintenance.* She grinned at him. *Hope that's okay.*

He blinked at her, pure joy moving through him. *I can't think of a better person to do that,* he said. *You're incredible.*

He leaned down and touched his lips to hers, wanting to feel that amazing, weightless, joy of being in love. Now, he could only hope and pray that Lacy fell completely and hopelessly in love with him too, and that his family, or the busyness of the academy, or the stresses of their lives would bring them closer together...and not drive them apart.

Chapter Thirty-Four

W illa tied up the loose ends in her office at the
church as quickly as she could. Her emotions
wobbled, and she felt like she might start weeping at any
moment. She usually loved Sundays after a sermon, and
she'd sit in her office, sip tea, and make notes of the impres-
sions she'd gotten that day or ideas she could turn into
another talk.

Today, she didn't do any of that, and instead grabbed the
keys to her car and stepped next door to her brother's office.
"Mitch and Lacy are coming for lunch," she said. "So I can't
stay."

"I wouldn't expect you to," Patrick said, barely looking
up. "Your other kids are leaving soon to go back to college,
right?"

"You could come to lunch," Willa said.

Her brother often did join her and Cactus up at the

ranch. Every day, she thanked the Good Lord Above for her brother, that he'd brought her to this small town where she had found a community of cowboys to preach to.

He'd been Willa's strongest support—outside of her husband—for a great many years, and she mourned the fact that he had gotten married and divorced young, never had children, and never been remarried.

She'd encouraged him to date in the beginning, but the more Patrick put her off, the more Willa realized that she was simply irritating him, and she'd stopped. He seemed happy in his small house almost smack dab in the middle of Three Rivers.

Willa offered him a smile when he looked over to her. "I think I'll pass," he said. "My throat is feeling scratchy, and I have a meeting with a young couple who thinks they want to get married this fall." He grinned at her, and Willa nodded as she pushed away from the doorway.

"All right," she said. "But you're always welcome."

"I know," he called after her.

Willa moved as fast as she could out to the rear parking lot and headed up to the ranch. She'd promised Mitch she wouldn't make anything special for him and Lacy, and she contemplated breaking that. She easily had the ingredients for pepperoni pizza quesadillas—one of Mitch's favorite foods—and though she didn't have the sweet Hawaiian rolls, she could easily make the ham and cheese egg sandwiches he loved out of English muffins.

She tightened her grip on the wheel and said right out

loud to herself, "You promised, and you will not be making anything more."

Melissa loved to cook, which meant she fit right in with some of the aunts, particularly Holly Ann, Etta, and Sammy. Willa had some pretty decent skills in the kitchen, and she'd taught all of her children to be able to take care of themselves, but the only time she truly enjoyed cooking was when it was for her children.

"You can't make him come home by making a pepperoni pizza quesadilla," she muttered. Intellectually, she was right, but her momma heart just wanted Mitch to be comfortable and happy.

He'd been coming up and visiting her and Cactus a couple of times a month this summer, and Willa could admit that something had healed inside of her as well. God had told her that even if Mitch never set foot inside a church again, he was still loved. She could still love him, and of course, God still loved him.

She and Melissa had spent the past couple of days putting together casseroles and freezer meals, and baking quick breads and sourdoughs for her and Chaz to take back to college. They'd be leaving this weekend, taking Burch and Hank with them, along with Judge and Mister and Cactus to help move them all in to their new apartments.

Willa couldn't really help carry boxes, and she could barely go up stairs faster than a toddler. So she'd volunteered to stay and clean the Edge Cabin from top to bottom, and then go see Mitch at his academy after his seventy-one students had moved in. As far as she knew, only a handful of them had gotten permission to move in on Friday night, with the rest arriving on Saturday. She expected it to be full chaos, and she wanted to be present for every minute of it.

Mitch would undoubtedly tell her not to come, and Willa hoped she could appeal to Lacy's softer side and get an invitation.

She pulled around to the side of the Edge Cabin, leaving the spot in the back for Mitch. Cactus had pulled right in front of the barn, where he usually did.

Willa could admit she had been surprised to see her husband at church today too. Though he was not Mitch's biological father, he possessed the same restless spirit that Mitch did, and while her husband was faithful and believed in God and lived an exceedingly chaste life, he didn't love coming to church.

He read a variety of religious texts, and he'd always led their family in choosing good, serving others, telling the truth, and honoring their ancestors. Willa had learned through Cactus that the outward appearance of attending a meeting did not indicate their inner conversion to Christ.

She wasn't sure why she had never extended that same courtesy to Mitch. Truth be told, when she'd seen Cactus hugging her son after the meeting, she'd realized that she had been blaming him for some of Mitch's absence. Her son had grown up here at the Edge Cabin since the age of ten, when Cactus had welcomed him with open arms and a quick mind that had learned sign language as fast as he possibly could.

He'd gotten Mitch all of the resources he needed,

including a hearing dog, and out of the two of them, he'd flown back and forth to Virginia dozens of times when Willa had only gone three times: one time each for Mitch's graduations.

But Mitch had grown up watching Cactus stay home from church on Sundays. She knew her husband had often volunteered to work on the Sabbath, simply so he wouldn't have to come to church. Yes, sometimes there were true emergencies that couldn't be helped, and none of the Glovers made it to church, and as she walked around the front of the house to enter through the door there, the Lord chastised her again.

She stepped inside and found Chaz and Melissa sitting on opposite ends of the couch, both of them bent over their devices.

"Where's Daddy?" she asked.

"Out in the barn," Chaz said. "Making sure there's room for Mitch's dogs. He's bringing all four." He grinned like this was great news.

Willa had no idea what to do with eleven dogs, even for a couple of hours. She looked toward the back of the house, and while she didn't want to go back outside, she headed that way anyway.

"Mitch and Lacy will be here soon, Mel," she said. "Is there anything we need to do for the food?"

"I've got it handled, Momma," Melissa said, and instead of entering the kitchen and looking around for a job to do anyway, Willa simply nodded and went outside again. She indeed found Cactus in the barn moving around dog beds.

He'd set out four more water bowls, as if dogs needed their own personal dish, and she noticed that extra leashes had been hung on the hooks near the entrance.

Her voice stuck in her throat, and Willa cleared it.

Cactus looked toward her, straightening from pulling the corner of the dog bed into place. "What's going on?" He always knew when something stormed inside her, and Willa limped over to him and took his face in both of her hands.

"I have been blaming you for something that is not your fault, and I'm sorry."

He blinked at her, though he had to be used to these kinds of statements. She'd given him many over the years, and sure enough, he softened and took her in his arms.

"Well, I hope whatever it was, it wasn't too bad."

She shook her head and closed her eyes, breathing in the scent of dirt and straw and cotton and underneath all of that, her dear husband's cologne. He touched his lips to hers gently and said, "Mitch texted five minutes ago that they were in the truck."

"Perfect," Willa said. "I'll go get the table set."

Cactus had needed a lot of forgiving over the years, and yes, sometimes he did things that upset his wife that she needed to move past. Usually, he knew what those things were, and after a day or two—or sometimes a week or two—of him grumping around and glaring, they'd finally talk it out.

But today, she had given him no indication at all as to

what she'd blamed him for, and Cactus turned back to arranging the beds and horse blankets for the dogs. He couldn't think of anything, and he'd simply wait for Willa to tell him when she was ready.

Mitch probably wouldn't let his dogs out of his sight, and while Cactus usually brought a couple of his into the house, with extra bodies in the small cabin, he didn't want anyone to trip over a canine.

He already missed Chaz and Melissa, and they hadn't even left yet. When they did, he and Willa would go back to being empty nesters, and they'd fill their days with a long morning walk, him taking care of his dogs, her working on a sermon or a charity knitting project, and he'd go around the ranch and see where his hands were needed.

He hadn't been brought up idle, and while he did slow down in the afternoons these days, he had no idea what he'd do at home all day. Bear seemed to fill the time, as did Ranger, but Cactus hadn't been able to get himself into full retirement yet.

He stayed out in the barn, fiddling with the fans until Mitch and Lacy arrived. Then he framed himself in the doorway and watched his dear boy drop to the ground and hurry around to get Lacy out. His dogs made no noise whatsoever, though Mitch had not put them in the back bed where Cactus would have made his ride. Oh no, Mitch's dogs were divas, and they got to ride in the air-conditioned cab.

Cactus liked this view of his son interacting silently with Lacy as he said something. Lacy spoke back to him, and while she usually vocalized what she said, this time, she didn't. Cactus could understand ASL just fine, but he didn't care what they said to one another. He only cared about how they *acted*, and he could see clearly that Mitch had totally fallen in love with Lacy Hayes.

He dated a lot growing up, and for the first few years out of high school, and a ton in Virginia. When he'd turned thirty, about five years ago, he seemed tired of the game, and when Cactus had asked him about it, Mitch had said his PhD program was far more rigorous than he'd anticipated. Then, he'd returned to Three Rivers to get the academy started.

A pureness radiated from Lacy as she stood out of the way so Mitch could get his dogs down. He blew the whistle twice, and one right after the other, the four canines hopped to the ground, moved around him, and sat in front of him. Lacy giggled and bent down, giving them all love while Mitch fed them treats from his pocket.

He'd brought William up to the ranch with Champ before, and Cactus loved that golden retriever. He knew of the other two dogs, as Mitch had brought them by as puppies, but he hadn't seen them work in a couple of months now, and he pushed out of the doorway and started toward Mitch and Lacy.

"Mitch," he called, because he knew that would cause his dogs to alert him, and all four of them did, nosing or pawing at him, and then turning and facing Cactus.

He'd put all of his dogs in their kennels, and he lifted his hand as he greeted his son. *Can I bring mine out? Or would you rather I not?*

Yeah, I want them to meet other dogs, Mitch said, and Cactus waved at him over his shoulder as he turned around. Footsteps crunched behind him as he went back into the barn and lifted the latch that would open all of the doors on the kennels of the seven dogs he owned.

Once upon a time, his boys had slept in the barn, and Cactus could admit that he'd gotten more dogs to fill the void that his children had left when they'd grown up and flew the coop.

"Whoa, whoa," he said, and he held up both hands as hundreds of pounds of dog flesh came roaring out of the kennels. "Sit, sit—stay." He growled at the dogs, and to his great relief, they all sat and waited, some of them sliding down to their bellies.

Mitch entered the barn with his dogs unleashed, and Lacy said, "Wow, Cactus, look how many dogs you have."

He glanced over to her, just as Mitch said something, and the two of them laughed. Cactus raised his eyes at his son and Lacy reached up and tucked her hair and looked over to Mitch.

I just said, it's a good thing Momma's a patient woman, Mitch said.

You have four dogs right now, Cactus told him. *When Momma and I got married, we only had two.*

And mine, Mitch said. *So three.*

Cactus slung his arm around his son and squeezed his

shoulder. He wanted to ask him how he was doing. He wanted to ask him what he thought of church. He wanted to ask him why he had shown up that day. Cactus himself hated questions, and he hated nosy family members who couldn't seem to get the hint that he didn't want to answer them, so he said nothing, and let Mitch introduce his hearing dogs to the farm dogs.

Noses started sniffing, and tails wagged as they moved around one another and got familiar. After he saw Lacy wipe the sweat from her brow, he said, *Momma is probably going nuts inside. Let's go eat.*

Lacy led the way out of the barn, and Mitch put the whistle in his mouth and did a series of tweets, which called his dogs back to his side.

I'll make them lay down in the living room, he said.

Okay, I'm sure it'll be fine, Cactus told him, and then they followed Lacy toward the Edge Cabin for lunch...with eleven dogs in tow.

Chapter Thirty-Five

L acy wasn't sure if she should just go up the back steps and into the cabin, but Cactus didn't call out from behind her, and both cowboys had decided to bring up the rear. She saw and felt all kinds of doors opening in her life as she went up the few steps to the small back porch. It had clearly been extended, as newer wood ran along the back of the house and then expanded out to a much larger deck on the western side.

She'd lived with and worked with Mitch for twenty months now, and he'd never once brought her home.

And why would he? she asked herself. Even as far as the two of them dating went, they'd only been seeing each other for ten or eleven weeks now. Of course, they worked in close proximity to one another, and she knew him quite well from that.

She reached for the door and opened it as if she'd

come here dozens of times before and knew exactly where to go and what to do. The sound of a microwave beeping greeted her from inside, as well as a cold blast of air conditioning.

Praise the heavens, she thought, because they'd been standing out in that sweltering barn for the last five minutes, and Lacy had thought she might melt.

"There you are," Willa said, her hands moving along with her mouth. "How many dogs are we bringing in?"

"Mitch is just bringing his," Cactus called. "I'm leaving all mine in the barn."

"There's some good news," Willa said under her breath, and she stepped into Lacy, her arms wide. "Are you a hugger?" she asked.

"Yes, ma'am," Lacy said, and she moved into Willa's arms. Nothing was ever as good as being hugged by a mother, and even though Willa wasn't Lacy's, she felt the same level of care and love from her.

"Oh, it was so good to see you today," she said. "How did you like the sermon?"

Lacy stepped back, glad when Cactus went by them and Mitch crowded into her personal space. This time, she didn't mind how close he wanted to be to her. She glanced over to him, almost expecting him to answer the question before her, but he simply looked down at her.

Embarrassment ran through her when she couldn't recall anything Willa had said that day. "I have to admit," she said. "It was a big day for me to even be there, and...." She trailed off, not wanting to say anything bad about

Mitch, but she *had* been distracted by him and wanting to interpret for him.

"I don't think I was able to listen as much as I will next time," she said.

Momma loves teaching the parables, Mitch said with a grin, and then he moved over to his mother and took her into a hug. She laughed as he held her and motioned to say hi to Chaz and Melissa.

Lacy had seen him in full grump mode during big family parties, and she liked this more smiley side of him in a small setting with everyone who could communicate with him.

Melissa protested as he tried to hug her while she stirred the gravy, and he stuck his finger right in it, as if it wouldn't be hot at all.

"Mitch," Melissa complained, but he simply laughed again.

"Don't antagonize your sister," Willa said. "Come sit down and tell us what's going on at the academy."

I don't want to talk about work, Mitch said, shooting a look over to Lacy. *We have a rule.*

"A rule?" Willa raised her eyebrows at him, and then Lacy. When neither of them spoke, she added, "Well, do tell me what the rule is."

When we're not at work, we don't talk about work, he said. *Because I don't want to work twenty-four-seven, and neither does Lacy.*

She put a thin smile on her face, sure his parents were used to him saying exactly what he thought. He turned his back on them and moved the dogs into the living room.

Lacy smiled at Cactus, though the man intimidated her a little bit. "He works with the dogs every day," she said. "For a couple of hours in the morning, and then we've been running quite crazy to get everything ordered and organized for the move-in. Now that that's done, we'll turn our attention to all the student assignments, and then once we open, it'll just be staff meetings, his Tuesday night classes, and the dogs." She smiled over to him and added, "He loves those dogs."

"He's so good with them," Cactus said. "And he's going to bless a lot of lives with a hearing dog."

Lacy nodded, because she believed the same. She watched as Melissa took the pot of gravy over to the table and clapped her hands. "It's time to eat," she said. "Everybody come sit down."

In addition to getting all of his dogs while they'd been at home, Mitch had put on his vibration watch, which meant he knew that something or someone had made a sound behind him. He looked over his shoulder, and Lacy gestured for him to come sit down.

He didn't quite have Sunshine where he wanted her, and he took a few extra seconds to do that while Chaz and Melissa sat on one side of the big table. Cactus and Willa sat at the head and foot, leaving the other side for Mitch and Lacy. With his dogs finally settled, Mitch came over and took her hand at the same time he leaned in and pressed a kiss to her cheek.

Looks like we have a whole feast here today, he said, as he pulled out Lacy's chair for her and helped her get settled.

She wasn't sure if he could feel the tension in the room or not, but it cut through her like a chainsaw and thickened the air into gravy.

He sat down and picked up his napkin and looked around. *What?* he finally asked, glancing from his father to his mother. *Are you going to make us go around the table and say something we've been thinking about?*

His mother only smiled and shook her head. *They used to do that,* Mitch said. *Usually when some of us weren't getting along. They'd make us go around and say all the things that we were upset about or that we needed cleared. Those weren't my favorite dinners.*

"We had a lot of people living in a small space," Willa said. "Different personalities and whatnot."

"I can only imagine," Lacy said. "Mitch said that you guys adopted some kids."

"Yes, three," Cactus said.

"Let's pray," Willa said. "We can talk while we eat."

"Yes," Melissa said. "I made Swedish meatballs and mashed potatoes, and they're not good cold." She glared at Mitch, and he held up both of his hands.

Hey, it's not my fault that we're not eating.

"You're the one still talking," Melissa said.

Fine, I'll stop talking, he said back.

Lacy could only imagine a dinner where Cactus and Willa made them all go around and say what they were upset about. She found herself grinning and grinning and grinning, and when Mitch looked at her, his eyebrows went up and that head tilted adorably to the side, clearly asking her, *What are you grinning about?*

She simply shook her head and then bowed it as Willa started to pray. She reached for Mitch's hand under the table and held it in hers tightly, feeling so blessed to know him and be here with this family after a Sabbath Day where she hadn't run away from the things that made her uncomfortable, scared, or nervous.

A couple of days later, Mitch grunted as she put her palm against his chest and pushed herself up. They'd been lying in the shade for the past hour, and these lazy afternoons were some of Lacy's all-time favorite activities. She got to be with the man she was steadily falling in love with, and they talked with their hands in the air and their eyes on the skies. And then they settled into silence, simply comfortable with one another.

The Panhandle breeze rippled through the grasses, keeping them cool too, while Mitch's dogs lay in the shade beside them.

We have to go, she told him. *You told Link and Misty we would be there at six.*

It can't be that time already, he said.

It's five-fifteen, she said. *And I want to change my clothes before we go.*

He groaned as he sat up, and she grinned at him. She'd really enjoyed herself at his family dinner on Sunday afternoon, and she'd thought briefly about writing about her feelings in her journal. In the end, she'd dismissed the idea in favor of ice cream sundaes with Mitch and a walk with the dogs out to the pond.

Only a couple of days had passed, and the itch to write down her feelings and thoughts had started clawing at her. She really loved the idea of a journal, because she wanted her feelings to be valid, even if she looked back on them in ten years and realized how silly she sounded.

In that moment and on that day, she had real things she was thankful for, real things she worried about, real goals and ambitions and dreams. Journal writing had always been the best way for her to bleed the bad things out of her life, and put them on paper and in ink where someone else could deal with them and manage them.

As Mitch pulled her to her feet and then started to fold the blanket, Lacy had the idea that she needed to get a *new* journal. She didn't want to use the one that she had quit using several years ago—at Landon's request. She had a *new* life now, in a *new* place, with a *new* man, and she wanted to start in a *new* book.

She'd lived in Three Rivers long enough to know where to go, but she could also buy a new journal online and probably have it here by the weekend.

She and Mitch would be finalizing room assignments tomorrow and making all the move-in packets in the next couple of days, and Lacy had not been planning a trip to town. So an online order it would be.

Back in the house, she hurried upstairs to change her

clothes, and as Mitch drove them to Shiloh Ridge to have dinner with Link and Misty, Lacy used the quiet moment to tap on her phone and find a journal that she liked. The cover boasted purple leather with a snowy white ribbon and beautifully lined pages. Lacy put it in her cart and checked out just as Mitch turned onto the ranch. She looked over to him, and he looked at her, his eyebrows up.

I just bought a new journal, she said. *I'm going to start writing again.*

He smiled, reached over, and took her hand in his. He lifted it to his lips and pressed a kiss to the inside of her wrist. *That's great news, baby.*

They passed under the arch, and Mitch turned left to go up into the hills. They passed the party barn where Lacy had attended his uncle's birthday party, as well as the wedding luncheon. The hill steepened, and Mitch went past trees on the left and right, almost to the top of the hill before he made another right turn.

A house came into view on the side of the road, and it was clearly under construction.

"Oh, wow," Lacy said to herself.

Mitch pulled in beside another truck. *They're doing an add-on—two more bedrooms and a bathroom,* he said. *As well as digging out a partial basement, since the house is on a hill.*

That'll be nice, Lacy said.

They've already got two boys, Mitch said. *And a third on the way.*

Is it a boy or a girl? she asked.

Mitch shook his head, his expression full of personality. *I don't think they know. She's due in a couple of months.*

Lacy had seen Misty at church, of course, and yes, the woman was clearly pregnant. The front door opened, as Mitch said, *This is called the Top Cottage.*

Do all the houses have names? she asked.

Just a few, he said. *The Homestead, Bull House, the Ranch House, the Edge Cabin, and the Top Cottage.*

Nerves reverberated from him, and she reached over and took his hand in hers. He turned toward her, something anxious and vulnerable in his expression.

Are you okay? she asked.

You know this is a big deal for me, right? he asked. *Me bringing you to the ranch to meet my parents, hang out with my best friend.*

She nodded soberly. *Yes, I think I know what a big deal it is for you.*

I can't say things the way you do, he said. *But I want you to know I'm listening to you, and I think you've told me that family is important to you and you want to be involved in mine.*

He was so expressive as he spoke, ending on a big question mark with his eyebrows.

She nodded. *That's right*, she said. *Why be alone when you have so many great people around you?*

I also wanted to tell you something, he said.

Lacy swallowed, because Mitch's confusion and vulnerability had just been masked by his grumpy cowboy persona. He glanced out the windshield, where two little boys jumped up and down at the top of the steps, waving for him to come in. He smiled at them and waved and pressed his palm toward them a couple of times, which Lacy knew to mean, *I'll be there in a minute.*

He hung his head for a brief moment, and then lifted his eyes back to hers. *You told me that you're falling in love with me, and I didn't say it back, and I just want you to know that I feel the same way—I'm falling in love with you too.*

You're falling in love with me? she teased.

All the way down. He grinned too and leaned toward her as movement on the porch told Lacy that Link and Misty had come outside too.

Since they had an audience, Lacy kissed him quickly. *Let's go, cowboy. They're waiting for us.*

Chapter Thirty-Six

"All right," Lacy said, as she held up a tablet. Mitch couldn't help but beam with pride at his beautiful girlfriend. She and Jacob were presenting for the small ranch owners' meeting, and Mitch was proud of both of them.

Jacob had been nervous and at the house all morning, going over the presentation with Lacy. Mitch didn't know what he was so nervous about. He could speak and sign, and he knew a lot about maintaining the physical facilities of a large operation. Just because he had to deal with dorms, which included laundry facilities and bathrooms and kitchens, instead of barns didn't mean he didn't know what he was talking about. The others in the room had to maintain calving sheds and milking pens, barns, stables, *and* their own homes.

Mitch had seen Lacy and Jacob make this presentation

twice now, and both times it had landed right around sixteen or seventeen minutes. "We're going to start by asking anyone who has any contractor or business that they know and like for plumbing, landscaping, general handyman repairs, HVAC, veterinary care, or if anything else that you might need help with on your ranch, to type it in here. I'm going to—" She shot a glance over to Mitch. "I mean, Mitch will—"

Her shoulders came up and then sank back down, and her brother stepped to her side. "It's a list we'll send out to everyone," he said. "It doesn't have to be just for physical facilities. Mitch will have access to it. And of course, you all have Lacy's number now, so you can contact her anytime as well." He nodded at his sister, and she gave him a grateful smile.

"I'll start it right here." She handed the tablet to Finn, who pulled out his phone before he started typing.

"One of the first things I did when I got to Signs for Success," Jacob said. "Was to make a schedule. I don't know how many of you have found this helpful, but with a lot of facilities that need to be maintained, it's good to have a general schedule—kind of like cleaning your baseboards once a year or washing your windows every other year." He looked over to Lacy, who nodded. "So you should have routines for checking your fences and your buildings for leaks and pests and rodents. That way, you'll be able to find things that are compromised before they're too bad, and get them fixed."

"It's just like vaccinating your cattle or branding

season," Lacy said. "We do those things for animals, but sometimes we forget that where they live is just as important."

They paused, their eyes flying to someone in the audience. Mitch looked around him as others started to laugh. His eyes quickly went back to Lacy, and she said, "Alex just said that if you have a schedule, you won't end up with a whole nest of mice in your barn like him."

Mitch smiled too, and Jacob continued with the presentation. He talked about how water damage was one of the worst things that could happen on a farm and that roofs needed to be checked so that hay and straw didn't get moldy, and pests didn't multiply. The tablet went around, and while Mitch could certainly add names to it, because he'd worked with a lot of people in the last couple of years as he'd built his academy out of bare dirt, he simply passed it to Brandon. He could add to it later after this meeting, as that was Lacy's tablet, and it would be going home with them.

Brandon looked at it blankly for a moment as well, and then passed it to his brother Dawson.

If Mitch didn't have Jacob working for him, this meeting would have brought him to his knees, and he sat there for the rest of the presentation with pure gratitude streaming through him. When they finished, the other farmers started asking questions, and Clara Jean had said they would move their news to the end of the meeting so that Jacob and Lacy could leave if they wanted to.

They didn't, and Mitch actually thought for a moment that he could send Jacob in his stead to these meetings and still get the information he needed. The moment he thought that, though, his heart crushed in on itself, because then he wouldn't get to see his friends.

He glanced around the room, realizing that, yes, all of these men and women had indeed become his *friends*, and this meeting wasn't a chore, but something he could find joy in.

They moved from the row-style seating to a table, and he sat next to Jacob, while Lacy sat across from them. Paul outlined his wife's favorite names for their baby boy that was coming around Thanksgiving. Alex said he and Nikki had an appointment with their specialist in Amarillo for their first ultrasound next week to see how their baby was doing.

"I keep trying to get Misty to learn the gender of our baby," Link said, a wide smile on his face. He lifted his sub sandwich to his mouth, and Mitch switched his eyes back to Lacy. "But she won't do it."

Lacy signaled laughter, and she wore a smile on her face as well.

"So you must have boy names and girl names," Finn asked.

"Yep," Link said.

Mitch lost track of the conversation as he bent over his food, but Lacy kept signing to both him and Jacob, effortlessly alerting them as to who was speaking and then signing what they'd said.

Henry and Angel were going to have another baby come March, and Mitch applauded for them, just like everyone else. It seemed everyone around him had a wife and family except for him, and he looked to his left and found Link looking at him.

What? he asked his cousin.

I'm wondering what you think about me and Misty setting up Jacob.

Mitch turned his whole body toward Link, to shield the conversation from Jacob. *What do you mean?*

I mean, Misty's best friend from Houston is coming back to Three Rivers. Remember, she lived here with Janie?

Oh, sure, Mitch said, though he had trouble recalling what Janie looked like in that moment.

He's gotta be almost thirty, right? Link asked.

Jacob was seven years younger than Lacy, Mitch knew that. He did the math quickly in his head. *I think he's about twenty-seven,* he said. *Maybe twenty-eight.*

Janie's only thirty-two, he said. *And Misty thinks they'd be super cute together.*

Does she know sign language? Mitch asked.

Link shook his head, which caused a frown to appear between Mitch's eyes. *I don't know,* he said, trying not to let it irritate him. How would Janie possibly communicate with Jacob if she couldn't speak sign language? It wasn't something that someone could pick up in a couple of days, either.

I'll ask Lacy what she thinks, Link said.

That irritated Mitch, but he chose not to argue. Jacob's best bet to find someone to be with would be at Signs for Success, but Mitch didn't have to educate Link and Misty about that.

He actually felt proud of himself for holding his tongue

and not trying to educate the world on what a deaf person needed. For all he knew, Jacob would be perfectly fine teaching someone how to sign and communicate with him.

He'd been in Three Rivers for over a year, and Link had never seen him go out with anyone, hearing or deaf.

He'd dated plenty of hearing people over the years. In fact, Mitch had always known that he would marry someone who could hear.

When it was his turn to say news, he looked at Lacy, and their grins seemed to widen at the same time. *Our faculty have arrived at Signs for Success*, he said. *Our students start arriving tomorrow and should all be here by Saturday night. Classes start the following Monday.*

"I signed up for your adult beginning sign language," Libby said, and Mitch turned and looked down the table to her when Lacy had signed it.

You did? Why?

She glanced at Lacy and then back to him. "Tyson Greene is deaf in one ear," she said. "They're bringing him home in a couple of weeks, and I thought it might be good to learn some sign language."

Finn leaned forward and grinned at Mitch as well, but he had to look back at Lacy to get the message. "His parents are really excited that there's a Deaf academy here, and they're hoping that he'll be able to learn some sign language as well."

Mitch nodded, something surging and moving up his throat that he couldn't name. *I'm glad he's coming home soon*, he said. *He's healing up all right?*

He had to wait for the questions to be conveyed, and then Lacy said, "Finn says yes, he's doing well."

Henry said, "God is good," and murmurs of assent went around the group. Mitch nodded his agreement to such a sentiment, and then he deliberately didn't sit and watch Lacy to know every single thing that was said in the room.

Sometimes it was simply too exhausting, and sometimes he simply wanted to sit with something inside his own mind.

When the meeting had ended and everyone stood around, mingling and chit-chatting, Mitch's grumpiness couldn't be contained any longer. He held up the keys and waved them at Lacy. *I'll wait for you in the truck.*

She nodded, moving right back to her conversation with Clara Jean and Tate. They still had plenty of work to do that day, as they'd practiced their presentation all morning while Mitch had tried to finalize the student dorm assignments.

They still had seventy-one packets to put together, key cards to distribute, signage to set up—*and lunch to order,* he reminded himself. He didn't want anything to be hard for anyone moving in at Signs for Success this weekend, and his impatience grew the longer he waited for Lacy and Jacob to come out of the grocery store.

When they finally did, he felt a little wild inside, and he breathed in deeply and held it—a practice he'd read about online. Navy SEALs did it to focus their minds, and it was called box breathing. He blew out his breath for eight counts and then held it for another eight. He closed his eyes and tried to center his thoughts, making himself a window where anything irritating, frustrating, or annoying could simply flow through him, the way sunlight moved through glass.

Everything will be fine. The packets would get put together, and they only needed six ready for tomorrow anyway. Mitch simply needed to *breathe*, and he gave himself the space and time to do that, hoping it would make him into the kind of cowboy who Lacy would want to be with, who others could approach without being afraid, and who God wanted him to be.

The following morning, Mitch's impatience had returned. He'd texted Lacy four times before she'd responded, and then she'd said, *Give me ten minutes.*

It had never taken Mitch more than ten minutes to walk in from the administration building, and he couldn't continue his dog training unless he had a voice. He could do a lot with the dogs with a whistle and his hands, but some things simply required a person to say something or do something. He'd been relying on Lacy for those things.

Today, Mitch wanted her to work with the dogs inside the house while he rang the doorbell on the front porch. It was important that they alert their handler, no matter who it was, whenever they heard a sound. He'd left Sunshine and Maven in the backyard, and he'd even looped Champ's leash around a doorknob in the kitchen because he wanted William to alert to the doorbell today...by himself, for someone new.

Finally, the front door opened, and William alerted him. He turned around and found Lacy entering, a stack of folders in her hand.

I can't find the printouts, she said. When she seemed a little frustrated, Mitch immediately felt bad that he'd called her away from her work.

I just need you for fifteen minutes, he said, and he quickly ran through where he would be and what he needed her to do. She set the folders down on a couch cushion and sank onto the other end of it.

He crouched down in front of his dog and gripped William's collar on either side of his neck. He looked into his eyes, and then looked over to Lacy. He pointed to her, and she patted the couch cushion for William to jump up next to her. He did, and he was a super cuddly dog, so he half laid in her lap and leaned against her side as he sat there and looked at Mitch.

Wait till you hear the doorbell, he told Lacy. *If he doesn't alert within two seconds, he's failed. He should come over to the door as part of the alert. He should alert you with a physical touch, and then immediately go to the door.*

She nodded, and Mitch turned to leave the house. He gave her a couple of seconds, and then reached up and tapped the doorbell. He assumed it worked, and several seconds later, Lacy pulled open the door.

He didn't alert, she said.

He didn't? Mitch asked, and he looked down at William. *He's standing right there.*

He just ran straight for the door, Lacy said. *But he didn't alert first. I think he's—*

Let's try again, Mitch said, and he pushed William back toward Lacy and reached to bring the door closed between them. Then he pressed the doorbell again.

This time, Lacy yanked open the door, her expression broadcasting her anger. *You didn't even wait for us to take one step away. He's standing right here next to the door. How is he supposed to run toward it?*

Move away from the door then, Mitch said, and he stood outside in the heat as Lacy turned around and stalked away from the door. William looked at her, and then Mitch, clearly confused about where he should be

He pointed to Lacy once, twice, and three times, and William trotted over to her. He sat practically on her feet, and Mitch closed the door again. He took a deep breath, paused for longer, and pressed the doorbell, sending up a prayer that his dog would do what he had been trained to do.

Of course, Mitch had trained him with a whistle and a hand signal, and a deaf person would not be able to hear the doorbell. They relied on *their dog* to know when something happened and to alert them of it.

Lacy once again pulled open the door. *He alerted this time, but he didn't go toward the door.*

So he knows how to do both, Mitch said. *But he's not doing them together.*

I don't think he's ready for this, Lacy said.

Irritation drove through him. *I know what my dog is ready for.*

Do you? she asked.

It's a good system, he said. *It's just a matter of consistency and repetition.*

He whined *when he alerted me,* she said, her signs getting larger. *And then he just sat there staring at me. That doesn't tell me where I'm supposed to look if I can't hear where the noise came from.*

He glared at her. *Let's just try again,* he said.

Fine. Lacy's signing had gotten a little sharper too, and she turned her back on him and walked away again. Mitch caught sight of her turning toward him and cocking her hip out in challenge just before the door swung closed.

He breathed. Paused. Pressed the doorbell.

Nothing happened. No one came. He waited and waited and waited some more, and finally, he opened the door and peered inside.

He found Lacy only a step or two away from where she'd been, pointing toward the door and talking to the dog. He waved his hands and rushed toward her. *You don't talk to him.*

She didn't see all of his signs, and when he got there, he stepped in front of her, boxing her away from William.

He's not ready for this, he thought. He pointed the dog into the kitchen, and the golden retriever turned and went, his tail low.

He turned back to Lacy. *You don't talk to him. A deaf person might not be able to talk to him. I can't talk to him.*

I know that, she said. *I told you he wasn't ready. You're not listening to me. You're not in here. You don't see what he's doing and not doing, and you don't believe me when I tell you.*

Whoa, now. I believe you, he said, searching her face for the root of this problem—and he didn't think it was the dog.

I'm trying to help you, but you're so focused on doing it your way that you're ignoring everything, including me.

I just sent him away, Mitch said, gesturing toward the kitchen afterward. *What do you want me to say? You're right? Fine. You're right. He's not ready. We tried* three *times for crying out loud.*

Do not yell at me, Lacy said, ice in her expression. *I'm doing* exactly *what you told me to do, and I'm giving you the information you need, and you didn't listen.*

She was yelling by the time she finished, and she stepped past him and toward the hallway that led to the stairs.

He growled, knowing he was far too frustrated to keep talking to her, but he couldn't let her just walk away either. She didn't like that, and Mitch rolled his eyes as he turned to follow her. He grabbed her elbow just at the bottom of the steps and said, *Wait, wait, wait.*

She went up two steps and now that she stood eye level with him, she glared even harder. *I'm going to take a break,* she said. *So that I can figure out what to do and decide what I really want.*

What does that mean? he asked, his heartbeat suddenly thumping hard against his ribs.

I don't want to talk to you right now. That's what it means.

With that, she turned and marched up the steps, and it wasn't like Mitch could call after her that he was sorry, though the moment she disappeared around the corner, he was deeply sorry.

And increasingly annoyed with himself that he'd let his temper get away from him—again.

Chapter Thirty-Seven

Brandon pulled up to Duke and Arizona's house, knowing exactly how dinner would go. Arizona worked here on the ranch with Duke part-time, as well as on her family ranch part-time. Duke, Dawson, and Brandon, as well as all four of Duke and Arizona's kids, worked the ranch, especially in the summer.

School didn't start for another two weeks, and Duke was putting all of his kids through the wringer to get as much done before he lost a lot of their labor.

They'd started to build a two-bedroom, two-bath cabin across the road for Shiloh and April to live in. Neither one of the girls had left the ranch to go to college, and neither one wanted to. They'd be moving into that cabin, and Dwayne, their oldest son, was moving in with Brandon. They had one more boy still at home—Dallas—who had three more years of high school left, and then Hidden Hills really would be a family ranch, as they all stuck around to work it.

Brandon sighed heavily as he got out of his truck and moved to the back of it to get out his blue heeler. He'd missed Dawson's dog when he'd married Caroline and they'd started their life together, and his orange tabby cat, who wouldn't even walk on grass, simply wasn't enough for Brandon.

He'd had Beacon for a couple of years now, and he followed Brandon up the walk to the big house that Duke and Arizona lived in.

He wouldn't come in the house, but he lay down in the shade and panted while Brandon knocked on the door and then walked in. His suspicion that Arizona had come back to the house to cook dinner came true when he smelled something meaty and rich floating on the air.

"Do *not* tell me you made stew," he said. "It's the middle of August, for crying out loud."

He found his brother's wife standing in the kitchen, and Arizona wasn't that much older than him. Maybe fifteen or sixteen years at the most, but she smiled at him with all the kindness and warmth of a mother.

"There you are," she said. "And yes, I made stew." She gave him some of her redheaded attitude and then drew him into a hug. "You won't get bison stew like this if you leave the ranch."

"I don't even like bison stew," Brandon said as he stepped back.

"Oh, you're such a liar." Arizona swatted at his chest.

"It's your favorite food, and you don't even know how to make it."

"I have my mother's recipe," he shot back.

"Are you two arguing already?" Duke asked as he came down the hall, tucking in his shirt. He'd clearly come off the ranch early as well, as he'd already showered. "Hey, brother." He grabbed onto Brandon and hauled him in for a hug as well.

"No kids tonight?" Brandon asked.

"We gave 'em a bunch of money and told 'em to go to town," Arizona said with a grin. "They're getting dinner and going to a movie."

"So you can stage an intervention with me." He wasn't asking, though he did raise his eyebrows as a punctuation mark.

"It's not an intervention," Duke said. "You knew about it."

"You can totally have an intervention if someone knows about it," Arizona said.

"Can you?" Brandon asked. "Because usually it's a bunch of friends and family getting together to confront someone about something that they might be doing to harm themselves, and that person usually doesn't know about it."

"Dawson said you've got a job down in Boulder Creek," Duke said, ignoring him completely.

"Yeah," he said. "There's a bunch of farms down there, and they need some people for a couple of weeks to help with a controlled burn, and I got the job."

"You've got a job here," Duke said. "There's a ton of work at Hidden Hills right now."

"And always," Arizona said.

"I just don't think Hidden Hills is for me," Brandon said, and he couldn't quite articulate why he felt like that. He only *knew* that his future did not live on this land. "You guys don't really need me here."

"We absolutely need you here," Duke said. "If you leave, then I have to hire someone else. You work full-time, brother." He turned away from the sink and leaned into the counter that housed it. "I don't want to pay someone else to work my land. I want you to do it."

Brandon rolled his neck, trying to find a way out of this situation. "You've got your boys now," he said. "Dwayne's not in school anymore. He replaces me."

Duke's jaw tightened, and he looked over to Arizona, because Brandon's argument held water, and a lot of it.

"Are you going to buy your own place?" Arizona asked.

"I can't afford to do that," Brandon said. "I mean, I love living here, but I don't really have any skills to get another job and save money, and you guys have always provided a good living for me—for real. I'm not ungrateful. I'm really not."

"No one's saying you are," Duke growled.

"Well, you're acting like I committed a crime," Brandon said. "I know my future isn't here, Duke, and I don't know where it is, but I'm gonna go wherever the work is and pray for the best."

Arizona stood near the fridge, frowning at him as well.

She turned toward her husband, and they both softened at the same time. "We're not happy about you leaving," she said. She moved toward him and ran her hand up the outside of his arm. "Because you've been so invaluable to us. You're family, and we love you." She moved her hand to cover her heart. "It makes me hurt that you don't feel like you belong here."

"It's nothing to do with you." Brandon swallowed hard. "It's just—I'm almost thirty-six. I'm not married. I don't want to live with my eighteen-year-old nephew, although Dwayne's great; he's awesome. I love him. I don't...."

He blew out his breath, because he simply felt like he'd picked up a shovel and started digging his own grave. "I've been feeling like this for a long time," he said. "About a year. And it's confirmed to me more and more that there's some-where else for me, and I don't know where it is, and I might have to work really hard to find it."

"God will guide you," Arizona said.

It took every ounce of willpower inside Brandon's body not to roll his eyes. He glanced over to Duke, who had once done some pretty bad things in his life, lost his faith, and left town. Brandon hadn't done anything like steal a bunch of money from the neighboring ranch, but he still felt completely lost and like God didn't hear him and certainly wouldn't lead him where he needed to go.

"I used to believe all that," he finally said, ducking his head to hide his face behind his cowboy hat. "But I've been out with so many women that I'm not sure I believe that God will put me where I need to be."

He shrugged one shoulder and glanced at his sister-in-law. "I'm just working around town for a while, odd jobs here and there."

"So you'll be down in Boulder Creek for the first two weeks of September?" she asked.

"Yes," he said. "And during the next couple of weeks, I'll be looking for something after that."

"So you're just going to move from job to job to job?" Duke asked, a measure of disgust in his voice. "This doesn't sound like a life, brother."

"It's better than working as a third-string cowboy on a dead-end ranch."

Arizona sucked in a breath, and Brandon shook his head. "That's how it is for me, you guys, and it's nothing to do with you. It's nothing to do with Dawson. I know you own this place, Duke, and I know it will go to him when you're ready to retire. All of that is fine with me—one hundred percent—but you have to understand where I'm coming from too, and I'm third string."

"It has to go to someone after Dawson," Arizona said, her voice pitching up.

Brandon zeroed in on her, "Yeah, and that person will be Shiloh or April or Dwayne. It won't be me, because I'm only two years younger than Dawson, and you think that I'm gonna outwork him?" He gave a mirthless laugh. "Please. Everyone knows I'm the play-baby of the family, and I just need to find something else to do with my life."

A long pause filled the kitchen, and then Duke opened a cupboard and took out some plates. He set them on the counter and returned to get bowls. "Maybe you could go to school."

Brandon met his eyes and shook his head. "I'm no good at school, brother." Brandon had started being really honest with himself this year, and it sounded a bit harsh when spoken out loud.

But it was the truth nonetheless.

"What did you do after you left the ranch?"

Duke's expression darkened, and now he used his cowboy hat to hide his face. "I wandered," he said. "Moving from job to job, city to city." He looked up, a fierce determination in his eyes. "That's how I know it's no life to live."

"Well, I'm not moving city to city," Brandon said. "I'm looking for work around here, and there are plenty of ranches who need cowboys like me."

"I just don't get why it can't be ours," Duke said.

"I don't either," Brandon said, throwing his arms up. "I honestly don't. I'm just trying to follow my gut here."

Arizona nudged him over to the table and said, "Sit. Let's eat."

She brought over the pot of stew, while Duke put down a cutting board with a round of bread and a serrated knife. They moved around Brandon, not speaking as they populated the table with food. A few minutes later, they joined him, and Duke reached over and clapped him on the shoulder.

"I just don't want you to go, and I'm hoping that you'll know how much we love you and need you here at Hidden Hills. And that you can always come back. One text." He held up one finger, his eyes blazing and his voice tight, tight, tight.

"*One text*, and you come back."

Brandon's emotions wavered, and he couldn't get his voice to work, so he simply nodded. Arizona wiped her eyes, and honestly, Brandon felt like doing the same. He'd be here at the ranch for another couple of weeks, and then he'd be working for a conglomerate of ranches who were doing a controlled burn in a small town about an hour southeast of here.

And after that...Brandon really didn't know, and he hoped something else would come up before then, so he didn't have to come back to Hidden Hills with his tail tucked between his legs.

Chapter Thirty-Eight

"Oh, they're here," Finn's momma said, and he abandoned his phone immediately.

He left it sitting on the couch with Edith and Brielle, and said, "Here we go."

"You're going to rush out there with everyone?" Edith called after him, and Finn reached for his cowboy hat and stuffed it on his head.

"Yep," he called out over his shoulder as he followed his parents out the door.

He'd seen many family parties and whole ranch luncheons served from this deck and on the grass down below—and Tyson Greene had been a part of all of them.

"I texted Libby," Daddy said as a big luxury SUV came to a stop in the driveway.

"Oh, I hope the trip was okay," Momma fretted, and

Finn felt her love and compassion for their friends deep in his soul.

"Finn," Libby called, and he hung back to wait for his sister as she came in off the ranch.

"Rusty's coming over from the stable," she said. She carried their baby, Nora, in a sling against her chest, and Finn found his little niece asleep.

"Uncle Pete and Paul and two of the counselors are coming over from Courage Reins," she said. "And Aunt Chelsea and Henry are bringing over the food now, so it'll be a big homecoming."

Finn grinned at her, and they faced the SUV and watched as all the doors opened.

Ethan got out of the driver's seat with his wife, Brynn, emerging from the passenger door. No one got out of the back passenger door, and someone Finn couldn't see joined Ethan on his side of the vehicle—probably Carolina, Tyson's older sister.

She'd left the ranch and gotten a degree in cyber security and now worked at a firm in Austin. Sure enough, the blonde-haired woman came around the back of the SUV with her father, and Brynn eased into the space of the open back passenger door.

Tyson, who'd inherited more of his daddy's darker features, took a painstakingly long time to get out of the car, and his mother balanced his walker in front of him, and then gave him a crutch as well.

He'd broken his left leg in four places and was still unable to put any weight on it whatsoever. He hobbled forward, and even from several yards away, Finn could see the angry red marks up his arm and neck and the way his left ear seemed a little bit lower than his right. The whole left side of his body seemed to sag as if he couldn't use it at all, and Finn reminded himself that he had been paralyzed for a while.

A lot of that feeling had returned, and the doctors had said that Tyson would most likely make a full recovery with possibly a limp, and of course, the hearing loss as the only long-lasting injury.

Ty smiled at Momma, who leaned in and brushed her lips across his cheek. She started talking as she turned to go back to the house. Brynn and Carolina stepped in line with her, and Finn could only marvel at his mother as she went by, rattling off all of the things that she had stocked the basement with for Ty's triumphant return.

Ethan and Brynn would be living there with him, and with no stairs to navigate and a full kitchen, three bedrooms, and two baths, they should be comfortable enough. Daddy finished shaking Ty's hand, and he looked over to Libby and Finn. In a miraculous gesture, he smiled, and that got Finn to move forward.

"Hey, brother," he said, hoping to treat Ty as normally as possible. "Long trip?"

"I never want to get in a car again," Ty said.

Finn shook his hand. "Well, I'm real glad you made it."

"Me too," Libby said. "Oh, it's so good to see you, Ty. We've all been so worried about you." She knew how to say all the right things too, and she turned and walked slowly with Ty and his daddy toward the house.

"Ethan," Finn said. "Should I get some stuff out of the car?"

"Yeah, all of it needs to be brought in." Ethan sounded tired and only managed to flash Finn a half smile before he turned back to his son.

Finn moved to the back of the SUV and opened it. He found all the third-row seats down, and the vehicle packed to the top with suitcases, boxes, and bags. Exhaustion pulled through him too, but he reached for the first bag and set it on the ground beside him.

"They made it," Uncle Pete said, drawing Finn's attention. He, Paul, and Henry had just arrived, and relief filled Finn.

"They just got here," he said.

"Yeah, we saw him walking in," Henry said. "I gotta say, he looks pretty good."

"He can't use that left leg at all," Paul said. "What are you talking about?"

"He's upright," Henry said. "His lungs work."

"They need all this taken in," Finn said before the brothers could really get arguing. "I'm sure Brynn will tell us where it goes."

Finn picked up another suitcase and started toward the house. He had no idea why some people had to go through such physical turmoil. His own daddy had been in a tank accident during his time in the Army and still walked with a limp, an ever-present reminder of the pain and suffering he'd been through.

Finn had served in the Army, as did countless others, and he'd come home unscathed. Plenty of men and women rode in the rodeo and didn't have to be paralyzed on their left side, or break their leg in four places, or lose the hearing in their left ear.

So why did Tyson have to suffer that? Couldn't God have protected him?

Finn didn't understand the complexity of the world or how life sure seemed to go well for some people and totally not for others. Whenever his mind moved into this spin, he reminded himself that he had a loving Heavenly Father and that all things combined together for his good.

He moved in and out of the basement, carrying in bags and boxes. He'd just set one down in Ty's room when the man came out of the bathroom.

"Heard you got your own place," he said.

"Yeah," Finn said. "It's about thirty minutes on horse-back, but it borders Three Rivers. It's pretty great." He stood out of the way so Ty could shuffle into his bedroom. He groaned as he got himself in bed, and Finn watched as he tried to get the pillows in a pile so that he could put his leg up.

"I can help." He moved over to do that, catching the way Ty's face turned a ruddy red and he looked away.

"Henry said you're doing great," Finn said.

"Henry doesn't know anything," Ty barked the words

and glared at Finn. "I'm completely useless, and I'm going to be like this for a long time."

"Nothing is completely useless," Finn said easily, adopting some of his mother's chattiness. "Unless you're talking about mushrooms, then yes."

Ty blinked at him, and then he started to laugh.

Ethan entered with a duffel bag, which he sat on the floor near the door. "What's going on in here?"

"Finn's just being funny," Ty said.

Not on purpose, though Finn *had* hoped that he could raise Tyson's spirits with a joke about fungi.

"Your mother's getting the kitchen unpacked," he said. "I'll help you in here."

"You mean you'll do it," Tyson said. "It's not like I can do anything, so you can't *help*."

Ethan stared at his son with a hard look in his eye. "Yeah, that's what I mean. Finn and I are going to do it."

Finn swallowed because he didn't want to be in the middle of this. He turned away and opened the closet, where he found a plethora of empty hangers waiting for clothes.

"How's Dusty feeling?" Ethan asked as he handed Finn a shirt.

"He's doing lots better now. Thanks," Finn said. "We had to take him to the doctor and get a nebulizer, but they think the worst of it has passed."

"That's great," he said. "I'm glad."

Finn nodded, trying to find something that he could ask

Ethan. "My daddy said you might want someone to take your dogs full-time."

"Yeah," Ethan said.

"I know we could do it," Finn said. He took another shirt from Ethan and threaded the hanger through the neck hole. "We've got a whole farm of animals, and my boys take good care of our dogs. Two more would be nothing."

"I can't ask you to do that."

"Of course you can," Ty said. "Tanner can't keep taking care of him. You might as well give them to Finn."

"Oh, no, you don't have to *give* them to me," Finn said, shooting a look over to Ty. "We'll just keep them until you're ready for them again."

Ty sighed and closed his eyes, and Finn met Ethan's. He said nothing, for which Finn was eternally grateful, because he wouldn't want someone to talk about him as he lay in a bed either. But Finn understood Ty was simply suffering mentally and emotionally as well as physically.

"I know Garth's always looking for a good dog too," Finn said. "It's up to you. Just trying to be helpful."

"I know," Ethan said. "And we're real grateful. I'll talk to Tanner and see if he can bring them out to you."

"I can text him too," Finn said. "I'm pretty sure I have his number."

Ethan nodded, and they proceeded to unpack Tyson's clothes while he pretended to be asleep. When they finished there, Finn found the basement apartment had been put together by Momma, Brynn, and Libby, and he was no longer needed.

With heavy feet and a heavier heart, he went upstairs to get his wife and kids. He sighed as he sank down onto the couch beside Edith and lay his head against her chest.

"He is hurting," he said. "And it makes me hurt."

"Oh, I'm sorry, baby," Edith said as she combed her fingers through his hair. She lifted his phone. "Tanner texted you something about when he can drop off two dogs."

Finn lifted his head and looked at his wife, finding that her accusatory stare made him smile. "Yeah," he said. "Surprise. We're getting two new dogs."

"Two new dogs!" Theo yelled, somehow hearing that when he didn't hear anything else. "Two new dogs, two new dogs," he started to cheer and chant, and Edith raised her eyebrows.

"What's two more dogs at our zoo?" Finn asked. "You're not really upset about this, are you?"

"Can I get another dachshund?" she asked.

Finn simply tipped his head back and laughed.

Chapter Thirty-Nine

This will be my last journal entry. Lacy read in the journal she'd found from her previous marriage to Landon, her previous life.

He doesn't like me writing in the journal, though I don't think I'm saying anything bad, but I respect him. And I don't want to have something like writing in a journal be a source of contention between us.

It's been a difficult couple of weeks as I've been studying for my state exam, and Jacob hasn't been able to get the help he needs at the doctor. We've all been praying for extra help, and I do feel more peaceful and like I'm in the Master's hands. And I suppose I can't ask for more than that.

I don't know if I'll write in this journal again, but if I do, I'll write a detailed update of everything that has happened since.

Lacy looked up from the journal and shook her head as

tears started to press into her eyes. There was no way she could ever write enough journal entries to say what had happened in the past three and a half years, and she didn't even want to.

The person who had written that journal entry was someone else, though she recognized her handwriting.

She closed the journal and set it aside, a fleeting thought in her mind that she should get rid of it. What did she need it for?

She couldn't quite make herself do it, and instead, she reached for the new purple, leather-bound book she'd received over the weekend.

Despite the tension between them, Lacy and Mitch had had a great moving weekend for their students. She'd attended church on Sunday alone, and she opened the journal that she'd started that day.

I went to church again today, she read. *This time alone. Mitch and I aren't talking much past what we need to for work, and I suddenly find myself very lonely again, isolated on the third floor and eating out of my mini fridge when I haven't done that all summer.*

Pastor Knowlton spoke about learning to love yourself despite your imperfections. It was exactly what I needed to hear.

I know Mitch is working hard with the dogs and with the academy. He's always quick to apologize and make things right. For the past few days, I've been questioning whether I should stay here at Signs for Success.

It's open now, and he can find someone else to do what I

do. The problem is I love it here. I love Three Rivers. I'm glad that I get to work with my brother. I love our faculty members and our students, and what scares me the most is that I think I'm in love with Mitch too.

We had one little fight about his dog training, and I know it won't be our last if I stay with him.

Pastor Knowlton suggested we close our eyes and picture Christ—however we see Him—and then make a list of things in our life that we're really good at, things that we could improve, and things we need to stop doing altogether.

Lacy looked up and out the window. It overlooked the side of the house, and if she stood, she could look to the right and see the academy with its green lawn extending behind it. If she looked left and used her imagination, she could get to the pond in the corner of the property. Right now, she just took in the blue sky with the gently waving trees in the distance.

She closed her eyes and replaced the picture of this perfect midsummer day with Jesus Christ. Her mind always went to Him holding a lamb, a piece of framed art that had been in the church where she'd grown up.

Christ didn't look at the viewer, but instead, His loving attention was down on the lamb as He cradled it in His arms, protecting it from anything bad that might happen. As a child, Lacy had imagined herself as the lamb, safe and comforted and loved in the arms of Christ.

She opened her eyes and looked down at her journal again, to the list she'd made. She'd written that she was a very good interpreter and an ally to the Deaf Community.

She was extremely good at organizing things, paying attention to details, and making others feel welcome.

She'd like to improve her relationships with her parents, as well as find a way to balance work and personal life better. She couldn't keep working twelve hours a day.

She wanted to put God first, and she'd made a sub-list for that one that included reading her scriptures daily—even if it was only one verse—attending church as often as she could, and continue listening to her podcast.

Below that, the next item on Lacy's list was getting to know more of Mitch's family.

She paused there, because she'd written this two days ago, on a day when she hadn't even spoken to Mitch. Not even one word. That line alone told her that she didn't want to leave Signs for Success, that she wasn't going to run away because she and Mitch had disagreed over something simple.

A sob choked in her chest. Lacy didn't need to keep reading her journal. She'd started on Sunday and gone through the things the pastor had asked her to. The next entry was actually backdated to move-in weekend, which had gone extremely well.

Every faculty member had been present and full of charm and a welcoming spirit. All of their seventy-one residents now lived on site, and Lacy absolutely couldn't wait to get to know them all better. That too spoke of her desire to stay and not let something simple come between her and Mitch.

Her advanced sign language classes were on Wednesdays and Saturdays, but Mitch's beginning course ran Tues-days and Thursdays.

She flipped the page and picked up her pen. *Well, the second day of classes has begun,* she wrote. *In fact, it's almost over. Our celebrations hotline is a big success, and we've had half a dozen texts today from students talking about the first day of their classes on this, our first B day at the academy.*

I can't wait for Friday at eleven o'clock, when we'll get to read some of those celebrations and celebrate as a unit our first week here at Signs for Success.

I'm also excited to report that I have decided to stay. Not only that, as soon as I'm done writing here, I'm going to go meet Mitch after his first beginning sign language class and do anything I can to make things right with him.

Her hands started to shake, but she pressed on. *I'm in love with him, and I want to build a life and a family and a legacy with him. I know he's stubborn, but so am I, and some-times that's a really good quality in a person.*

They get things done, and they have passion for the things they believe in. I can't stand not being able to talk to him and ask him about his first day of class, because I know he's been nervous about it.

She smiled. Just the way he'd been trying to get out of it for the past couple of months had told her that.

Hopefully, I'll be able to report tomorrow of a blissful makeup session, where Mitch takes me and all the dogs out to the pond and confesses that he loves me too, and that we have a shared desire to work together, build this place, have chil-dren, and live happily ever after.

Lacy lifted her pen, because she had just written down her biggest dream of all time: To live happily ever after with her cowboy Prince Charming, and all of his dogs.

She wanted that so badly that tears filled her eyes. She let them track down her face for just a moment. Then her stomach growled, and she glanced at the clock, seeing that Mitch's class would end in only two minutes. She quickly slapped the journal closed and stood from the desk.

She hurried to change into something just a little bit cuter and more professional than a t-shirt with an ice cream cone on the front of it. She tried to be presentable and professional whenever she left the house, as she would see students and faculty members, and they often asked her questions and still needed help.

She slipped on a pair of sandals and hurried downstairs. The house sat in silence, another indicator that Mitch wasn't there, and she hurried across the front lawn to the sidewalk of the academy.

He'd been assigned their main theatre for his class, as it had the highest enrollment. They required all of their academy members to take beginning sign language at least once a week, though Mitch offered it twice.

Lacy wanted to do assessments with each of them, so she could place them in higher classes and understand where they were in their language development, so they could continue to provide for their needs.

The theatre held three hundred people, the maximum capacity of the academy. Mitch had planned to include community classes to be held in the hall as well.

Lacy knew something was wrong when she rounded the corner and found the theatre doors open. She didn't see anyone coming out or going in, and it seemed like class had already ended.

"And some time ago too," she muttered to herself. She felt certain she would have seen students leaving otherwise, or mingling in groups talking after class. She continued on anyway and went right into the main hall.

It sat empty.

Frustrated, she blew her breath out and wiped her hand through her hair, her mind racing as to where Mitch might be right now. He had an office at the house, as well as one here in the administration building, and she headed that way.

The door was locked, the window dark.

"Where is he?" she asked herself.

She went back to the house, because she'd finished work for the day and she didn't want to get stuck over here in conversations, even if she would enjoy them. Instead of going inside, she walked down the side of the house to the backyard, where she half expected to see Mitch out in the training enclosure with Sunshine, Maven, and William.

He was not there.

None of the dogs were there.

Great, she thought. *He's probably out with them in the wilderness.*

Mitch could use some personal and work balance as well, but Lacy wasn't going to tell him that. Instead, she returned to the house, praying that he would be there, radio blasting, making dinner.

He was not.

He loved those dogs like children, and he let them sleep with him sometimes, so Lacy paused on the landing outside his door and reached for the doorbell. She pressed it once and then again, and listened to the bell ring throughout the apartment. She didn't expect to hear any barking, though Sunshine sometimes still alerted with her voice.

She waited, the anticipation inside her building and building and building. She didn't know where to go next, and she didn't want to text him and say, *Hey, where are you?*

She wanted to *see* him. She wanted to *touch* him. She wanted him to crowd into her personal space and cling to her the way he did that made her feel so needed, and necessary, and loved.

He didn't answer the door, and with disappointment mingling with heartbreak, Lacy turned and headed back to her third-floor apartment. He'd return sooner or later, and since Mitch certainly wasn't a quiet man, Lacy would hear him when he did.

"Please give me enough courage to go down and see him when he gets home," she prayed, because she felt like she'd used up every ounce of bravery she had.

And Mitch was MIA—which meant her heart felt like it had been hollowed out of her body as well.

Chapter Forty

Mitch stood in front of the floral case at Wilde & Organic, searching for the flowers that Lacy loved best. He couldn't go through another restless night without making things right between them.

They'd made it through the move-in and their first two days of class, which meant all of their students had had all of their classes at least once, except for Advanced Sign Language, which Lacy would do tomorrow night and then Saturday morning.

Mitch wanted to sit in on her class, but he didn't want her to be nervous or upset with him. He hadn't seen her in the kitchen once since their argument on Thursday afternoon, and all of their other interactions had been breezy and professional—right back to the way they'd been when he'd asked her out the first time and she'd rejected him.

His heart ached and his limbs felt so heavy attached to

his body. Finally, his eyes landed on a tulip bouquet, and a new measure of peace entered his bloodstream. He reached for the flowers and found the vase to be solid and textured against his palm. Bright yellow, pink, white, and purple tulips filled the vase, along with some greenery, and while Mitch found them to be the most common flower that would grow anywhere, Lacy adored them.

She'd mentioned it once, as they lay in the shade out by the pond, that they were just "so happy" and they always made her smile. He hoped they would tonight as well.

He'd dismissed his class a half-hour early, his heart just not in it, and their introduction to the class and to each other done. He had more he could teach, as Mitch had taught many sign language classes in his life, but he'd simply wanted to get all of Lacy's favorite things and go up to the third floor and apologize.

He'd beg if he had to, and he'd been praying for five solid days that God would make Lacy's heart soft and forgiving, and that He wouldn't take her from him.

Please, God, he thought again as he moved over to the bakery. He found the rolled chocolate cake filled with vanilla-chocolate-chip frosting that he'd bought accidentally once—and which Lacy had loved.

He walked the perimeter of the store, picking up the prepared meals that she liked and the sunflower crunch salad and even a blanket and then a white noise machine from the specialty aisle.

She could run that at night so he wouldn't wake her when he got up too early and slammed pots and pans around the kitchen. *Or maybe you could just not do that,* he told himself.

He felt like this summer had changed him from the blunt, grumpy cowboy to a more compassionate, more patient academy headmaster. He knew that transformation had come by being Lacy's boyfriend and nothing more, and while they hadn't officially broken up, he certainly didn't feel like they were together.

He checked out, loaded everything into the truck, and moved to the back of it to steal some comfort from his dogs. They all came to greet him, and Sunshine licked his face and neck. He chuckled and didn't correct her, because while he believed Sunshine had the potential to be a hearing dog, he had worked with enough of them now to know that it would simply take him too long and too much effort to get her there.

He hadn't told Lacy yet, because he didn't want to get rid of Sunshine. He wanted her to be their family pet, while he continued to work with William and Maven as hearing dogs.

Mitch had a long list of things he needed to talk to Lacy about, because he also thought William would be perfect for Jacob, and he wanted to start working with Jacob and William together. Then the dog could learn Jacob's name and alert to it. He also wanted someone besides him to start learning how to train the hearing dogs, as that was a vital part of his academy that he absolutely would not compromise on—education for the Deaf and Hard of Hearing, community resources for everyone, and hearing dogs.

Mitch told his dogs to sit down with the required hand signal, and they did. He got behind the wheel of the truck and set his sights back on Signs for Success on the west side of Three Rivers. His heartbeat picked up the pace the moment he turned onto the gravel lane.

He'd prayed and prayed for a smooth opening, and God, in all His mercy, had granted it to him. He felt selfish as he looked at the gleaming windows of the house where he lived and asked for more.

I don't need her to hear me, he prayed. *I just need her to be heard, and I need her to understand that I listen to her. I do value her voice. I want her and need her at the academy, but more importantly, I want her and need her in my life, as my family. I want her and need her in that house as it becomes ours.*

He wanted to move all of the business out of the house and over to the education building, where it belonged. He wanted to remove the doors from the second- and third-floor apartments and just have a house with Lacy—as her husband and partner, her best friend, her lover.

He swallowed as he pulled into the driveway and parked next to her SUV. He let the dogs down and then gathered the flowers and the groceries from the back of the truck. He got everything inside in one trip, though his muscles strained against the weight of a week's worth of food, a heavy vase of flowers, and the blanket and white noise machine.

Still, he managed to get it all up to the third floor, and he started unbagging it, setting out the box with the white noise machine, as well as a sleep mask and a box of earplugs.

He laid out the furry blanket and put the flowers in front of it. The groceries he stacked on the other side, and he wadded up the plastic bags and shoved them in his pocket. He looked around at all the things that he'd gotten and then looked at Lacy's closed door. He wanted to take an axe to it and kick down all of the walls that had been erected between them by his careless behavior.

Hey, he told himself. *Even if she doesn't take you back, at least you'll have done your best to make things right with her, and maybe you'll be able to sleep.*

His self-loathing had reached an all-time high on Sunday, and he'd gone to his parents at Shiloh Ridge and confessed everything to them.

Your daddy was like a bull in a china shop, his momma had assured him. *But he always apologized, and those words go so far, Mitch.*

I did apologize, Mitch had said.

Sometimes they don't hear it in the heat of the moment, Daddy had told him. *And you can't control her. You can only control yourself, so do everything you can to make it right, and then you'll have to see what she says.*

It was time to see what Lacy would say.

Mitch stepped forward to knock at the same time the door opened. Lacy carried a red suitcase in her hand, and Mitch's heartbeat accelerated at the same time it dropped to the soles of his boots.

His presence stopped her forward momentum, and

shock coursed across her face. She stepped back, her grip on the suitcase unwavering as she said, *Oh, I didn't know you were here*, with tight hand movements.

Mitch could not believe she was leaving. She hadn't texted him or said a single word. Desperation, combined with his anger, held him in place, his hands mute at his sides. He forgot all about everything that he'd purchased and brought to the third-floor landing until Lacy's gaze dropped to it and she looked around.

Their eyes met, and he asked, *Are you leaving?* his movement somewhat angry.

Lacy set down the suitcase. *What's all this?*

Are—you—leaving? Mitch asked again, giving more of a pointed punctuation with his hands. She couldn't leave, and Mitch drew in a deep breath, ready to do whatever it took to get her to unpack that suitcase and stay.

The problem was the irritation that ran through him. He'd be completely off script now, but he decided he didn't care.

Desperate times called for desperate measures—and Mitch was one desperate cowboy.

Chapter Forty-One

Lacy took in the joyfully smiling tulips and the soft, gray, fuzzy blanket. She noted that he'd gotten the chicken parmesan with stuffed shells, along with several other prepared meals, and her favorite salad. And that rolled chocolate cake she adored.

A box sat by the blanket, and she wasn't quite sure what that was. She couldn't hear much past the pounding of her heart, and she couldn't look away from Mitch as he started signing frantically.

You can't go, he said. *I know I said some stupid things and I acted kind of rashly. I apologize, and I will apologize again and again and again. Please don't go.*

He gestured wildly, his desperation coming out through his hands. *I dismissed my class early, and I went to the store and got everything I could think of that you love. I know it's stupid, because it's just a bunch of stuff from Wilde &*

Organic. We can go to the mall or to dinner, whatever you want.

He reached out and took the suitcase from her. *I just don't want you to leave.*

She tilted her head at him, wondering if he didn't want her to leave, because he needed her for Signs for Success, or because he wanted her as his wife.

I'm desperately in love with you, he said next, answering that silent question. *I haven't been able to sleep much for the past several days, but I know how I feel. You're everything I want in a partner, in a friend, and I think you'll make an amazing wife and mother.*

I want you to call me on my bad behavior when I upset you or when I'm being grumpy. I can't promise you that I won't act like that. I wish I could, but I can't.

He started to get a little bit out of control again, and Lacy shook her head and waved her hands to get him to stop.

I am not asking you to change who you are completely, she said.

I have been trying, he said, the expression on his face so serious and yet so hopeful.

I know you have. She stepped out of her apartment and moved right over to him. *Do you know what I did tonight?*

Mitch frowned at her, even as she put her hands against his chest. It felt so good to be touching him again, and she leaned into him, hoping he would put at least one arm around her. He didn't ask her to continue. He simply watched her and waited.

She hoped her hands would be calm and gentle as she spoke. *I got a new journal on Saturday*, she said. *I've been writing in it. It's like—* Her hands hovered in midair as she struggled to find the right words.

It's like a new beginning for me, she said. *A new life, a new book. New stories to experience and write down.* She smiled up at him, hoping he understood all she was trying to say. *I love writing in a journal.*

You've said that, he said.

At church on Sunday, Pastor Knowlton asked us to make a list of things we wanted to work on, things we needed to do to improve, and what we were already really good at. I did all of that, she said. *And it became abundantly clear to me that I belong here, not just at Signs for Success, but with you.*

His eyebrows went up, as Mitch was always so expressive.

I'm in love with you too, Lacy said. *And I spent some time this evening trying to find you, so that I could tell you*

You came to find me? he asked.

Your classroom was empty, she said. *No one came to the door. You weren't out in the dog enclosure, and your office was dark.* She looked down at the gifts he'd brought her. *You don't have to bring me stuff, you know.*

I felt stupid just showing up and saying, I'm sorry, he said. *I said it that day, and I texted it to you, and I just wanted you to* hear *it this time.*

She nodded, tears filling her eyes. *I hear you, Mitch. Did you hear me when I said I love you?*

A small smile tugged up the corners of his mouth. *Yeah, I heard you.*

Did you really? she teased, leaning in. *Because you haven't kissed me yet. You haven't wrapped me up in your strong cowboy arms.*

She took a breath as new electricity flowed through her the moment Mitch finally brought his arms around her, and a sense of belonging and warmth moved through Lacy in the most delicious way.

You—You're really good at showing *me how you feel, and I'm really good at telling you how I feel, and I want us to kind of meet in the middle.*

I love you, Lacy Hayes, he said. *And I was going to stomp into your apartment and unpack whatever's in that suitcase to make you stay. I would have offered you more money, and gotten down on my knees and begged, and promised you the world.*

Lacy smiled up at him. *You've already given me the world, Mitch, because you've given me your heart. You—*

I'm going to kiss you now, he said, and he moved his hand to brush her hair back off the side of her face. Tingles and sparks moved down her neck, and Lacy let her eyes drift closed. The anticipation of being held by and kissed by and loved by Mitchell Glover more than she could handle with her eyes open.

In true cowboy fashion, he took his sweet time lowering his mouth to meet hers, but when he kissed her, every other thought flew out of Lacy's mind. She simply wanted to be in this moment and not worry about writing it down for later, or riddling through how she felt.

She'd done that work, and she was in love with this good man, and she wanted to build her life with him here in Three Rivers at Signs for Success.

Mitch kissed her like he wanted all of those things too, and Lacy clung to every one of them.

A half-hour later, they sat on the back deck, her with a plate of chicken parmesan and cheesy stuffed shells, and him with meatloaf and mashed potatoes. Champ lay right at Mitch's side, with William beside him, and the other two dogs over by Lacy.

So you don't think you can train Sunshine as a hearing dog? she asked.

Mitch shook his head and took another bite of food.

She can be my dog then. Lacy grinned at him.

He raised his eyebrows and then rolled his eyes. *Sure, she can be your dog.* His hands spoke playfully, because they both knew Sunshine would be Mitch's dog forever and ever.

Lacy nudged him with her shoulder. *What else do we have to talk about?*

They'd been talking nonstop since she'd taken everything into her apartment, and then he'd brought the food downstairs to prepare it for dinner.

He glanced over to her and set down his fork. *I want to move anything business out of the house and over to the administration building. I have an office there now, and we have a conference room over there too.*

Lacy nodded as Mitch continued to speak. His hands moved faster the more excited he got about something, and she grinned as she tried to keep up.

I want to take down the doors on the second and third floor and make this house just a house—our house for me and you. I'm not super patient, though I'm working on it, but I want to get married fast, unless there's some reason that you don't want to. I mean, I haven't even met your parents. Maybe I should do that.

His thoughts seemed to be streaming out of his hands the moment he had them, and for some reason, that made Lacy giddy with happiness.

Oh, and I want William to be Jacob's hearing dog, he said. *I want him to start working with me to learn how to train the dogs, and I want to start training William to alert on Jacob's name.*

Mitch tilted his head to the side, his expression so earnest. *Do you think he'd want a hearing dog? Maybe he doesn't even want one.*

His hands finally dropped to the table, and Lacy reached over and covered them with both of hers.

Jacob loves this place as much as I do, Lacy said. *I think he'd be absolutely thrilled to get a hearing dog and to start learning how to train them.* Tears filled her eyes. *Thank you so much for including him.*

I love your brother, Mitch said. *He's a hard worker and a good man.*

Lacy nodded, because Jacob was both of those things—and she loved that Mitch had seen them.

What about the wedding? he asked. *Do you have some grand dreams of what you want?*

Lacy smiled, and she got up, abandoning her food, and went to sit on his lap. He grinned at her and said, *I love being close to you.* He pressed a kiss to her neck and then her jaw.

I know it's fast, but we know each other really well. We've lived together for almost two years. You're the love of my life, and I want you on the first floor in our new master bedroom, me and you.

Me and you, she said back.

She touched her lips to his and kissed him sweetly, softly, trying to decide how selfish she could be. As she pulled away, she realized she didn't want anything more than what God had already given her—this beautiful house, the gorgeous land, the academy...and Mitch.

We can get married anytime, she said. *As long as it's not in the spring.* She'd married Landon in the spring, and he'd died then too. She wanted her marriage to Mitch to be the most joyous thing of her life, and that meant it couldn't happen in the spring.

So...like, this weekend? Mitch asked, his lopsided smile coming to his face.

She pushed against his chest. *I need enough time to get my parents here and buy a dress.*

I can take care of everything else, Mitch said. *We can*

have tulips everywhere. We can get married right here at the academy, in front of the fountain.

Lacy nodded, because that sounded amazing. *And all the dogs can be your groomsmen,* she said. *And your mother will do the ceremony.*

Mitch nodded, suddenly serious. *I adore you,* he said. *Are you sure you can put up with me?*

She grinned at him and took his face in her hands. *I'm sure.*

Then she kissed him again, the electrifying union between them only the beginning of something absolutely amazing.

Chapter Forty-Two

M itch sat in the back row in the main theatre where he'd taught his beginning sign language class yesterday. Tonight, Lacy led the advanced ASL course, but Mitch had been totally engrossed in his phone for most of the lecture.

Class ends in fifteen minutes, he said. *Can I get a sound-off for who's here?*

He'd invited everyone with the last name of Glover, anyone from Seven Sons Ranch, Three Rivers Ranch, and the small ranch owners' group, to come to Signs for Success that evening.

Yes, he and Lacy had only been back together for about twenty-four hours now, but Mitch had spoken true when he'd told her he was impatient when it came to making her his.

He'd taken his dogs to the mall that morning for their

"training" to buy a diamond ring, and all four of them approved of the diamond he'd purchased.

He'd asked his aunts to buy every tulip in town, and Aunt Ida, Aunt Etta, Aunt Sammy, and Aunt Montana had taken him very seriously. The real champion had emerged in Aunt Dot, who owned a landscaping company and had called her flower supplier that morning. She'd gotten a *truckload* of tulips here from a warehouse in Amarillo.

We're here, his father said. *Me, Momma, Mel, and Chaz.*

Mitch's smile touched his mouth—and his heart. His siblings coming home from college mid-week was a big deal, and it meant a lot to him to have them there.

Out on the quad, Uncle Bear said. *All the Walkers are here, a bunch of people from Three Rivers Ranch, all the boys from Hidden Hills and Golden Hour.*

And the folks from the apple orchards, Aunt Sammy added.

Henry and Angel are on their way, Finn said. *They might be a few minutes late, and I'm sure you know how Henry feels about that.*

He'd added a smiley face with its tongue out, and Mitch almost started laughing. Henry would be irate, Mitch knew that. He really liked Henry, because he had a short fuse he was working to lengthen, the same as Mitch.

When he added horses to Signs for Success, he fully planned to have Henry and Angel come help him with them.

My parents are here with me, Jacob said. *My mother*

can't wait to meet you in person. He also included an emoji, but his was an extra-wide smiley face.

Mitch's heartbeat thumped a little harder in his chest, and he looked up to where Lacy demonstrated how different facial expressions could actually enhance or change the meaning of certain signs. His pulse settled down at the mere sight of her, and he let himself soften into the version of himself that didn't have to hold everything so tightly, who didn't have to be one-hundred-percent right and heard all the time, who could slow down and listen and hear another person's point of view.

He thanked God for bringing her to Three Rivers, to Signs for Success, to him.

He added to his gratitude the fact that everyone who loved her had literally dropped everything in their lives to be with them in the quad that evening.

Mitch couldn't comprehend all the things that people had juggled and rescheduled to be there with him and Lacy that night. He simply knew and recognized it was a lot, and he thanked the Lord Above for making it possible.

If her parents hadn't been able to make it, Mitch would've waited to propose until they could. But Jacob had called them, and he and Mitch had explained everything, and they'd immediately booked a flight to Amarillo. Jacob had gone to pick them up this afternoon.

Mitch had bought a lot of Lacy's favorite things yesterday, hoping to at least show her he was willing to make a gesture to keep her at his side. Tonight's proposal was more about showing her how loved she was—by more than just him. That she had become an integral part of so many lives here in Three Rivers, and that she didn't have to be lonely ever again.

Mitch could admit it was a nice reminder for him too. Texts continued to flow in, and when Lacy ended class a few minutes later, Mitch thanked the stars in heaven—and God—that a few students went down to the front to speak with her. That would delay her a bit, and Mitch could stall her even further. Hopefully, that would give Henry and Angel enough time to arrive, and he realized he hadn't heard anything about the catering either.

His phone vibrated again, and he couldn't stop the enormous smile from spreading across his face at the tulip display out on the quad. Mitch's surprise proposal wouldn't be much of a surprise, and he didn't care one whit. Aunt Etta stood beaming with the flowers, which his aunts and probably a whole bunch of his cousins had used to spell out the words "Marry Me."

He sent a thumbs-up to Jacob privately, who would text everyone at Signs for Success about an impromptu event happening on the quad and inviting them all to come to participate.

Food just got here, his momma said. *They're setting up the tents and tables on the grass across the street.*

Relief painted through Mitch, because Lacy's favorite restaurant required twenty-four-hour notice for meals serving more than one hundred. With everyone Mitch knew in town, plus all of his students and faculty, he needed to feed twice that many mouths. He'd gone by the restaurant the moment they'd opened that morning, shown them the diamond, offered to double their fee, and begged.

Thankfully, good people still existed in the world, and Lacy would have her gourmet meats with the raspberry barbecue sauce and all the best Texas sides.

They should be ready by the time the proposal is over, Momma added, and Mitch decided he'd have to catch up with all the texts later. He stood and shoved his phone in his back pocket. His dogs came with him as he went down the steps to the front of the theatre, the view from above so different from leading the class as the professor.

He waited near the first row while Lacy finished talking to the students, and then he grinned at her and swept his arms wide. *You did it*, he said. *Amazing class.*

You think so?

He took her into his arms and leaned down to kiss her. *Yes, it was amazing*, he said. He stepped back and ignored the way William nosed the back of his thigh. Yes, he knew his phone had vibrated. No, he wasn't going to look at it.

His pulse thundered through his body as he laced his fingers through Lacy's and tugged her toward the door. *Let's go sit on the fountain and reflect.*

She glanced over to the stack of folders on the counter there, and Mitch quickly said, *We can get them on the way back through.*

Lacy's office sat in the heart of this building, as she had quickly become the central figure of Signs for Success. Mitch took her up the steps and out to the arced foyer beyond the theatre. Only a few steps would have them outside, and Mitch swallowed hard as he went that way.

Whatever happens is what happens, he thought. *People, food, dogs, Lacy. It'll all be exactly as it should be.*

Dozens of people lingered on the benches and paved area leading to the fountain—Jacob's text had worked. Everyone grinned at him and Lacy with pure sunshine and stardust in their expressions, and Mitch gave their bright energy right back to them.

What's going on? Lacy asked with only a few steps remaining to the fountain. She looked over to Mitch, who nodded his cowboy hat to the left. He took her that way, knowing the moment she saw the non-student and totally-Glover crowd—and the tulips—that she'd stop. She did, and Mitch stepped away from her slightly and let go of her hand, so he could indicate her with both hands, as if she were a celebrity.

He grinned and grinned, so happy when Lacy brought her hands to her mouth and covered it, her surprise obvious and complete.

He looked back out to the quad and found every person applauding—in sign language.

Every—single—person held their hands up in the air, their fingers outstretched and shaking. Mitch's vision filled with the fluttering movement, a sea of waving hands.

It was a beautiful and unified expression of appreciation and support, each person contributing their own visual cheer to the collective celebration of this moment.

Before he could stop himself, tears spilled out of his

eyes. In that moment, he realized all of these people loved *him*. They'd come for *him*, though he'd arranged for them to be there for Lacy.

Lacy stepped in front of him, blocking his view of all the celebrating cowboys and students. *I love you so much,* she said. She wiped his tears, and pure humiliation flashed through him. There one moment and gone the next. He could be vulnerable in front of her, in front of everyone here.

I love you, he said. *I told you I wasn't patient when it came to being with you, and your parents could be here.*

My parents are here? Lacy turned around, and Mitch moved to her side. She turned toward him with joy emanating from her every pore.

I love you, he said again, facing her and turning her to look at him. Everyone in the quad could still see them, and Mitch suddenly needed to get all these words out.

I want us to live together in a whole new way. I see so many kids in our life, from those who come to the academy to get their education, to our own children, to puppies and kittens and whatever other kind of baby animal you want.

Lacy wore the most beautiful smile and wiped her eyes. Mitch caught movement out of the corner of his eye, and he turned to find his mother moving so she could translate for the crowd. One of Mitch's professors handed her a micro-phone, and he returned his focus to Lacy.

I got all your friends, and family, and flowers. Every-thing, so you'd know it's not about me buying you a white noise machine, but that you have so many people who love you right here in Three Rivers. We want you here, and I would literally die a miserable death without you.

He took both of her hands and beamed at her. He then turned the pair of them toward the huge tulip display and swept one hand toward it.

So will you marry me?

Mitch watched as all the Glovers raised their fist to their hearts, their family pledge of solidarity and support, a gesture filled with absolute love. Mitch made it back, and he looked over to Lacy, who wept openly.

She nodded and said, *Yes!* her hand practically flapping. *Yes, yes, yes, yes, yes.* She was still saying it when Mitch swept her into his arms and kissed her, this woman he'd fallen for in so many ways.

With so many people watching, he didn't take things too far, and he pulled away and said, *I love you,* just one more time. He wanted to tell her over and over, because it felt so amazing to say it and feel it at the same time.

And the best thing Lacy had ever said to him happened with enthusiastic movement of her hand matched with her mouth: "I love you too."

He slid the diamond on her finger, and together, they faced the crowd he'd gathered to the quad to witness his proposal. They all loved him and Lacy too, and Mitch could only press his lips to Lacy's temple as she held up her hand and flashed the diamond at his family, their students, and her parents.

* * *

Oh, my heck! Mitch is grumpy and blunt and impatient...in all the best ways! I hope you enjoyed seeing him and Lacy open their Deaf academy, as well as all the updates on the Glover Family! Oh, and I hope you loved your stay in Three Rivers!

I just love them. If you did too, **please leave a review on Amazon, Goodreads, BookBub, or my online Book Shop!**

And keep reading for the first two chapters of the next book in the series, THE COWBOY WHO BELIEVED AGAIN, featuring Brandon Rhinehart as he tries to find somewhere to belong...and it could be the last place he expects. **You can preorder it now by scanning the QR code below with your phone:**

Sneak Peek! The Cowboy Who Believed Again, Chapter One:

B randon Rhinehart walked into the cabin he'd once shared with his older brother—and whom he now shared with Dwayne.

"Howdy," he said as Dwayne tucked in his shirt and re-buckled his belt.

"I'm heading back out to the fields," Dwayne said with a straight face. "I just had to use the bathroom somethin' fierce."

Brandon grinned at him. "I'm not your daddy, my friend." He pulled open the fridge and got out a couple of cans of sparkling water. "I'd enjoy the air conditioning and cold water while you can."

"Are you done for the day?"

Brandon shook his head as he snapped open the first can of water. Sometimes he put energy packets in them to give them flavor, but today, he simply tipped the can back and started guzzling. Finally satiated, he slid the other can to Dwayne. "Nope. I'm just in for dinner, and then I'll be out to relieve you."

They'd been assigned opposite schedules for the harvest, as Brandon didn't like getting up early, and Dwayne couldn't sleep past five a.m.

"One more hour," Dwayne said, and he faced the front door with determination in his dark eyes. Then he swiped the water off the counter and took it with him while Brandon chuckled.

Dwayne had not lived outside of his childhood home for long, and he still struggled to do whatever he wanted as an adult. Brandon knew he wasn't the greatest influence on the young man, as he lived his life exactly how he wanted. He ate when he wanted to eat, drank what he wanted to drink, went to bed when he wanted, and got up when he wanted. He also had an extreme sense of duty, and he'd never had a problem taking an assignment.

Brandon had never had a problem getting a date. Or having friends. Or much of anything. He was easy-going and personable. He worked hard, and he loved Texas, his parents, his family, dogs, chickens, horses, and cats.

His happy-go-lucky life had taken a turn for the worse in the past couple of years, as Brandon's desire to meet someone he fell hard for and spent the rest of his life working to make happy grew, and grew, and grew. He wanted children, and a house he didn't share with another male family member, and land he could cultivate with his own hands.

"The land is out," he told himself as he pulled a fried chicken meal out of the freezer. "But you might be able to get the rest."

Of course, he'd gone on a female fast recently, choosing instead to order his groceries and household items online and picking them up from the safety of his pick-up truck. He'd stopped using TwoCents, as well as any dating apps, to meet women. He just needed to figure out where he should be, and then he could get back to dating.

With his hot fried chicken, gravy, and mashed potatoes, Brandon settled at the table with another can of sparkling water. This time, he slapped a packet of grape powder against the edge of the table, then ripped it open and poured it into the can. The resulting bubbling made him smile, and he picked up his fork to eat dinner.

Instead of scrolling apps for a date, Brandon had started looking at the temporary job boards for farms, ranches, and any other outdoor operations surrounding Three Rivers. He'd worked as far as Pampa, an hour straight south, and out at a one-man operation west of town that he'd used the west exit of the ranch to get to faster.

Everyone needed help at the harvest, but Brandon had committed to Duke and Arizona that he wouldn't go bring in someone else's crops. Harvesting was the hardest work a cowboy did, and Brandon had his fill of it here at the Rhine-hart Ranch just fine.

Since Brandon looked at these listings every day—sometimes multiple times each day—he recognized the jobs he'd seen before. Then his eyes caught on a new listing, and he put a bite of food in his mouth and lifted his phone closer to see it better.

Winterizing Help Needed.

He tapped to open the listing to see more details, wondering what would be required. His heartbeat started to pound when he saw this was a "minimum three-month position, with possible long-term work for the right fit."

Room and board included, and Brandon forgot completely about his microwavable meal. The listing said he'd have his own cabin to live in on the property, with his own garden space if he wanted it.

This is a homestead, the listing continued. *I can't pay you much, but I need help getting the animal pens shored up and repaired for winter, winterizing fields, cutting down trees for firewood, and possibly drilling a well.*

"No water," Brandon muttered to himself, because he could read between the lines.

I have chickens who produce plenty of free eggs, and a garden and greenhouse that produces vegetables year-round. I'm looking for someone who can help get more pastures and enclosures built, so I can add turkeys, goats, and cattle for milk and meat. My goal is to be completely dependent on the land, and anything we can raise and grow here is free for the person who can help me get my homestead to this point. Serious inquiries only, with the understanding the salary will be low.

A name and phone number sat at the bottom, but Brandon couldn't see it right now, as he wasn't logged in to the job board. He did that and found a female name sitting there: Lenore Sawyer.

He tapped on the phone number and his phone brought up the option to text or call. In this moment, the fact that Brandon would rather call than text reminded him of how he was closer to forty than thirty, and he lifted the phone to his ear as it started to ring.

The sun stayed up pretty late still, and Brandon could also get up earlier to make it to an interview should he get one. He left his dinner on the table and went to sit in front of the computer, because he'd be able to see the schedule here at the ranch easier that way.

"Hello?" a woman answered.

"Hey, there," Brandon said easily. "This is Brandon Rhinehart, and I just saw your help wanted listing on the Temporary Rancher's Forum."

"Sure," the woman said easily, and Brandon relaxed a little bit. "You saw the part about a low salary?"

"Yes, ma'am," he said, though the voice didn't sound much older than him, if she was at all. He had a little bit of savings, as he lived rent-free and had worked on the family ranch for literally his whole life.

"I can pay you seven hundred and fifty dollars a month," she said. "I'll give you the three months cash up front, when you sign the contract to work with me through February first."

"So the job starts November one?" he asked.

"Yes," she said. "I can be flexible on that, though, as I know most cowboys are working the harvest right now."

"Is your harvest done?"

Lenore cleared her throat. "Uh, yes," she said. "I didn't have much."

"Okay." Brandon could hear so many things in her tone, and he narrowed his eyes at the screen as he pulled up his calendar. "I'd love to come see the place, check out the cabin, and go over more details of what you need to make sure I have the skills to do the job."

She hesitated, which also set a red flag flying in Brandon's mind. He looked down at the keyboard, waiting.

"Okay," she said. "I'll send you a pin, because I'm obviously off-grid."

"Obviously," he said. "Do you have generators? Solar power? Anything like that?"

"I run on generators," she said. "Though I have the capability to get solar set up...if I can get the help."

Brandon nodded, and he'd roughed it plenty of times in his life. He couldn't imagine living without water and power for very long, though, and he understood the need Lenore had to get her infrastructure set up.

"What about tomorrow morning?" he asked. "I work the later shift on my family ranch, so evenings would be harder for me. Not totally out of the question, but harder."

"Tomorrow morning is fine," she said. "Eight? Nine?"

"Where you at?" he asked, because travel time would factor greatly into what time Brandon could meet.

"My place is northeast of Three Rivers," she said. "About thirty or forty minutes."

He whistled, because he currently lived about that far

southwest of Three Rivers. "Hoo, boy," he said. "That's probably a couple of hours for me."

"Really? Where are you?"

"My family owns the ranch just south of Shiloh Ridge," he said, because everyone in the Panhandle knew Shiloh Ridge.

"Oh, that is far."

"I can do it," Brandon said. It would simply take a text to Duke to let him know he wouldn't be able to work until noon. "Let's say nine, and I won't stay long, so I can get back here."

"It won't take long," Lenore promised. "I'll send you the pin and see you in the morning."

"Sounds good." Brandon added a, "See you tomorrow," and hung up. He put his interview and homestead visit on the calendar that his whole family could see. Then he texted Duke, Dawson, his daddy, and Zona. They all wished him well, and Brandon sat back, feeling more peaceful than he had in a while.

Then his alarm went off, his stomach growled, and Brandon realized he'd spent his dinner break setting up an interview for another job instead of eating.

"Oh, well," he said, quickly throwing his uneaten meal on the floor for Dumpling to finish for him. He'd eaten on the go before, and he grabbed a bag of beef jerky and a protein bar on his way out the door to relieve Dwayne from the fall Texas heat and harvest.

* * *

The following morning, Brandon leaned forward as he muttered something about whether this was the right road to take or not. He'd been bumping along at a snail's pace on a rutted dirt road for at least twenty minutes now, and he feared his GPS would give out at any moment, leaving him lost and stranded in the wilderness north of town.

He made the turn, hoping it was right. Relief edged through him as the arrow on the map pointed toward the pin Lenore had sent him. Only another minute passed before he drove past a chunk of trees that needed to be thinned and onto the homestead.

He pressed on the brake as all new emotions stomped through him. This place didn't need a *little* bit of work.

"This place should be condemned," he said right out loud. None of the fences stood up straight, and piles of lumber, plastic containers, and other debris littered the side of the road where he'd been driving. Chickens roamed freely in the yard, and two dogs got to their feet as the front door of the cabin opened.

A woman came outside, and Brandon eased his foot off the brake to get his truck moving forward again. He came to a stop next to her truck, glancing over at it too. The vehicle had to be at least fifteen years old—just like everything else here.

Brandon honestly wasn't sure if he could revitalize this place. Perhaps this woman and her husband or other hired help, plus him, could make some headway. But if she had other help, why did everything here look like it had been put together with string and toothpicks?

And why would she have put up a job listing?

He peered through the windshield as the woman came down the front steps. She had pretty blonde hair swinging in a ponytail, and Brandon sucked in a breath as he recognized her.

"The woman from the hardware store," he breathed out, refusing to let his lips move. She kept coming, and Brandon unbuckled his seat belt and dropped to the ground.

Their eyes met, and she came to a complete stop too, and Brandon knew why—she recognized him too.

All he could do now was pray she didn't have any friends in town and hadn't heard of his reputation with women.

Sneak Peek! The Cowboy Who Believed Again Chapter Two:

L enore Sawyer was having a week filled with shocking things. First, that anyone had responded to her ad on the temporary job board. She'd been using other sources to try to hire somebody, but they'd all fled once they found out about the low salary. Lenore had finally decided to just be super honest about it and see what happened.

So Brandon's call yesterday had taken her by surprise in the first place. Secondly, he was the first person who'd been able to find the homestead. She'd managed to get two other people to respond to ads on TwoCents, but neither one of them had been able to navigate their way here.

She knew she lived off-grid, but how hard was it to use your phone's GPS to navigate to a pin? Obviously not that hard, as Brandon Rhinehart had done it.

Of course, Brandon Rhinehart looked to be the type of

cowboy who could do anything, and that was exactly what Lenore needed.

Third, he hadn't run screaming off the property yet. That alone was shocking.

And while Lenore had definitely been praying more than she ever had in the past two months since she'd run—literally—into Brandon in the hardware store, she doubled down now, begging God that he wouldn't jump back in his truck and hightail it out of there.

She could barely believe it that the only cowboy who'd managed to look past the low salary and get himself here was the handsome man she'd made a fool of herself with. She'd counted on never seeing him again, and yet there he stood in the flesh, reaching down to pat Admiral. Once Susie-Q saw he wasn't a threat, she went over to greet him as well.

He doesn't have much time, she reminded herself, and she stopped staring and stepped forward. "I'm Lenore Sawyer."

"It's great to meet you. Again," Brandon said easily, a quick smile coming to his face. Oh, so he was an optimist, and Lenore actually found herself returning the smile, because she definitely needed an upbeat outlook to get this place in shape. He shook her hand and then pulled away, tucked his hands in his back pockets, and looked around.

"She's in rough shape right now," Lenore said, deciding that the honesty about the low salary had gotten him here, and perhaps if she just laid everything on the line, he would stay.

"Yeah, I can see that," Brandon said. "You live here by yourself?"

"Yes," Lenore said. "My momma and daddy passed away a little over a year ago."

Brandon's wandering eyes came back to hers and locked into place. "Oh, I'm real sorry to hear that," he said. "My daddy's getting a lot older, and I don't know how much longer he'll be with us."

Lenore nodded, accepting his condolences. "I'm really good with gardening," she said. "I have a big garden that I just harvested, and I've managed to build a greenhouse onto the back of my cabin that will get sunshine all winter."

"That's great," Brandon said.

Lenore turned and faced more of the homestead. "But I can't keep my chickens contained, no matter what I do, and I lose a couple every month to predators."

Brandon nodded and fell into step beside her as she started away from the cabin. "What kind of predators you got?" he asked. "You talkin' coyotes or hawks?"

"It's the birds that get them," she said. "But I have seen coyotes and foxes out here as well."

He nodded and kept looking around. Lenore knew he was the kind of man who would catalog everything. She tried not to feel like he was judging her, though he had to be. She'd done her best, and she'd gotten to the point where she simply couldn't do more. She'd swallowed her pride and asked for help. Thankfully, the usual humiliation she felt at having someone come to the homestead and see its condition only stayed for a moment.

"I have the space for turkeys," she said. "And goats, which would give more eggs and more milk. And long term, I want to add a couple of beef cattle that I can raise each year for meat and a dairy cow for milk."

"Mm hm." Brandon said nothing, and she thought he probably hadn't wanted to speak out loud so that his disbelief wouldn't shine through. But Lenore didn't know how to keep living if she didn't have dreams.

And the idea that she could get the homestead to the point where it could support cattle and goats meant that it could support her—and that she wouldn't lose it. She'd written that down on a whiteboard in her kitchen, and she'd magneted pictures of beef cattle and dairy cows and goats, turkeys, chickens, and even ducks to it.

"I wouldn't mind putting a pig on the property either," she said. "I have twenty-five acres."

They reached the barn, and Lenore didn't have to open the door, because it hung sideways on its hinges. "This got broken last week," she said. "When we had that terrible wind."

"Sure," Brandon said, keeping his answers short and clipped.

She led the way into the barn and found it easier to confess her lack of skills when she wasn't looking directly at such a handsome man. She told herself she would have trouble admitting this to anyone, not just Brandon. But he'd shown up in jeans and a gray t-shirt with a hiking boot print on the front, the biceps far too tight around his muscles. He wore a dark brown cowboy hat and boots, and she actually couldn't wait to see him really dirty.

She tamed her thoughts and continued. "I'm not real great with a hammer and nails," she said. "So repairing structures and building new ones is difficult for me. I need help organizing the barn and making it more functional, so I can bring the animals inside during storms. I need the chicken coop redone and fenced, so that the birds can't get in from overhead. I want a turkey enclosure, goat pens, and a pasture properly fenced. I may not be able to afford the animals for a while, but that would give me physical facilities for them, and...."

She trailed off, so many things already having been spoken. She turned to face him, fierce determination coming into her body and soul. "And I can't do it. I've tried and I've failed multiple times. My daddy got hurt about a year before he died, and me and my momma did our best, but neither one of us could keep up with the physical demands of the homestead."

Brandon wore sympathy in his gaze too, but also something strong and fierce in the set of his jaw. "Yeah, my daddy got old real fast," he said. "So I understand what that's like."

"Yeah, but you're able to help," she said. "Actually help."

"I've got two brothers as well," Brandon said.

Aha, Lenore thought. *That's why he doesn't want to work his family ranch.* She'd intended to ask him why he wanted this job, but now she didn't have to.

"How good are you at building things?" she asked. "And with a chainsaw?"

"I can do all that for you, so it won't be a problem." He gave her a tight smile and added, "My brother is excellent at farm management. I can ask him what he would do out here to make things easy for you, getting animals in and out, storing feed and supplies."

She nodded, not quite daring to hope that his offer to ask his brother meant that he would take the job. She didn't want to waste either of their time, and she turned back to the entrance of the barn as she asked, "Are you considering the job, or are you offering so you won't feel guilty when you drive away?"

"Wow, someone's honest," he said from behind her, a light laugh following. "I'll join you there, Lenore—this place needs a lot of work."

"Don't I know it," she grumbled, barely loud enough for herself to hear.

"I'm not sure the two of us can even get it where you want it in three months," he said.

Lenore wasn't sure of anything other than the fact that she couldn't do this herself. She only had enough money to pay him for three months, and then she'd have to hire herself out to other operations, so that she could feed herself and keep the land. She'd toyed with that idea plenty already, because there were always places looking for good people.

"You said you had the capability for solar?" he asked.

"Yeah," she said. "My daddy had these big wheels from an old sprinkler system, and we got the solar panels for free when a neighbor threw in the towel and left their homestead."

"Oh, that's nice," Brandon said.

"Yes." It had been nice, but the solar panels had been leaning up against the side of the barn for years now. She led him outside and around the corner and indicated them. "Daddy's idea was to build a rotating panel with these that we could adjust to the angle of the sun throughout the year that would feed our generator and store power in batteries as well."

"You got the batteries?" he asked.

"Two or three is all." She kept it to herself that eventually, if she could get this place more operational, she'd be able to afford more. "I've been charging my phone in my truck," she said. "By driving to the truck stop and back." She cleared her throat. "That's where I shower too."

She found herself drawn to him again, and their eyes met. "Full disclosure, there's no running water here. I have to haul it all in for drinking, and it makes bathing a little bit difficult."

"Shower at the truck stop's only—what?" he asked. "Four-fifty?"

She nodded, her jaw tight because it was four-fifty to take a shower.

"How far is the truck stop?" he asked, though he had to have passed it on the way up.

"Thirty-five minutes," she said. "I get all my potable water there as well, and they have a pretty decent little grocery section that I buy meat out of." She turned away from the solar panels. "Your cabin is over here."

She led him across a parched piece of land that could

probably be brought back to life. But Lenore poured all of her energy into the greenhouse and the garden, and she let the rest of the land do whatever it wanted. The second cabin on the property sat nestled back in the trees, about fifty yards from the barn, and closer to where Lenore thought she might be able to drill for water. She'd keep that to herself for now, because she didn't even know if Brandon would agree to come work for her.

"I'm afraid it's as neglected as a lot of the other parts of the homestead," she said. "I lived here for a little bit, and the cabins are at least the two things that won't fall down."

Brandon said nothing, which actually said a whole lot. She could feel his doubt kicking up behind her as she walked up the front steps. His boots clunked against the solid wood as he joined her, and he actually stomped on the porch and said, "Huh, you might be right."

"My grandfather was a master carpenter," she said. "He built both of the cabins."

"Not the barn?" he asked.

"The barn was here before my grandparents bought the homestead." Lenore nodded to the door. "I'll let you go in and explore by yourself. It's two bedrooms, two baths. The idea was that a small family could live here, or two cowboys as hired help."

Brandon took a couple of steps toward the door and then turned to face her. "Are you hiring two cowboys?"

"No," she said. "I can only afford to hire one, and only for three months." She'd made that very clear, hadn't she?

"Good," Brandon said. "I'm sick of sharing a cabin with someone." He muttered something else that Lenore didn't quite catch as he turned and opened the cabin door. It sailed open smoothly, like melting butter, and Lenore smiled at the truth she'd spoken. Her grandfather had built the cabins to last, and even if they were the only two structures on the homestead that didn't seem like they were one breath away from collapse, that made Lenore happy.

She sat down on the front step, glad when Susie-Q came up the steps to meet her. Admiral stayed down at the bottom, where he lay in a patch of shade and simply kept watch. She wasn't sure how long Brandon stayed inside, taking in the mess that was the cabin, but when he returned, he settled onto the top step beside her, a sigh hissing out of his mouth.

"There's more," Lenore said without looking at him. "I've got piles of tires sitting around that need to be disposed of, and debris and other materials that we need to organize and perhaps use."

"I'm sure," Brandon said.

"You've probably seen enough to know whether you want to commit yourself to this purgatory or not." Lenore looked over to him and smiled, something hopeful raising the corners of her mouth. "You don't have to decide right now, but you're the only cowboy who's managed to even find the homestead...so if you want the job, it's yours."

He gave a couple of curt nods and then got to his feet with a groan. "I'll think about it," he said.

Lenore wanted to ask for more than that, but she actually couldn't, so she joined him, and they walked in easy silence back to her house and his truck.

"Well, you've got my number." She tried not to let her heart crash to the ground when all he did was grunt, but it did anyway. Something hot and sizzling still passed between them, but Brandon didn't seem to react to it at all. Perhaps he couldn't feel it. Maybe he had a girlfriend or even a wife. Lenore's gaze dropped to his left hand, but she didn't find a ring. *Doesn't mean anything*, she told herself. Lots of cowboys didn't wear their wedding bands, as they worked so much with their hands and got dirty and banged up.

"I have your number," he said now. "I'll be in touch." With that, he got in his truck, started up the engine, and backed away from the cabin.

Lenore stood there, all the stars in the heavens falling to the ground—and bringing the sky with them. He simply *had* to take the job.

Her desperation lifted on the air like a foul scent. Then Brandon's brake lights came on, and he brought his truck to an abrupt halt. Lenore's heart started to pound, but she didn't dare hope for anything, and besides, Brandon didn't get out of the truck and stride back to her and tell her he'd take the job.

She folded her arms, trying to keep her emotions stable, as she waited for what he would do next.

* * *

Why did he stop? What is going to happen?! Find out in THE COWBOY WHO BELIEVED AGAIN - you can preorder it now by scanning the QR code below with your phone:

The Cowboy Who Came Home: A Second Generation in Three Rivers Ranch Romance™ (Book 1): He's been serving in the military for a decade. She's been quietly grieving a devastating loss. When Finn and Edith reunite in small-town Three Rivers where they grew up together, can their second chance romance provide hope, healing, and the happily-ever-after they both crave?

Scan this QR code with your phone to see this series in eBook, audiobook, large print paperback, or regular paperback:

Be sure to check out the other three series set in the beloved town of Three Rivers too!

Meet the cowboys who started it all at Three Rivers Ranch! Scan the QR code below with your phone to check out this complete series.

Scan this QR code with your phone to see and order this series in eBook, audiobook, large print paperback, or regular paperback:

1. Second Chance Ranch
2. Third Time's the Charm
3. Fourth and Long
4. Fifth Generation Cowboy
5. Sixth Street Love Affair
6. The Seventh Sergeant
7. Eight Second Ride
8. The Ninth Inning
9. Ten Days in Town
10. Eleven Year Reunion

Seven Sons Ranch in Three Rivers Romance™ Series

Meet the cowboy billionaire brothers at Seven Sons Ranch! Scan the QR code below with your phone to check out this complete series.

1. Rhett
2. Tripp
3. Liam
4. Jeremiah
5. Wyatt
6. Skyler
7. Micah
8. Gideon

Shiloh Ridge Ranch in Three Rivers Romance™ Series

Become a Glover Lover by reading all the Glover Family romance & family saga at Shiloh Ridge Ranch! Scan the QR code below with your phone to check out this complete series.

About Liz

Liz Isaacson writes inspirational romance, usually set in Texas, or Wyoming, or anywhere else horses and cowboys exist. She lives in Utah, where she writes full-time, takes her two dogs to the park everyday, and eats a lot of veggies while writing. Find her on her website at www.feelgoodfiction-books.com.